Praise for Stephen McCauley's
THE MAN OF THE HOUSE

"Charming . . . A wry, bittersweet look at the importance and impossibility of father-son relationships . . . The writing is seamless, the story never lags, and it is filled with eccentric characters and observations that you'll find yourself reading aloud."

—Susan Kelly, *USA Today*

"A comic novel about human predicaments . . . McCauley has mastered the small yet perfect comic gesture. . . . Readers will welcome back the rueful and rumpled comic vision that is unmistakably his own."

—Meg Wolitzer, *The New York Times Book Review*

"A wry and melancholy comedy of modern manners . . . A lovely, funny book that represents an impressive strengthening of McCauley's themes and talent."

—*Kirkus Reviews*

"Fine, funny and appealing . . . *THE MAN OF THE HOUSE* is consistently compelling in its depiction of the intertwining relationships between Clyde's friends, neighbors and relatives. . . . A talented and winning writer."

—James Ireland Baker, *Time Out New York*

"A painful, humorous look at life as a grown-up, where great expectations give over to silent resignation . . . Clyde's observations are witty and right on target."

—Helen A. S. Popkin, *St. Petersburg Times*

"Irresistible . . . McCauley's latest and most emotionally complex probe into family dysfunction."

—James Patrick Herman, *Elle*

"A hilarious new tale of wit and woe . . ."

—*Genre*

"[A] wry vision of the way we live now . . . funny, bright, fast-paced and populated by attractive characters . . ."

—Francine Prose, *Newsday*

"McCauley has a gift for creating characters who are wry, amusing, compassionate and genuinely smart."

—*Mademoiselle*

"McCauley has a great eye for nuance and a great ear for dialogue. . . . [And] a real talent for searching out the flaws in people that make them truly interesting . . ."

—Fred Goss, *The Advocate*

Books by Stephen McCauley

The Object of My Affection
The Easy Way Out
The Man of the House

Published by WASHINGTON SQUARE PRESS

For orders other than by individual consumers, Pocket Books grants a discount on the purchase of **10 or more** copies of single titles for special markets or premium use. For further details, please write to the Vice-President of Special Markets, Pocket Books, 1633 Broadway, New York, NY 10019-6785, 8th Floor.

For information on how individual consumers can place orders, please write to Mail Order Department, Simon & Schuster Inc., 200 Old Tappan Road, Old Tappan, NJ 07675.

the man of the house

stephen mccauley

WASHINGTON SQUARE PRESS
PUBLISHED BY POCKET BOOKS

New York   London   Toronto   Sydney   Tokyo   Singapore

In memory of my real father
and for Sebastian

A Washington Square Press Publication of
POCKET BOOKS, a division of Simon & Schuster Inc.
1230 Avenue of the Americas, New York, NY 10020

Copyright © 1996 by Stephen McCauley

ISBN: 0-671-00225-2

First Washington Square Press trade paperback printing November 1996

10 9 8 7 6 5 4 3 2 1

WASHINGTON SQUARE PRESS and colophon are registered trademarks of
Simon & Schuster Inc.

Cover design by Brigid Pearson
Cover art by Terry Widener

Printed in the U.S.A.

THE MORNING LOUISE MORRIS'S LETTER arrived announcing that she was coming to town, I was sitting up in bed, rereading *Wuthering Heights*, trying to think of something meaningful to say about it to my adult education class that week. It was a little after ten, and already it was warm and comfortingly humid. It had been a steamy, wet summer, with one day more insufferably torpid than the next, but it was just past the middle of August and I'd grown used to the weather. I liked to think that putting up with it stoically would build character, a quality I couldn't afford to pass up, whatever the price. I'd turned thirty-five that spring, so I figured it was now or never on the question of character.

My quarters in the two-story apartment I shared with Marcus Gladstone, an old friend of mine and a onetime lover of Louise Morris, were the three converted attic rooms under the eaves of a busted-up, vinyl-sided house outside Harvard Square. Throughout the summer, they were stifling and smelled of tar and cedar, as if the roof were cooking right above my head and about to burst into flames. But there was something about the almost suffocating closeness of the rooms that appealed to me. I could sit up in bed and, with a few careful adjustments, touch all the walls around me. Marcus, who had a bedroom and study on the floor below, was too tall, considerate, and lazy to climb the steep staircase to my lair, so in addition to everything else, I had almost complete privacy. I'd moved in with Marcus two years earlier, after the breakup of a relationship, desperately longing for and dreading privacy. There's a fine line between the gorgeous luxury of not having to account for your time and the loneliness of knowing that no one cares what the hell you do with it, and some days—most days, I suppose—I wasn't sure which side of it I was on.

When I heard the mailman pounding up the front steps of the house that morning, I got out of bed, slipped on a pair of jeans, and headed for the door. I always raced for the door as soon as I heard the mail arrive. Like a lot of basically unfulfilled people with too much time on their hands, I'd fooled myself into believing that A Perfect Life and I were separated by nothing more substantial than a postage stamp. Maybe there was money in today's mail, or an offer of a job in...Rome, let's say—a teaching position at some undemanding American school that provided its staff with rooms in a crumbling villa with views of the Forum. Or, equally likely, maybe Gordon, my ex, had come to his senses and written to tell me he'd made a mistake in leaving, the very words I'd been waiting to hear from him so I could finally forget about him and move on.

As I walked past the bureau I had wedged into one corner under the eaves, I caught a glimpse of myself in the mirror and stopped short. The problem with having a housemate as handsome as Marcus was that I sometimes took his face as standard issue. Then I'd walk past a mirror and have to suffer through the comparison. It wasn't that I had any desire to carry around the burden of Marcus's languid blond beauty; it was just that lately, the few things I'd once considered assets in my appearance were beginning to work against me. The lean and hungry, unkempt, and addled look I'd cultivated throughout my twenties was beginning to read like desperation and indigence as I stepped into my mid-thirties. At a certain age, the unkempt and hungry look is attractive only if you're neither, and the truth is, I was at least a little of both. Even my eyeglasses were turning against me. Almost daily, the black, clunky things I'd been wearing for years appeared less and less East Village and more and more Steve Allen. I'd chosen them years earlier as a fashion statement, but I'd made a mistake and now it looked as if they'd chosen me. The depressing part was, I was stuck with what I'd made myself into and I couldn't pretend that it was only a matter of minutes before I turned everything around and started getting expensive haircuts and flattering eyeglasses. Some things have to be hammered out in youth. Past the age of thirty-three, no one ever becomes stylish or takes up smoking or develops a passion for John Steinbeck. Besides, considering the astonishing number of people I knew who'd been plowed under before making it out of their twenties, aging felt like a privilege, the kind of privilege you should complain about only in private.

I tripped down the two flights of stairs and pushed open the door to the tiny entryway of the house. Donald Gern, our downstairs neighbor, was standing there leafing through a stack of mail.

"Can't see a thing in here," he said. "Like trying to read in a freaking cave."

He held an envelope at arm's length and squinted until his gray eyes disappeared. Cracked stained-glass panels in the front door of the house blocked out a good deal of light, but even on the bleakest winter mornings I'd had no trouble reading the mail. Donald always went through this showy routine in my presence out of what I assumed was a combination of self-consciousness, lack of social skills, and discomfort at being trapped in a confined space with a known homosexual.

Donald had moved into the first floor about six months earlier. The apartment was one of those badly painted, peculiarly laid out places that attract oddball transient renters. In the time I'd been living in the house, over half a dozen people had moved in and out of the apartment—mostly, as far as I could tell, math geniuses with greasy hair, the type who graduate from college with honors and high expectations, have a nervous collapse of some kind, and end up collecting comic books and working at copy shops. Donald Gern didn't exactly fit the mold, but he didn't exactly break it. He was a big man, over six feet tall, with a blocky body that could have been fat or muscular but didn't seem to be either. I'd once seen him barechested in the backyard; he had a massive, undefined torso, the kind of pale, hairless body you expect to see on an extra in a black-and-white biblical epic.

This morning, he had on a pair of dark pants, a white shirt, and a knee-length white lab coat. He worked in Boston at what he described as a "clinic" that treated baldness, thinning hair, and other untreatable maladies. In the short time I'd been acquainted with him, I'd become obsessed with his profession. I assumed it was pure quackery and was amazed at how unabashed he was about the whole thing. Whenever I mentioned his job to him, he grew serious and grim, in a pompous, self-righteous way, as if we were discussing oncology. On the other hand, I was beginning to grow concerned about the possibility of someday going bald myself, and I was always looking for signs that there was a shred of validity to what he did, in case I needed his professional help. In daylight, his own hair looked to be the color of a Band-Aid, but in this dim light it looked pink. It lay across his head in one limp flap, like a leaf of lettuce flung on top of a grapefruit. Was it real? A toupee? The result of some unsuccessful surgical procedure? These were questions that, I'm ashamed to admit, I pondered when I could have been pondering the meaning of life.

"Off to work?" I asked him.

"Double shift," he said. He shook his head grimly, like someone recounting last night's body count in the emergency room. "Eight patients back-to-back. We're understaffed, but I'll tell you, it's tough to find qualified trichologists." He glanced at me without lifting his head. "You know anyone looking for a job?"

He asked in such a deadly serious tone, the offer seemed ominous. "Not offhand," I said.

10

"Everyone's unemployed, but when you come up with a job offer, you can't find a warm body." He examined an envelope intently. "Looks like one of you boys is popular. Handwriting's a lady's, too, unless I'm mistaken."

He tucked the letter under his arm and continued to go through the stack. He had one of those ageless baby faces. His eyebrows were so light they were almost nonexistent, and his mouth was as puckered and tiny as a Kewpie doll's. At first I assumed he had a thyroid condition—the thinning eyebrows, the awkward bulk, the sluggish Bride of Frankenstein walk suggested as much. More recently, however, I'd noticed a look of unmistakable sadness on his face when he thought he wasn't being observed, and I suspected he might simply be lonely. Still, he had an irritating way of treating both Marcus and me like children, even though he was probably younger than both of us. I wanted to demand that he hand over the letter immediately, but I couldn't think of a way of doing so without acting like a peevish child and justifying his condescension.

When he came to the bottom of the stack, he looked up. "Shucks, I guess no one keeled over and left me a million bucks." He surrendered the letter. "Maybe you got lucky."

"I'm not sure you'd call it luck," I said. "It's from my sister." There was no return address, but Agnes always wrote our surname, Carmichael, in huge block letters, a reminder that I had familial obligations.

"I always wished I had a sister," Donald said, shaking his head sadly. "Other than the one I have, I mean."

As I started to back toward the door, another letter fell out of the pile of catalogs and magazines Donald was holding and fluttered to the floor. He uttered one of his genteel curses, picked it up, and handed it to me. "I guess I missed one in this fricking light." He opened his door. "See you 'round, buddy," he said.

He slipped into the apartment and slammed the door, leaving behind the citrus-and-sawdust scent of his aftershave and the powerful adhesive smell of hair fixative.

In the past month or so, it had begun to worry me that I had such a strong interest in and identification with Donald. I suppose he was the person others fear they will become if they don't hurry up and get their professional life together or inherit some money or, at the very least, dig up a spouse of some kind. The week before, he'd told me that he was planning to have a cookout in the backyard and would keep me posted on the date. "No big deal," he'd said, "just a bunch of losers sitting around getting drunk. You guys should drop down."

Unfortunately, it was the best offer I'd had in weeks.

The second letter Donald had turned over was addressed to me in Louise Morris's scratchy handwriting. I hadn't heard from Louise in a while, not since she'd written more than a year earlier, to tell me she was moving to Seattle. I stuck it in my back pocket as I walked upstairs, intending to save it as a reward for reading the missive from my sister. Agnes had left a couple of messages on my answering machine in the past week, but I hadn't returned them, largely because she'd said: "It's about...Dad." Both Agnes and I tended to hesitate before calling our father "Dad": the term didn't quite fit somehow, but "Father" was too formal and we were too intimidated by him to call him by his first name. Discussing our father was low on my list of ways to brighten up the day. I could already feel myself starting to resent Agnes for reminding me of his existence.

The house Marcus and I lived in had been built sometime in the late forties, a standard, uninspired two-story dwelling with an attic, a little front porch, and a mattress-size backyard, just right for the optimistic postwar family moments before the flight to suburbia shifted into high gear. There were four houses identical to ours on the street, but we had the distinction of having in the tiny front yard an immense pine tree that was gradually chewing up the foundation. The tree, so out of proportion to the yard, added a look of neglected beauty to the bland exterior of the house and the romance of pine needles clogging the gutters and littering the front steps. Over the years, the interior of the place had been reconfigured, renovated, and neglected by a series of owners, and as a result, many of the rooms were oddly shaped, with staircases and doors that led nowhere, windows sliced in half by a cabinet or makeshift closet, and moldings and wainscoting that disappeared unexpectedly into a wall. We were only a few blocks from a neighborhood where professors and lawyers lived in leafy quiet, but our street was crowded with noisy, pessimistic post-Reagan families in constant financial turmoil and personal crisis, who, inexplicably, drove cars plastered with bumper stickers for Republican candidates and assorted right-wing extremist causes certain to make their lives even more unbearable than their constant public brawling indicated they already were. All the fathers had the bloated look of heavy drinkers or steroid abusers, and the teenagers walked around day and night as if they were trying to decide whether to shave their heads or commit suicide. The mothers were either morbidly obese or amphetamine-thin. The former made rare public appearances, and the latter tended to spend eight or nine hours a day washing clothes at the laundromat on the corner, hooked up to Walkmans.

Our house backed up to a fancy grocery where Julia Child, who lived part time on the other side of the tracks, was rumored to do her shopping. She'd been my favorite TV star as a child, long before I learned, with some dismay, that she was a real person and not an invented character. The breakup that precipitated the move in with Marcus had been a fairly traumatic one, and I'd initially spent hours wandering the cramped aisles of the store, picking up tins of snails and caviar and other expensive, fishy items, all in hopes of catching a glimpse of the French Chef. For some reason, I thought it would be reassuring: Gordon may have left me, but goddamn it, Julia Child and I shop together. Finally, I gave up the pursuit and started shopping at a chain supermarket, where no one famous was rumored to shop but where they did give double value for coupons.

When I got upstairs, Marcus was standing at the stove in a pair of madras designer boxer shorts and beat-up tennis shoes. Marcus was not athletic; the fact that he wore out tennis shoes with such regularity only fueled my suspicion that he spent an inordinate amount of time wandering the streets of Cambridge when he claimed to be in the library researching his thesis. He was constantly broke, but he had an amazingly large and eclectic underwear wardrobe, because not one of his girlfriends had ever given him anything other than intimate apparel as a gift. I considered telling him I had a letter from Louise and then thought better of it. Marcus couldn't understand how I'd remained friends with Louise when he had not. It made perfect sense to me, since she and I had been friends from the start, while she and Marcus had been lovers, a more tenuous and opportunistic connection, and one which rarely endures.

I lowered one of the matchstick blinds to filter out the sunlight and dropped onto the nubby orange sofa we'd placed against one wall of the enormous L-shaped kitchen in an attempt to fill space.

"Not good for the springs," Marcus said. He was pouring water over the coffee grounds, slowly and methodically. Coffee was the mainstay of Marcus's diet, and he'd turned the production of it into a fetish.

"They're shot anyway," I said. "We should go out and buy a new one."

"We should," he said, without conviction. "I was thinking that the other day. We should get a new thing for the living room, too."

"Good idea," I said.

What "thing" for the living room he was talking about I couldn't imagine. There was no possibility of our buying a sofa or a table or any "thing" for any room in the house, because we operated on the assumption that our arrangement was temporary. The arrangement of two romantically uninvolved men living together is always considered temporary, unless they're brothers, in which case it's assumed they're insane and the arrangement is therefore permanent.

There was something so embarrassingly intimate about the two of us doing housecleaning as a team that walking into a department store together and arguing over upholstery was clearly out of the question. So we stuck with the sofa we had, which we'd found on the sidewalk. My guess was the previous owner had been a junkie.

I'll get one humiliating fact out of the way now and confess that once, many years earlier when I first met him. I'd been infatuated with Marcus, knowing very well that he was diligently heterosexual. He had those dashing looks, and the faint traces of a Southern accent around the edges of his vowels, and a quiet, seductive manner that made you think he was keeping some great secret you just had to find out. Fortunately, the infatuation had faded. You can't sustain a sexual attraction over the course of a long friendship any more than you can sustain a long friendship without some flicker of sexual attraction. In any case, it was a relief to me now that when I looked at Marcus, I could appreciate how stunning his looks were and still feel an element of revulsion at the thought of going to bed with him.

I draped my legs over the arm of the sofa—a knotty-pine appendage with cigarette burns—and studied the envelope from my sister, daring myself to open it.

"Do you think Donald wears a wig?" I asked.

Marcus looked up from his coffee production. "Donald's hair isn't something I've given a lot of thought to."

"No," I said. "I haven't given it much thought, either."

Marcus poured himself a cup of coffee and casually said, "Why? Do you think it's a wig?"

"Who knows? It could be anything up there."

"The color's a little odd, isn't it?"

"Pink," I said, warming up. "And sometimes it seems to change shades right in front of your eyes. Have you noticed that?"

Marcus shook his head. He sat down at the kitchen table, wound his legs together, picked up his coffee cup, and sipped with the slow, subdued pleasure of an addict. To his credit, Marcus had developed his addiction to caffeine long before it became a fashionable, socially acceptable substitute for nicotine addiction. Now that secondhand-smoke activists had diverted attention from real health hazards, such as auto emissions and ozone depletion, it was no longer possible to stop the world for ten minutes by lighting a cigarette in public. Coffee, a more dangerous and malodorous drug, had stepped in to fill the void.

Marcus's mother was of Dutch ancestry, and his father was from rural Virginia. He had the dramatic, rough-cut features of a peasant from a Brueghel canvas combined with the blond lankiness of an American Gothic. His face was sunken and sallow in the most flattering ways possible, with the high forehead of an intellectual and the full lips and protuberant ears of a sensualist. Something for everyone, in other words, providing you didn't dig too deep.

"I don't want to talk about Donald's hair, Clyde. I had a tough night last night. Just when I thought things were going smoothly enough with Nancy to finally let me concentrate on the thesis. Where were you, anyway?"

"Movies," I said. A lie, but my disorganized attempts at having a sex life were my own business. I'd spent a portion of the night with Bernie, a waiter and Gordon look-alike who sometimes called me when his lover was out of town. "What happened?"

"Nancy left me. She said I wasn't giving her enough emotional support." He looked up at me—mournful, sincere, a pout on his big, lovely lips. He had thin, dirty-blond hair that he kept at shoulder length. A hank of it swung down to cover half his face, and he pushed it back behind one of his teacup-handle ears. "Would you please tell me what the hell that's supposed to mean? Emotional support?"

"You're asking the wrong person," I said. "What do I know?"

What I knew was this: in the two years we'd been sharing the apartment, there had been at least five of these brief, passionate affairs, usually with young graduate students Marcus met in the Harvard libraries. He seemed to attract inexperienced scholars who were still judging books by their covers and were taken in by the deep-set eyes and the hollow cheeks—as I'd been, and as Louise Morris had been, too. A few months down the road they'd leave, making similar charges about Marcus's inability to give himself to them. They missed entirely the significant point, which was that he had given as much of himself as there was to give.

I dreaded each new relationship, knowing that sooner or later I'd end up sitting around the depressing little maple table in the vast, depressing kitchen, listening to how detached Marcus was (something I already knew) and being asked if I, in-house expert on the subject, thought Marcus was really attracted to men (something I doubted, although he clearly didn't mind being *attractive* to men). Inexplicably, most of these women were involved in the field of Gay Studies, an academic pursuit that baffled me. I always asked polite questions about their work, hoping for gossip on the sex lives of literary or historical figures, and was invariably treated instead to a lecture on power dynamics, images of sadomasochism and bondage, and gender identification in the novels of George Meredith and Jane Austen, or even, God forbid, in *Beowulf*—all delivered in a language that sounded only vaguely like English.

"I'm beginning to lose hope," Marcus said, his coffee cup perched at his lips.

"Don't do that," I said. "You're too young to lose hope." In fact, as Marcus rapidly approached forty, he was statistically the right age to lose hope.

It's unfair but true that it's fundamentally impossible to have much sympathy for handsome men.

I tossed Marcus Agnes's letter. "From my sister," I said. It was too early to read it myself. I loved Agnes, but communicating with her sometimes caused me to sink into a swamp of guilt and sadness that cost me an entire day. As for whatever it was she had to say about our father, well, the only two options were bad news and worse news, and since I wasn't on mood-stabilizing drugs, I didn't feel like hearing either. I sometimes thought about trying mood-stabilizing drugs, but unfortunately I'm of the generation that only feels comfortable swallowing organic vitamins or street drugs.

"Agnes!" Marcus said, brightening and tearing open the letter. "I haven't seen that poor kid in months."

As long as a woman wasn't a serious candidate for romance—

if, for example, she was almost his age or not enrolled at Harvard —Marcus was so emotionally available and supportive, he could have hung out a shingle. And there was no mistaking the fact that Agnes was not a serious candidate for romance.

The envelope from Louise contained a short note scrawled on a piece of motel stationery.

Dear Clyde, Greetings from, let's see, where are we? The car has a problem I couldn't fix, so we're stuck here for a few days. (Actually, I could have fixed it, but I didn't have the spare parts on board.) Ben's been using his free time researching flea collars. Know anything about dogs?

Remember when I said I would never come east again? Well, guess what? *Never* turned out to be not so long as I thought. I suppose it never is. I got a grant from a prominent academic institution in Cambridge that's generous to women, and here we come. Don't worry, I've lined up a sublet. I should have contacted you sooner, but things got hectic. I'll sign off as soon as you tell me Ben and I are going to love living there and everything's going to be wonderful. Oh, don't bother—I wouldn't believe you if you did. Complications abound. I'll tell you when I see you.

Yr frnd, Louise Morris

It was a pretty dull letter, by Louise's standards. She was a writer, a novelist, and occasionally her letters had a stylized quality that made me suspect she might be trying out on me material she planned to use later in her fiction. I would have objected, but the letters were usually entertaining. Besides, I'd assumed that the most intimate part of our friendship was long over, and I was perfectly content to accept my demotion from confidant to audience.

In any case, I was pleased to hear that Louise was coming to Cambridge. Visits from old friends have a way of cheering me up, especially if the old friends don't need a place to stay and they bring with them the promise of drama I can become involved in at a safe distance.

For the past twelve years, Louise had been leading a peripatetic life, drifting up and down the West Coast with her son, Benjamin, picking up teaching jobs and freelance writing assignments and, from time to time, restaurant work. I'd read all three of her novels, of course, but I'd been so busy trying to read between the lines for information about her life and some veiled portrayal of me, I'd had a hard time following their plots. Actually, they were pretty plotless, and I couldn't help but think that, enviable as it was, her meandering life must be, too. She was a respected writer, the type whose name sounds vaguely familiar to most readerly individuals, even if they've never gone so far as to actually read one of her books. At one time, I'd had aspirations in a literary direction myself, so I derived vicarious pleasure from the publication of her work. And because the books sold modestly, I didn't have to get caught up in the petty resentment and envy that a truly major success would have provoked.

I'd last seen Louise six years earlier, when she was living in San Francisco and Benjamin was a charming little neurotic who never cracked a smile. He was one of those bright, unsentimental kids who can break your heart with their eagerness to appear adult and make you believe they're on top of the chaos of their lives. It was only the second time I'd seen her since we'd graduated from college. Mostly, we kept in touch through postcards, sporadic bursts of letters, and late-night phone calls, although the calls had ceased since she'd given up drinking a few years earlier.

"That Agnes." Marcus sighed. "We really should visit her."

In the excitement over Louise's letter, I'd forgotten all about my sister. I'd been trying to forget all about my sister for quite a few years now but had never succeeded in doing so for more than a few hours at a time.

"She says you never return her calls. She says she thinks your father's getting worse. And you're not being helpful with the cookbook. What cookbook's that?"

"You don't want to know."

Marcus looked at me with his big-eared, wounded expression

that said: I'm white, middle-class, overeducated, and devastatingly handsome. Pity me! It always got to me.

"The cookbook is a metaphor," I told him.

"Ah," he said, and nodded. Whenever I came to a dead end with Marcus, I threw in the word "metaphor." Marcus was very susceptible to metaphors or even the mention of metaphors. I was more susceptible to similes, which perhaps says something about the difference in our personalities, although I'm not sure what.

After my mother's sudden death a couple of years earlier, Agnes and I had found among her papers a shoe box filled with odd, handwritten recipes she'd dreamed up in the last year of her life. Agnes was trying to organize them, in the hopes of having them published. I'd read several of the recipes and saw them as testaments to how overworked and uneasy our mother had been at the end, and possibly how emotionally unstable. What other explanation was there for "Tuna Cookies," "No-Bake Meatloaf," and "Wonder Cake," a bizarre concoction made from chocolate syrup and slices of white bread flattened with a frying pan? I had an abundance of memories of my mother, with her unfortunate but appealing I Suffer, Therefore I Am philosophy and her I, Doormat demeanor. She was small in stature, soft-spoken, had a perpetually crestfallen expression that Agnes had inherited, and dark, nearsighted eyes she'd passed on to me. Not counting cafeteria workers, she was the last woman in America to wear hair nets on a daily basis, delicate little things that came in plastic envelopes and, before she stretched them over her thin hair, looked like dust bunnies. She was Italian, second-generation but still with a flair for grand gestures and big, emotional outbursts that I saw as a confused blend of opera, papal edicts, and devotion to those gorgeous Italian saints, bloodied and beatific. More or less everything made her weep: commercials, greeting cards, thunderstorms, all music—from the most sacred to the most insipidly profane. But her emotional extremes had been diluted over time by my father's icy evasiveness, her disappointment over the bitter failure of Agnes's marriage, and the strain of trying to accept me with compassion and understanding. In her last years, floods of tears and religiosity had given way to the bland suburbanization that makes clean laundry a moral imperative. She started shopping through the mail, cooking out of cans, and watching Mass on TV with the washing machine churning in the background. She clung to the Catholic sense of doom and punishment while she lost her belief in redemption. At least, that's how I interpreted it. She'd been a mild, uncomplaining, and unfulfilled woman, and I'd loved her enormously. A few minutes after every phone conversation I'd ever had with her, she'd called back to add some irrelevant bit of news, as if she just couldn't stand the finality of hanging up. It plagued me to think how miserable she must be with the finality of death.

To my knowledge, she hadn't even been sick when my father called me at seven o'clock one morning in the middle of a howling blizzard and ordered me to get a haircut.

"Haircut?" I'd croaked. "What do you mean?" I assumed it had something to do with the snow, although I couldn't imagine what.

"Haircut! Never heard of it?"

"But why?"

"Because your mother died in her sleep last night," he said, "and I want you to look respectable at her funeral."

My mother's recipes alluded to big family gatherings with grandchildren, nieces, nephews, in-laws, and all kinds of relatives she lacked or had no contact with. I sometimes thought of them as messages from beyond the grave. I'd read a number of them, hoping they might contain clues about a secret illness or otherwise explain her death, but I'd only found evidence of her frail state of mind.

She had only one sibling, a bachelor brother named Raymond. Raymond lived in an apartment no one in the family had ever visited in Revere, a run-down beach town north of Boston. Raymond himself was pretty run down, one of those Italian guys who, because they're emaciated, are often told they look like the young Frank Sinatra. Raymond's life, like the lives of male librarians and priests, was regarded with respect and suspicion, as if there were something noble but pathetic about his existence, better left described in big, broad, blurry generalities.

Uncle Raymond showed up at my mother's funeral, wraithlike and hacking, dressed in a suit that didn't fit, his skin scrubbed raw as if he wasn't used to bathing. He sat next to me on a funeral-home folding chair and, between coughing fits, pointed to my father and said: "He's what killed her."

Given the strained relationship I had with my father, it was tempting to believe this was true, but I don't think it was. I doubt it had been a particularly happy marriage—I'd never seen either of them laugh or even smile in the other's presence—but over the years they'd eased into a state of morbid dependency and resignation, like two people clinging to each other on the tilting deck of a sinking ship. Worse things than antipathy have been confused with love. As far as I know, there were no incidents of significant violence, death threats, or suicide attempts in nearly forty years of marriage.

I'd loved my mother deeply, and when she died, I was desperately sad. But because there wasn't anything unresolved between us, it had been easy to let go of her. It's the nightmare you wake up in the middle of that haunts you throughout the day. Now my thoughts about her were dominated by images of her small body frantically trying to make a stab at immortality by compiling her recipes, those weird combinations of pulverized crackers and condensed soup and salad dressing put to uses that approached science fiction.

"I see what you mean about the metaphor," Marcus said. "I think you're right. It's all about food, isn't it?"

"Most cookbooks are."

"Let's go to New Hampshire and cheer Agnes up. It might make me feel better to be around someone as unhappy as she is."

Marcus got up and went to the stove, dragging his feet in his beat-up sneakers, drowning in sweet self-pity over the departure of Nancy. For mysterious reasons, Marcus took comfort in thinking of himself as the victim of a cruel and chaotic universe. He was amazingly passive. It was a quality that attracted intellectual women, although it added to his air of unemployability.

"I'm off to the library," he said. "Christ, I hope this thing with Nancy doesn't set me back. I really think I was on the verge of a breakthrough."

Marcus was thirty-nine. He'd completed his course work for his Ph.D. in experimental psychology ten years earlier and had been trying to write his dissertation ever since. As far as I could tell, however, he was no further along than on the day he started. He was filled with maudlin regret when he talked about what his life might have been like if he had finished his dissertation, and with vague hopefulness when he dared to mention what it might still be like if he finished it now. His research and his thesis had something to do with the significance of the frown in human relations, but what, exactly, I can't report. No one in the history of the human race has ever been as boring as Marcus Gladstone was on the subject of his dissertation. The mention of it seemed to send him into a stupor, as if he'd been injected with some powerful narcotic. He started to drawl and drone, and his eyes drooped. Listening to him, I sometimes felt as if I was literally going to lose my mind.

Marcus had been a gifted child, raised by gifted parents in a variety of academic settings. His parents were both professors, and he'd been brought up being assured by them that he would achieve great things in life, that his future was filled with bright promise. Now, he sometimes confessed, he was beginning to think they'd been wrong all along.

I had a different but related problem. I'd never been told by anyone that I would achieve great things, and I was beginning to think everyone had been right.

Marcus bolted down another cup of coffee. "Who's that other letter from?"

"Louise Morris," I said. "She got a grant. Radcliffe, from the sound of it."

"Ah, well, women have these grant networks all sewn up. Don't ever bother applying for a grant unless you're a woman."

"I'll keep it in mind."

"I suppose I should write a novel. Is she going to look us up?"

"It sounds like it."

He chewed this over for a moment. "I never should have told her I loved her on our first date. That's why she hasn't kept in touch with me. You know that, don't you?"

"I didn't know you were in love with Louise."

"I wasn't. But I misread her, thought she was one of those dreamy girls who'd like to hear gushy pronouncements. I'd better read one of those books she wrote before she gets here. One more distraction I don't need. Maybe you could give me a plot summary."

Like most of the academics over thirty I knew, Marcus rarely read. One of the apparent advantages of being well educated at a young age is that you get all of that out of the way early on.

"I'll loan you one," I said.

"She was a blonde, wasn't she?"

"Redhead."

"That's right. Redhead. And you're sure she never based a character on me? I wonder if I should be insulted. Funny, isn't it—I've never been attracted to redheads. Something too ghostly about them. Does she still have her kid with her?"

"Of course she does. Why wouldn't she?"

He downed the rest of his coffee and clenched his lips around his handsome, horsey teeth. When he recovered from his caffeine spasm, he said, "I don't know. All those years . . . Maybe the father came along to claim him. I guess it doesn't usually work out that way, does it?"

"No," I said. "I guess not. Not usually."

"French, wasn't he? Something like that?"

"He was. If you believe her first novel."

"You can pretty much take all fiction as fact, Clyde. It's the other stuff you have to wonder about."

SPENT THE REST OF THAT WARM MORNING reading an enormously long biography of an Australian painter I'd never heard of and whose work, judging from the plates stuck between the endless pages of text, was cloying and uninspired. The paintings were mostly muddy landscapes—the kinds of things Cézanne might have painted if he'd been instructed by one of those TV art teachers who paint with knives, spatulas, meat cleavers, and other kitchen utensils. Which is not to say I didn't find the book fascinating. In fact, I find most biographies fascinating and often read as many as two or three a week. It's encouraging to be reminded that even the least eventful and interesting lives can count for something in the history of the human race. And it's satisfying, in a greedy, vengeful way, to be reminded that the most eventful and interesting lives usually end tragically.

I suppose I read so many biographies because I was trying to understand how people stumbled through their days and their failures and spun their miseries and despair into great art or pathbreaking science or profound enlightenment. There were lessons to be learned, I hoped, principles I could apply to my own plodding existence. I likened the process to studying the training schedule of Olympic swimmers. But I was always tripping over the most lush, lurid details—Edith Wharton's furniture, Nureyev's dick, Freud's cocaine, Garbo's diet —and coasting through the rest.

By afternoon, I figured it was time to attack my sister's letter, and I put aside the Australian painter and prepared myself. I had a complicated system of fans in my attic rooms, which I moved from window to window and from floor to bureau to bookshelf, depending on the time of day and the angle of the sun. They didn't really keep me cool, but they blew around enough dust and stale air to create the illusion of a breeze. Besides, all that plugging and unplugging and opening and closing of windows distracted my attention from any discomfort caused by the heat. I sprawled out on the daybed in my study, set a heavy cast-iron fan on the floor in front of me, and took Agnes's letter out of the envelope.

There it was, right at the top of the page, her sad, infuriating letterhead:

FROM THE DESK OF
AGNES CARMICHAEL, CO-PRESIDENT
E AND A RESOURCES, INC.

In the mid-eighties, shortly after Agnes's divorce had been finalized and she'd moved into a town house development in southern New Hampshire, her friend Elizabeth (E) had persuaded her to give up her successful nursing career to start E and A Resources, Inc. For a substantial fee, E and A would line up baby-sitters, keep fresh-cut flowers in your bedroom, buy a Christmas present for anyone on your list, make arrangements for your five-year-old's birthday party, and so on. They'd done reasonably well for a while, but as the economy started to slide, their business had suffered huge losses. With half the state of New Hampshire unemployed, who was going to pay E and A to hire a clown? E.A.R. had gotten into the more mundane housecleaning and laundry end of things, and a few months earlier, E had convinced A to go in on some weight-loss-supplement pitch. I was worried that it was only a matter of time before my sister joined a neo-Fascist direct-sales company and was out peddling cosmetics door to door. As it was, she had to take occasional retail jobs at department stores and a few shifts at one of the many nursing homes near her condo just to afford the business. And to keep up with the financial demands of caring for our father in his supposedly numbered days.

No doctor had been able to explain our father's mysterious, selectively debilitating illness. William, always a stocky, robust, unyielding man, had worked in the insurance industry for twenty-five years. He'd sold off his business early and bought two sporting goods stores, both of which had eventually burned down under highly suspicious circumstances. It was after the second fire that he began to have amorphous health complaints and refused to leave the house—unless he wanted to. Our mother ended up waiting on him day and night, right up to her death. My father's doctor, a peculiarly hostile man in his seventies, was never more specific about my father's illness than to say that he was incapable of taking care of himself. Agnes had insisted he move into the basement of her town house rather than face the horrors of a state-run nursing home, which, according to his doctor, was the only alternative. The facts of my father's financial situation were as difficult to untangle as the plot of *Bleak House*; he alternated between claims of poverty and hints that he'd made out like a bandit on the fires.

He was mercilessly demanding of Agnes, and although she got no thanks for anything she did, she refused him nothing, from running errands to cooking meals to paying him a small monthly allowance. Part of me was sorry for all Agnes had to endure, but part of me was fiercely jealous; my father never asked me for anything and never accepted anything I offered him. My contributions to his allowance were made under the table to avoid an ugly scene. I'd come to the distressing conclusion that I didn't have anything he wanted, or worse still, that he didn't want anything I had. He was unabashedly homophobic, but I had to remind myself that being heterosexual hadn't done Agnes all that much good.

Agnes's letter fluttered in my hand every time the fan rotated in the direction of the daybed, but I couldn't bring myself to read past the letterhead. I put the thing away, promising to read it before nightfall—or at least before dawn—of some day in the next week. I went over to my stereo and put on a scratchy recording of musette waltzes. Louise Morris, who knew of my fondness for the bright melancholy of accordion music, had turned me on to French dance hall tunes years earlier. As the afternoon wearied on, and I carted around the heavy fans, I played the record over a dozen times and thought more and more about my old friend and the period of my own life when we'd been close.

Louise and I had been in English Lit together my freshman year of college. A thin girl with fine copper hair and pale skin, she was always rushing into the room late or leaving early, knocking over a chair and apologizing loudly. She tended to dress in very practical, androgynous clothes—chinos, thermal T-shirts, work boots, bulky sports jackets—that somehow looked provocative on her, drew attention to her lean, clumsy body instead of hiding it. She rarely spoke up in class, but when she did, she made the kind of pithy, mildly ironic comments that can easily be interpreted as condescending or brilliant and, either way, turned most of the other students against her. There was always a lot of eye-rolling after Louise Morris made one of her literary comments: "I don't find Ophelia at all sympathetic. If she were alive today she'd be teaching aerobics." When she took more than a few sentences to make a point, she tended to ramble and let her hoarse, raspy voice trail off into silence in the middle of a thought.

The professor, a young man with the harried look of someone who'd fallen behind on his reading ten years earlier, had a fawning appreciation of her. He became rapt when she spoke and was visibly distressed when she left the class early. I don't think that helped her popularity much, either.

I was taken with Louise from the first time I saw her stumble into class, tousled and boyishly pretty and smelling of cigarettes. She had a pocket watch she was always pulling out to check the time, as if she had some important place to go, a real life outside of school she was eager to get back to. I had no life outside of school—or in it, for that matter—which heightened my fascination with her. I'd gone to college primarily as a way of distancing myself from my father, partially at his expense, and had forgotten that it involved studying and attending lectures and feigning an interest in the future. It was a state school in western Massachusetts, one of those bursting-at-the-seams places with the atmosphere of an overcrowded city in which no one has a job. Freshman year, I lived in a dormitory with thousands of teenage rowdies who spent most of their free time knocking down walls and throwing furniture out of windows. I suppose I could have found a niche into which I might have fit—a social group that catered to insecure, inarticulate, introverted homosexuals, let's say—but for months I got lost whenever I walked outside the dorm. Then, too, I seemed to be constitutionally incapable of fitting into groups: I alternately feared being rejected by them or losing myself in their claustrophobic warmth. The first months I was in school, I felt most comfortable at football games; I didn't care a thing about competitive sports, but I could sit in the middle of thousands of screaming fans and feel simultaneously surrounded and utterly alone.

I used to see Louise in the library, in a back corner of the top floor, where I studied and napped. I'd glimpse her leafing through old botany texts, books about birds, and poetry anthologies she routinely picked off a table of discarded tomes. We nodded at each other for weeks—more than once, she'd tripped over my feet when she was rushing into class—but neither one of us spoke.

Halfway into the semester, on an afternoon when I was trying to study, I was roused from my stupor by the sound of a man talking in a strained, choking whisper. "I have to go back to her," he was saying. "Considering everything, it wouldn't be fair not to. It wouldn't be right."

I turned around and saw a dark, brooding man sitting on the edge of a low table. He was wearing a paisley shirt with a big white collar and an ugly gold chain around his neck, items that made him look ruggedly handsome. I was just beginning to learn that the simplest way for masculine men to project masculinity is by dressing in cheap, slightly effeminate clothes. Louise was curled into a corner of the sofa in front of him, a book open on her lap. There were tears rolling down the man's face. I don't think I'd ever seen a man crying before, and the sight of him shocked and excited me in some strange, erotic way. I wished *I* could make a dark, brooding man weep merely by sitting in front of him with nonchalant disregard. It's relatively easy to make someone happy, but only the truly desirable can make loved ones miserable.

He reached out and took Louise's hand. "But who's going to take care of you?" he asked.

"Oh, I'll be fine," she said. "Really." She took back her hand and closed her book. "You just should have told me you were married, that's all. What are you going to name the baby?"

When he left, she looked at her pocket watch and went back to her reading.

I moved over to the opposite end of the sofa where she was sitting and rested my feet on the table, next to hers. She had on a pair of engineer's boots that made her feet look absurdly big and her legs spindly. "You recovered from that quickly," I said.

She had very pale blue eyes and a spray of freckles across her nose. When she smiled, I noticed that she had a slight overbite. I've never understood why people go to such great lengths to perfect their features when it's the imperfections that make a face memorable and appealing—the bumpy nose, the crooked mouth, the uneven eyes. Louise wasn't exactly beautiful, but something in her face drew you in. She had long eyelashes that made her look attentive and innocent and contrasted sharply to a pallor that made her look prematurely world-weary. "Poor Larry," she said hoarsely. "He's left with a bigger mess than I am."

"His wife?"

"His pregnant wife. You see, he had bad skin as an adolescent. It's made him unbelievably insecure."

I've always had a fondness for acne scars, except on the shoulders, which is where I have them. "Even so," I said, "he should have told you he was married."

I thought of marriage then as an exotic drunken brawl in which a man in ugly shoes and a woman in a girdle hurl insults at each other and make hollow threats. Not pretty, but glamorous somehow, like Joan Crawford in her horror-movie incarnation. In any case, not something to be taken or betrayed lightly.

"I told him that," she said. "Did you hear me tell him that?"

"I did."

"I wouldn't have gotten involved with him if I'd known." She started to loosen the lacings on her enormous boots. "On the other hand . . . maybe I would have." When she bit down on her lower lip, her overbite became more apparent and appealing. "You never say anything in class."

I was pleased that she'd noticed. "I usually don't get to the reading on time."

"Oh, that doesn't matter. You just listen for a while and then take a position that contradicts everything everyone else has said. You have to make it completely insupportable if you want professors to think you're a genius. You're gay, right?" she asked, without any hint of judgment, and then started to tell me about an ex-boyfriend of hers she thought I might like to meet. I was happy she accepted it so calmly, but I was a little disappointed that she'd stolen the fanfare and drama of revealing to her the central secret Fact of My Life, the only Fact of My Life that I was aware of at the time. Before I even had time to comment, she changed the subject again. "It's for the best it's over with Larry."

She had on a long-sleeved T-shirt, and she pushed the sleeves up to her elbows. I was surprised by the frailty of her arms; the bones of her wrists stuck out and her skin had a skim-milk cast. Her pale eyes began to wander around the room and settled on a shelf of books behind us. It was obvious she was about to cry. It was one thing to watch a stranger cry from a safe distance, but to sit beside a weeping acquaintance was a different story. "You'll have a lot less trouble without him," I said quickly. "No relationship, no demands. You'll probably get better grades."

"No, no," she said. "I get good grades anyway. It's because I don't really care about them. If I cared about them, I'd be flunking out. As long as you don't want something too passionately, it's bound to come your way sooner or later."

We studied together for the rest of the semester, and by Christmas we were fast friends. We shared a sublet that summer, a dilapidated apartment with a view of the Berkshires, and we split the cost of a used Volkswagen van. Louise had taken a job in a drugstore. She had a half-baked idea that she might like to go into pharmacology. It was a hot summer, the air still most days and the mountains shrouded in thick haze. I found a job working on the grounds of a vast resort hotel. I didn't have any half-baked ideas of going into the hotel business, but there was an atmosphere of sexual possibility on the wide, shady porches and in the steamy, fragrant gardens which excited me, even though the furtive glances suggested more than they ever delivered. In the evenings, Louise and I would drive our van into the mountains to cool off and watch the sunset. She was usually on her third beer by the time I got home from work, and eager to talk as we watched the valley turn red and then purple and then fade away altogether.

Louise had been an illegitimate child, a category her son, Ben, would have fit into if it still existed, which, for all practical purposes, it no longer did. She'd been raised by an aunt and uncle, and although her childhood had been happy enough, it was obvious she considered herself an orphan. She had a mania for self-sufficiency, which sometimes amounted to finding someone to take care of her.

She always had admirers, mostly men in their late twenties, men with jobs and cars who were drawn to her resourcefulness and probably all that trembling loneliness that was peeking out from behind her front of bold independence. Usually, though, her admirers had a wife or girlfriend in the picture, someone who wasn't quite an ex, and most of her relationships evolved into one-sided friendships. Louise got calls at I A.M. from former boyfriends who were a little drunk and wanted to tell her how wonderful she was and how they wished things had worked out differently. She often seemed dismayed by her relationships, but it was clear she would have been terrified by a man who didn't have other irons in the fire, other lives to live, and other women to marry.

She smoked too much, drank too heavily, could be frustratingly stubborn, and sometimes, in a room full of people, she seemed to drift away, as if she were attending to a secret sadness. Once, when I asked her if she was happy, she said, "I'm not destined for a big hilarious life. You can tell that, can't you?"

It was true. She wasn't morose or self-pitying, but she had the demeanor of someone who was resigned to making the best of a bad situation.

One hot afternoon at the end of that first summer we shared an apartment, I went into Louise's room and lay down on the bed beside her. She was reading and smoking, and I watched her for a while as her eyes moved across the pages. She'd cut her hair off that summer, making her look even more careless about her appearance and more dashing as a result. There was an exhaust fan in the window, spinning the smoke into a thread and sucking it out of the room. The summer was nearly over. Our van was up on blocks in the driveway beside the house, and the tenants we'd sublet from were due back in a week. I was moving to a small room in a boardinghouse, and Louise was moving into an apartment with a girlfriend.

After a while, Louise put down her book and rested her head on my shoulder. "I don't think I'll ever be a pharmacist, Clyde."

"The amazing part," I said, "is that you ever thought you would."

"Look, man, it's a living. I have to worry about making a living.

I guess I thought it was a practical career I could tap into. Counting out pills. I thought I'd like it. Now I think I'll end up doing something very impractical."

"I think that's a good idea, Louise." I'd never really understood people with practical goals. The premed students with their chemistry books and the eerie economics majors with their statistics and bar graphs seemed to exist in a parallel universe, one I wouldn't have known how to enter even if I'd wanted to. "Did you have a particular impractical field in mind?"

"I might write, for instance," she said.

"A good choice. You can string that one along for decades."

Like everyone else who's read a novel, I'd considered this option myself, but I'd concluded it required too much stamina. Despite her exhausted appearance, Louise had stamina. I was waiting for some unsuspected talent or ambition—an aptitude for physics, let's say, or the ability to play the piano by ear, or a desire to speed skate competitively—to rear its head and lead me on. If none of it worked out, I figured I could always go to law school.

For me and Louise and for everyone we knew, the world seemed filled with unlimited possibilities. But when we said, as we often did, that anything could happen, even the most cynical of us said it with the vain optimism that's one of youth's most dangerous blind spots. Certainly in those days, and for a few promiscuous years after, there didn't seem to be such things as mistakes that couldn't be corrected or diseases that couldn't be cured.

The summer after graduation, Louise and I shared another apartment, a bigger one than the first, but without a view. In September she was going to France, where she'd lined up an au pair position, and I was heading off to Chicago to enroll in the first of many graduate programs I'd never finish. For three months, I felt caught in a no-man's-land between the home I'd grown up in and couldn't go back to and the one I wanted to inhabit but didn't yet know how to create for myself. If a picture fell off the wall, Louise and I left it on the floor. I didn't bother to shelve books as I finished reading them; I'd just heave them into a corner, where they'd be easier to pack.

Some nights, I'd come home from work late and Louise would sit me down in the kitchen and tell me, lucidly and in extraordinary detail, about a story she was writing or was planning to write. It took me a while to realize that this outpouring of detail, her most enthusiastic talk, usually meant she'd been drinking. She was one of those unusual people who seem to be more clearheaded when slightly drunk, even though her pale eyes got red and her lids heavy. I didn't think anything of it at first—careless inebriation is another privilege of youth—and besides, nothing seemed to matter very much that summer. We were both in limbo. But after a while, it began to dawn on me that I often saw her drunk but never saw her drinking. It was the loneliness of the whole enterprise that worried me.

Marcus lived in a basement apartment in our building. He'd graduated from Amherst when Louise and I were freshmen at our school. He was already practicing the hanger-on skills he'd perfected by the time I caught up with him again, years later, in Cambridge. We'd watch him coming and going through a little screened porch on the front of the house. He was blond and deeply tanned, and in those days, he walked with a healthy dose of self-assurance. Late in the summer he started coming by the apartment for coffee and asking Louise out to the movies.

One night when Louise and I were having dinner, she asked, apropos of nothing, "Do you think I should?"

I knew exactly what she meant. The question of whether or not she'd sleep with Marcus had been hovering since we first noticed him. "Go ahead," I told her. "I would. You're leaving, he's leaving. What could be more romantic than that?"

For nearly a month, I'd been having a torrid love affair with a man I couldn't stand the sight of. It seemed entirely possible to be passionate about anyone, as long as you were fairly certain you wouldn't have to look at him after a set date.

I don't think Louise's affair with Marcus lasted more than a couple of weeks. By early September, Marcus had packed off to Harvard. Louise and I put our belongings on the sidewalk and sold them. I drove Louise to the airport in Montreal and waved to her as she boarded the plane. She had two suitcases, both small, and was wearing a pair of overalls. She was proud of the fact that she was traveling light—undeserved pride, as I was soon to find out.

I heard from her only once when she was in France, a cryptic postcard that was all weather and paintings. When she returned, she sent a letter from California. "I'm a bilingual mother, Clyde. I've moved out here for a while. Probably forever."

I never thought all that much about Ben's paternity. Louise had told me his father was an Australian she'd met in Paris and had lost touch with by the time she discovered she was pregnant. Reading between the lines of her first novel, you had to assume the husband of the family she worked for in France, a chubby doctor, had fathered her baby. I suppose I accepted the truth as some hazy confusion of the two stories; Ben was enough like Louise in appearance and demeanor to make the question seem irrelevant somehow. Besides, the idea of simply not having a father had always struck me as enviably uncomplicated.

That afternoon as I lay in my cramped attic rooms with the black cast-iron fan clattering on the floor in front of me, and all that waltzing accordion music playing in the background, I entertained myself by guessing what complications she might be alluding to. But finally I put the letter aside, reminding myself that Louise had a streak of drama she loved to play on.

WOULD GLADLY HAVE SPENT THE NEXT
several days or weeks—or however long it took Louise to drive across the country—thinking about my
old friend and her life, largely because the whole
business demanded so little of me and provided a
distraction from those things that demanded more.
For example, Agnes and the bundle of family misery
she was carrying on her shoulders. Several days after
her letter arrived, I finally got around to reading it.
It was typical of my sister's notes and her style of
communication in general: reproaches disguised as
apologies, cries for help disguised as gentle reproaches, and an overriding tone of despair that was
barely disguised at all. She'd begun one sentence: *As
for Barbara,* but then had drawn three lines through
the words, as if she couldn't bring herself to discuss
her teenage daughter. The only point she made
clearly was that our father seemed to be getting
"worse" and she needed to talk about the situation
with me. But even this wasn't as unequivocal as it
seemed. When dealing with matters paternal, Agnes

spoke in coded language. It was possible that "worse" meant sicker, but she usually used the word when she meant to say that he was becoming more demanding and critical of her than ever.

I phoned Agnes several times over the course of the next few days. She always picked up after half a ring, a sign that she'd been waiting by her office phone, ready to pounce on a potential client.

"E and A Resources, Inc. Can I *help* you?"

The flutey forced cheerfulness in her voice and that bright uprise on "help" got to me every time. I wanted to start all over again— not with the phone call, but with my whole life. As soon as I heard her greeting, I hung up.

What finally compelled me to go through with contacting Agnes was a dinner I had with my friend Vance Merkin.

Vance was one of several people I'd met through my former lover Gordon and the only one I continued to see on a regular basis. Gordon himself had been a twenty-four-year-old law student when I met him. He was standing behind me in line at a cash register in the Harvard Coop, delivering a nonstop monologue to a friend, a rant that swooped dizzyingly from environmental law to Latin American politics to infamous celebrity fashion faux pas. He had a rumbling voice that was excessively deep in an unconvincing sort of way, as if he was pulling in his chin to strangle his larynx and collapse down into a lower register. The voice was completely at odds with his outrage over what some minor movie actress had had the audacity to wear to the Oscars four years earlier and made him sound like a truckdriver with a Liz Smith complex. When I finally turned around, I saw a short, chunky guy in a loose summer shirt, a pair of saggy seersucker shorts that made his legs look about as long as his forearms, and cheap plastic flip-flops. He had a sloppy, slatternly demeanor—shirt half tucked in, hair rumpled —that immediately fired my interest. There can be something mesmerizingly sexy about laziness, particularly if it's combined with intellectual curiosity and manic, gossipy talk. His shirt revealed a gentle roll of stomach, another plus. I'm not especially partial to fat, but owing to my general insecurity, I prefer going to bed with men who have convex guts, since they're more likely to mistake my emaciation for a washboard stomach.

Gordon and I went from the cash register to a coffee shop to cohabitation just like that, one two three.

I blamed the eagerness with which I leapt into love with Gordon on a lack of attentiveness. Less than a year before we met, I'd managed to extricate myself from a devoted lover and believed that I wasn't looking for another relationship and wasn't due to find one, a relaxed state of mind that made me especially vulnerable to bumping into one headfirst.

We lived together for two years, and then Gordon graduated from law school and from me at roughly the same time. He left me after delivering a speech that sounded suspiciously like one I'd heard at his commencement exercises. New Beginnings, Looking Ahead—god-awful greeting-card sentiments he'd obviously taken too much to heart. I was considerably more shattered by his departure than I ever would have guessed. I'd have guessed that our relationship was almost at the point of dying peacefully in its sleep anyway. We'd traveled the predictable route from passionate groping at the movies to eating dinner watching TV. I'd begun to clench my teeth when I heard a sentence that started, "If you don't mind me saying so" or "Don't take this the wrong way." I found it more and more difficult to say "Drive carefully" when Gordon left for a trip.

But the sense of rejection I felt at his departure was so complete and overwhelming, I was still reeling from it two years later and trying to figure out a way to patch my wounds. It was obvious, even to me, that my reaction to his leaving was so out of line with what I'd been feeling for him that he must have tapped into a deep reservoir of hurt that had been waiting to drown me for years. Still, the only way I could think to make things right was to keep my love for him alive in some locked chamber of my heart and pretend that he'd made a gross mistake and was bound to come back to correct it. When he did, well, then we could get down to the business of going our separate ways.

I knew better than to talk with friends about my lingering feelings of affection for Gordon; it's considered chivalrous to maintain feelings for a former lover only if you're the one who ended the relationship in the first place or if, as is so often the case these days, you've been widowed.

I broke the rule of discretion only with Vance Merkin. He and Gordon had been friends in law school and still saw each other at lawyerly functions. And Vance was in no position to pass judgment on me. For the four years I'd known him, he'd been obsessing over a young man with whom he'd had an unconsummated seven-month relationship. If my attitude toward my ex was pathetic, at least it wasn't as pathetic as his. He'd arranged his whole life around his obsession with Carl in a way that I probably would have found frightening if it hadn't suited my purposes so well.

Vance and I met from time to time at a restaurant in Boston's grimy financial district, a neighborhood tucked between the fashionable shopping streets and the waterfront. The restaurant was close to where Vance lived, but he insisted upon going there not for convenience but because Carl had worked in the kitchen for three months more than a decade earlier and one of the ancient waitresses claimed to remember him.

I had a genuine fondness for Vance that went beyond the connection with Gordon. He'd graduated from Yale at twenty and Harvard Law at twenty-four. He was still under thirty (although he looked a good fifty) and was making well over a hundred grand a year. Most of his income was spent on dinners, clothing, and the expensive gifts he lavished on Carl's mother, a widow who lived in a suburb north of Boston. (Carl himself had departed for a commune in San Francisco long before I'd met Vance. According to Vance, he'd discovered he had bone cancer and had moved to the West Coast to spare his mother the pain of watching his illness progress. According to Gordon's rumor mill, Carl was perfectly healthy and was simply fleeing from Vance.) Vance had boundless neurotic energy and great intelligence, both of which he squandered on trivial concerns. Above all else, he was a kind man and, like all kind people, pleasant to be with and mildly depressed.

I met him on a balmy August night, after nearly a week of aborted calls to Agnes. I'd taken the subway into Boston and, an hour past the agreed-upon time, was still waiting on a corner near the restaurant. The streets in that part of town were always empty in the evening, and the whole city took on a pleasant deserted atmosphere I love—as if a bomb had wiped out the crowds but the subway was still conveniently running. The swath of sky visible between the granite buildings had turned bright purple as the sun set, a fleeting few minutes of magenta beauty.

I'd taken a seat on the sidewalk with my back pressed against one of the crumbling gray buildings and immersed myself in the last chapter of *Wuthering Heights*, trying mentally to compose a lecture on it for class. Not that I needed to worry. I'd been teaching a series of unrelated courses at the adult ed center for several years, and experience had taught me that it didn't matter all that much what I said. Few of the students who enrolled in the classes actually read the assigned books, and a small percentage of those who did had any interest in discussing them. Whether I talked about Cathy and Heathcliff or Ishmael and Ahab or Batman and Robin, the class would listen in polite silence for about ten minutes. Then someone would ask an irrelevant question and the group would debate an amorphous topic unrelated to the book in question. The week before, in the middle of my halting lecture on narrative structure, someone had initiated a discussion of sex education in elementary schools that had gone on for the better part of an hour.

But I was determined to do justice to the ending. A teacher can get away with any number of fumbled inanities and inaccurate statements about a book as long as he's brilliant about the ending. Or at least coherent.

My stab at having a life of the mind was cut short by a taxi making the corner at the far end of the street. It came to a halt in front of me, and Vance burst from it as if he'd been shoved from behind. He bounced across the street and embraced me, rattling off a long, incomprehensible list of apologies.

Vance had my unimpressive height and was, to be kind about it, stout. Since getting hired at a prominent law firm, he'd taken to wearing extremely expensive business suits he had made for him by a tailor in Italy. Despite the extravagance, his wardrobe didn't really complement his personality or his bulk or the pink puffiness and almost feminine smoothness of his face. He ended up looking like someone in costume: specifically, a girls' field hockey coach in male drag. He also had the unfortunate habit of wearing hats, usually big, loud ones that sat on top of his head as if they had landed there and were about to take possession of his body. Tonight he had on a large panama with the brim turned down. The hats were a too obvious bid for Personality, something Vance was hardly lacking, but because he was terribly vain about them, I always felt obliged to comment.

"That's some creation," I said, straightening out the brim.

"No, no, no, no," he rattled. He tended to speak so quickly, he sometimes sounded as though he were singing a patter song from a Gilbert and Sullivan operetta. "It's all wrong for me. Too much panache for my small head. I bought an identical one for Carl's mother. I thought it would be cute, the two of us in identical hats. The creep won't wear it. Oh, Clyde, not *Wuthering Heights.* Read it when I was twelve and desperately wanted a nervous breakdown. It glamorizes languishing in bed with a wasting disease. Well, look what we're dealing with now. My poor Carl." He took a triangle of chocolate out of his jacket pocket and popped it into his mouth. "Beautiful sunset, wasn't it?" he mumbled, melting the candy in his mouth.

"I only saw that much of it," I said, pointing to the sky between the buildings.

"That was the best part. How are you, dear? Hold this, will you?" He handed me his briefcase, slipped off his suit jacket, and began fiddling with the suspenders that were tented out over his impressive stomach. "Monstrosity, aren't I? Gained fifty pounds since last Tuesday. Why the hell did I just eat that chocolate?" He wiped his mouth with an initialed handkerchief. "Compulsive eater, that's why. Why couldn't I have been addicted to crack or something slenderizing? Well, I'm going on a diet next week."

Vance tended to flatten any possible comments about his rapidly increasing girth by bringing it up first. It wasn't clear to me what he was doing with his suspenders, but I had the feeling he wanted to exhibit his belly, show me what he thought of as the worst of himself right off so I wouldn't think he was trying to hide something.

"What's in here?" I said, hefting the briefcase.

"Oh, who knows. My secretary loads it up every night before I leave. I must have a lot to do tonight. Did I tell you about my new secretary? Dead ringer for Carl's mother. Hell of a lot more on the ball, though. I should have bought the matching hat for *her*. Shall we go in?"

The restaurant was one of those dark, paneled Boston eateries that cater to elderly Brahmin businessmen. The light of day never reached the far corners of the room, creating an atmosphere of impenetrability that I suppose was reassuring to those who didn't want to be reminded of the changing world on the other side of the heavily curtained windows. The dining room smelled of starched linen and grilled meat. The decor hadn't been altered in decades, and the staff, mostly white-haired and glum, appeared to have been suspended at age sixty-three. Because the restaurant catered to a lunchtime crowd, it was almost always empty when Vance and I ate there, a fact that contributed to the general gloom. The hostess waved to us from across the room as we walked in, and we seated ourselves at the corner table where we always sat.

Vance settled in clumsily, jostling the table with his belly. He loosened his tie, readjusted his hat to a more jaunty angle, and shook out one of the enormous starched napkins. "Here comes the grim reaper," he said, waving brightly to Beatrice, our perpetually dour waitress. She came toward us, not so much walking as tipping from side to side on her spindly legs.

When she'd finally made it to our table, Vance grabbed her hand. "They've been working you too hard as always," he said. "Pull up a chair, Clyde, and let Bea sit down for a minute. Doesn't she look adorable? What's that perfume you're wearing? I love it. Give me the name before we leave, and I'll bring you a few bottles next time we come."

Vance had an extraordinary ability to charm older women. Once when I'd first met him, he'd helped an elderly, shaky woman with too many groceries negotiate a busy intersection in Harvard Square. By the time they'd crossed the street, she'd offered to rent him the attic of her Brattle Street mansion, and he'd spent the remainder of his law school career there.

"Carl always said you were an angel to him when he worked here. The least I can do is bring you some perfume."

To her credit, Beatrice was wary. "Feisty little guy that one was," she said blandly. She had on hot-pink lipstick that arched up off her thin lips in a heart shape, like a child's drawing of a mouth.

Vance nudged me under the table.

I have no idea what Beatrice thought of Vance, but I'd come to the conclusion that she had absolutely no recollection of anyone named Carl. The first time Vance had mentioned him, I suspect she'd gone along to be polite. The nonspecific little compliments she continued to toss out were obviously motivated by business sense. Vance regularly dropped twenty-five-dollar tips, even though the heavy food was undistinguished and we usually sent our plates back half full.

"Feisty," Vance said. "He *was* feisty, wasn't he? A bundle of energy. His mother claims he was always sluggish. Can you believe it? You haven't heard from him, have you, hon?"

Beatrice pursed her pink lips and touched the froth of white hair hovering over her head, as if to make sure it was still there. "Now that you mention it . . . no, no I haven't. Maybe next week."

After we'd ordered, I sat back and asked Vance if he'd seen Gordon recently. I always tried to get that part of the conversation out of the way early on, just so it wouldn't be buzzing around the table, distracting me from other topics. It seemed the only decent thing to do, since Vance insisted on paying for the meals we ate together.

"Little Gordie," he said fondly. "I saw him at a fund-raiser a few weeks ago, poor baby. He's not happy with that man, Clyde— you know that, don't you?"

I shrugged. "Between you and me," I said, "how could he be happy?"

"What's-his-name is deadly boring, isn't he?"

What's-his-name was Michael, the brawny accountant Gordon had been living with for nearly a year. "Deadly. How does Gordon look?"

"He looks fine," he said, snapping a bread stick in half and dipping it into a pot of processed cheese, "as far as looks go. I could do without the crew cut and the muscles. That style is so ridiculous on men. Much better on dykes. I hope they don't have a gym out at Carl's commune. It's unhealthy, in the long run." He peered into the pot of cheese, munching. "No flavor, no texture. I feel like I'm eating used chewing gum."

"Gordon's searching for meaning," I said. "Literature to psychology to law school to the gym. A downward spiral. Next it'll be religion, you watch. He's the kind of lost soul those religious vipers prey upon."

"I heard a rumor What's-his-name is a Republican."

"I suspected as much, to tell you the truth. Gordon should have stayed with me and let himself sit with his unhappiness. This is a phase, you watch."

"Of course it is, dear."

It was a mystery to me why I was consoled by these conversations with Vance, since I knew he was only telling me what I wanted to hear and I believed a mere fraction of what I said myself. I considered his feelings for Carl to be so neurotic they were almost grotesque, and I suspect he felt the same way about me. But we had a bond of insincere acceptance.

"It's tragic," Vance said. "Like Carl, out at that commune. His own mother admits it. Says Carl would have been a lot happier if he'd stayed in the East. Sharing a bathroom with fifteen people! Never complains, though. Never mentions a thing about his health to the mother."

When Beatrice had delivered the unappetizing plates of beef, Vance sat looking at his despondently. With the shadow from the brim of his hat falling across his fleshy cheeks, he looked like a cross between Dietrich and Al Capone.

"Don't look at me like that," he said, "or I'll have to get a drink, and then you'll be sorry you came."

"I thought you were on a no-booze diet."

"Carl's mother knocked me off the wagon. I've got to stop taking her out to dinner. Thank God she goes for those cheap suburban places with the big parking lots. Early-bird special for six ninety-nine. Of course, it costs me fifty bucks in cab fare every time I take her out."

At least twice a week, Vance took a taxi to the suburbs and treated Carl's mother to dinner at the restaurant of her choice. "Maybe you should get a driver's license," I suggested.

"I'd love to, but I know so many cabdrivers now I'd feel I was letting them all down. When is Miss Morris arriving in town?"

"I have no idea. Soon, I imagine."

"Do you think you could talk her into coming to my book group? I haven't been to a meeting in two years, and dragging her in might be just the coup that would let me start up again."

Like virtually everyone else in Boston, Vance was a member of a book discussion group, one of those organized gatherings that sounded a lot like dinner parties to me and resembled my classes at The Learning Place. Vance never attended meetings of his group because he had a crush on one of the other members and got too nervous in his presence to talk articulately. Still, he read more than anyone I knew or had ever known, although when he found the time, I couldn't imagine. In addition to working sixty hours a week, watching every television show in existence, taking on a significant number of pro bono cases, and eating compulsively, he went through two or three novels a week, everything from Flaubert to the kinds of lowly romances that had driven Emma Bovary over the edge.

"You're trying to exploit her success," I said sternly. "Anyway, she's not going to any book groups until she's given a lecture at one of my classes."

Vance looked at me pityingly and shook his big head. He was unabashedly critical of my job. A couple of years earlier, he'd made use of some connections he had at a private school outside the city and, after helping me to plump up my résumé, had finagled me an interview for a teaching position. But that had been right around the time that Gordon had departed and I'd moved in with Marcus, and I hadn't followed through on any of it. He was always offering to reopen the doors for me, but I never felt as if I was quite ready. The headmistress was one of his sixty-plus-year-old female friends, and he routinely warned me that if I didn't make some move soon, his connection was likely to take her retirement and move to Florida. Frankly, I was more concerned that if I didn't make a move soon, I would cross over into that pushing-forty age group that's viewed suspiciously at job interviews, especially if the job involves working with minors.

Vance took off his hat and scratched his scalp. Because he constantly wore hats, everyone assumed he was bald, but he had a full head of tight brown curls. For years, I'd been trying to encourage him to get a shorter haircut or have his hair straightened; the curly mop made him look especially matronly, a little like Margaret Rutherford, give or take a couple of decades. "I suppose Louise will want to start up another torrid affair with Marcus the minute she arrives in town," he said mournfully. Along with everyone else I knew, Vance was fascinated by Marcus.

"I seriously doubt it," I said. "I don't think she cared that much about him to begin with."

"Are you *sure* he doesn't walk around the house stark naked day and night, taunting you with his body, humiliating you and begging for admiration?"

"I'd have noticed by now."

"I suppose so. Oh Christ, why did I order this side of beef? My arteries are hardening just looking at it. Did I tell you Carl's mother calls herself a vegetarian? It's the new trend out in the 'burbs. They think it's healthier to say they're vegetarians, even though they still eat chicken, pork, beef, lamb, veal, and anything else that had a face. Oh-oh, better start eating—here comes the living dead."

After Vance had assured Beatrice the food was delicious and she'd tottered off, he pushed his plate away from him. He put on a pair of tiny Ben Franklin spectacles, read the ingredients list on the bread stick wrapper, and began a ravenous attack. Dipping into the pot of cheese, he sighed and said tonelessly, "I saw your delightful father at one of the restaurants Carl's mother insisted we go to."

"My father?"

He nodded. "And one of the worst restaurants, too. All they had on the menu was Boston scrod. Will you tell me what's wrong with this city? I'm giving serious consideration to moving to New York. I've even got a lead on a great two-bedroom. Do you think Carl's mother and I could get along?"

"Doubtful," I said. "And I don't think it was my father you saw at the restaurant. He's a semi-invalid. He's supposedly dying. I've told you that."

"It definitely was him, dear. Same guy I saw at your mother's funeral. The one who asked you, right in front of me, if I was a 'lesbo,' remember? Did wonders for my self-image. He was having a grand old time with some babe and a youngish man who looked like her son."

As far as I knew, my father hadn't so much as cracked a smile in twenty-five years, not counting laughing at someone else's misfortune.

" 'Babe'?" I asked. "What do you mean, 'babe'?"

"Some creature in her late sixties. Same age as Carl's mother. A lot better-looking, too, but don't ever say I told you so. Frightening hairdo, though. Cotton-candy-in-a-tornado look. Very in, in the 'burbs."

"What do you mean, 'grand old time'? And 'youngish man'? How young? How do you know it was her son?"

Vance put his panama hat back on his head and cleared out a space on the table in front of him. He pulled a handful of sugar packets out of their container and started to arrange them on the starched white tablecloth. "Here's the booth Carl's mother and I were in. Here's the booth with your father and the babe. Here's the waiters' station. I could see the Boston scrod on their plates. I thought about going over and introducing myself, just to bug your old man, but Carl's mother hates it when I leave her alone, even to go to the bathroom. They were having a little party. Your father ordered some champagne, and they were toasting the son. Your father had his arm around the son's shoulder. More than that I can't tell you. What's the big deal?"

"The big deal," I said, beginning to think that maybe there was some truth to what he was saying, "is that he's supposed to be dying. And broke, too. So what's a penniless dying widower doing out with a babe and her son? Ordering champagne?"

"What was I doing out with a horror like Carl's mother, poor dear? What are you doing out with me? Oh, Clyde, find me a nice boy. I'm so lonely. No, no, no, never mind. It wouldn't work out. I've got to start that diet tomorrow. Don't they give any courses in bulimia at The Learning Place?"

"Not that I'm aware of. Though I'm sure they've considered it."

"Do something else with your life, will you, Clyde? Oh Christ, here she comes again, the zombie parade. Order some dessert or something, anything to boost the bill a little."

When I'd left Vance and taken the subway back to Cambridge and climbed up the creaking flight of steps at the back of the house to my attic rooms, I reread Agnes's note. But I couldn't find anything in it to indicate that Dad had been going out with any babes, no matter how carefully I read between the lines.

I called Agnes.

Now that E and A Resources, Inc. was closed for the day, she answered the phone with a halting hello, as if she was expecting a heavy breather or a death threat. My sister, like most people who reside in communities far enough outside the cities to be considered safe, lived with one foot in a perpetual panic attack.

"Agnes," I said. "It's your brother."

"Clyde?" she asked, as if there were another choice. Agnes was always stating the obvious, an indication of her touching insecurity and an altogether infuriating habit.

"I got your letter," I said calmly. There was no point in trying to be direct with Agnes, since it made her even more nervous.

"I had to send it, Clyde. You weren't returning the messages I left on the machine. I wish you'd let me know if that answering machine is broken. I sent in the warranty on it—"

"The machine is fine, sweetheart. It was the perfect gift. I just haven't had a chance to call, I've been so busy, with teaching and all."

"Ever since you became a professor, you've been too busy for everything."

"Please, Agnes," I said. Considering the circumstances at the so-called Learning Place, "teacher" would have been bad enough.

It was still quite warm, and a humid breeze was blowing through my rooms. I could hear a couple of the neighborhood teenagers issuing threats to each other and a few of the nasty dogs behind us barking. "How's the business going?" I asked.

"Well, Elizabeth's optimistic about the vitamin sales. I'm still not sure. The pills are a little hard to swallow. They're biggish. I hope that doesn't hurt business."

I didn't say anything. The vitamins bore an unsettling resemblance, in size and color, to dog biscuits. Scurvy was a more appealing option than trying to gag down one of those every morning. "What's all that noise?" Agnes asked. "It sounds as if someone's being attacked by animals."

"I'm sure it's just people attacking each other. What's going on with . . . Dad?"

She let out a long breath, as if she were practicing her yoga. Agnes, the least physical person in the universe, had signed up for a yoga class last January. She claimed that it had changed her life, although there was no evidence to support the claim. "Oh, Clyde. I'm not sure, but I think he's getting worse."

"How do you mean worse?"

"I mean sicker. More cranky, snapping at me all the time, complaining about meals. And he says his allowance isn't enough. I might have to ask you to pitch in a few more dollars."

"Agnes," I said, "has he . . . has he been going out more?"

"Why would you ask that?" There was an edge of hysteria in her voice. Agnes lived in fear of conspiracies and inexplicable coincidences. I blamed our Catholic upbringing.

"No reason. I was just wondering."

"Well, as a matter of fact, he *has* been going out more. I think he's going for some kind of treatments he doesn't want to tell me about. It fits with his whole mood."

"There are some other possibilities, you know."

"Such as what?"

"Well, maybe we should sit down and go over this situation again."

"Situation?"

"He's been living with you since Mom died. Maybe it's time to review the options."

"If you're talking about a nursing home, Clyde, I won't. I just won't. I couldn't live with myself, and neither could you."

Agnes's voice was getting chirpy, as if she was about to burst into tears. She had a way of bursting into tears or fits of inappropriate laughter, sometimes in the middle of a sentence. She'd inherited this trait, along with her insecurities and her bad digestion, from our mother. I tried to change the subject, but the options weren't promising: her business, the cookbook, her daughter. One topic seemed as perilous as the next.

"I was thinking about coming up for a visit," I said. "I could try and see what's going on with him."

"Please. When?"

Faced with the prospect of actually setting a date, I felt my stomach start to tighten and the first knot of a headache take shape behind my eyes. "I don't know," I said. "Maybe sometime before Thanksgiving?"

"Thanks*giving?* It's not even September. What about tomorrow night?"

"I have plans," I said.

"Oh. Are you seeing Gordon?"

"Gordon? Gordon and I haven't been living together for two years, Agnes! I wish you wouldn't keep mentioning *Gordon!*"

"Don't jump down my throat, Clyde! I'm under a lot of stress. If it weren't for the yoga, I don't know where I'd be."

Because Agnes, although accepting of me in a broad, sentimental way, had never quite been able to grasp the concept of a relationship between two men, she'd never been able to understand that Gordon and I had broken up. Because I had never been able to understand that we'd broken up, either, I found her constant mentions of him especially annoying and gratifying. "I hope you're being careful, whoever you're going out with."

Agnes's safe-sex lecture. She was always cautioning me to be careful, and I was always advising her to take risks.

"Maybe in a couple of weeks," I said, worn down by the pleading in her tone. "I'll talk it over with Marcus. He mentioned he'd like to come."

"Oh, Clyde, I'm sure you must have misunderstood. Marcus is probably too busy with Harvard and girlfriends to visit *me.*"

"Well, maybe he won't."

"Why are you so discouraging? I'd love to see him. He's always so cheerful and Southern."

"Cheerful" was Agnes's highest compliment. As far as I could tell, it meant someone who made her forget for a moment how unhappy she was. I still hadn't broken the code on "Southern."

We set a date. I said goodbye and started to hang up.

"Oh my," Agnes sighed.

That remorseful, crushed sigh put my older sister right there in my bedroom: low ceiling, sloping walls, scattered socks, Agnes, and me. Agnes wore a fragrance she referred to as a "splash" called Summer Meadow, and I could practically smell its sweet scent, and I wanted to hold her hand and let her have a good cry and try to make everything all right for her. "What's the matter, sweetheart?" I asked.

"Oh, nothing. Just . . . everything."

"Agnes," I said, "it's going to be fine. One of these days, everything is going to turn around."

"I just wish I had a nice beefsteak tomato to have for lunch tomorrow," she said.

On that note, I decided to hang up and did.

T RAINED STEADILY ALL MORNING THE DAY
Louise arrived in Cambridge, one of those drumming, insistent rains that signal the hesitant approach of a new season. It wasn't quite two weeks since my dinner with Vance, but already summer seemed to be losing its sweaty grip.

After talking with Agnes, I'd attempted a few calls to my father, but hadn't succeeded in going through with them. My father's telephone style was to pick up the receiver and, instead of saying hello, to wait in stony, indignant silence for the intrusive caller to announce himself first, a test of wills. I always felt as if I was being sucked into that silent void on the other end of the line and hung up, exactly the effect my father hoped his intimidation would have. But in addition to my being intimidated, there was a small part of me that feared he might hang up if he recognized my voice. Oddly, I always felt sure he knew it was me anyway, and after every attempted call, I came down with a crushing headache.

There must have been a small leak in the roof

above my attic rooms, because whenever it rained, a brown, oblong water stain in one corner of the ceiling deepened in color and spread. I loved to lie in bed and read, with the rain driving against the leaking roof. The morning Louise arrived, I looked up occasionally from a stultifying biography of an opera singer to watch the slow progress of the seepage. It was tremendously reassuring to me to know that no matter how bad the situation got, I would never have to fix it. I'd called the landlord two years earlier. I'd done my duty. If the roof fell in, it wasn't my concern. It made me feel secure, lying there, watching someone else's house deteriorate around me while I read about someone else's deteriorating life.

By early afternoon, the storm had passed and the sun had come out. The steam was rising off the soaked pavement when Louise called. I was shaken by the sound of her raspy voice, now only a mile or so away. Her voice had a way of pulling me back in time, since, despite my ongoing fondness for her and the distant way I kept up with her, our friendship existed in the past.

"I can't believe you're so close," I said. "I really can't."

"Neither can I, Clyde. Tell me I haven't made a hideous, irreparable mistake I'll regret for the rest of my miserable life."

"Of course you haven't," I said. Louise was always looking for reassurance, although she never accepted any. "Why would you think that?"

"We unloaded the car and the house is filled with boxes UPS dropped off weeks ago and I've got a stiff neck and the trip is over and now we have to start living. It's daunting."

"But you're an expert at this sort of thing," I reminded her. "You've been relocating for years."

"I think that's what makes it so difficult. The thrill is gone. I used to feel like an old hippie, but today I just feel old. Will you come over and tell me it's fine? It really is a beautiful place, a total fluke I landed anything this nice from three thousand miles away." She lowered her voice to a hoarse whisper. "Ben loves it, even though he won't admit it. Come before we both lose our enthusiasm, shredded as it is already."

I copied down her address and told her I'd be over in a few hours. I could have left right then, but it was the middle of the day, and I didn't want to make a bad first impression by having it look as if I didn't have more important things to do. Or at least other things to do. Already I could feel the gaps in my résumé open wider beneath my feet. In the dozen years since graduation, Louise had racked up quite a list of accomplishments—books, offspring, foreign languages, and teaching credentials. The most I could point to was a series of failed attempts at advanced education, one relationship I hadn't been able to stay in and a more recent one I hadn't been able to leave, and a few trial memberships at health clubs. I'd done some traveling, too, but travel on an otherwise unimpressive résumé looks like what it usually is: an attempt to give the appearance of forward momentum to a life that's really at a standstill.

I'd recently come to the conclusion that much of the stop-and-start quality of my experience thus far (with the emphasis on stop) could be traced back to my inability or unwillingness to really participate in anything, even my own life. I'm not a joiner. I have all the instincts of an outsider, but saying even that implies membership in an avant-garde, bohemian sort of society that I didn't fit into, either. In my worst, most self-pitying moments, I felt as if I were doomed to live in the off-season, like a tourist on a round-the-world journey who arrives at every port a month after the shops have been boarded up, the restaurants closed, and the crowds dispersed for a more agreeable climate. My timing was off, my instincts were awry.

I'd vowed that if I ever made enough money, I'd get into therapy and try to move past my neuroses, but I only made the vow because I was fairly certain my financial status wasn't likely to change soon.

I'd always been pretty skeptical about the whole therapy industry anyway. It reminded me of a course I'd taught at The Learning Place, called "Telling the Truth: How to Keep a Journal." It had attracted the most blatantly dishonest and self-dramatizing students I'd ever had, the only kind of people, when you came right down to it, who'd bother to keep a journal in the first place.

In the late afternoon, I walked to the address Louise had given me. It was still quite warm, but the rain had indeed driven in a new weather system, and there was a suggestion of fall in the air, a ripple of cool I felt whenever I passed under the shade of a tree, something wistful in the angle of the sun. I saw several moving vans circling the streets, ruthlessly pulling up over curbstones and lopping off the branches of trees, a sure sign that summer was ending and another wearying influx of hopeful students was under way. It was demoralizing, the sight of all that intelligence, beauty, and human potential that washed into town every September, all that Harvard brilliance scrambling to find something significant to do with itself. I liked living in a college town—good movies, good bookstores, great trash on the sidewalks in May—but for my next life I'd make it a junior college with a bad reputation that attracted only slackers. It would be a relief to be surrounded by people whose lives I could more easily understand and who didn't have quite as far to fall when they fell from grace.

Louise's sublet was in one of the many hidden pockets of Cambridge in which the air is usually cool and fragrant and the architecture grand and eccentric. Her house was located on the far end of a dead-end street halfway up a steep, shady hill. As directed, I looked for a towering yellow Victorian with a white picket fence. At the corner of the fence, nearly hidden under the sagging branches of an enormous hydrangea bush, was a gate with the number 17½ artfully painted on it. I pushed this open and entered a sprawling garden lushly overgrown with end-of-summer flowers: white and magenta phlox and black-eyed Susans and tall spikes of purple loosestrife. The carriage house sat at the back of the garden, at the end of a narrow flagstone path. It was a tiny building, the same shade of yellow as the main house, with a steeply pitched roof and wide windows glinting in the sun. The front of it was covered with morning glory vines and ropes of autumn clematis. It was one of those overdone renovations with *Investment* emblazoned across every clapboard, but I was so charmed by the sight of it, I didn't notice and almost stepped on a small brown dog that appeared to be doing somersaults in the middle of the path.

"Sorry about that," I said.

The dog looked at me with a submissive, cowering glance, tail tucked under and head down, as if I'd threatened it with a club. It seemed to be part terrier, not much bigger than a good-size cat and so scruffy and bowlegged it must have been the product of a furtive, lustful coupling behind a breeder's back. Its fur was dark brown except for two beige forelegs, light stripes above the eyes that looked exactly like eyebrows, and a tuft of beige fuzz that stood up on its head and gave the creature the look of something drawn by Dr. Seuss, or maybe by one of his less talented imitators.

I crouched down to pat it, but the poor mutt whimpered, dived into one of the flower beds, and started to kick up the dirt around a cluster of snapdragons with a demented fury, as if it were digging its own grave.

As I approached the house, I heard the voices of a man and a woman, arguing. I knocked hesitantly on the door. A woman shouted, "It's open!" in a very unwelcoming tone, and I walked into a tiny, book-lined study, the floor of which was strewn with balled-up newspaper and overturned cartons.

The woman who'd shouted me in was talking in an equally unfriendly tone to someone else: "I don't understand why you didn't solve this before I got home, Thomas. *That's* what I don't understand."

There was a sound of gurgling, like a baby spitting up, and then a man mumbled something.

I followed the voices into an open, high-ceilinged room flooded with hazy late-afternoon sunlight. Louise was sitting on a long bamboo sofa with her feet thrust out in front of her and crossed at the ankles and her arms folded across her chest. She had on a pair of rumpled khakis and a big white T-shirt. She was barefoot. For reasons she'd never made clear, she'd always claimed to hate her ankles and her feet. It was one of the few complaints I ever heard her make about her appearance, but in the time we'd been friends, she'd made it frequently. The sun was striking one side of her face, and she was squinting into it. She looked exhausted. There'd always been something luminous about Louise's pallor, but now the sunlight was being decidedly unkind to her, making her skin look as lifeless and rumpled as her khakis.

She smiled at me vaguely and waved without unclasping her arms. It was a mercifully anticlimactic greeting. I hate big hellos and all goodbyes.

Standing on the other side of the room was a tall woman, in a gray skirt and a silk blouse, and an addled man, balding on top, ponytailed in back. He was bouncing a baby, whose face was so pink and contorted it looked as if it was about to explode.

"Who's this?" the woman asked. She looked at me with a fixed, blank expression, but the question didn't seem to be addressed to anyone in particular. She was one of those no-nonsense types who make the world go round and resent having to drag the dead weight of the rest of us behind them.

"This is Clyde," Louise said. "A friend of mine." Her voice was raspier and even more hoarse than it had sounded on the phone, as if she were thoroughly worn down. I realized I'd made a big mistake in waiting so long to show up. Clearly, her frayed enthusiasm was all gone. "You don't mind if I have visitors, do you?"

"Oh boy, another victim," the woman said. "I only wish Thomas had settled this before I got home. That isn't unfair, is it?"

She looked at me when she said this, but it wasn't a question so much as a reproach to her husband. I had no idea what to say or do with myself, so I sat on the sofa next to my old friend.

"Oh, Clyde," Louise said quietly, "those glasses."

"Awful?" I asked.

"Terrible. They make you look asthmatic."

All my concerns about seeing her again vanished. There's really nothing more intimate than the right kind of insult. I leaned over and kissed her. She put her arm through mine and nestled against me. Her hair, her clothes, and even her skin smelled heavily, though not unpleasantly, of cigarettes.

"We have a rule about pets," the man explained to me, shifting the baby from one arm to the other. "It's the garden. The gardener, actually. I'm Thomas. My wife, Camille." He walked toward the sofa and extended his hand but, remembering the baby, retreated back to his corner. He had on short pants, white athletic socks, and a pair of those ghastly New Age sandals with nubby rubber soles that look like a bed of nipples.

"Are you also a writer?" Camille asked me. Her tone was intimidatingly impatient, as if either a yes or a no answer would be equally predictable and boring.

If you could look past her sedate outfit and sensible jewelry, you could see that she was quite young, probably not thirty. Somehow, I'd gone directly from feeling at a disadvantage because I was younger than those in authority to feeling at a disadvantage because I was older than those in authority.

"I teach at The Learning Place."

Husband and wife exchanged glances. It was the first indication of compatibility I'd seen, and I found it reassuring, despite the fact that I was the butt of their mutual disapproval. I should have said, "I teach in Cambridge," and let them think I was a tenured Harvard professor trying to be modest.

The baby's face was getting redder and more bloated, like an overinflated balloon. Suddenly, she popped: her eyes and mouth flew open, and she flung herself against Thomas's shoulder and let out a tremendous wail.

Camille and Thomas returned to recriminations in what was, apparently, their private shorthand: "Yes, at three..." "At three!" "But she didn't even..." "Oh, I'm tired of that excuse..." "All right, but where does it get *me?*"

I felt Louise relaxing against my shoulder, as if she was sighing with relief that the couple was distracted or possibly that she wasn't one of a dueling couple herself, a favorite theme with her.

"Just take her outside," Camille said. "It's obvious I'm going to have to deal with this anyway."

"I'm sure we'll be seeing more of you, Clyde." Thomas was shouting over the baby's cries. "That . . . school's in the neighborhood, isn't it?"

But before I could answer, Camille nodded significantly at her husband, and he walked out. Camille's shoulders dropped and she flopped into a chair near the sofa. "The baby takes after her father," she said. "And that's not meant as an insult." She removed a pair of tiny pearl studs from her ears. "I suppose you think I'm a horrible person, Louise, making a scene about a little dog."

"My son thinks you're a horrible person," Louise said. "Not me."

"I'm constitutionally incapable of giving in. Plus, I don't like animals." She slipped the earrings into the pocket of her skirt. "I'm just not interested in all that fur and panting. I might as well be honest about it."

She had a very practical haircut, a drip-dry bowl cut, and didn't appear to be wearing makeup. Up and out of the house in half an hour, that type. Unless I was mistaken, the marriage was one of those teacher-student flirtations that had gone way too far.

Louise was nervously shifting her weight on the sofa, as if she was trying to prevent herself from pouncing. Her face was considerably leaner than the last time I'd been with her, her flesh settled in closer to her bones, and despite her pale-blue eyes, and that appealing tomboy's overbite, and the freckles scattered across her nose, she'd lost her carefree girlishness and, to my disappointment, had finally, visibly, become a full-fledged adult. She reached into a canvas bag at her feet and pulled out a pack of Marlboros. "We found the dog after I talked with you about the sublet. I wasn't keeping anything from you intentionally." She produced a large ceramic ashtray from her bag and set it on the coffee table. "You didn't say anything about smoking."

"I'm not saying anything now."

"Well, good. Now, are you going to let me talk you into the

dog or not? Because if you're not, we can save ourselves a lot of time."

Camille shrugged. "I'm not." She said it so casually, the dog was clearly a lost cause.

"Fine," Louise said. "Give us twenty-four hours and we'll figure something out."

"Fine. Let us know if you need anything. You might as well come straight to me, since Thomas is useless." She started to head out, then stopped in the doorway. "By the way," she said, "we read one of your novels in my book group. The one about the baby. We all loved it. The group can't wait to meet you."

❧

Louise threw herself into the chair Camille had been sitting in. It was a big, overstuffed thing, its maroon slipcovers printed with ivory peonies, and although it had propped Camille up as if she were a queen on a throne, it seemed to swallow Louise whole.

"Is this a big crisis?" I asked her.

"It could be." She arranged her legs under her, carefully hiding her feet. "Oh, Clyde," she said hoarsely, "I've really fucked everything up, haven't I? Tell me I haven't, even if you don't believe it."

"You haven't," I said.

"Of course I have. And I wanted us to have one of those phony, huggy reunions." She lit her cigarette and scattered the smoke with her hand. "Awful part is, I like that kind of woman: bossy, knows what she wants. Why shouldn't she? Well, she isn't going to step on my toes. No way, man. She picked the wrong person to wrestle with." Louise looked around at the chaos of boxes and newspaper and heaps of clothing. "I wonder if I kept a copy of the lease."

A door slammed on the floor above, and Benjamin came pounding down the staircase. He had a defiant gait, but it was obvious from the smudges on his cheeks and the drained look in his eyes that he'd been crying. Although he still looked like a little boy, he was virtually unrecognizable from the last time I'd seen him. He was gangly now, and awkward, with the slumped, self-conscious posture I'd noticed on my niece, Barbara: an adolescent's conviction that every move is being watched by an interested adult, which, at the moment, was absolutely true.

He had Louise's pale skin and lank red hair and a cluster of freckles on each side of his face, right along the cheekbones. His nose was broad and soft-looking, as if it hadn't quite taken shape yet, and his ears stuck straight out from his head, like two little red wings. He was dressed in an absurd pair of dark-purple shorts that hung down below his knees, a big black T-shirt, and an enormous pair of green sneakers. He looked like a scarecrow some-one had thrown together too hastily and hadn't given an adequate portion of stuffing. Standing in front of Louise with his arms folded resolutely across his chest, he snapped his hair out of his eyes. "I just want you to know one thing," he said. "It's all of us or none of us. I'm not kidding. I'd rather have myself put to sleep than him."

"I doubt it will come to that, sweetheart. Can't you even say hello to Clyde?"

He nodded at me with his eyes averted. "Hi, Clyde," he said shyly. He had a surprisingly raspy voice, as if he had inherited or was imitating his mother's.

"You look like a whole new person," I said. "Since the last time I saw you. Do you remember? I came to visit when you lived in San Francisco."

"Benjamin remembers everything, so watch what you say around him," said Louise. "He's grown, Clyde. It happens at his age. Fortunately, he'll never outgrow those clothes he's wearing, unless some sort of glandular disturbance kicks in."

Ben had those weirdly shapeless legs all kids his age seem to have as they start to shoot up: protruding hipbones, knees, and ankles, with a couple of slim, undercooked baguettes in between to separate them. But it was more than his height; the proportions of his face had changed, and despite his coloring, he didn't look all that much like Louise anymore. There was a grave, handsome set to his features that was all his own.

"I'm five seven almost," he said. "But let's not change the subject, all right?"

"All right, sweetheart." Louise was holding her cigarette between her middle and ring fingers, and the smoke was drifting up into her eyes, causing her to squint. Her hair was stringy, as if she hadn't washed it in a couple of days. Once, slightly greasy hair had made her look nonchalantly glamorous, but it wasn't a look she could really pull off anymore, just as I could no longer skip shaving for a weekend without looking like an unwashed speed freak by Sunday night. "I just need to figure something out."

Benjamin went to one of the wide, sunny windows and looked out for a moment, checking on the dog, I suppose. Then he came and slumped down on the sofa at the opposite end from me, his arms across his chest once again. "We can't dump him after we rescued him. He's our responsibility."

"He's awfully melodramatic, isn't he? I don't remember saying anything about dumping anyone. We have to develop a plan."

"You and your plans, Mom. She's always developing plans. That stupid motel cabin in Indiana. That was some plan. Wow."

She stubbed her cigarette out in the big ceramic ashtray. "You can't blame me for that, kiddo. You have to be fair about the way you spread around blame."

"Well, it wasn't my idea. She has bad judgment sometimes. She almost burned the place down."

I nodded, even though I didn't know what they were talking about and neither of them really seemed to be talking to me. Their conversation was taking on some of the coded intimacy of their landlords'.

"How did I know the oven wasn't working?" Louise asked. Then she and Benjamin exchanged glances and broke into laughter. Benjamin rocked forward and crumpled up on the cushions, and his hair fell all over his face. He sat up again and pushed it behind his big ears, a gesture that struck me as terribly familiar, for some reason.

When he'd gone outside to play with the dog, Louise curled up into a tighter ball on her chair and stretched her T-shirt over her knees. I'd forgotten how small she was, possibly because I'd always thought of her as so self-sufficient and accomplished. Folded up on the chair like this, she didn't appear to be much bigger than her son. "Do I look like an old woman to you?" she asked abruptly.

"You look wonderful." I wasn't sure if that was true, but since her day was turning out to be such a bust, I figured the least I could do was offer a facile compliment.

"But older?" She was holding her chin at a slight angle, and I couldn't tell what she wanted me to say.

"Maybe a bit."

"I'm glad." She let her chin drop. "I hated being young. I hated everything about it. Almost everything." She lit another cigarette, inhaled deeply, and swallowed the smoke as if she were downing one of Agnes's monster vitamin pills. "Days like today, I wish I was still drinking. I didn't say that. Well, I said it, but I didn't mean it."

"How about this," I suggested. "You meant it, but you're not going to act on it?"

"That's even better." She eyed me through the smoke of her cigarette in a friendly, critical way. "You need sprucing up, Clyde; not that I'm one to talk. You look like you've been working too hard."

"It's probably allergies," I said. I'd picked up on this latest cultural trend—the allergy problem—as a way to publicly explain away every sleepless night, stomach upset, and other disorder that was obviously and embarrassingly psychosomatic in nature. It was doubtful anyone believed it, Louise least of all, but it was an effective conversation-stopper. "What's the dog's name?" I asked.

"Otis. We found him in a rest area off the highway, tied to a picnic table and shaking. A case of abandonment, which is probably why I let Ben take him in. I agree completely with Camille on the subject of dogs, but this wretch got to me. Believe it or not, he's in better shape emotionally than when we found him." She uncurled herself and smashed out her cigarette, jostling the big ashtray and spilling ashes onto the top of the coffee table. "Let me show you the rest of the place, in case we get chucked out tomorrow."

She took me by the arm and led me through the square, bright rooms of the carriage house. The whole place was furnished in a style that made it look like a sun room in a 1930s summerhouse, with faded floral cushions and toss pillows, wrought-iron tables with tile tops, and cabinets and bureaus covered in weathered, chipped paint. In addition to the living room and the study through which I'd entered, the first floor housed a spotless kitchen and, in the back, Louise's bedroom. There was a door beside her bed, which led out to the rear of the garden. She opened it, and the room was flooded with the smell of damp earth.

Battered as some of the furniture was, the house itself appeared brand-new, the walls freshly painted in various shades of white and the floors desperately clean and polished. It felt solid and secure, and when Louise shut the door again, there was a little sucking sound, as if the house were sealing itself off from any assaults by man or nature. The place made me feel momentarily ashamed of the dilapidated wreck I shared with Marcus. Ben's bedroom, the only room in the loft, looked out on the garden. Unlike the rest of the place, his room was neatly arranged. The bed was made, the pillows were plumped, and the doors of the two closets tightly closed.

"Obsessively tidy," Louise said, when she saw me looking over the neat stacks of records in the corner. "He's compensating for all our moving by keeping strict control over his own stuff. That's my analysis." She sat down on the edge of the bed and started to pick at the fuzz on a red plaid blanket. "Poor little Ben," she said, with some combination of pity and sarcasm.

I went to the window and looked down at the garden. "You'll never find any place nicer than this, you know."

"Thanks for reminding me. Maybe Camille will move to Colorado tomorrow."

"It's more likely you will, with your track record."

"I suppose you're right. But not tomorrow. The grant keeps us here until the end of December. After that, I haven't decided. I have the option of hanging on to this place for a while. The tenant's on a research grant in North Africa."

Ben was sitting on a rusted metal chair on the lawn below, holding a red rubber ball in his hand. His baggy clothes had settled around him, as if they were melting into a puddle on the chair. The scruffy mutt was eyeing him warily with his head down, trying to figure out what new kind of torture was being planned for him. When Ben threw the ball, the dog cowered and snuck off into the bushes. I felt a horrible pang of sadness, not for Louise or Ben, but for the pathetically insecure animal. Like a lot of people who know something is missing from their lives but can't figure out what, I frequently contemplated checking out death row at the Animal Rescue League to find myself a grateful canine companion. It seemed a lot more straightforward and manageable than trying to find a lover or spiritual fulfillment.

"I could take Otis for a while," I said. "We have a yard behind the house. The whole neighborhood's basically a pound." Most of the troubled families on either side of us had at least one dog, usually a fierce pit bull or German shepherd with a threatening two-syllable name: Rambo, Uzi, Killer, Bullet.

"No garden?"

"Marcus tried to grow a patch of marigolds back in May, but it was taken over by weeds before Memorial Day."

She smiled at this and looked away. She propped herself up on the bed, with her hands out behind her. For a minute, she looked very much as she did in one of her book-jacket photographs, pretty and bemused and a little too posed to look entirely sincere. "She knows how to take a picture," Vance had said after looking at the jacket of her last novel, but I wasn't sure he'd meant it as a compliment. "So how is Marcus, anyway?" she asked.

"In the middle of a few crises, as usual."

"Women?"

"Women, dissertation, poverty. Are you looking forward to seeing him again?"

"I wouldn't put it that way." She started to rap her fingers against the blanket and let her head drop back. "You might say I'm dreading it."

"There's not much to dread, is there?"

"More than you think," she said, and snapped her head up. "Listen, you don't have to take the dog. I'll figure out something else. I really will."

"I want to. Will Ben go for the idea?"

"You'd better present it as the best thing for the dog. Make it sound as if it's all for the dog's sake. Whatever you do, keep me out of it."

$\backsim$

I've always found it unnerving to be around children, especially intelligent ones who can't be fooled and haven't yet learned the social usefulness of lying. They have a way of looking directly at you and then quickly away, as if they've spotted something hideous, better left unacknowledged.

So when Louise had gone out to buy food and Ben and I were left sitting opposite each other in the living room, I found myself squirming on the sofa. I'd brought up the idea of taking Otis temporarily, and Ben had immediately retreated into brooding silence. To fill space, I'd asked him what he thought of the house. He'd given me a suspicious glance through his bangs, as if to say: You already know, so why ask? Now he was settled into the overstuffed maroon chair, silently patting the cringing dog.

"Did Louise write dog food on that shopping list?" he asked abruptly.

"I'm sure she did," I said. "It was a pretty complete list."

"She never gets the right kind. She always buys the most expensive one, which he doesn't even like. I should have gone with her."

I assumed this meant he was as uncomfortable with me as I was with him. At least he had the dog to pet. I resorted to tying and untying my sneakers in order to keep my hands occupied, and each time I retied them, they got a little tighter. A few more minutes, and my feet would start to swell. Otis was peering across the room at me, his big watery brown eyes suspicious, his ears flattened back.

"Is he a fussy eater?" I asked.

Ben obviously considered the answer to this question one more thing that was none of my business, since he didn't respond to it. "I almost flunked out of school in Seattle. That's one of the reasons we left. Did Louise tell you?"

"She didn't."

He nodded—proudly, it seemed to me. "She had a horrible boyfriend, too."

"She didn't mention him, either," I said. "What was his name?"

Ben set Otis on the floor, lifted his rear end off the chair, and pulled a piece of paper out of his back pocket. He unfolded it carefully and smoothed it out on his lap. "His name was Dale. He wanted to marry her. Louise wasn't interested. I made a list of all the breeds Otis might be. I'll give you the top ten."

He read through the list of breeds, giving me a detailed explanation of how Otis fit into the characteristics of each. I listened with as much enthusiasm as I could muster, which, frankly, wasn't all that much. As far as I could tell, the dog was mostly a mix of assorted toy terriers, with some long-haired dachshund tossed in around the ears. Personality traits were irrelevant, as the creature had clearly been traumatized out of anything but the most rudimentary self-preservation reflexes. But as I listened with drifting attention, I realized that Ben had lapsed into a list of dos and don'ts related to care and feeding. Apparently, I'd missed some connecting link in the conversation in which he'd given his approval to my taking the dog.

"Don't hit him," Ben said. "If he starts to bother you, just shout at him and he'll crawl off under a bed or something. I'll take him out for walks in the afternoon." He folded up the paper and slipped it back into his pocket. "Do you think you could maybe give me a key to the apartment?"

"I'll have an extra one made," I said.

"You should let me know which rooms are off-limits," he said.

"None, I think. But I'll check with Marcus."

"Doesn't he go out to work during the day?"

"Well, he goes out," I said. "Look, Ben, I hope you don't think I'm taking your dog away from you."

"You're just trying to help. I think it's the only solution at the moment, don't you?" He'd inherited his mother's matter-of-fact attitude toward solving problems. He hooked his hair behind his ears and gave me a very thoughtful and unnerving glance. "To tell you the truth, I'd rather you take him than someone he was going to get really attached to."

I nodded distractedly. I was so preoccupied by those oddly familiar ears that I didn't get around to feeling insulted until later.

MARCUS WAS SITTING AT THE KITCHEN TABLE, folded over a cup of coffee with his legs wound together, studying a newspaper. Marcus read the newspaper irregularly. Often, he'd pick up an old copy in the hallway or from the top of the trash and read it from cover to cover, completely oblivious of the fact that it was days or even weeks old. "Did you hear?" he'd ask, and then recite some piece of news that had been debated by two-thirds of the population for weeks. I always try to keep up with the news, especially the local news, so that if I'm called for jury duty I can legitimately claim a bias.

Without looking up from the paper, he said, "What's with the dog?"

"I'm taking care of it for a while," I said. I knelt down on the floor and unhooked the leash. He'd seemed surprisingly inept at being walked, stopping one moment and racing ahead the next, then abruptly sitting on the sidewalk as if waiting to be bludgeoned. Now he stood in the middle of the room for a moment, perplexed. The tuft of sandy fur on top of his head made him look especially pathetic, and I patted it down gently to try and grant him some shred of dignity. He darted his eyes from corner to corner and whimpered, then started to shake and wheeze.

"Whose is it?" Marcus asked.

"He belongs to Louise's son."

"Small," Marcus said, even though, as far as I could tell, he still hadn't seen him.

Otis began circling the perimeter of the room, anxiously peering into the corners and sniffing. He stood on his hind legs to try and see over the top of the trash can and ended up tipping it over, a catastrophe that induced more wheezing.

"Is he housebroken?" Marcus asked.

"Supposedly," I said.

"I guess it doesn't matter much at that size whether he's house-broken or not. Seems pretty skittish, though." Marcus looked up for half a second as the dog crawled out to the center of the floor. "Cute," he said, and immediately went back to the paper. "How's Louise?"

"She seems to be doing pretty well. She's going to call you tomorrow to see about getting together for lunch."

Finally, something had captured his interest. He folded up the newspaper and began making faces at Otis.

"Freaky, aren't they?" Marcus said, pointing his chin at Otis. "Little hairy emotional creatures. Had one when I was a kid. It got struck by lightning when it was swimming in the river. Big tragedy. I wonder if that has something to do with my procrastination." Marcus was always bringing up some occurrence of this nature. None sounded very likely, but because I was a Yankee, I felt I had no right to doubt the truth of any eccentric, folksy thing a South-erner told me. "Well, I'm no good with dogs," he said, "so don't count on me." He opened up the newspaper again, wrapped his hair around his big ears, and started to read. "What's the kid look like?"

"A little like Louise." I paused. "A little like you, as a matter of fact."

He laughed, obviously flattered in some way. "Don't pin that on me. I've never even been to France."

It was nearly midnight when I finally decided I couldn't wait until the next day to confront Louise. I walked back to her house, along the shadowy, leafy streets—no moving vans or giddy students now —and quietly pushed open the gate leading into the yard. The second floor of the carriage house was dark, but a thin yellow light was spilling out of the study. I peered in; the room was empty. I walked around to the corner of the garden off Louise's bedroom. She was there, sitting on a lawn chair, her feet up on a round wrought-iron table with a candle burning in the middle. There was a trellis overhead, dripping with grapevines and clematis, and the air smelled sweet, from the white flowers and the pot she was smoking.

She didn't seem especially surprised to see me. She waved toward an empty chair across from her and handed me the joint.

I sat down and shook my head disapprovingly, then took a hit, and, holding the harsh smoke in my lungs, said, "You could have told me about Ben, you know. I can't believe you didn't."

Louise's hair was still damp from a shower, and when she reached out to take back the joint, I could smell the scent of lemony soap rising off her skin. "It's not fair to burden people with your secrets, Clyde."

"But it would have been worth the burden, sweetheart. All these years, I could have known more about Marcus than he knows about himself."

"Everyone knows more about Marcus than he knows about himself. Or they did, in the days I knew him. I'll bet somewhere deep down you suspected anyway."

She was wearing a shapeless black jersey dress, with a big gray sweater on top. Her skin was pale, almost luminous against the black dress and the dark. After a few more hits of the pot, I felt something inside me let go, and I sank back against the cushions of the chair and drank in the still night air. A phone rang in one of the houses behind us, but no one picked it up.

"It was his ears," I said. "He has Marcus's ears. His mouth, too, but it was the ears that tipped me off."

"Oh, the ears, right. I'll bet I found those attractive on Marcus. But Ben might outgrow them, don't you think?"

"Marcus didn't."

"I've spent so many years thinking of him as mine alone, I hate the idea of sharing his genes with anyone."

"Does Ben know?"

She shook her head and slipped a roach clip onto the end of the joint. "He pretends he doesn't care. But he asks about his father sometimes, mostly in discreet non sequiturs he slips into conversation, trying to trip me up. 'That Austrian guy who was my father,' he'll say, and then wait to see if I correct him and say 'Australian.' "

"Do you?"

"Not as often as I used to," she said quietly. "I didn't know a twelve-year-old boy without a father would look so different from an eleven-year-old boy without a father. He's sadder than he used to be. He hated Seattle, didn't get along in school. The grant came through. It seemed fate was arranging a convergence."

She had a plan of action, and she related it to me as we sat there with the galaxy of waxy flowers drooping overhead. She wanted a commitment from Marcus, not to support Ben financially or to be a father in any traditional sense; she had no illusions about renewing a relationship with him, and no interest. She simply wanted Marcus to be a reliable presence in Ben's life, no matter what was going on in his own.

I found myself growing sad as I listened. Among other things, it was hard for me to imagine Marcus being a reliable presence in anyone's life. I'd romanticized the idea of Louise as a single mother just as I'd romanticized her own orphaned childhood. But now all the relationships and connections struck me as dubious and up for grabs. One thing I'd learned from reading hundreds of biographies is that chaotic, ill-defined relationships, appealing at the start, don't age well. I'd also learned that it's almost always a mistake to bury part of the truth—not for any moral reasons, but because eventually someone feels compelled to dig it all up and expose the whole mess to sunlight.

"But it might work out, don't you think?" she asked. "Marcus will probably be relieved I didn't tell him sooner. And Ben's bound to understand, especially since I'm the one who pays his allowance."

"You might be right." She smiled faintly when I said this, exposing her overbite and some ghost of the puckish girl she'd been so many years earlier. Her optimism—part dope and part desperation—was infectious, if not exactly convincing. "I'm sure you're right."

She shrugged. "All I can do is try. It worked out with the dog, didn't it?"

"Magnificently."

"You're a liar, Clyde. That's why I knew I could count on you."

❧

I had a key made for Benjamin and put it on a chain with a tag shaped like the head of a dog. When I presented it to him, he glanced at the tag, slipped it into his shirt pocket, and thanked me without looking at me, as if he was mortified by the sight of the Day-Glo plastic mutt. My niece had had a similar reaction to a dinosaur watch I'd given her for her eleventh birthday, some mix of being insulted at my estimation of her maturity and embarrassed on my behalf for my awful taste.

"I know it's hideous," I said, trying to recoup, "but I wanted to make sure the key didn't get lost, and it was the only one I could find. At the last minute. Before I gave it to you." I'd spent half an hour poring over a rack of the tacky things in a pet shop and was pleased and proud when I found one that vaguely resembled Otis.

"It's okay, Clyde," Ben said. He pulled a key chain out of his pocket, a stylish silver item that looked as if it had been crafted from the handle of an antique spoon. There were at least a dozen keys attached. "I'll just put it on with the rest of these. I collect the keys from the places Louise and I have lived."

I nodded and watched as he hooked Otis up to his leash and led him out.

Ben came by every day after school, let himself in quietly, left with the dog, and returned a few hours later. He was so cagey about his comings and goings, I thought it best to leave him alone. I watched him from my top-floor window. The poor dog seemed thoroughly confused about where he belonged and whose orders he should obey. He often looked back at the house as they headed off, as if trying to determine the likelihood of returning. The one time I'd scolded him for knocking over a stack of books, he'd cowered so pathetically I hadn't had the heart to do it again. Now, whenever he stumbled into a mishap, I found myself apologizing profusely, begging him to crawl out from under the bed and stop wheezing.

Ben had been coming to the house for about a week when I ventured downstairs to talk with him. I'd seen him returning from his walk with Otis and timed my arrival in the kitchen to look like a chance meeting. But when I got there, he was sitting on the nubby orange sofa, undoing Otis's leash and listening to Marcus. He smiled at me and looked away.

Marcus didn't hear me come in. He was standing at the stove, going through his ritual afternoon coffee production and relating some variation on the implausible tale of the dog who'd been killed by lightning.

"It nearly killed *me*, I don't mind telling you that. Of course, I always had a way with animals. Don't know what it is, but they all seem to gravitate to me. I guess I should be flattered, right? What's the name of that dog of yours again?"

"Otis," Ben said.

"My brother's name is Otto," Marcus said. "Same kind of idea, wouldn't you say?"

Otto was Marcus's older brother, an equally handsome but more motivated academic, whom Marcus usually preferred not to mention except in some faintly disparaging context like this.

When he finally finished with the coffee, he took a cup of it to the maple table and nodded at me as he sat down.

"You're home early today," I said.

He hooked his hair behind his ears and sipped. "Everyone deserves an afternoon off now and then. I was just talking about my dog."

"I heard."

"He's got his mother's hair, doesn't he, Clyde?"

"He does."

"I always loved Louise's red hair. We used to be great friends, your mother and I." He picked up a newspaper that had been sitting on the table for at least a week and started to read. "She's probably told you all about that. We're having lunch next Thursday. Can't wait to see her, actually. Rehash the good old days. I think they were good, anyway."

He started talking about his career at Amherst, a self-aggrandizing, revisionist version of history if ever I'd heard one. I couldn't tell if Ben was listening or not; he appeared to be preoccupied with Otis, but every once in a while he'd nod his head and look over at Marcus. Studying him? Weighing the credibility of what he was saying? I couldn't tell. I myself was too preoccupied with comparing their features and contemplating the strange, immutable bonds wrought by something as cold and mathematical as genetics.

When Marcus had finished leafing through the paper, he folded it and wrapped up his life story. He put his hands behind his head and looked across the room—a confused, vague glance. The few weeks in any given year when Marcus wasn't involved in a relationship, he wandered around the house like a man suffering from memory loss, lifting up the cushions on the sofa and staring into empty cabinets, trying to remember where he'd left his . . . well, something. He was usually saved from this fruitless search by the appearance of an eager, impressionable young woman.

He recovered from his identity crisis and shook his head. As he was walking out, he turned to Ben and said, "You ought to teach that pup a few tricks. Make him earn his keep. Right, Clyde? Now, tell me your name again?"

Ben sat in silence for a few moments after he'd gone. "Is he a Southerner?" he finally asked.

"He is," I said. "But sometimes he's more Southern than other times. You'll like him once you know him better."

"He doesn't seem like Louise's type."

As I remembered it, Louise had fairly eclectic tastes. But it didn't seem like an appropriate comment, so I changed the subject.

THOUGHT IT WAS AN ESPECIALLY WONDERFUL class tonight," Eileen Ash said.

I was standing behind the table at the front of the classroom, stuffing my books and papers into my backpack. I looked up at Eileen and bared my teeth, hoping the expression would pass for a smile. Eileen Ash had stayed behind after every class to offer some congratulatory comments on my performance. Because no class ever seemed any better than another (although some, like tonight's, were clearly more disastrous), I felt mildly insulted by the praise. Either my skills were so minimal that Eileen felt bad for me, or she was so desperate to make the most of a bad situation that she'd actually managed to convince herself.

Eileen was one of an even dozen students who'd signed up for "Love and Marriage, Horse and Carriage: Relationship Issues in Some Nineteenth-Century Novels," and the only student who'd bothered to attend all three meetings thus far. She was a tall, angular woman with graying hair she wore parted down the middle and turned under at the chin. Tonight she had on a loose Indian print dress made of light cotton and cinched at the waist with a multicolor belt that looked like it had been woven by a peasant living at a high altitude in some impoverished nation. Despite a degree of frailty suggesting a few too many liquid lunches, there was something energetic and almost athletic about Eileen; she had enormous green eyes that gave her narrow face an equine beauty, and I could picture her a decade or so earlier downing cocktails at some horsey gathering in Greenwich or the Berkshires. In class, she often remarked that she loved the books we were reading, although she never said anything specific enough about them to indicate that she'd read them. Still, her enthusiasm was genuine, and she was always eager to help me out by leaping in during embarrassing silences, usually with the all-purpose comment, "I keep wondering if things are so very different today."

Eileen and her husband, a Harvard professor so famous even I had heard of him, lived off Brattle Street in a rambling mansion hidden behind a softly rounded privacy hedge. During the first five minutes of the very first class, Eileen had offered to hold a party at her house at the end of the term. "To give us something to look forward to," she'd said. She'd intended no offense, but I'd felt defeated by the comment. As a result, I harbored a slight resentment toward her, which I hadn't been able to shake.

"I thought it was a particularly *relevant* class tonight," she said. "Especially for poor Mallory. It's awfully sad, isn't it?"

"It is," I said. "But we don't know, things might work out for her."

"I hope so." Eileen clasped her book to her chest, and I noticed that the volume she'd brought to class was *Jane Eyre*. At least she was in the right ballpark. "But the chances are slim, aren't they? Look at this class alone. How many divorced?"

"Quite a few." I should have known the exact number, since every member of the class had announced his or her marital status on the first day and many continued to slip barbed comments about "my first wife" or "that ex-husband of mine" into virtually every statement they made.

"Nine," Eileen said. "Imagine that. Nine out of twelve. Not very encouraging."

Indeed not, but you'd hardly call the class a random sampling of the population at large. The title of the course, which had been manufactured and handed to me by the admissions board of The Learning Place, almost guaranteed a disproportionate number of students from broken marriages.

I attempted a casual glance at my watch by pushing my glasses up on my nose with the back of my wrist. I'd let the class out early, but it was now a little after seven, and Marcus was probably out front, waiting to depart for New Hampshire.

"I shouldn't be keeping you," Eileen said.

"No, no," I said. "You're not."

"You don't need to be polite with me. We're old friends, Clyde. I don't have anything urgent to discuss, I just wanted to tell you how much I'm getting out of the class and maybe go over a couple of details for the party. It's only a few months away, so I really should be lining things up with the caterer. Don't you think?"

"Maybe we should plan a simple potluck event," I said. Personally, I had no interest in planning anything, but since the party had become the centerpiece of the entire class, I felt some responsibility to get involved.

"Oh, no, I don't think so. Those can be so depressing, all those blocks of cheese. I'm just not sure if there are any vegetarians in the bunch. With your permission, I'll take a head count next week."

"That would be fine," I said, We were supposed to begin discussing *Cranford* the following week, but I could tell that a good portion of the class would be spent on menu planning, if I played my hand right.

She tilted her head to one side, smiled graciously, and walked out, leaving behind a faint smell of hyacinth.

Maybe it didn't matter what she was getting out of the class, as long as she was getting something out of it. Anyway, I had my own concerns that night, specifically trying to figure out how best to confront my father about his mysterious social life. I was so nervous about the visit, I'd barely been able to see straight for the last half hour of class. I hitched my backpack up to my shoulders and walked around the room, closing windows and turning off lamps.

The Learning Place was one of two adult education centers within a one-mile radius of Harvard Square. It was the newer of the two, the less academic and the more elegant. The promotional material for the school made much of the fact that it was housed in an immense Greek Revival mansion on nearly an acre of meticulously landscaped grounds. As I made my way around the perimeter of the room, checking that all the windows were latched, I looked down on the expansive back lawn. It was a warm September evening, and the sky to the west was a sunburn shade of pink. A gentle breeze was rustling the leaves of the beech trees along the side of the house, filling the air with a wonderful chattering. There was a sunken garden below the window, in which a teacher was holding a class amid a profusion of dying purple flowers. Men and women were draped across the lawn chairs, most holding paper cups containing, in all likelihood, an alcoholic punch. There was something languorous and soothing about the scene, like an autumnal lawn party—albeit an especially dull one.

The classroom itself was immense, with a bay of curved windows at the back. I conducted my lectures from behind a nineteenth-century walnut library table at one end of the room, while the students sat in front of me in an assortment of bow-back Windsor armchairs. The rest of the antiques—everything from a primitive pine chest to a thousand-pound French commode with ormolu plaques that was undoubtedly worth more than I made in a year—were pressed against the walls, giving the place the haphazard elegance of a museum storage room.

Because I'd been teaching at the school for a while, my classes were frequently scheduled in that desirable room. It was dominated by a five-foot-high oil painting that hung from the front wall, one of those dark, slightly dreary turn-of-the-century portraits of a dour-looking woman in a black dress, with a huge white jabot spilling over her bosom. Her hands were folded primly on her lap, and time had faded her complexion and eyeballs to a shade of ocher that suggested jaundice. She sat there, territorial and grand, and from time to time I could hear her clucking her tongue in disapproval of something I'd said: "Mr. James wasn't like that at all, certainly not when I met him." No one knew who she was, but it was apparent to me her first name couldn't have been anything other than Edwina. I sometimes turned to her for moral support when the conversation turned to the truly irrelevant: "It's the nineties, Edwina, what can I tell you?"

The Learning Place had opened its ornate doors six years earlier and immediately made a name for itself by offering courses that managed to sound both intellectually challenging and embarrassingly trendy. Everything from literature to exercise was offered up with a healthy, enrollment-boosting dose of pop psychology. "Haute Cuisine for the Hungry Heart," "The Peter Pan Syndrome in the Novels of George Eliot and Gail Godwin," "Kundalini Yoga for the Suddenly Single." I was usually given a time slot and a course title and left to figure out the rest for myself.

Not that I was about to start a campaign to raise academic standards. I was qualified to teach at The Learning Place because I was a generalist, or, to be honest about it, an expert in nothing. In my twenties, I'd begun graduate programs in everything from Art History to Education, and even though I hadn't lasted past the first semester of any of them—or even past the first two weeks of a couple—I could legitimately say I'd "done graduate work" in an impressive number of fields and make myself look appealing to a school that cared a lot more about surface area than depth. I wasn't getting rich on what I was paid, but I was paid more than I was worth, the one sure measure of success.

Tonight's class had been typical of my teaching experience at The Learning Place. I'd begun the evening by offering a fairly concise and insightful analysis of the ending of *Wuthering Heights*, a minilecture on the nature of passion and romantic love. Admittedly

I'd culled most of my major points from the liner notes of an Edith Piaf album I'd taken out of the library, but it seemed to me it was coming off pretty well. I had the feeling, at one moment anyway, that the students were actually listening, leaning forward in their seats and listening. My big mistake had come in pausing to ask if there were any questions on what I'd said thus far. Tim, an aspiring actor and one of the few members of the class who was younger than me, asked if I knew anything about a remake of the movie *Oliver Twist*. Dorothea, a retired schoolteacher who appeared to have enrolled in the course for the sole purpose of finding fault with everything I said, corrected a comment I'd made the week before about the date of Branwell Brontë's birth. In the ensuing silence, Eileen Ash had sighed loudly and commented, apropos of nothing in particular, "I wonder if it's all so different today."

Discouraged but undeterred, I'd shuffled my notes and prepared to forge ahead. Mallory White, sitting in a far corner of the room, had cleared her throat and said, "Well, since we're all being so wonderfully honest with each other in here, I think it's only fair that I mention something . . . in case I seem a little *off* tonight."

There was a stir of curiosity, and the other eight students turned in their seats to get a better look at Mallory. From what I could remember, Mallory had attended only the very first class. She'd worn a pair of gaucho pants and sandals and a lot of noisy wooden jewelry. She'd sat in the back, said nothing, and left during the break. According to Eileen, who claimed to know something about almost everyone in the class, Mallory was in her late forties, a therapist. "I've heard she has a lovely office," Eileen had said, "with lots of pillows and Kleenex."

"Please go ahead. It's important to be honest in your opinions and observations about the books," I said, knowing very well that the odds of whatever was coming being about *Wuthering Heights* were about one in a thousand.

"Thank you, Clyde. It's very kind of you to say that." She paused, slid a couple of thick bracelets up to her elbow, and said, "Well, the fact is, I discovered last March that my husband has been having an affair, and I still haven't been able to put it all in perspective. It's been a difficult period for me, and these wonderful books just resonate."

There was a rumble of disapproval. Brian shook his head and said, "I know where you're coming from on this one. The unfaithful spouse, the whole bit. Believe me, I've been there."

Brian was a dashing man, probably in his late fifties, who showed up midway through each class in a business suit, his hair slicked back matinee-idol style. When he spoke up, it was usually to announce, with a boastful expansion of his chest, that he hadn't read the book because he'd been too busy at the Boston law firm where he was a senior partner. The question of why he'd bothered to take the class in the first place was answered by his constant references to the difficulties a busy, successful divorced man had in meeting women.

I could accept that most of my students in most of my classes were recovering from marriages gone bust or relationships gone sour, but how was it statistically possible that they were all the wronged parties?

I turned to the wall to see how Edwina was taking the subject of marital infidelity, but her expression was inscrutable.

"I'm sorry to hear about your husband," I said to Mallory. I was, too, even though Mallory, who was adjusting a necklace made of massive carved wooden beads, didn't seem especially shook up. Taking courage from Edwina, I added, "Let's go back to the point I was trying to make earlier."

Everyone who'd been eyeing Mallory sympathetically turned a hostile gaze in my direction, and I recoiled.

A man whose name I'd never been able to remember announced that he'd taken both sections of "Processing," the most popular course in the school (running neck-and-neck with "Processing Food," a discussion group on eating disorders). "I think it might be helpful to Mallory," he said, "if we did some role-playing. To help sort things out."

Mallory seemed delighted by the suggestion, and the remaining hour or so had been spent on "building trust," deep breathing, and improvisational acting exercises.

In the years I'd been teaching at The Learning Place, I'd discovered that classes usually went this way sooner or later. Most students signed up to show off what they knew about subjects they'd already studied elsewhere, to discuss their personal problems, to make a romantic connection, or some confused combination of all of the above.

The irony was that the further from the subject the classes veered, the more likely it was that I'd receive glowing reports from my students. I'd figured out that the best way to secure my job was to take a back seat whenever possible—a lesson I'd foolishly forgotten that night.

IT WAS WELL AFTER SEVEN WHEN I FINALLY stepped outside and strolled down the brick walk to the street. My car was pulled up to the curb, and Marcus was sitting in the passenger seat, looking at himself in the rearview mirror and fiddling with his aviator sunglasses. He gave me a quick glance and then went back to the mirror.

He looked astonishingly cool. Astonishing because Louise had arranged to meet with him that afternoon, ostensibly to tell him about Ben. I'd expected to see him slumped over the dashboard, riven by self-pity.

"I figured you'd want to drive," he said calmly.

I slid behind the wheel and buckled on the seat belt. In fact, I wasn't particularly fond of driving and took a great deal of pleasure in being a passenger, even when the driver was as inconsistent and distracted as Marcus. But some combative masculine pride prevented me from sitting in the passenger seat of my own car while another man took the wheel. Especially when I was headed to see my father. Especially when the other man was handsome and straight. And Marcus was looking particularly handsome and reedy tonight. He had on a green-and-white-striped dress shirt and a pair of rumpled khakis. With his aviator sunglasses and his long blond hair combed back, he looked like an aging British rock star making a stab at middle-class respectability. He'd obviously dressed for Louise.

I was dying to know how things had gone, but since I was unsure how much Louise had told him, I figured it was best to wait in silence. As I drove through the crowded streets around Harvard Square, dodging the college students and the wobbly bicyclists, Marcus peered out the side window mournfully. "I've been in this town too long," he said. "Kids on bicycles."

"Everyone who lives here feels they've been here too long," I said. "Especially the kids on bicycles."

"Do you?"

I considered this for a moment. "I suppose so. That's why I'll probably never leave." There's something relaxing about feeling you've been in a place too long and have exhausted its possibilities. You don't have to rush around visiting museums, and you can set aside expectations of having your life transformed by new scenery.

"I don't see how that helps me," Marcus said.

Frankly, I didn't, either. But clearly, help was not what he was looking for.

When we got onto the highway and had reached cruising speed, he turned to me. "I assume you know all about my talk with Louise."

"Not all."

"But some?"

"The basic outline."

"Christ," he shouted, his voice filled with more emotion than I'd ever heard him express before. "What a thing to do! Not even tell me about my own kid!" He slammed his fist against the dashboard, and the glove compartment door burst open. A stack of road maps slid into his lap. He seemed confused for a moment, all his emotion derailed. He carefully arranged the maps in a neat pile and put them back in the glove compartment. "I mean, why would she do that, Clyde?" he asked quietly. "Why?"

"She rationalized it somehow. She thought it was the only fair thing to do. I can't remember the exact reasoning."

"I don't think she can remember the reasoning, either. I don't think there was much. The poor kid thinks his father is some Austrian vagabond."

"Australian."

"And she tells me *now*, the worst possible time. I get over that thing with Nancy and really start to settle into the dissertation, and this comes up."

Marcus's talk about his dissertation was like any obsessive-compulsive behavior—unconscious, pointless, and slightly embarrassing. The kindest response was to ignore it.

"Do you know what you're going to do?"

"What can I do? I'm going to talk to him. I told Louise to give me a few weeks to get my head together about this and then I'd talk to him. He seems like a sensible kid, doesn't he?"

"He strikes me as pretty mature."

"Kids usually like me, don't they?"

If you included most of his girlfriends in that category, the answer was a resounding yes.

I looked in the rearview mirror. Behind us, a driver was frantically flashing his high beams, signaling me to let him pass. In other circumstances, I might have given in, but I was going close to the speed limit and the driver was clearly working himself into a frenzy, so I decided to hold my ground out of spite.

"Monica and I used to talk about having kids. Funny how things never work out as planned."

The driver behind started to blow his horn in the same frantic way he was flashing his lights. It occurred to me that this was exactly the kind of pointless traffic squabble that ends in gunfire these days, and I swerved into the middle lane. Marcus clutched the dash. "I wonder what Monica's up to these days. Maybe she has a family of her own."

Monica was one of the few women his own age Marcus had been serious about. They'd met in graduate school as equals. She was one of those intellectually intense honey-blond beauties with insomnia and the forward momentum of an ocean liner. In less time than it generally took Marcus to get out of bed, Monica had researched, written, and found a publisher for her dissertation. It was a wild take on George Eliot, one of those academic books with a thesis so improbable and scandalous, it made Monica an overnight sensation in English departments across the country. When it became obvious to her that Marcus was terrified of testing his assumed brilliance by actually getting to work, she'd broken off their engagement and accepted a position at a prestigious school in Illinois. The last anyone had heard from her, she was in the middle of one of those juicy, gossip-driven tenure battles that seem to be the only topic of interest among academics past a certain point in their careers.

In my bleaker moments, I wondered if Marcus's attitude toward Monica wasn't just a variation on my own attitude toward Gordon.

"You're probably in shock," I said. "It'll take a while for the reality to sink in."

"It better not take more than a couple of weeks. He's bright, isn't he? Benjamin?"

"Seems to be."

"Why'd she have to name him Benjamin? I had a math teacher in junior high named Mr. Benjamin. I hated him. He always made fun of my ears."

"He probably wanted to get in your pants," I said.

This seemed to perk him up some. "You think that was it?"

When I looked in the rearview mirror again, I saw that whoever was now behind us was flashing his high beams in the same manner as the other driver. I pondered the likelihood of there being two psycho killers on the same road at roughly the same time, then decided not to risk it and pulled to the right once again.

"Your driving's a little rough tonight," Marcus said.

"Would you rather be gunned down by a lunatic?" I asked.

Marcus took off his sunglasses and stuck them in his shirt pocket. "Are you nervous about having dinner with your father?" he asked.

"Let's not get psychiatric," I said. The truth was, the thought of sitting across a narrow dinner table from my father for over an hour made me feel extremely vulnerable, especially since the table would be laden with sharp objects. I wasn't sure who I was afraid would pick up a knife first. It had taken me over an hour to dress for class, because I knew where I was headed afterward. When visiting Dad, I always tried to dress in a way that made me look professional but not pretentious, masculine but true to myself, clean but not obsessively so. The whole quandary over wardrobe was a joke, because all my clothes were pretty much the same—jeans, T-shirts, and thrift-shop sports jackets with a few minor variations in color for seasonal adjustment. And no matter what I wore, my father always managed to find something to criticize in a particularly humiliating way that struck me as unjust but accurate and left me longing to heap my clothes in the backyard and burn them.

For the past few days, I'd been scanning newspapers and magazines, trying to put together a portfolio of safe, uncontroversial topics to discuss over dinner. But the more scanning I did, the more hopeless I felt. Everything from international news to the pet column in the Living section of the *Boston Globe* looked like fertile ground for William to turn critical, me to turn self-righteous, Agnes to turn neurotically sentimental, and Barbara, her daughter, to turn. The only thing my father and I had in common was a loathing of the Red Sox, but unfortunately, they'd been on an uncharacteristic winning streak, so even that wasn't without its difficulties. I had a fleeting thought that perhaps we could continue the discussion of Marcus's problems through much of the meal, but that wouldn't work, either. Despite ample evidence to the contrary, my father refused to believe that Marcus, or any other friend of mine, of either sex, wasn't gay.

"You know, you've got it lucky in a lot of ways, Clyde. You can go out and have meaningless, impersonal sex behind a tree whenever you want and then get on with your life. You don't appreciate the perils of heterosexual sex."

"Whatever they are, I'll take them over AIDS any day."

"All right, but you can have safe sex. For me, there's no such thing. Someone either wants more from me or less from me or is having a kid. It's a scary world out there. I envy you."

"Of all the insensitive things you've ever said, that ranks up there among the worst." Secretly, though, I was flattered that he assumed I could have sex anytime I wanted, even if it was meaningless and impersonal. As far as I'm concerned, no sex is meaningless and impersonal—although I've been told that after ten years of marriage, it's pretty close.

I reached down and switched on the radio. *All Things Considered* was on, a translator speaking over the barking of dogs and distant gunfire somewhere in the strife-torn world. We had another ten miles or so before we got to Agnes's, and there was always the possibility I'd find a topic for dinner conversation at the last minute.

Agnes lived eight miles over the New Hampshire border, about forty-five minutes from Boston—actually, half an hour if, unlike her, you were capable of driving at the speed limit. She was closer to the center of downtown than many of the city's suburbs, but because she had a New Hampshire address, she insisted upon claiming that she lived "in the country." "It's lonely up here *in the country.*" "It's not as easy as you'd think, raising a teenager *in the country.*"

Her "country" residence was a town house in a development called WestWoods. I found the name of the place a constant irritant. Where were the woods? Any trees within miles of the development had long since been chopped down to make room for the endless strips of shopping malls and factory outlets and condo clusters. And west of what, exactly? There didn't appear to be a companion development called EastWoods.

Within minutes of the exit, I was trapped in a confusing maze of on-ramps and cloverleafs and garish neon signs pointing to fast-food restaurants, budget motels, and car dealerships. It was hard to know what to make of this place. It wasn't a city and it wasn't a suburb and it certainly wasn't rural. Although the population density was probably second only to Calcutta, you never saw humans in the open air here, unless they were riding in a convertible with the top down. There were no sidewalks, no parks, and only an occasional patch of grass, usually with an enormous sign planted in it. If, for reasons that were hard to imagine, someone wanted to walk from his condo to one of the gargantuan discount drugstores, let's say, he'd either be mowed down in traffic or be asphyxiated from exhaust fumes.

This was a world of vast parking lots connected to one another by roads that, due to congestion, often looked like vast parking lots. Every motel, restaurant, pet shop, and cinema was part of a national chain, giving the whole area a surreal atmosphere of being everywhere in general and nowhere in particular. Once in a great while, you'd come upon a shabby luncheonette or a dimly lit variety store, establishments that might as well have been archaeological finds from some ancient lost culture.

"Do you know where her place is?" Marcus asked. He was hunched over the dash, peering out the windshield.

"I'm having a little trouble seeing." There didn't really seem to be day or night here, just a perpetual pink-and-purple twilight created by the spotlights in the parking lots and the flashing neon. "Look for a movie marquee done up like a sign for an Adirondack lodge."

There it was, glowing in the distance: "WestWoods." And underneath that, in lowercase letters: "a place to live." Insipid, yes, but I suppose it gave the residents some help in figuring out what the hell they were doing there.

I made the turn and headed up the winding drive. WestWoods was perched atop a hill, or, more likely, a pile of dirt left by some nearby construction project.

"She's in number fifty-seven," I told Marcus.

It was bad enough that the developer had built over three hundred identical units, but most of the residents had individualized their homes in exactly the same way. Above virtually every door was a flag printed with an autumnal tree. In winter, the flags had snowmen, in February, valentine hearts, in spring, baskets of flowers, and so on down through the whole cavalcade of seasons and holidays.

Although the residents lived in intimate proximity, no one seemed to know anyone else. I'd visited Agnes one summer afternoon and spent a few hours sitting around the complex's overchlorinated swimming pool. Nearly a hundred people were stretched out on lawn chairs in identical Lycra bathing suits, smearing themselves with the same brand of sunscreen, all reading the same paperback novel and ignoring one another. My impression was that suspicion, envy, fear, and bottled-up rage at the world in general kept socializing down to a bare minimum.

PARKED THE CAR IN THE VISITORS' LOT, AND
Marcus and I trudged up the steep drive. Agnes was waiting at the top of her steps, wearing an expression of indignant bewilderment. "Why did you leave the car out there? There's a spot right in front," she said.

"I forgot about that."

"Oh, Clyde. Now everyone's probably calling the police, saying two strange men are walking the grounds."

"Please, Agnes." She had on a little white scarf tied jauntily around her neck, a red jersey, an immaculately white pair of shorts, red socks, and gleaming white sneakers. The alternating bands of red and white made her thin body look like a candy cane come to life.

"Well, there have been some break-ins recently. Even out here. I suppose I'll get blamed if anyone's car gets stolen tonight. I'm so glad you could come, Marcus!"

She extended her hand to Marcus just as he was

stepping in to embrace her, and their bodies collided in a clumsy exchange that made them both stiffen.

Physical awkwardness can be winning in some people, but in the case of Agnes, I found it heartbreaking, as I did most things concerning her. At a dinner party she'd thrown years earlier, she'd attempted an affected curtsy in greeting a guest and ended up twisting her ankle. Afraid of spoiling the evening, she sat through the entire meal in excruciating pain, then called an ambulance as soon as the last guest had departed. It was the kind of catastrophe I was always expecting with my sister.

Agnes and I embraced awkwardly. I could feel the delicate bones in her back through the thin material of her jersey. Her whole body seemed to be vibrating slightly with pent-up nervous energy. I held her for a moment, wishing I could calm the motor running inside her, but I was quickly overcome by the scent of her perfume. Summer Meadow: honeydew and cloying lilies, with the harsh chemical undertones of insect repellent.

"I like your hair," Marcus said, as Agnes led us into the town house. "It was much longer the last time I was here." His slight drawl had become more pronounced in a decidedly forced way: "Ah lahk your hair."

"I thought it was time for a change," Agnes said. She flung out her hand. "So I had it all chopped off." Agnes was always asserting that it was "time for a change" or that some action or event had transformed her life; on the whole, though, her life seemed remarkably, depressingly steady. "Take a seat, and I'll get you something to drink."

"Nothing for me," Marcus said. He sat down on the edge of the sofa and clasped his hands nervously. "I've had a rough afternoon. I think I just need to . . ." His voice trailed off.

Agnes stood perched, waiting for him to finish the sentence. When he didn't, she looked at me for help. The best I could do was shrug.

"It sounds like you need a drink," Agnes finally said. "What about you, Clyde?"

"I'll have a diet Coke."

"A diet *Coke?* You guys! I opened a bottle of wine for you." She stomped her foot in mock outrage, a particularly ineffective gesture considering the ultrawhite sneakers.

"All right," I said, "we'll try the wine."

"You'll probably hate it. I know Marcus is a connoisseur."

"Only of coffee," Marcus said.

He was trying to be charming, but Agnes's face fell. "All I have is instant," she said. "I wish you'd told me, Clyde. And Marcus has had a bad afternoon. You'll have to tell me about it, Marcus, once we get rid of Clyde."

I paced around the living room, suddenly unnerved at the sight of Agnes's furniture. Everything in the room—the chairs, sofa, end tables, magazine racks, lamps, and bookcases, even the mirrors and picture frames—was spindly wicker. Everything was fragile, uncomfortable, and determinedly light; it made me want to cry.

Five years earlier, Agnes's husband, a ridiculous person named Davis, had left her, announcing that he had to "find himself." He'd actually used those words. As he'd explained it to me, "I went from being a perfect son and perfect student to being a perfect husband and father. Now I need to find myself and figure out who I am." I'd listened in astonishment, torn between anger and embarrassment at this inversion of early-women's-lib jargon. The whole rant smelled of budget psychotherapy. Among other things, his claims of perfection were entirely gratuitous. As for finding out who he was, the process turned out to involve nothing more soul-searching than moving into a garish singles complex built around a health club, going on a lot of ski weekends in Montreal, and ignoring the impediments of his former, perfect incarnation—his ex-wife and daughter, for example.

Agnes moved into WestWoods shortly after the divorce. She'd bought all this breezy furniture as a way of proclaiming her delight at her newfound independence. "It's time for a change, a whole new beginning," Agnes had said, although the beginning of what had never become clear.

"Why are you pacing?" Marcus whispered.

"I'm restless," I said. "This wicker makes me restless."

"That's ridiculous."

"Look around. One match, and we'd be reduced to ash in seconds."

"Just sit down, will you? You're making me nervous. And believe me, I'm nervous enough already."

"No whispering in there," Agnes called out from the kitchen.

I sat on one of the chairs. The seat was too short and the flowery cushions were too big, and I felt as if I was being thrown onto the floor.

Agnes came in with a tray of glasses and an open bottle of wine. She set the tray down on the unsteady wicker coffee table and poured. "You were so late," she said, "I had a taste already."

I took a sip of the wine; it was so chokingly sweet, the room began to spin.

"Tell me the truth, Marcus: it's horrible, isn't it."

"It's fine," he said. "It's very good. Exactly what I needed."

"He's just saying that, isn't he, Clyde?"

"He means every word, sweetheart." And then, because the subject couldn't be avoided indefinitely, I said, "Where's . . . Dad?"

Agnes had her glass to her lips. She held up her hand until she'd taken a delicate sip. "Downstairs. I told him you wanted to talk with him." She dabbed at her mouth with a napkin, and I immediately felt a wave of resentment toward her roll in.

"Why did you do that? You didn't make it sound important, did you?"

She shrugged. "I didn't make it sound like anything, Clyde." She was sitting sideways on the far end of the sofa, with only one leg resting on the cushions. She looked at Marcus and forced a laugh. "I hope you're hungry, Marcus."

"I'm famished." Marcus's face was frozen in a grin that made him look like one of those handsome, distressed perfume models. Aside from an occasional game of squash, he never exercised. His stomach had no definition to speak of and his chest was concave, but he'd been blessed with wide shoulders that filled out the striped shirt and made him look naturally fit. "I met someone for lunch, but I wasn't able to eat."

Agnes set down her wineglass. "Oh, dear," she said. "I wish you'd told me, Clyde. I hope there's enough for all of us."

"I'm sure there's plenty. It smells absolutely wonderful."

"Well, I'm not all that hungry myself, so I won't eat much. And Barbara probably won't do more than nibble."

"Clyde mentioned she was anorexic," Marcus commented brightly, as if praising an accomplishment.

"That was *years* ago," I said. "Around the time of the divorce."

Barbara had gone through a period of pushing food around on her plate for a couple of months, lost twenty pounds, and then took up shoplifting. We were all relieved when her weight returned to normal, but it seemed perfectly in character that she wasn't able to sustain her interest in even a behavioral problem for more than sixty days.

"Her father bought her a microwave," Agnes said, "and she eats most of her meals in her room."

Once she'd headed off to the kitchen, Marcus whispered, "You don't have to be so critical of the poor kid. She's doing her best."

"I know that," I said.

"It's not her fault," he said.

"I know that."

"She just needs a little appreciation." Marcus stood and poured his wine back in the bottle, then walked into the kitchen. "Ah you makin' one of your mothah's recipes?" His voice was sounding more like Tennessee Ernie Ford's every second.

The drawling mention of the disastrous cookbook was enough to propel me down the staircase to the basement, where my father had been in residence for two years. It was one of those iron structures that wind down in a tight, narrow spiral, and it always made me feel as if I was heading into the hold of a doomed submarine.

The "ground floor," as it was euphemistically called by the real estate developer, consisted of a two-car garage, a small bathroom, and the room that had once been Agnes's office and was now our father's lair. In all seasons, the basement was damp and chilly, a little like an underground cave, and it still smelled of poured concrete.

From behind the door, I could hear the sound of a television. I braced myself and knocked softly. When there was no response, I pushed the door open. My father was sitting in a chair crammed between the wall and the bed, his eyes glued to the television screen. His face had a grim, ashen look, and despite the fact that he was clearly breathing, I felt a ripple of panic and relief at the thought that perhaps he was dead.

"What's on the tube?" I asked.

He shushed me and pointed to the TV with the remote control. "Look at that moron," he said, "spinning that goddamned wheel."

I turned to the screen and watched as a group of hyperactive game show contestants applauded and bobbed up and down, with lights flashing on and off behind them.

"Go ahead, fatso," my father said, "spin the wheel."

The wheel stopped on a slot marked "Bankruptcy," and my father broke into hearty laughter. "Good for him. I hope they take his house away from him." When a commercial came on, he switched off the sound and turned to me in silence, waiting for something: a greeting, a reproach, a handshake? I never knew what was expected of me, although he always expected me to show respect by making the first move.

I opted for the obvious and asked him how he was feeling. One thing I had to say for my father's mysterious illness was that it gave me a conversation opener.

"I'm feeling lousy. How do you think I'm feeling, stuck down here in this dungeon?"

"You look well."

That much was true. Whatever the nature of his sickness, it didn't seem to hurt his appearance. He'd always been a tall, solid man with wide shoulders and big features—a thick nose with a cleft in its tip, heavy brows that seemed to get lower every time I saw him, as if they were threatening to pull his whole forehead down over his eyes. He was wearing a sleeveless T-shirt, and his arms looked massive, even now. His face was always imprinted with a look of disgust, the corners of his mouth pulled down and his lower lip folded over, as if he'd just stepped in dog shit. It worried me that there was no sure way to know if he wore this expression when I wasn't in his presence.

He grunted at me and switched on the sound again. "Why the hell should I look good? I'm half dead and I'm stuck down here listening to those two fighting day and night. I told your sister she was spoiling that girl."

"Barbara?"

"Who else? Well"—he shrugged—"her father was a loser, so why should she be any different? Leaving him was the only smart thing your sister's done."

"I think he left her, Dad."

"Well, for Christ's sake, can you blame him? Here we go." He pointed at the TV. "I hope this moron loses his shirt."

For as long as I could remember, my father had been addicted to television game shows, mostly because they confirmed his belief that the human race was made up of a bunch of brainless fools.

I sat down on the edge of the unmade bed. The room was almost chilly, despite the warmth of the evening. It smelled of some combination of concrete, gasoline from the garage next door, and whiskey, probably from the half-empty glass on the bedside table. I knew I should make a stab at defending Agnes, but it was a relief to have him criticizing someone other than me.

I think I suffered from some peculiar strain of amnesia when it came to my father. I had detailed memories of my dull childhood —school anxiety, friends who'd betrayed me, trips to the heart-breaking local zoo/death camp, fights with Agnes, books my long-suffering mother had read to us, the whole suffocatingly boring Kodachrome slide show—but when it came to my father, I couldn't remember much about him before he'd turned bitter and scowling. From time to time, I tried to conjure up happy memories, but I invariably decided to leave well enough alone, since it was certainly possible that none existed. What I was most aware of was a vague sense of wanting something from him, but what, I didn't know.

The show was winding up for its splashy finale, a lot of swirling lights and a parade of automobiles and bedroom sets and hotels in Hawaii. My father shut off the sound and rotated his upper body slowly and stiffly. He reached behind him, plucked the glass off the table, and turned back to the television.

"What's that on your wrist?" he asked.

I checked. "My watch?"

"Oh. I thought it was a bracelet."

"Come on," I said. "It's one of those things you tell time with. You're wearing one, too."

"Don't get bent out of shape. I just asked."

Surreptitiously, I looked down at my wrist. I was wearing a gaudy gold knockoff I'd bought on the street the last time I'd been in New York. It was too big for my bony wrist, but it kept remarkably good time. I snaked my hands around the back of the chair, slipped it off, and snuck it into the pocket of my sports jacket. "Dad," I said, hoping to call a truce, "Agnes is making dinner. Are you coming up to eat?"

"I ate already. I can't rearrange my whole life just because you decide to drop in once every decade."

"You're exaggerating," I said. "I was here five years ago."

There was something morbidly institutional about the room, with its vertical blinds and its blank white walls. Down at the far end, a set of sliding glass doors led out to a miniature sunken patio surrounded by a cinder-block wall. It was an odd little well, with a concrete floor covered in mildewed AstroTurf. In winter and spring, it was freezing and flooded, and in summer, it trapped heat and formed a primitive convection oven. There was a plastic lawn chair flung into one corner and a rusting gas grill in the other. Agnes had brought the grill with her from the house she and Davis had lived in, but because she thought of outdoor cooking as a man's job, the thing had never been used and sat there brutalized by the elements, a monument to Agnes's failed marriage and general loneliness. I felt a sharp stab of pity for my cranky old man. No matter how you looked at it, he was not in an enviable position, even if it was one he'd made for himself.

"I'd come more often," I said, "but I've been busy teaching. I haven't had much free time lately."

"Did you get tenure yet?"

"It's not that kind of teaching job."

"Ah." He nodded and turned away in disgust. "So what you're trying to say is, you didn't get it."

"I guess that's right."

He turned down his lower lip and shook his head, and I felt my shoulders slide under the weight of his disappointment in me.

"I'm thinking about applying for a different kind of teaching job," I said. "At a private high school. I've got a few connections."

"Are you crazy? You can't change careers at your age, Clyde. You're stuck. Live with it. Even if you don't have tenure, there's a chance they might not fire you for a while."

He was sipping at his drink, slowly but without evident pleasure. Vance must have been delusional. It wasn't possible that anyone as disgruntled and perennially miserable as my father could be whooping it up under any circumstances. He drained his glass and held it up. "There's a bottle on the floor behind the chest. Get it for me and fill this up."

For as long as I could remember, my father, an avid though not wildly excessive drinker, had kept his liquor bottles in odd, out-of-the-way places—the back of a cabinet under the kitchen sink, the far reaches of a closet in the front hall, with the detergents and bleach near the washing machine. It might have made some sense if he were a secretive drunk, but he made no attempts at hiding his drinking. In fact, Agnes and I had always been enlisted in digging out his stash. I pushed aside the chest of drawers, one of those blond, pressed-wood, cheap-motel creations, and rummaged around on the floor for the bottle. Even though a headache was beginning to trickle down the center of my forehead, I felt useful for the first time since entering the room and buoyed up by the boost in status I was getting from performing this humiliating chore.

As I poured whiskey into his glass, he said, "So Agnes tells me you want to 'talk' with me."

"She asked me to," I said, eager to shift the blame. I passed him his drink. "She's worried you might be leaving the house for some secret late-night medical treatments."

"I'll tell you what she's worried about—she's worried I'm going to die and leave my money to someone else."

He frequently made these scurrilous accusations of gold-digging, even while he pleaded poverty. The whole thing was so ridiculous, I suddenly craved a drink myself. But I screwed the cap on the bottle, set it on the floor, and pushed the chest back against the wall. Although my father viewed my lack of interest in booze as suspect, the few times I had taken a drink in his presence, he'd indicated that the lapse was another sign of my moral and physical weakness. I sat down in a chair near the door, the big bed a buffer between us. "She's not worried about money. She pays you an allowance. We know you got wiped out in that last fire."

"The beautiful part is, Clyde, that neither one of you knows anything for sure. I could be sitting on a million-dollar insurance settlement." He seemed absurdly pleased by this comment. He took a big ugly gulp from his drink and turned back to the muted TV. "Now that we settled that, is there anything else you wanted to 'talk' about?"

"As a matter of fact, there is. A friend of mine said he saw you out at dinner with a couple of people a few weeks ago. Some seafood joint. If that's true, Agnes would be relieved to hear it. And I would, too."

"First of all, what friend of yours?" he asked, as if this were the relevant point.

"My friend Vance. You don't know him."

"Someone I don't know is spotting me at restaurants? Wouldn't hold up in a court of law, would it?"

"I knew he was wrong, but I figured it couldn't hurt to check."

"I don't remember saying he was wrong." He wrapped his lips around the rim of his glass and took another swallow.

"You mean he was right?"

"I don't remember saying that, either."

I stood up and started toward the door. "I think you should reconsider and come up for dinner. It would mean a lot to Agnes."

As I was about to walk out, he said, "Where are you running off to?"

There was such an unlikely, uncharacteristically plaintive tone in his voice, I stopped short and turned back to him. He seemed to be slumped in his chair now, his neck bent as if those heavy brows were pulling his whole head into his lap.

"You act as if I didn't love your mother. Well, I did. And no matter how I felt about her, I stuck by her."

I never had doubted or even given too much thought to his love for my mother, possibly because contemplating their relationship in any way struck me as too morbid.

"My friendship with Diane has nothing to do with your mother."

Diane? "Diane?"

"That's right. And don't go broadcasting the name around up-stairs."

"So are you . . . dating her?"

"I'm thinking of asking her to move in."

"*Here?*"

"That's what I said, isn't it?"

I looked around the tiny room. "Where?"

"Look, I'm not asking for your advice, Clyde. I'm just telling you."

"But Dad . . ."

"Don't go pulling a guilt trip on me. We're trying to help her kid out. He had everything under control, putting some money aside; next thing you know, they've got him on some rap about being a deadbeat dad. It's none of the government's goddamned business. Just don't go telling Agnes about this!"

"Don't you think she's going to find out if someone's living here?"

"I'll cross that bridge when I come to it. In the meantime, I don't feel like dealing with her hysteria. I'll just tell her it's a nurse."

The light in the room was beginning to grow gray, as if a fog were seeping in the sliding glass doors. I felt I was suffocating in the dank room, slipping away into the fog. I promised him I wouldn't tell Agnes and tried to convince him one last time to come upstairs for dinner. "My friend Marcus is here," I said, an unlikely inducement.

"The loser with the phony Southern accent? No way. I've got to make a few phone calls. Tell Agnes to bring me down a beer. There's not even room for a refrigerator in this dump."

When I got back upstairs, Marcus was setting the dinette table and Agnes was taking a roasted chicken out of the oven. She handed me a carving knife and said, "Here. Men seem to be able to carve better than women. How was he?"

"Engrossed in *Wheel of Fortune.*"

The chicken was so dry it was practically crumbling. I'm not sure why it is that some people seem to be incapable of cooking, but Agnes was one of them. Even if she followed the directions on a box of cake mix down to the last quarter teaspoon of oil and second of baking time, there was a problem. The idea that cooking requires love is absurd. Cooking requires confidence.

She looked at her watch and put her hand on her hip. "But *Wheel of Fortune* went off the air ten minutes ago."

"Well, he got engrossed in whatever came on next."

"*Entertainment Tonight?*" Agnes had a way of scouting out the most irrelevant side to every issue, something I was not in the mood for. The conversation with my father had left me jittery and confused, exactly as if I'd just had two cups of coffee too many. "I don't think it makes much difference," I said.

"But he usually hates that show."

"Agnes . . ."

"Agnes was showing me some of your mother's recipes," Marcus said. He was folding cloth napkins and carefully placing them beside the plates. "They're unique."

"There's a reason for that," I said. I handed Agnes the plate of chicken, which looked a lot like a plate of heaped-up sawdust.

"I showed him the No-Bake Cake Pie," Agnes said, "and for your information, he thought it sounded delicious."

"Is that the one with the cookies?" I asked. It was a preposterous recipe that involved smashing up a bag of chocolate-chip cookies with a hammer, mixing in a lot of peanut butter and junk food, and then pressing the glop into a big pan and smearing a can of frosting over the top. "Perfect for long holiday weekends," my mother had written, "when the family raids the icebox for snacks after the touch football game." I hated to think of my mother sitting around the kitchen table dreaming up these absurd fantasies, depicting the family as a less political version of the Kennedys.

"Oh, Clyde," Agnes said calmly, "would you mind going upstairs and getting Barbara? I called her on the phone, but her line's busy."

I could tell by the forced nonchalance of her voice that Agnes was determined to stay out of the line of Barbara's fire. Not that I blamed her.

I walked upstairs with dread, hoping my niece was in a good mood. All the hallways of the condo were painted the most gratingly powdery shade of blue imaginable, the visual equivalent of air freshener, and I felt as if they were closing in around me, conspiring with my headache to crush my skull.

As I was about to knock on Barbara's bedroom door, I heard her talking and stopped to listen for a second. "Don't buy it from him," she said. "I can get you a much better deal."

I knocked.

"Listen," she said, "I gotta go. No. Uncle, I think. Yeah, tell me about it." Then she opened her door and stood holding the knob. "Hi, Clyde." She leaned in and kissed me on the cheek.

The kiss was so disarmingly genuine and so shy, I felt like a horrible curmudgeon for having any doubts about her. The truth was, she could shift from impossible teenage delinquent to adorable little girl and then back again, all in the course of a single sentence. Much depended upon the company.

She had on an enormous pair of denim overalls, a flannel work shirt with sleeves hanging down over her hands, and a pair of tattered blue sneakers. Her hair was unnaturally black and hacked off in an alarming fashion, the sides long, the back cut to the middle of her head, so that she appeared to be wearing a Halloween fright wig that didn't fit. I couldn't really tell through her clothing, but she seemed to have filled out some since the last time I'd seen her. In contrast to her hair and clothes, her plump face looked soft and angelic. But on closer inspection, I saw that what I'd assumed was a pimple on the side of her nose was a gold stud poking through her flesh.

"How's it going?" I asked. I often found myself trying to sound as casual and hip as possible when I talked to Barbara, even though I had very little idea of what casual and hip sounded like to a fourteen-year-old these days.

Barbara shrugged. Behind her, the room was a tangle of electrical wires from a television, a boom box, a telephone, an answering machine, a computer, and the aforementioned microwave. The faint smell of popcorn wafted out into the hallway. The powdery blue walls were covered with spray-painted graffiti. "Did you do that?" I asked, nodding toward the black lines.

"Yeah." She stepped out into the hall and slammed the door behind her.

"It looks great," I said.

"Whatever."

"I like your . . ." I pointed to my own nose, not sure what to call her piercing. "Did it hurt?"

"I put ice on it first."

"You did it yourself?" I got the creeps cutting my own fingernails.

"A friend helped," she said, apparently assuming that I'd find this reassuring.

Barbara started down the stairs ahead of me, clumsily bouncing from step to step. "How's teaching?" she asked, without turning around.

"It's all right," I said. But as soon as I'd uttered the words, I felt a sudden solidarity with her, a desire to confess all. "Actually," I said, "the classes aren't going too well. The school's a bit of a joke."

"All schools are, Clyde. We're having metal detectors put in next month."

"Metal detectors!"

"I know—pathetic, isn't it? All you have to do is have someone pass the gun through the bathroom window once you're already in."

Marcus was standing behind a chair in the dining area. "Wow," he said, "look who's all grown up."

"I'm working on it," Barbara said in a bored, suggestive tone. She sat down at the table and, without rolling up her sleeves, managed to grab a piece of chicken and pop it into her mouth.

Agnes came in from the kitchen with a plate of vegetables, carrots and broccoli in such fantastically uniform pieces it was hard to imagine they weren't plastic. "Oh, honey, that shirt," she said. "You're dressed for midwinter."

"What am I supposed to be? Naked?"

"Isn't there something in between?"

"Like what? A lame scarf around my neck?"

Agnes took a seat, and Marcus and I followed her lead.

"Did you show Clyde your paintings?" Agnes asked.

"They're not *paintings*," Barbara's evil twin growled.

"They're wonderful," I said.

Barbara reached across the table and grabbed another piece of chicken with her invisible hand.

"I didn't know you were an artist," Marcus said.

"She's a very good one," Agnes said, and passed me a plate of sawdust.

Barbara rolled her eyes. "She's pissed off because I painted on the walls. You ought to be happy, Mom. At least I didn't do it on the *outside* walls."

"I don't think the neighbors would have appreciated that."

"Like we know the neighbors."

"I thought you were friends with that girl on the A side of the complex. Ginny Monte, isn't it?"

"Right. Like I'd ever be seen with her. You just want to meet her father."

"How's the chicken, Marcus?" Agnes asked, carefully avoiding eye contact with her daughter. "I hope I didn't overcook it too much. Someone told me that two people in the complex died of salmonella last month, so I kept it in an extra hour."

"It's superb," Marcus said. "I had a grandmaw used to make it just like this." The last I'd heard, the only grandmaw he'd ever known had been a physicist.

Agnes sloshed more wine into her glass. "Marcus was telling me about your writer friend," she said. "Louise Morehouse, is it?"

"Morris. How much did he tell you?"

"I mentioned that she'd come to town. That's all."

"I wish you'd invited her, Clyde. I'd love to meet her. You gave me her books. I adored them. Of course, I don't remember a thing about any of them."

"I don't know why you bother reading, Mom, since you forget everything about the books two days later. I mean, I wouldn't even bother."

"It passes the time," Agnes said.

"That's why you do yoga. That's why you do everything. I mean, why not just take sleeping pills and go into a coma for a few weeks? That'd pass the time."

"I hope I get to meet Louise. And that dog sounds a*dorable!*"

I began describing one of Louise's novels, while Marcus picked nervously at his food.

A light went on in Agnes's head: "I remember the wonderful little baby that poor girl has. It was so sad. Or was it funny?"

Marcus looked across the table at me. He put his hands to his temples and applied pressure, as if he were trying to squeeze a pimple.

Barbara, who seemed lost once attention had drifted away from her, pushed back the long flaps of hair covering her ears, revealing a fleeting glimpse of the shaven sides of her head. "I mean, the one time I made the mistake of going over to see Ginny Monte, her father practically raped me. Good luck with him, Mom."

"We were talking about something else, dear."

"I think me almost getting raped is more important."

"I think you're exaggerating just a bit, honey."

"No, I don't think so, Mom. I think I'd know when someone's practically trying to rape me."

"Marcus," Agnes said, "would you pass the chicken to Barbara so she can put some on her plate."

"Oh, right," Barbara said. "Like we sit down with napkins every night and have dinners all the time."

"Sometimes we do," Agnes said. "Sometimes we even eat with forks."

"I mean, why do we have to be so civilized all of a sudden, just because Clyde and *Marcus* are here?" She said Marcus's name in a provocative singsong, and a flush crept up Agnes's chest, past the scarf on her neck, right to her jawline.

"So tell us about these metal detectors," I said.

"It's so sad. You move up to the country to get away from all that," Agnes said, "and you just can't escape it. It's the saddest thing I've ever heard."

"Right, Mom. Teenagers are committing suicide all over the world every minute of the day, and a metal detector is the saddest thing you've heard."

"I'm sorry, but I think it's sad, honey. I think it's tragic."

"Oh, right, and Ginny's dad cornering me against the refrigerator is just fine."

"Listen, Barbara," I said, "why don't you let your mother off the hook for one night. Give her a vacation."

Barbara looked up at me and then at Marcus. There was something ominous in her silence, and I began to wonder if intervening had been such a good idea.

"So," she said, popping another piece of chicken into her mouth, "are you two, like, *boyfriends?*"

Agnes slammed down her fork. "That's it," she said. "I've had it. I've *had* it."

"What'd I say?"

"Forget it," I said.

"I can't forget it," Agnes said. "How can I forget it when I can't forget it? When I get reminded of it every minute of every day— how unhappy she is, how every word out of my mouth is wrong, wrong, wrong!" Her voice was going shrill, as if she was about to burst into tears.

"I don't even know what you're talking about," Barbara said. She rolled up her sleeves and put a slice of chicken on her plate and started to cut it with her knife and fork.

"Please leave the table," Agnes said.

"What'd I *say?*"

"Go to your room and heat something in that oven your father gave you."

Barbara stood up and knocked over her chair. It fell back against the floor with a thud. "It's always me, isn't it?"

"As a matter of fact," Agnes said, "it usually is."

There was a loud banging from the basement, my father pounding on the ceiling. "The devil is calling you down to *hell,*" Barbara shouted, and bounded up the stairs.

I remembered his beer. "I'll go see what he wants," I said.

"No, no, no," Agnes said. She wiped at her eyes with her napkin and threw it on top of her uneaten food. "I'll go." She untied the white scarf from around her neck and stuffed it into the pocket of her shorts. "He can be so awful sometimes. What did you find out, Clyde? Is he all right? Did the doctor tell him something he isn't telling me?"

I cleared my throat. "Well, no, not really. I think he's just going through a phase."

There was more angry rapping from below, louder this time. "He has a stick he pounds with," Agnes explained. "It's very convenient. What do you mean, a phase?"

"I think he's doing better."

Agnes looked at me sadly. Though I could tell she didn't believe me, she had no alternative but to accept what I said, at least for the moment. She disappeared down the winding metal staircase. Marcus pushed his plate away from him. "Jesus Christ," he said, "I hope Louise's kid isn't angry like that. You think it's because the father walked out on them?" He paused, then looked at me defiantly. "You can't say I walked out on anybody. You can't accuse me of that." He shook his head. "Poor Agnes. How much older is that girl than Benjamin?"

"We'd better leave," I said, and started to gather up the dishes. The condo was quiet in an eerie, insulated way. I began to experience some of Agnes's panic, not at the thought that the outside world might start climbing in the windows, but at the realization that there was no obvious way to climb out.

FOR SEVERAL DAYS AFTER THE VISIT TO NEW Hampshire, I stumbled around my cramped rooms in the apartment, trying to decide what to do about the situation with my father. Of course, the decision-making was complicated by the fact that I really didn't know what the situation was. Was he actually planning to have this woman move in with him? Was he playing Agnes and me for fools by pleading illness and poverty while trying to set up his girlfriend's son? Or was he the one being played for the fool? After all, who in her right mind would move into that dank basement voluntarily? Maybe the whole mess was a feverish delusion brought on by a combination of alcohol and fumes from the garage and the mildewed AstroTurf.

I kept planning to tell Agnes, but I didn't go ahead with my plans. Like my father, I didn't want to have to deal with her hysteria. Mainly, however, I was enjoying sharing something with . . . Dad, even this absurd deception. My father and I had shared only one other secret that I could remember, and that dated back to around the time I was twelve. He and I were working on a lawn mower in the garage one rainy afternoon when he got up, walked to a corner, and pissed on the filthy, oil-stained floor. Looking over his shoulder, he said, "Don't tell your mother I did this."

Four days after the visit, I got a call from him. It was early morning, and I was lying in bed reading the biography of a movie star who was dead or nearly dead (I was two hundred pages from finishing it and didn't want to skip ahead and spoil the surprise ending). I always felt a slight surge in my chest when the phone rang unexpectedly, probably because I was hoping it was Gordon, calling to arrange a get-together or something even more improbable and longed for: a reconciliation. The biography was basically a list of sexual conquests, with a few references to idiotic, forgotten films thrown in for bulk, so my romantic fantasies were running especially wild that morning.

I picked up the phone and gave a few quizzical hellos without getting a response. It wasn't until I heard wheezy breathing on the other end that I suspected my father.

"Dad?" I said. "Is that you?"

"That's right, it is," he said, as if I'd challenged him.

Since the only other time he'd called me was to announce my mother's death, I immediately assumed disaster and asked him what was wrong.

"Nothing's wrong. Why would it be?"

"I don't know, I just thought ..."

"Are you trying to tell me you told Agnes about Diane?"

"Agnes?"

"You mean you did!"

"No, no. I didn't say a word to her."

"Good. Don't," he barked, and hung up.

I replaced the receiver gently. It had never occurred to me before that he might have my phone number written down somewhere, and I was delighted to think he did. Perhaps it was alphabetized in some book. Was I listed as Clyde, or was our last name in there, too? Perhaps he'd put "son" in parentheses, as a reminder. For a full ten minutes after the call, I felt so warm and connected, in a welcome-home, chestnuts-roasting kind of way, I couldn't even read. I suppose I should have felt more loyalty to my poor dead mother, at least a few moments of outrage on her behalf, but after all, she was dead, poor thing. Eventually, I put the book aside and went downstairs to make myself a huge breakfast.

I was still feeling elated early the next morning, when my father phoned again. I suspected it was him this time, so I decided to try his own telephone technique and, instead of saying hello, remained silent. I considered it a triumph that he was the first one to give in and say, "Is that you?"

"Who wants to know?" I asked, curious to see if the question would corner him into an admission of paternity.

"Don't give me that bullshit," he said. "You know who it is. I'm calling to ask you about your rent. Diane's son is thinking about moving to Cambridge, and we're trying to figure out what it's going to cost him."

When I told him what I paid, he blew out his breath and said, "For that dump?"

"But you've never been here," I reminded him. "I've never described it to you."

"Believe me," he said, "I can imagine."

That was pretty much the extent of the conversation, but it left me with the same combination of hope and despair and the altogether pathetic feeling that there was something flattering about the fact that Diane's son—Roger, I learned in the course of the brief volley—was thinking of moving to the same town I lived in.

I should have directed some of my anxiety toward reading the rest of the books for my ailing class and preparing a few lectures in advance, but I wasn't up to it. The week after Mallory's big announcement about her husband's affair, she'd come to class carrying a picnic basket of food she'd purchased at a nearby gourmet shop. She'd arrived twenty minutes late, projecting the flushed enthusiasm of a minor celebrity making an appearance at a charity auction. "Just pretend I'm not here," she'd said, interrupting my introduction to Elizabeth Gaskell. She unloaded the picnic basket on the marble top of the French commode. One by one, heads turned in the direction of the food as the sweet, buttery smell of pastry drifted across the room.

Aside from a few dismissive comments about the book's title ("Sounds more like a chocolate bar") and a consensus that it was of unimpressive length, *Cranford* was scarcely mentioned, no matter how many times I tried to intervene.

Tim, the would-be actor, brought up a television movie starring Marlo Thomas that had aired the night before, which, it turned out, everyone else in the class had watched. Split personalities were debated for almost an hour. I was incapable of contributing much to the discussion, since I'd called a phone sex line and had missed the last half of the movie.

I could see the next two months of classes taking shape in front of me. Dorothea, the retired schoolteacher, had passed around a sign-up sheet for bringing in snacks and beverages for the rest of the semester, and Eileen Ash had taken her poll of vegetarians (one hypoglycemic who wanted to be counted as a maybe, and one lacto-ovo macrobiotic). The competitive spirit was building; the food would get more and more elaborate, culminating in Eileen's catered extravaganza. Brian, the divorced lawyer, announced that he was going to talk to the administration about setting up a grill in the garden when it was his turn. "Let it be known, ladies," he crowed, "I can cook."

When I described this to Marcus, he offered his standard metaphor theory: "It's all about food, Clyde."

I spent my mornings reading more and more movie star biographies, while Otis looked on sheepishly from a pile of blankets I put out for him in the corner. I was beginning to get used to his presence in the house, although we hadn't established much of a relationship. Sometimes when I looked at him, all timid and doe-eyed, I felt saddened by his evident insecurity about where in the world and to whom he belonged. I could easily drift off into a lurid, tear-jerking fantasy of his abandonment under a picnic table beside the highway, station wagon of screaming children pulling away and so on.

Of course, I hadn't completely ruled out the possibility that his depression was primarily the result of lying about in the apartment, observing me.

Mostly, however, I'd begun to organize my days around Benjamin's eerily prompt afternoon arrivals. He came by the house to collect his dog at two-fifteen every afternoon, give or take no more than a few minutes. The world is divided into people who tell time in minutes and those who tell time in blocks of half an hour or so. Ben was obviously in the former group. But even so, I wondered if he didn't have a friend or two with whom he might occasionally fight after school or sneak off somewhere for a cigarette.

Otis had a preternatural ability to distinguish Ben's tread, for he always perked up as soon as Ben's foot hit the bottom step. The dog had long strings of fur that hung off the tips of his ears. When he stuck out his ears to capture sounds, the strings hung straight down and made him look even more like a frayed piece of clothing. But he seemed confused about what he should do when Ben showed up: bound out of my rooms and fling himself down to the second floor to greet his master, or crawl under the bed. Usually he looked at me, whimpered, and licked his chops, as if waiting for instruction. There was no question that the dog had been traumatized, but all I had were odd clues that didn't add up to much. What could it possibly mean that every time Marcus started to make coffee, the dog ran to the third floor and crawled onto his blankets? And what was his apparent water fetish all about? Each time I turned on the shower, Otis dashed into the bathroom and sat in front of the tub panting expectantly, ears straight up to the ceiling.

As soon as Ben came into the house, he'd call Louise and recount some bit of news about school in a grudging tone. As part of her grant, Louise had been given an office in a building outside Harvard Square and had been told in an amazingly subtle but unambiguous bureaucratic way that she was expected to spend the bulk of her time there. After the call, Ben would take Otis out for a walk, sometimes not returning until after five. I had no idea where they went, but since Louise seemed satisfied that he could take care of himself, I didn't think it was my place to be concerned. Still, the sight of Ben loping up the street, baggy clothes swimming around his body and Walkman clamped to his head, Otis dragging along beside him, brought back all the aimlessness of my own childhood and all the lonely disappointment. I had to keep reminding myself that it couldn't mean anything to Ben that Marcus was spending increasingly long hours at the library, despite his resolution to get to know his son.

A couple of weeks after his initial talk with Louise, Marcus still hadn't shown any signs of sitting down with Ben. Most alarming of all, his golden hair was getting noticeably more unkempt, as if he hadn't been combing or shampooing it with any regularity. Ordinarily, delight in casually maintaining his appearance was one of the things that held Marcus together. As he was wandering out of the house one morning in a bleary-eyed, caffeine daze, I stopped him to ask how things were going.

"Which things?" he asked.

"Well . . . academic things," I said, figuring it was best to start with the predictable.

He leaned against the doorjamb and ran his hand through his greasy hair. He had on a maroon V-neck sweater with moth holes around the waistband, a piece of clothing he usually wore only when he was housebound with the flu. Over his shoulder, he was carrying a gray canvas briefcase that Monica had given him when he began work on his dissertation. It was stained and tattered, the strap frayed and one of the zippers broken. There was a wad of unpromising-looking, dog-eared papers sticking out of the top. "I feel as if I'm on the threshold, Clyde. I really do. A few steps, and I'm in there. It's all so clear in my head, I know I'll be able to knock the thing off in a few months once I actually begin. It's a surprisingly hot topic right now."

I nodded, afraid to say anything. I wasn't even sure how the frown qualified as a "topic."

"I'm putting off talking with, you know, Benjamin," he said. "Just until I get my foot in the door. Just until I feel secure about the beginning. Another week or so is all."

Then he hoisted his ratty briefcase up on his shoulder and left.

One afternoon, after Ben had made his call to Louise but just before he left for his walk, the phone rang. We were in the attic room I did myself the favor of calling a study, and I was bent over the record player, attempting to move the needle beyond a scratch without making it worse. I was trying to interest Ben in accordion music through subliminal suggestion. Whenever he was around, I put on albums of musette waltzes and Argentinian tangos and even some insipid but virtuoso recordings of Lawrence Welk playing polkas and pop tunes. Thus far, he hadn't commented on the music, and I couldn't tell if he hadn't yet noticed it or was simply trying to be polite. Either way, I was sure that eventually, unless I'd completely misjudged him, he'd fall for the combination of giddy circus wheezing and the heartbreaking chords that I found so haunting.

"Do me a favor," I said on the third ring, "and answer that."

He picked up the phone, said hello a few times, and then held the receiver out to me. "No one's there."

"That's my father," I said over my shoulder. "Ask him what he wants."

He put the receiver to his ear and then said to me, "He says to pick up the goddamned phone yourself if you want to know what he wants."

"All right. Tell him to hold on a minute."

"He said to hold on a minute," Ben repeated. Then, obviously answering questions, he said, "It's Ben. My full name? Benjamin. Oh, well, Benjamin Morris. I'm twelve." He put down the phone and shrugged. "He hung up."

A few minutes later, the phone rang again. "You'd better get it this time," Ben said, and left with Otis for one of his long, mysterious strolls.

"I'm not going to ask who that is," my father said, "but who is it?"

"A friend's son," I told him. "He comes here after school to walk his dog."

"You're running a day care center now?"

I knew it was only a short step to accusations of child molestation. Still, I hadn't heard from him in over a week, and I was happy he'd called. For some reason I couldn't quite explain, I was proud of the fact that Ben knew my cantankerous old man was phoning me in the middle of the afternoon. "Was there something you wanted to tell me, Dad?"

"Diane and I are going to the Cape for a night next month, and I want you to explain it to Agnes."

"Explain it? How?"

"Well, obviously not by telling her the truth. I could do that myself."

"Forget it, Dad. There's a limit." I wasn't sure there was, but it seemed to me it was in my best interest to say so. As soon as I'd said it, though, I could feel his disgust draining through the line and tried to make amends. "Why don't you tell her you're going to visit Uncle Lon?"

"Ha! I wouldn't even lie about visiting that rat."

Uncle Lon was my father's younger brother, a gaunt, towering loudmouth who'd made money on a variety of real estate deals that were constantly under investigation. He had three bibulous daughters who, much to my father's delight, were always in trouble —everything from drunk driving to "female problems," aka abortions. Lon was steadfast in his devotion to his "girls," and they doted on him, between drinking binges and court dates. My parents had lived a few miles from Uncle Lon and company for decades, but the brothers hadn't seen each other in nearly ten years. Once, in the middle of an Easter dinner, Lon had accused my father of burning down one of his sporting goods stores—a generous accusation, since it was obvious to anyone who knew anything about the situation that he'd burned down both. My father had countered with a snide comment about Tina. Lon made a tearful defense of his beloved youngest daughter, dragged his wife out of the house, and the two hadn't spoken since.

One of my father's chief concerns when he discovered I was gay was that Lon would find out and have something else to hold over his head.

"You know, that might not be a bad idea after all," my father was saying. "It's not like Agnes would dare call Lon to check up on it. Thanks."

Later in the afternoon, when Ben stopped in to drop Otis off for the night, he hung around the kitchen, rearranging the dog food on the shelves. He seemed to be waiting for something. Finally, when he was at the door and about to leave, he said, "Do you like your father, Clyde?"

"Like him?" I asked.

He nodded, his lank red hair falling over his left eye.

It had never occurred to me to think about whether or not I liked my father, possibly because it was so clear I didn't and possibly because it seemed an entirely irrelevant question. One thing was certain: I'd never been able to talk myself out of wanting to be liked by him, even if he wasn't terribly likable himself. "You wouldn't call us friends," I said. "Why do you ask?"

"I don't know," he said. "I was just wondering."

After a couple of weeks of watching Benjamin wander out in the afternoons, I took to going for long walks myself, hoping to bump into him, or at least to catch sight of him in some corner of the city.

It was, by this time, getting toward late September, and although the days were still warm, the afternoons frequently turned windy and damp. A faint trace of the spicy rot of autumn—dying leaves and decayed flowers and the heavy sweetness of pine needles—had begun to scent the air, giving the whole pursuit an especially melancholy tone. But for more than a week, Ben and I had no chance encounters, and since I wasn't ready to contemplate the humiliating absurdity of trailing boy and dog, I was about to give up.

And then one afternoon as I was wending my way back toward the shabby neighborhood where Marcus and I lived, I cut through the yard of Radcliffe College. The yard was a quiet, soothing oval of pampered lawn ringed by impressive Gothic Revival buildings, which, unlike their immense Harvard counterparts, were small enough to exude an unintimidating charm. When, years earlier, I'd worked at a bookstore in the Square, I often took breaks there and napped in one of the several gardens tucked into shady alcoves behind the brick walls surrounding the school. The sounds of traffic and pedestrians filtered into the yard, but muted and serene so that it was like being in a grassy clearing listening to the sounds of a football game from a distant stadium. (Another advantage to living in a college town is easy access to a lot of nicely tended grass, secret gardens, and public toilets.)

The library at Radcliffe was reputed to have the world's largest collection of cookbooks, a fact I'd once made the mistake of relaying to Agnes. She'd lit up at the prospect of our mother's recipes being housed in such a renowned institution. "Mom would be so proud," she'd said, and had gone back to her insane project with new determination. Actually, the idea of "Oh-So-Simple Spaghetti Sauce" ("Mix one bottle of 'catsup' with two cups of 'water,' one cup of sugar, pinch of 'herbs' and stir") being housed at Radcliffe excited me, too, but I wasn't about to admit it to anyone. A few days after my abortive visit in New Hampshire, Agnes had sent me a note saying that she was disappointed I'd left so abruptly. "We were having such a fun time," she wrote, without any apparent irony. She'd enclosed a couple of new recipes she'd come across and wanted to know if I thought she should include them. One in particular caught my fancy:

Corn Flake Balls

ingredients:

1 box "Corn Flakes"
1 can "cling" peaches in syrup
1 jar cocktail cherries
2 boxes lime "Jell-o"
4 cups sugar
2 big bottles corn syrup
3 7/8 cups mayonnaise

"Crush" cereal with hammer or empty red wine bottle. Chop peaches and cherries into nice "chucks," retaining liquids for later. Meanwhile, make "Jell-o" using extra sugar and syrup. Stir pulverized cereal, fruit chunklettes, and liquids into the mixture. "Fold" in the "mayo." When "Jell-o" has hardened, form into balls with ice cream scooper or melon baller.

These keep for months in the "fridge" and make colorful "snacks." My grandchildren are just thrilled when they visit for the weekend and I serve them these for breakfast, afloat in a bowl of "milk."

Cutting through a side yard, I started to imagine this recipe among the volumes of world cuisine, and within seconds I was leaning against the wall, gasping for air, thinking about Agnes and my mother and those ridiculous balls of Jell-O floating in milk, forlornly waiting for Barbara or *anyone* to come along and admire them or appreciate them or at the very least eat them.

It was then that I spotted Ben. He was stretched out on his stomach on the grass, propped up on his elbows, reading. Otis was keeping watch beside him, and when the dog saw me, he started to wag his tail, the first sign of pleased recognition he'd ever shown. I immediately felt revived.

It was after four, and the wind had shifted east and begun to blow in from the ocean, salty and damp. The remaining sunlight in the garden had narrowed to one bright corridor on the grass, and Ben was lying in it, facing away from me, a bed of dead daylilies near his head. Something in the sight of him, stretched out and reading like that, made me feel I'd snuck up on him unfairly, and I turned away and hurried across the yard and out one of the wrought-iron gates.

When Ben showed up with Otis late that afternoon, I was sitting at the table in the kitchen, eating a bowl of cereal. He had on several shirts—a black T-shirt and a long-sleeved flannel shirt and, over that, a short-sleeved white dress shirt—and his face was pink from the breeze.

"It's getting cool out there," I said. "You'll have to cut your walks short, won't you?"

"This weather won't last. There'll probably be another long stretch of warmth. New England is famous for that."

Ben had told me that he researched all the places he and Louise moved to. He knew more about the climate and topography of New England than I'd learned from a lifetime of living there. We were, he explained, in a period of deceptive cool that usually occurred this time of year and seldom lasted more than a few days, a week at most.

He went to one of the cabinets and pulled down a box of dog food, filled Otis's dish with it, and made him sit for a moment before putting it on the floor. We'd agreed that he would feed the dog in the afternoon, although I'd started to sneak him treats from my plate just because I couldn't resist the look of hungry pleading in his eyes. "I think Otis likes the cold," he said. "He's more lively in this weather."

"He's lively around you," I said. "Around me, he sleeps. Why don't you sit down and have some cereal?"

He looked at me through his bangs and then snapped his hair off his face. "That's what I had for breakfast."

"That's what *I* had for breakfast," I said. "That's what I had for lunch. It's probably what I'll have for dinner. Take one of those bowls from the dish rack."

"I don't think so, Clyde. I already ate."

I shoveled in more of the cereal. It had been sitting in the bowl so long it had taken on the consistency of wet newspaper. "Where did you eat?"

"At a friend's house." He said it quickly and then turned to put away the dog food.

I'd felt such a pang of sadness at seeing him alone, hiding out in the garden, I'd stopped at a used-record store on the way home, one of a good half dozen in town that I frequented, and picked up an album for him. I'd bought it solely for the title—*Music for a Chinese Dinner at Home*—and the faded but still garish cover, a posed photograph so racially insensitive it defied description. Louise had told me Ben collected odd record jackets from the fifties, and I figured you couldn't get much odder than this. I had it in a bag on the table, and I handed it to him now as unceremoniously as I could, slightly embarrassed by the offering, by having any offering at all, and went back to my cereal.

"For Louise?" he asked.

"For you."

He fingered the bag for a moment. "Accordion music?"

"As a matter of fact, it isn't. I've temporarily given up on that. This is an unselfish gift, appealing to your interests, not mine."

He pulled the record out of the bag and smiled, briefly and hesitantly, when he saw the cover. I hadn't seen him smile very often, and for a few seconds he looked untroubled and happy, like a little boy. The skin around his eyes was so light and thin, it looked blue. As he smiled, some facial muscles tugged his ears forward, making them more protuberant and uncannily Marcus-like than usual.

He put the record back in the bag and mumbled a thank-you that sounded more embarrassed than pleased. "Where'd you find this?" he asked.

"I can show you, if you like," I told him.

We fell into a routine of going out together some afternoons and walking to one or more of the used-record stores in Cambridge or across the river and into Boston. On the whole, the record stores were dusty places with a damp-basement smell, most of them heaped to the ceiling with stacks of discarded LPs. The floors themselves were sagging under the weight of all that perfectly good vinyl, cast off by the lemmings who've been hoodwinked into believing that compact discs have superior sound.

The stores were always crowded with brooding shoppers who fit into one of three broad categories: young music student with, assuming he was white, dreadlocks; tweedy academic with bad eyesight; nervous, obsessive-compulsive opera fan with body odor and shoes worn down at the heels. Apparently, women don't buy used records, so the stores had the atmosphere of a faintly unwholesome men's club. I mixed right into the crowd because my glasses created an all-purpose weirdo look that was right for every occasion. Despite his sheepishness, Ben never seemed uncomfortable in these stores. He had the same self-contained quality Louise had had when I knew her in college: a way of carrying himself and moving through a crowd of people that made it clear he didn't really fit in but wasn't exactly out of place, either. He was fending for himself, an attitude most people seem to respect.

Louise often called me late at night, after Ben had gone to sleep. She'd drag the phone to a chair on the patio off her bedroom and wrap herself in a blanket. Her hoarse voice sounded even smaller and more distant as, in vague, reproachful terms, she talked about the book she was working on and lit one cigarette after another. Occasionally she'd comment on what she could see in the lit-up window of a neighbor's house.

Some nights I'd wander over to her neighborhood. Because my days lacked much in the way of formal definition, I'd long been a nocturnal walker, tromping around the streets of Cambridge after most of the city was dark. Somewhere in the city, there was always a fusty-looking person sitting in a window, bent over a book. I'd sneak through the garden alongside the main house like a thief, and if I saw lights on in Louise's study, I'd knock on the glass doors and lure her out.

One balmy midnight as we sat under the dying grape arbor, she said, "I hope Ben isn't taking too much of your time."

"Not at all. He's giving my life some shape."

I'd said it to be polite, because he was taking up an increasing amount of time, but as soon as the words were out of my mouth, I realized they were true. Perhaps that was why some people need children and pets and spouses, to bring order to the chaos of their lives. In a pinch, the pursuit of anonymous sex can function as a reasonable alternative, although it's complicated these days and it does require a fair amount of self-motivation.

"Shape?" Louise said. "Don't tell me that. I've spent the past twelve years trying to make sure my life is shapeless."

"Turning down marriage proposals?"

"Not many," she said. "None that would have lasted. Let's face it, I'll never marry."

"Why do you say that?" I asked as if I were shocked by the comment, but I'd thought the same thing for a long time.

"I'm not sure. Maybe I just like men too much. Every job I've ever had, I sit around and listen to women complaining about the men in their lives—how they don't like the way they smell or the way they think or how they slop down their food. They just categorically dislike the whole breed, give or take a few parts and pieces. And we all know that most men hate women."

It was true that most women I knew had little good to say about men in a general way and seemed to take rapacious pleasure in running down the entire sex. One of the chief drawbacks to a decidedly macho gym I'd joined had been having to listen to a lot of discontented straight men voice their bottomless rage and resentment toward the women in their lives as a way of veiling their fears of being rejected by them. Heterosexual relations are in such an appalling state in the country, it's a wonder anyone bothers to marry. If it weren't for the consumer frenzy for big dresses and creamy roses whipped up by those immense bridal magazines, I doubt anyone would. Of course, I have to admit I've heard gay men talking about women in disparaging terms, too, but it never seems quite as bluntly misogynist, since they're usually talking about their mothers.

"But somehow," Louise said, "all these people who can't stand each other end up having relationships. Rancorous relationships, it's true, but ones that endure. There's some element of passion missing in me, I think. I'm too calculating, especially since I stopped drinking."

I, too, had a theory about why it would be hard for Louise to form a relationship, but it lacked the irony of hers. My theory was that she was too independent, in a determined way, to really give herself over to anyone. She hadn't changed all that much from her college years, when she dated only men who were unavailable or otherwise engaged.

More important—most important—she already had a man in her life, or a male anyway, and I don't think she was ready to nudge Ben aside to make room for another.

On our walks to the record stores, Ben and I spent a fair amount of time talking about Louise. He spoke of her with what sounded to me like calculated annoyance. According to Ben, Louise had terrible problems disciplining herself to sit down and write; she was a sloppy housekeeper; she never dressed properly for the weather; she was an impractical shopper. But the real point of his comments wasn't to criticize his mother so much as to imply that he was the one who held her together. He listened to the weather reports in the morning to tell her if she should leave the house with an umbrella or a sweater. He curtailed her tendency to overspend. He was forcing her to cut down on her smoking.

"But what about you?" Louise asked. "You shouldn't be mooning over someone who left years ago. It's not healthy, Clyde."

"I realize. But I feel as if I can't go ahead with this unresolved relationship hanging over my head."

She looked at me warily in the dim light spilling out from her bedroom. I wasn't sure I believed it, either. I had a sense I'd fallen into a crack in the sidewalk somewhere a few years back and couldn't pull myself out.

"Marcus called to tell me he's putting off talking to Ben for a little while," she said. "Something about stepping into a room. I couldn't follow the metaphor."

"It has to do with beginning his dissertation."

"I figured. He should just write it."

"He should," I said. "But then it would be written, and where would he be?"

She pulled at her lip. "I think it's a momentary case of cold feet about Ben. Don't you?"

"Definitely momentary," I said.

"But definitely cold."

Every night when I visited her and we sat in her garden, a phone started to ring in one of the houses behind us. It rang ten or fifteen times, and no one ever picked it up. It started to ring now in the silence between us, a distant bell tolling out the time: fifteen o'clock. I hated the sound of that phone, ringing and ringing and no one answering it, all that wasted potential. When the phone stopped, Louise and I sighed together, and without saying anything more, I kissed her good night and left.

DONALD GERN, MY DOWNSTAIRS NEIGHBOR, struck me as one of those affable, basically kind-hearted, but socially inept people besieged by bad luck. The only sounds I ever heard coming from his first-floor apartment were those of falling pans and breaking dishes, followed by loud thumps, as if he'd slammed his fist into the wall in rage or frustration.

When, late in the summer, he'd mentioned his intention of having a cookout, I'd assumed that if he ever did get around to planning it, the event would be canceled at the last minute by a sudden, unseasonable weather disaster—tornado, massive electric storm, flooding—or possibly by some personal tragedy. It was hard to imagine that anything ever went well for Donald. The problem was that hair. One calamitously ill-advised affectation, like a ridiculous hairstyle, a propensity for cheap jewelry, or overdeveloped calves, can act as a magnet, drawing bad luck and misery. If Donald didn't have that idiotic flap of pink hair sitting on his head, he wouldn't be living in that grim apartment on the first floor. He wouldn't have his quack job, and he wouldn't dress in clothes that made him look like a cartoon baby.

Unfortunately, it's not possible to spot your own ill-advised affectations. If it were, I probably wouldn't have been living in the grim apartment above Donald or have my quack job or be scurrying around town awaiting the affection of a lover who'd dumped me, so I could turn around and dump him and get on with my life.

One morning early in October, Donald stopped me in the hall-way and handed me a couple of bills that had come in the mail that day. He had on his lab coat with a baby-blanket-blue sweater underneath, stretched tight across his chest. He was studying a catalog of mail-order food, one of many that came for the previous first-floor tenant. "The guy that lived here gets four of these a day. Must have been a real pig, huh?"

"I didn't know him, to tell you the truth," I said. "But he was awfully skinny." Most of the tenants in the building were physical extremes of one sort or another. Donald's predecessor had had the gaunt form and furtive demeanor of a male anorexic. I often saw him on the front steps of the house huddled over his food maga-zines, his legs tightly wound around each other like pipe cleaners. Along with most of the other residents, he'd had an inexplicable fondness for sheeny blue windbreakers. In many ways, Donald was the best of the bunch.

He looked at me, wide-eyed and sincere. "No kidding. Skinny! Maybe he read these instead of eating. Kind of like jerking off, but with food. You know what I mean?"

I nodded and reached behind me for the door to our apartment. I was never too keen on turning my back on Donald. It wasn't possible that anyone that ineffectual could be dangerous, but I hadn't completely ruled out the possibility that he had body parts stashed in his freezer. When he opened his own door, I was over-come by a wave of morbid curiosity. I craned my neck to get a better view inside. All I could see was a scrap of living room. From my vantage point, it appeared to be empty except for an ugly brown sofa that looked disconcertingly like a log and a big black box, probably the back of a TV console or a massive stereo speaker. A perfect suicide parlor.

Donald turned suddenly and caught me peering. "Oh, hey," he said, squinting through the gloom of the hallway, "I'm having my cookout next Saturday. The one I told you about. Finally got the fricking thing together."

"That's great!" I said.

"Yeah, well, I don't know about great, but come down anyway."

Because I felt so foolish peering into his apartment, I said, "I'll be there," as excitedly as if he'd just offered me two tickets to watch James Dean rise from the dead.

"Bring that kid, if you want."

"Ben," I said. "His mother's a friend of mine. I'm just taking care of his dog." I'd begun to wonder if the neighbors were talking.

"Bring the dog. Bring the mother—we need some more females. Some of us anyway. Me, I mean." He went into his apartment, humming to himself, turned, and said, "Listen, when you're trying to get that dog to obey you? Make eye contact and give him a few rewards—bones, hunk of cheese, crap like that. And let it out in the yard by itself every once in a while. Builds confidence." Then he slammed his door shut.

I stood in the hall, undone and defeated by the encounter, as I usually was when I bumped into Donald. How was it that he knew more about the care and training of dogs than I did?

Marcus was hunched over his coffee, leafing through one of the many academic journals he brought into the house. As far as I could tell, he had no interest in the articles they contained. He read them so he could dismiss the colleagues who'd written them and explain away the unjust circumstances under which they'd been published. For someone who'd chosen to enter the field of experimental psychology, Marcus was oddly disinterested in the workings of anyone else's mind or the circumstances of anyone else's life. He hadn't accepted the fact that being interested in someone else is generally a lot more interesting than hauling out a half-dozen fascinating experiences, vacations, and love affairs for the perusal of the gathered multitude. The advantage of having low self-esteem is that certain social graces come naturally. Marcus would listen to me yak, all right, just as he'd listen to his youthful girlfriends. But it was always with a slightly distracted, bored attitude, as if no one's problems but his own could be of any real significance in the world. This, like most delusions of grandeur and inflated-ego disorders, came from the misfortune of having had loving and nurturing parents. Marcus's attitude, if articulated, would have been: Gee, I'm really sorry to hear that, Clyde, but I have a one-in-fifty-million chance of being elected President, while you, like all homosexuals, most women, and Ted Kennedy, have none. So let me get back to my coffee.

"Donald's having his cookout after all," I said.

"Should be fun."

"Fun? You must be joking. It's going to be a bunch of losers sitting around getting drunk—remember?"

"You could use a better attitude about social events, Clyde, you really could. You never know who you're going to meet. Even in the most unlikely places."

Because Marcus was virtually incapable of expressing any of his emotions directly, I always had to read between the lines of what he was saying. And because, no matter what he talked about, he never really talked about anything other than himself, I found this minilecture on optimism suspicious. I sat down on the nubby sofa. He was still leafing through the dull journal, shaking his head in apparent dismay at what he was reading. But he didn't look quite as mangy as he had recently. A certain glamorous pallor had replaced the distressed flush of the last few weeks, and unless I was mistaken, he'd had his lovely yellow hair trimmed.

"How's the work going?" I asked.

"Better, I think. I've almost got the whole thing done. Chapter by chapter. It's just a matter of getting it down on paper."

Sometimes when I was walking to The Learning Place or wandering through the streets of Cambridge after midnight, I'd sing. In my head, I mean. There, my voice and phrasing were a synthesis of

Mel Tormé and Carlos Gardel. Innovative, emotionally compelling, flawless. The only time I stumbled was when I actually opened my mouth to utter a note. So it was, I imagined, with Marcus's dissertation. The more perfect it became in his imagination, the less likely it was the thing would ever get written, even a single paragraph.

"You should bring someone along to the cookout," I said, testing my suspicions.

"I might. On the other hand, I might just let her take the lead, see what happens."

"Probably a good idea. With someone her age."

He looked up from the article he was skimming. "Did I tell you about Sheila already?"

"No, no. I was just taking a guess."

"I'd never noticed her before. She started coming around my carrel." He shrugged at the inevitability of the whole thing. "You know, I've been meaning to tell you," he said, gathering up his papers. "I think I might be allergic to that dog. We should probably keep her out of my room."

Otis was sitting on the sofa, his absurd, tufted head moving back and forth from me to Marcus, following the conversation. I'd noticed that Marcus had increasing difficulty in remembering Otis's name and sex.

"I'll see what I can do about it," I told him. "But I'm taking him for assertiveness training, so I can't promise anything."

Later that day, I went to Louise's office. It was a small room on the second floor of a Colonial-style house in a cluster of houses owned by Harvard. The university owned mind-boggling amounts of real estate and was slowly but surely turning the city into Harvard World, a beautifully tended theme park designed around an academic motif. You couldn't walk across any corner of the sprawling campus without getting swept up in a throng of tourists listening to amusing anecdotes about the school's founder and snapping pictures of libraries and lecture halls. It was only a matter of time before they installed a monorail and a water slide.

The inside of Louise's building was a warren of tiny rooms and narrow hallways, noisy with the clicking of computers and the whir of copying machines. I climbed the steep staircase to the second floor and knocked on her door. She was sitting at her desk, staring at the opposite wall. "Take a seat," she said hoarsely, indicating a daybed littered with books and papers.

The whole room had the feel of massive confusion and chaos. Magazines and newspapers were stacked everywhere, cords and computer parts were scattered about, a toaster oven and a hot plate took up the floor in one corner. The drawers of a filing cabinet were open, revealing a coffeemaker and bags of English muffins. She had a few road maps stuck to the yellow walls, which somehow added to the atmosphere of confusion—all those crisscrossing black and red lines.

I cleared off a space on the daybed and sat down. "Cozy," I said. "The whole house is buzzing with creativity."

She looked over at me with undisguised dismay, her pale-blue eyes bloodshot and exhausted. "That's not creativity, it's neurotic energy. They're all nuts, the women in this building. Obviously, I can't smoke in here, which is fine, but the poet over there"—she pointed to the wall behind me—"told me I couldn't smoke in the yard behind the house because the smell was drifting in through her windows. And the one on this side is allergic to everything and breaks out in hives when I make toast."

"Too bad. I was hankering for one of those English muffins."

"Oh, good." She sprang up from her desk and ripped open a bag. "Let's make lots."

"Do you get any work done here?"

She pushed up the sleeves of her sweatshirt. "Of course not. No one does. Every bit of creative energy gets sucked up in the rivalries and complaints and endless rounds of gossip and breast-beating. Who got a bigger advance, a better teaching job, a roomier office. Thank God I'm basically a failure and have the least desirable room. And let's not forget the round-table discussions of Prozac dosages. It's a sham."

"So the novel..."

She slammed shut the door on the toaster oven and pushed a button, and all the lights in the room dimmed. Someone in the room behind me pounded on the wall. "All right, if you want to hear the truth, here it is: I got the grant because I told them I was writing a memoir about being a single mother. No one cares about novels anymore, Clyde. No one wants to wade through the obfuscations of fiction. Just pump out all the filthy facts, toss in a chapter on rehab, and wrap it up."

I nodded guiltily, thinking about my own reading list of late. Of course, I didn't entirely agree with her estimation. It struck me that as literature, movie star biographies, for example, are vastly underrated. Given a fitting course title, I could teach a superb class on the subject. With their tales of astonishingly abrupt physical transformations and meteoric shifts from poverty to wealth to poverty and so on, they rival the magic realism of any Latin American novel I've ever read. And trying to sift through the exaggerations, dodges, and outright lies of the subjects, the sources, and the hack biographers themselves requires as much intellectual engagement as it takes to read Kafka.

"So, you're not working on a memoir?"

She opened up a drawer of her desk, lifted out a stack of papers, and dropped it on the desk. "I don't know what it is. A big mess. Unpublishable hybrid."

"Why don't you just write a novel and pretend it's a memoir? People have been writing memoirs and pretending they're novels for decades."

"Too confusing. I might try my hand at a mystery. I'm in the mood to kill someone off." She tossed her manuscript back into the drawer. Fine wisps of smoke were starting to rise from the toaster, but when I went to the corner to unplug it, she told me to leave it alone. "Let her suffer," she said, pointing to the wall behind her. "Actually, she's out of town anyway."

When the toast was sufficiently burned, she yanked it out and spread it with something yellow and slick from a tub she kept in the bottom drawer of the filing cabinet. She sprawled out on the floor and picked at the bread. "At least the grant got you to Cambridge," I said.

"It did indeed. But is that a good thing? Marcus stopped by here a few days ago to tell me he needed a little more time before talking with Ben. He's on the threshold," she said, doing a fair imitation of his accent. "Right on the threshold."

"I think he might be starting up with a new girlfriend."

"Ah well, that makes sense, I suppose. Nothing like staving off impotence in one area by disproving it in another. But I can't be too critical of him. I'm the one who made the mistakes. He was an innocent bystander."

That was at least partly true. Marcus, with his wondrous passivity, had made himself a professional innocent bystander.

"The other day," Louise said, "Ben asked me if Marcus was gay."

"What was that all about?"

"Probably because you two share the house."

"One of these days, Marcus is going to have to reevaluate having me as a roommate."

Louise rolled over on her back and sucked at an unlit cigarette. "Don't you think *you* should reevaluate it one of these days? What keeps you in that place?"

"If I knew, I'd move out." Although I did have suspicions. There was something appealing about Marcus, beyond his looks and that irritating charm of his. I loved the way Marcus blathered and stumbled through life, like some fool tripping through a minefield and coming out unscathed. I suppose what it really was was that since Gordon had departed, and probably before that, too, I'd felt an especially compelling need to live my life as if I was waiting for it to begin. Like Marcus, I was in that odd state of suspended animation—waiting to graduate to the next stage of life. If I went out and got my own place and started to buy furniture that hadn't been cast off by some junkie who'd gotten his life together, it would be an admission that my own life had begun, and I suppose I'd have to take some responsibility for it.

By the following Saturday, I'd forgotten about the cookout. It wasn't the kind of event even I would live for.

The night before, I'd received a call from Drew and Sam, a couple of ferocious overachievers I knew, inviting me to a cocktail party at their South End condo. The invitation was such an obvious last-minute attempt at papering the house, I should have refused on principle. But I had so little respect for the hosts, I didn't really care about humiliating myself by accepting.

"Who's going to be there?" I asked.

"People you know" was the vague answer.

I wasn't sure if I was talking to Drew or Sam, but they were so similar, it didn't really matter. They were part of, and fairly representative of, Gordon and Michael's social circle. I had high hopes that my ex and his accountant would be in attendance. I tended to avoid that kind of gathering, but I figured that since I was making such progress with my father, I might give it a whirl with Gordon.

Drew and Sam lived in one of those superbly renovated brownstone condos that give me severe claustrophobia. The walls were painted in dark colors, so dense they seemed to absorb all the light and most of the oxygen. The artwork consisted of soft-core porn photographs tucked into lovely metal frames they didn't deserve. It would have been simpler and more artistically honest to tack up a few Polaroids of the neighbors exposing themselves.

Not only was Gordon *not* there, but after half an hour of forced, disjointed conversation, Drew and Sam brought out the VCR and showed a two-hour pictorial record of their recent trip to Brazil. The video was basically a modeling portfolio of the hosts wearing a variety of swimsuits, drawstring pants, and terry-cloth robes, a sort of home-movie version of the International Male catalog, with a few perfunctory shots of Poverty, Crime, and Nature thrown in for local color. The main, perhaps only, advantage of lousy eyesight is that it's possible, in these situations, to remove eyeglasses, stare at the TV screen, see a lovely pale-blue blur, and go into a state of meditative repose. The sole mention of my ex all evening was when Drew/Sam said that Gordon and Michael were coming over to see the video the following week so that they could plan their own, identical vacation. I left late, hungry and with the same sense of having pointlessly amputated a portion of my life I had had the time I sat through all four torturous hours of *Gone With the Wind*.

I was barely awake when the doorbell rang at eleven the next morning. I glanced in my bureau mirror on my way to the stairs, amazed at how increasingly unkind sleep was as I got older, as if someone came in every night to practice origami on my face while I slept.

My sister was standing on the doorstep, clutching an enormous shopping bag, her jaw clenched with anxiety, as if she were expecting to be assaulted by a gang of roving crack addicts. She hadn't been to Cambridge in nearly a year, claiming that visiting the city, along with flying, listening to the radio, and seeing the sunset, made her nervous. Since the New Hampshire visit, she'd had her hair cut still shorter, into one of those Peter Pan dos with a tiny sprig of cowlick sticking up in back. It made her neck look even longer, in a surprisingly flattering way.

I assumed disaster of some variety had brought her to town, so I tried to sound my most calm and upbeat.

"Agnes! What a surprise, sweetheart," I croaked.

An ambulance screamed a block away, and Agnes closed her eyes until it had passed and the sound had faded. She glanced behind her. "Do you think my car is safe out there?"

I peered around her. The car, a newish four-door sedan of no discernible make, model, or color, was pulled up to the curb right in front of the house. "They never ticket on Saturdays. Come in."

"I'm not worried about a ticket, Clyde. I mean *safe*. Is it *safe?*"

Sometimes I wondered if the kindest course to take with Agnes wouldn't be to act out her fears right off and get them out of the way—in this case, take a sledgehammer and smash all the windows myself so my sister could relax for the rest of the day, secure in the knowledge that the worst had already happened.

"I'm sure it's fine," I said.

"Well, it's important. Barbara's in there."

I looked around her again. There was no sign of my niece.

"She's asleep on the back seat. It's usually best not to wake her up. It tends to make her a little moody."

"I'll leave the door unlocked in case she wakes up and wants to come in."

"Oh, good. Well, unless you think that isn't safe."

Agnes talked about safety as if it was synonymous with happiness.

"We'll risk it this once."

I was so stunned to see her, it wasn't until we were upstairs and in the kitchen that I thought to ask her why she'd come. "The cookout," she said. "Didn't Marcus tell you he invited us?"

She asked this question in a characteristically incredulous tone, as if I'd just informed her that I'd never heard of Hiroshima or the Washington Monument. It wasn't until that moment that I remembered the event myself. "He invited you? But it's going to be unbearable."

"Well, he didn't think so. And he sounded as if it would mean so much to him to have us come, I didn't want to disappoint him."

Two nights earlier, Marcus had gone out on a date with Sheila, presumably at her suggestion, and he hadn't been home since. It was a good bet he'd forgotten about the cookout himself. "How," I asked, "did you talk Barbara into coming?"

"She insisted. There's a store in Harvard Square that sells awful, awful leather things. She wants a black leather vest or something. I can't worry about it, Clyde. I can't take the whole world on my shoulders. I can't be responsible for every mistake she makes."

"No," I said. "Of course you can't. Have a seat and relax."

She had on a pair of brown corduroy slacks with slightly flaring legs and a ribbed orange turtleneck jersey. Over the jersey she'd flung a truly horrid shawl, a crocheted brown-and-orange lap blanket kind of thing that could only have been purchased at one of those nursing home crafts fairs she attended on a regular basis. I'd yet to figure out why it was that Agnes always added to her outfits some accessory—a shawl, a scarf, an eight-pound brooch—so dazzlingly ugly even she seemed self-conscious about it. She peeled the shawl off her shoulders, practically lighting up the room with sparks of static electricity, and draped it over the back of a chair. "Oh, Clyde," she said, "a sofa in the kitchen. I'd forgotten how bohemian you are." She checked the cushions to make sure there wasn't anything unspeakable there and lowered herself down. "But it doesn't make sense. Why put a sofa in the kitchen? I've never heard of that."

There was a ticking of nails on the stairs, and Otis pranced into the room, sniffing the heavy honeydew scent of Agnes's Summer Meadow "splash." In the past week or so, the dog had begun to show some signs of increased confidence. He frequently roamed around the apartment by himself, and although he started out the night sleeping on his pile of blankets in the corner, I usually woke to find him curled up at the foot of my bed.

Agnes sat upright on the sofa and clutched the handles of her shopping bag. "Oh, that's the little dog. He's adorable," she said uneasily. "He doesn't bite, does he?"

"No, dear, of course not. Look at him."

He sat on his haunches in front of the sofa and eyed Agnes, his stringy ears pulled back and his nose twitching.

"What's he trying to say?" Agnes asked.

"I don't know. I think he just wants to say hello. Isn't that right, Otis?" I asked gooily. To my enormous satisfaction, he responded to my insipid tone by wagging his tail.

Agnes reached to pat his head, then snapped back her hand as suddenly as if she were testing an iron for heat. "He has eyebrows!" she said. The dog cocked his head to one side, lost interest, and checked the corners of the room for edible trash. Then he went to the chair with Agnes's shawl, flattened back his ears, and started to sniff.

"He isn't going to *do* anything, is he?"

"Otis," I said, and he turned his head toward me, "you aren't going to pee on Agnes's shawl, are you?"

He smiled and panted.

"Well, don't sug*gest* it, Clyde," Agnes whispered.

I pointed to the stairs and snapped my fingers. "Go," I commanded. He whimpered but headed back upstairs slowly, his body close to the ground. Only a few days earlier, he'd started obeying my commands, and I'd been basking in a testosterone rush since. It's obvious why dogs are such an appealing possession to the kinds of men traumatized by Hillary Clinton: loyal and obedient, not to mention that with a dog at your side, at least one set of balls is hanging out in plain view.

"I didn't think I should come empty-handed," Agnes said, "so I made some cookies last night." She sighed and pulled at the ribbed turtleneck, straightening out the lines running down her chest. "I'm afraid they got a little burned. I wonder if there isn't something wrong with the oven. I called the maintenance man, but they never come when a woman calls. A man calls—oh boy, they drop everything and run over as if it were a medical emergency."

"That bag is filled with cookies?"

"Not filled. I brought some beer, too." She reached in and took out a six-pack with five bottles in it. "Put these in the fridge, will you? Oh, what the heck, maybe I'll have one. It's almost noon."

I went to a cabinet to get her a glass, and while my back was still turned, Agnes said, "Well, don't make me feel like that, Clyde, I've had a long, exhausting drive. Barbara didn't fall asleep until we were in Cambridge."

"But I wasn't even looking at you, sweetheart. Honestly." I

handed her a glass. "Maybe you should ask . . . Dad to call maintenance, if a man's voice would help."

"I did," she said calmly. And then, so suddenly that it took me
a moment to realize exactly what had happened, she burst into
tears.

I retreated until I was backed up against the counter and could
do nothing but look on in horror. Agnes's whole frail body was
trembling. From outside, I could hear the sounds of Donald and a
friend setting up a table. They'd put one of Donald's speakers in
the yard, and "Jumping Jack Flash" was blaring from it, the high
notes crackling and the bass distorted. Sunlight was pouring in the
windows of the kitchen, too warm, bright, and intrusive.

I made a move toward Agnes, but she held up her hand to ward
me off, and composed herself as suddenly as she'd fallen apart. "I'm
fine, Clyde. I really am. I don't know what came over me." She
twisted off the bottle cap with the kind of confidence all her other
gestures lacked, poured the beer into her glass, and siphoned off a
layer of foam. "It's a lovely day for a cookout, isn't it?" she asked.
"Nice for this time of year. Anyway, I did ask . . . Dad to call
maintenance."

Then she began crying again, great heaving sobs this time.

"Oh, Agnes," I said. "What is it?"

The front door banged open, and Barbara appeared in the
kitchen doorway, her eyes still puffy with sleep and her face flushed.
She looked at her mother in disgust and pulled back her hair to
reveal the shaven sides of her head and a line of silver studs running
up her right ear. "Can I have that hundred dollars now?" she asked.

Agnes stomped her foot and, through a fog of tears and phlegm,
said, "No, you cannot. You can't even be civil. You didn't even say
hello."

"We made a deal, Mom."

"I said you could have seventy-five!"

Barbara sat on the opposite end of the sofa from her mother.
She was wearing the same baggy overalls and flannel shirt she'd
been wearing when I visited in New Hampshire. She crossed her

legs, resting one ankle on her knee. Sitting next to Agnes like that, so composed and solid, she looked particularly sensible, pincushion ears, nose stud, and shaved head notwithstanding. At moments, she had the kind of easy Gary Cooper swagger that was prized in women these days and considered despicable in men. "She's crying about Grandpa, right?" she asked. She reached over and took one of Agnes's hands in one of hers, a simple gesture of unexpected tenderness that flooded me with fondness for my dear, kind niece. "Did she tell you he's got a girlfriend?"

"Girlfriend?" I said, wondering if I'd let it slip.

"He does *not* have a girlfriend!" Agnes sobbed.

"He's got a girlfriend, Clyde. He's been sneaking her in and out of the basement. It's revolting."

"We've never met her," Agnes said. "She's his nurse."

Barbara tossed aside her mother's hand. "You're hopeless, Mom. I want that seventy-five bucks." She turned to me. "We made a deal. She thought it would look less pathetic running down here to see *Marcus* if she dragged me along. So we're helping each other out. Did she tell you she has to give Grandpa another fifty bucks a week?"

"Why didn't you tell me, Agnes?"

Agnes had calmed down enough to pour the rest of her beer into her glass. "I think he's paying the nurse," she said, "that's why he needs the extra money. But here's what really worries me, Clyde: he's going to visit Uncle Lon this weekend."

"Well, what's so bad about that? At least he's getting out." Since that ridiculous cover had been my suggestion, I felt some need to defend it.

"They can't stand each other! He's trying to make amends with everyone in the family. I got so nervous about it, I just couldn't stay out there in the country. I figured coming down here would be a distraction."

"I'm going back out to the car to sleep," Barbara said.

"Don't forget about the cookout. You haven't had lunch."

"I'll stay for food, but then I want that money." Barbara stood up and bracelets jangled down her arm under her bulky shirtsleeves. She lifted her hand and shook them back up to her elbow. A strong smell of patchouli oil wafted over to me.

As Barbara was heading out the door, Otis came into the room and made a hesitant approach toward her, taking a few steps forward, cringing and retreating, then making a new, more decisive advance. "Oh, look!" Barbara said, her voice suddenly the high-pitched squeal of a little girl. She lay flat on her back on the dirty linoleum and made whimpering, come-hither sounds until she'd enticed him to her side and then up onto her chest. He stood there, looking down into her face, and then started to lick her nose.

Barbara pulled at the tuft of fur on top of Otis's head until it was standing straight up. "A Mohawk," she said.

In addition to the cookies, which I didn't have the heart to look at, and the beer, two more bottles of which she drank in the next hour, Agnes had brought with her a copy of as much of the manuscript of our mother's cookbook as she'd typed out. "I'd appreciate it if you could pass it on to Louise," she said. "As a writer, she might have some suggestions." She took a sip of her beer and laughed self-consciously. "Who knows, maybe she'll want to show it to her editor."

"Don't count on it, Mom," Barbara said. Instead of going to the car to take her nap, she'd fallen asleep on the floor, with Otis on her chest. Every few minutes, she woke to criticize something Agnes had said.

"I'll give it to her next time I see her. It's possible she'll drop by this afternoon."

At this, Agnes seemed to grow distraught. She began to pluck at her jersey, as if she were picking lint from it. The prospect of having to face Louise, a celebrity author in her eyes, though one whose books she couldn't remember, was too much for her. She was pretty, sitting there with the sunlight slanting across her face and making her shorn hair look smart and shiny. If she'd been an actress playing a waif, she would have been charming right then, maybe even beautiful. But she wasn't acting, and her emotions were gnawing at her so obviously that, instead of pulling me in, the sight of her made me want to look away. I went and lowered the matchstick blinds, then sat next to her. "Don't worry about Louise," I said. "She's as insecure as the rest of us. And about . . . Dad," I started. She glanced up from her jersey, let her hand drop onto the wooden arm of the sofa, and began to run her fingers over one of the cigarette burns.

But I wasn't ready to confide in her yet, and because I couldn't think of anything else to offer, I asked if she'd like another beer.

Sometime after noon, Marcus did finally show up, but not alone. He stumbled into the apartment with a statuesque beauty attached to his left arm. It had turned into a warm day, and both of them were glowing and smelled strongly, pleasantly, of healthy, hard-earned sweat. It was obvious from the stunned expression on his face when he saw Agnes sitting on the sofa, and Barbara sprawled out on the floor, that Marcus had forgotten he'd invited my sister, had forgotten about the cookout itself.

But Marcus had a way of recovering quickly, at least in social situations. He pushed a hank of blond hair behind one of his big ears and, with an abundance of good cheer, said, "I am so glad you decided to come, Agnes. I was afraid you wouldn't. This is my friend Sheila."

Agnes, unsure of whether to stay seated or stand, attempted an awkward handshake, and Barbara waved from the floor without bothering to get up or even open her eyes.

Like most of Marcus's girlfriends, Sheila appeared to be somewhere between twenty-three and twenty-six, old enough to know what she was getting into but neither old enough nor young enough to care about the consequences. She was nearly as tall as Marcus and had a high, shiny forehead, ripe lips, and a jaw that was probably a little too long and square for the rest of her face but didn't detract from her overall radiance. Her hair was the color of cherrywood and fell almost to the middle of her back. When she reached out to shake my hand, a great Pre-Raphaelite curtain of curls fell across her face. She lifted a heap of it away from her eyes with the back of her hand, sighing as if it were a terrible annoyance. The gesture was so languid, even I wasn't immune to its sensuality. "Marcus has told me all about you, Clyde," she said.

"Are you at—at Harvard, too?" Agnes asked, slitting the label on her beer bottle with her fingernail.

"Art History," Sheila said. She looked down, and as she untangled a strand of hair from one of her bracelets, she rattled off a jumble of academic abbreviations: USC, Ph.D., UCLA, Ed.D., UC Davis. Agnes and I nodded as if we were following whatever narrative was buried under the list.

Barbara swam to the surface of consciousness. "Isn't it about time you, like, graduated, Marcus?" she asked. It was an unfair question, but then again, Barbara had been four years old when Marcus finished his course work.

"I'm getting there, Babs," he said. "One damned day at a time."

"Of course you are," Agnes said. "When she gets to college she'll understand."

"Right. Like I'd ever even consider going to college."

"What makes you think they'd let you in?" Sheila asked. She leaned against Marcus's shoulder, lifted a foot, and scratched her ankle. "So that's the little dog you're taking care of."

"It is," Marcus said. "Clyde and I are doing our best to keep him happy, aren't we, Clyde?"

"We are," I said. Marcus *was* doing his best, which was one of the things that made me so concerned for Otis and his master.

By one in the afternoon, a loud little group had gathered in the backyard. From the kitchen window, I could see bobbing heads and glasses of beer and occasionally hear a forced, braying laugh that had to be Donald trying to drum up a little merriment. "Why don't we just get this over with," I said.

I picked up Agnes's shawl and handed it to her, but she shook her head frantically, trying to disown the thing before anyone noticed it.

The afternoon was unseasonably hot, too hot for my liking, but far from the weather disaster I'd imagined. Marcus and Sheila went to change out of their sweaty clothes, but when, a few minutes later, their laughter drifted into the kitchen, I gathered up Agnes's bag of cookies and what remained of the beer she'd brought and led my sister and my niece out the door.

As we were clomping down the dark staircase, I said, as casually as I could, "Now, have either of you ever seen this . . . nurse of . . . Dad's?"

"His girlfriend?" Barbara said.

"We've never seen her," Agnes said. "She does her job, very professional. Is that girl a student of Marcus's?"

"No, Mom, she's his nurse. She's giving him his medication right now." Barbara turned to me. "They drive right into the garage, Clyde, and sneak into his cave down there. It's like they think they're in a James Bond movie, except in this case, no special effects and everyone's ugly."

"Well, let's not talk about nurses," Agnes said sadly. "Let's try and have a nice time at the party."

DONALD WAS WEARING A PAIR OF PALE, shapeless blue jeans with a signature and a horsey design stitched on the back pocket; his billowing sweatshirt was printed with an advertisement for some drinking establishment in one of the more depressing suburbs. The stereo was playing early Rolling Stones, the sound muffled and distorted, as if Mick Jagger were singing "Ruby Tuesday" with a sock stuffed in his mouth.

"I thought you'd left town," Donald said, grinning and slightly drunk. "That's what I would have done, if I'd looked out the window and seen this party."

He ushered us into the little yard with big welcoming gestures, hostly and grand.

"This is my sister, Agnes, and her daughter. They came all the way from New Hampshire," I said.

"I'll tell you something, Agnes," Donald said, with absurd sincerity, "I love the country, all safe and cozy." He ran his eyes up and down Agnes's slim body with a look that struck me as a cross between appreciative and leering. Then he snapped out of whatever pastoral fantasy was playing in his head and returned to his jovial self. "What's in the bag, sis? A present for me, I hope."

"Some cookies, but I'm afraid they came out a little overdone." She handed him the big shopping bag and folded her arms. "It's probably my oven."

"Cookies! Just what we need. The loser who was supposed to bring the food had an accident on the way over, so who knows when the burgers will arrive. Last I heard, they were still sewing Jerry up. The guy has an accident every time he pulls out of the drive. We'd better put these out, before the mob riots."

He took Agnes by the arm and led her over to a table against the chain-link fence. Four big, empty plastic bowls sat on top of the table, and a grill and a hibachi with nothing on them smoldered beside it. The only food on the premises appeared to be the potato chips and corn chips and similar greasy snacks spilling out of bags that had been ripped open and tossed onto a couple of lawn chairs.

"That's the *host?*" Barbara said.

"I'm afraid so."

Barbara rolled her eyes and surveyed the rest of the crowd with a grimace. It was a fairly dismal gathering of about twenty-five people, mostly egg-shaped men who looked as if they were trying to compensate for their height by living on weight-gain powder and following a poorly designed power-lifting regime. They were all wearing loose cotton pants resembling harem pants, in wild zigzags of lurid color. These had become popular attire for men in Agnes's neck of the woods in the past few years, possibly because all that loose, sagging cotton gave the impression of hidden assets. The women were gathered in a circle near the back door of the house, smoking cigarettes and casting wary glances at the eggs. Most of them had extraordinarily thin legs, which they'd encased in tight blue jeans, and they were all perched atop dangerously high heels. The yard wasn't too much bigger than our kitchen, and what little grass there had been early in the spring had long since been scorched and trampled. Even a group this small seemed jammed in, as if we'd all been herded and then locked into the wretched little pen. Donald had bought a few mums, which he'd left in their cardboard pots and stuck into each corner of the yard, a noble but failed attempt at dressing the place up.

"Pretty pathetic," Barbara said. "Why does everyone have such weird hair?"

The men did have amazingly similar, disfiguring haircuts: bowl-shaped around the top, with a curtain of stiff hair hanging down in back, like the shag cut Jane Fonda wore in *Klute*. The women had big, heaped-up hairdos, like headdresses from a Vegas night-club act.

"I'm going to get a beer," Barbara said, and lumbered off to one of the two kegs in opposite corners. Donald had already pumped a glass of beer for Agnes, and he had her backed against the chain-link fence, nodding intently as he listened to her talk. I couldn't imagine what it was they'd found to discuss already, at such length. I'd never figured out what to say to Donald once we got past hello, and Agnes usually lapsed into self-loathing silence in social situations. To be truthful, I felt a little jealous that each had found something in the other that I apparently hadn't been able to find in either. Agnes made a fluttering gesture with the fingers of one hand and then started to stir at the air as if she were beating an imaginary egg with a wire whisk.

Marcus sauntered into the yard and glanced around at the party. He'd put on a pair of shorts that came down below his knees, and there was something undeniably sexy, in a boring, pale sort of way, about his long, shapeless calves.

"Where's Sheila?" I asked.

"She's poking around in my drawers," he said, "looking for something summery to put on." Marcus had a way of unconsciously uttering god-awful double entendres, and even when I pointed them out to him, he'd shrug as if he didn't get my point.

"I wish you'd told me you invited my sister. I wasn't psychologically prepared."

"She called for you the other day and we got jawing and I guess I said something about it."

"Jawing?" You didn't "jaw" with Agnes. You tried to reassure and soothe her while she edged ever closer to a massive attack of hysteria. "You were flirting with her and then you forgot about her and showed up with this Sheila."

"Aw, stop talking like her brother. Anyway, it looks like she's got an admirer." His lifted his chin toward Donald.

"Don't be ridiculous."

The sun was blazing down on us, making the top of my head uncomfortably hot. Like Agnes, I was overdressed for the weather. I had on long pants and a bulky sweater and a pair of black shoes. After the middle of September, I start to feel inexplicably naked in shorts, no matter what the temperature is. Perhaps it was the heat, but the still air was heavy with the smell of cheap powdery cologne, rose and vanilla and spicy citrus, as if everyone's perfume and aftershave were mingling and merging and having a party of their own in a cloud above the yard.

"I'll tell you something, Clyde, I really think Sheila might be the one."

"The one what?"

"You can't believe how supportive she is of my work."

"Supportive" usually translated into reassuring Marcus that the brilliance of his dissertation was not dependent upon its ever being written.

"Maybe she'll help you get things rolling, and then you can sit down and talk with Ben."

"That's what I'm hoping, Clyde. It really is. That's the goal I'm working toward. It's helping me settle in. Is this the Rolling Stones? Why are they playing this old stuff? I hate that narcissist Mick Jagger, strutting around with a microphone."

I felt a tap on my shoulder. A man was standing behind me, clutching a plastic cup filled with beer. He had one of those bizarre shag haircuts, and a faint smudge of a mustache that looked as if someone had drawn it on with an eyebrow pencil and then done a bad job of erasing it. "How you doing?" he said.

I shrugged. I really wasn't in the mood for socializing just then, not that I ever was.

"Mark Greeley," he said, and held out his hand. "You're the guy from upstairs, right?"

"Well . . ."

"Donny said you teach at Harvard."

"No, no," I said. I pointed at Marcus. "He's doing a Ph.D. there, but I'm unaffiliated."

"If I was teaching at Harvard, I'd be bragging about it." He looked at Marcus and laughed. "Right?"

Marcus nodded, shrugged, and looked away.

Mark Greeley's harem pants were neon green with hot-pink stripes, and his T-shirt advertised a resort in Jamaica with the slogan "Rev Your Engines and Cool Your Jets." He had on a pair of black sneakers that made his feet look like mittened fists.

My eye started to itch, a problem I frequently have when I feel cornered. I reached up under my glasses to rub my eyeball and nearly knocked the frames off my face. This encounter was headed for disaster. I could smell it on his aftershave. "Is there any more beer in those kegs?" I asked.

Mark Greeley took a gulp of his own beer and said, "Anyway, I wanted to ask you a—you know—a little favor, since you teach there and everything. I'm trying to get into that Harvard Business School, and I was wondering if maybe you could"—he tipped his hand from side to side—"you know, put in a good word for me."

"Put in a good word?"

"Yeah, you know, pull a couple of strings."

"You've got the wrong idea," I said. "I really can't. I've got nothing to do with the school, and Marcus here is only a student—"

"I wouldn't say 'only,'" Marcus piped up. "I've taught several courses over the years."

Mark Greeley was staring at me and nodding in an anxious,

angry way, but I could tell he wasn't listening to a word. He had a case of steroid acne spread across his cheeks, which looked uncomfortable in the bright sun. "Listen," he cut in, "you guys have your thing, that's your business. I'm not worried about that. I just said put in a good word, no big deal. If I still don't get in, I'm not going to hold you responsible. I've got a lot going on in my life. So are you going to help me out or not?"

"Well . . . no."

He tossed his cup of beer onto the ground and stormed off. There was a momentary hush. One of the women in the smoking circle turned around and started to laugh. Mark Greeley pounded his fist against the fence and stomped out of the yard, banging the gate behind him.

"What the hell was all that?" I asked.

Marcus shook his head. "Terrible."

"I'll say." I looked around the yard, trying to calm down. Agnes, laughing at something Donald had said, seemed oblivious. Really, it was all her fault. If she hadn't shown up, I'd still be upstairs reading about Lauren Bacall. Or better yet, sleeping.

"It's just another example of how you get involved in everyone's tragic story, Clyde, instead of paying attention to your own."

"Involved? Don't tell me that was *my* fault!"

Marcus hooked his hair behind his ears and squinted up at the sun. He pulled a pair of aviator sunglasses out of his shirt pocket and slipped them on. "You have to start examining your own life a little more instead of getting involved with every person who wanders over looking for a kind word. Things have a way of working out if you give them time." He looked at me for a moment, letting this profound statement sink in, and then went to open the gate for Sheila.

Half an hour later, the food still hadn't turned up. Barbara, who'd remained stationed by the keg, refilling her glass frequently, was looking less restless than before but, amazingly, still sober. From what I'd seen, no one had dared speak to her. The entire time she'd been standing there, she'd been casting threatening glances to ward off any possible approach and proudly, challengingly, showing off her severe haircut, her piercings, and a frown that Marcus could have used as the basis for his entire dissertation.

Shortly after the incident with Mark Greeley, the teenage girl who lived in the house next door walked into the neighboring yard, set up a lawn chair, and stripped down to a Day-Glo–green bikini. She lay there in the sun, separated from the party by only a few feet and a chain-link fence. She'd even brought her own radio, a small boom box, which had much better sound quality than Donald's massive speaker system. A week earlier, I'd heard her father shouting at her in the middle of the night, threatening to have her arrested, for what I had no idea, although I'd stayed up for over an hour trying to find out. She seemed perfectly composed now. Once the guests had ogled her, they turned their backs, as if they were ashamed to be caught at this low-prestige event.

Donald had spilled Agnes's cookies onto one of the empty plastic plates. They looked more like brown Bakelite poker chips than food, but they'd been devoured enthusiastically. At least half a dozen people had made their way over to Agnes to compliment her on her cooking, and she'd thanked them with cringing gratitude. To my amazement, she seemed to have completely forgotten about Marcus and my father. With any luck at all, Dad would call the following week to tell me about his trip and to thank me again. At least it gave me something to look forward to.

It was hard to know what Sheila made of the event. Although Marcus had opened the gate for her, it was she who led him into the little yard with some of the vain pride I occasionally felt when I was out walking Otis: Look at me! Aren't I adorable because I've got an adorable dog at the end of this leash?

What she'd dug out of Marcus's drawers was a white sleeveless T-shirt that clung to her flat stomach and her breasts and a pair of long dark pants that looked so heavy and wintry, they made the T-shirt all the more provocative.

We engaged in a few minutes of strained conversation on her studies—landscape paintings of the Sung dynasty from a contemporary Western feminist perspective—before it became apparent to her that despite my broadly phrased questions, I hadn't even a remote idea what century we were discussing. "Marcus told me you teach at The Learning Place," she said, trying to rescue me.

"He would."

"I think that's great! Adult education is wonderful."

It was bad enough having people know what I did for a living, but having them praise me for it, the way you might praise a ten-year-old for his paper route, was truly humiliating.

When she and Marcus went to sit on the back steps of the house, Agnes squeezed her way through a group of men and leaned against my shoulder awkwardly. "They're in love, aren't they?"

"They are," I said. "But they're both in love with the same man, so it's bound to fail."

"Oh, Clyde, don't be a cynic. I'm so glad I came. I'm having a lovely time."

"You really are?"

"I really am."

"Well, I'm awfully happy to hear that, sweetheart."

"You have such nice friends. Even Barbara seems to be enjoying herself."

At the very least, Barbara was enjoying her bottomless cup of beer. She had her arms spread out along the fence behind her as if she were claiming that whole corner of the yard as her territory.

"I know I shouldn't let her drink, but I can't take the weight of the world on my shoulders, can I? Donald said everyone drinks at that age, so I shouldn't worry. I suppose he's right. He's cheerful."

"Donald?"

"Mmm." She put an arm around my waist, an affectionate gesture so badly executed she twisted her shoulder and had to retract it.

A few minutes later, I started inching my way toward the gate, hoping to slip out of the yard unnoticed. But when I turned to leave, Ben was standing there, half hidden by an immense hydrangea bush. He had on a big jersey with a pair of sunglasses sticking out of the pocket and absurdly oversize sneakers. I couldn't tell if he was spying on the pathetic spectacle or simply trying to get up the nerve to enter.

"I forgot my key," he said.

"You did? That's unlike you."

"I wasn't sure you were here."

"With a little luck, I won't be for long. Have you been standing there awhile?"

He shrugged.

I started to open the gate, intending to leave, but thought better of it. "Come in for a minute," I said. "There's no food and there's nothing for you to drink, but . . . I want you to meet my sister."

"Agnes?" he said.

"Very good. Half the time, I can't remember her name."

I unhooked the rusted gate and directed Ben to the corner of the yard where my sister was once again yucking it up with Donald.

"I bet I know who this is," she said. Her tone was uncharacteristically confident and buoyant, even a little teasing. "I bet this is Louise Morris's son."

"Benjamin," I said.

She stuck out her hand. "Well, I am very pleased to meet you. Did Clyde tell you I'm your mother's biggest fan?"

"I don't know. I guess so."

"Well, I am. You must be very proud of her."

"Hey, kid," Donald said, "tell Agnes here how I trained your dog to fetch a ball. I'm trying to impress her with my talents."

Ben nodded and then looked at me without saying anything. I'd claimed responsibility for teaching Otis his latest trick, a lie I'd felt justified in telling since I was the one who'd bought the ball. "It was a group effort," I explained.

Sheila and Marcus walked arm in arm through the cluster of chain-smoking women, as if deigning to mingle with mere mortals. When they reached us, Marcus put a hand on Benjamin's shoulder, a gesture of intimacy and ownership that shocked me. Perhaps it shocked Ben, too, for he turned around and stared up at Marcus with a sad, worried expression. "Sheila was just telling me she has a brother right about your age," Marcus said. "They're best friends."

"He's the main reason I hated to leave California," Sheila said. "And you, you remind me of him exactly. We send E-mail back and forth almost every day."

"Don't talk to me about computers," Donald said. "Gives me a headache just thinking about them."

"Isn't it lovely you're so close," Agnes said. She glanced across the yard at her daughter and sighed. "I wonder how things would have turned out if Barbara had had a brother."

"Where in California is he?" Ben asked.

"San Diego. Have you ever been there?"

"Me and my mom lived there for a year. But I don't remember it much."

"You were four," I said. It was a guess, but I figured it was closer than anything his father could come up with.

Sheila rested her head on Marcus's shoulder and squeezed her lips into a pout. "I'm sorry you can't keep your dog with you, honey. He's such a sweet little guy. Marcus is helping you take care of him, isn't he?"

Ben shrugged.

"We're working on it," Marcus said. He said it with so much conviction, I could tell he believed he really was.

Agnes introduced Ben to Barbara, who dismissed her mother and started talking with him animatedly, making discouraging faces at the adults. She finished off the beer in her cup and clomped over to our little group, with Ben trailing behind her. They hadn't been together more than a few minutes, but already she'd established dominance over him.

"We're walking up to the Square," she announced. "Does anyone object too much?"

"Oh, my purse is upstairs," Agnes said. "Barbara and I made a little deal—"

"Forget it, Mom."

"—that if she'd come down to Cambridge—"

"Mom, quit while you're ahead, okay? Anyway, I changed my mind. We're going to walk the dog and try to score some drugs. Just kidding." She snapped her head. "C'mon, Morris, let's go. We need your key, Clyde."

"I was about to leave myself."

"We should go, too," Sheila said.

"Got a feeling the ship's sinking, sis?" Donald asked.

"Not at all," Agnes said. "I'm having a wonderful time."

THE ROOM I GENEROUSLY CALLED A STUDY was small, low-ceilinged, and looked out to the side of the house and right over the rooftop of the gourmet grocery. There was a duct from the store's ventilation system below the window, and at odd hours of the day and night, mouth watering smells of baking bread and roasting coffee and chocolate belched out and seeped into the house. I used the room primarily for napping and other slothful midday activities, for while I found it depressing to fall asleep in my bed in the middle of the afternoon, I found it reviving to fall asleep in the study. I assume the only thing that kept Marcus from crashing into a suicidal slump about having accomplished nothing for a decade was the fact that he'd had the good sense to accomplish nothing in the library rather than at home. I'd furnished the room with a thin twin-bed mattress propped up on bricks and boards I called a daybed and a pair of overstuffed chairs with serious structural problems. I'd draped the chairs with Indian-print bedspreads—a decorative touch that's practical at age twenty but an admission of defeat at thirty-five. The chairs were so bloated and lumpy and lopsided, they sometimes looked to me like two fat, sloppily dressed drunks complaining to each other about the state of the world while slugging down another drink.

But the room had an undeniable charm, especially when something delicious was in the oven next door or when there was a power outage and it was too dark to see much.

A few days after Donald's cookout, Ben and I were sitting in the study. It was pouring, sheets of rain slamming against the window and drumming loudly on the roof. Otis's reluctance to go outside had convinced Ben to stay in for once, and he was sitting on the floor pulling knots out of the dog's wiry coat. I was eager to find out what Ben thought of my niece or at least what they'd done for the nearly two hours they'd spent together the afternoon of the cookout, but whenever I asked a question, he practiced the same kind of maddening evasiveness that Barbara herself practiced routinely.

"Do you know what it means when Otis rolls over on his back like that?" I tried.

Ben looked at me doubtfully. "I didn't know it meant anything at all."

"Sure it does. Everything they do has some meaning. Rolling over on his back is submitting to your will, his way of saying, 'You win, I'll do what you say.'"

"How do you know that?"

"I've been reading up on dog communication," I said.

Standing in line at the photocopier in the library, I'd thumbed through one dreary, cheaply bound book on canine behavior, all in an attempt to pick up a few fun dog facts I could impress Ben with. I'd found it far more interesting than I'd expected. I kept hunting through it, looking for explanations for Otis's behavior or tips on training, and ended up checking it out. I didn't want to show the book to Ben, because I was afraid it would make my knowledge seem less impressive, like revealing the mechanics behind a magic trick. I let the information sink in and then went back to the subject of my niece.

"So what did you two do?"

"Me and Barbara?" He shrugged. "We went to The Pit."

The Pit was a depression in a pedestrian walkway near the entrance to the subway in Harvard Square. It was usually jammed with a group of sickly teenagers with oddly colored hair and leather jackets and pierced eyebrows. I was so far removed from the current youth culture, it was impossible for me to read meaning into the hairstyles and costumes of the kids who congregated there, but the whole crowd exuded an air of lethargy that screamed elephant tranquilizers. I couldn't imagine Ben or even Barbara fitting into that scene. "What did you do there?" I asked.

"We didn't stay long. One of Barbara's friends was there, and she started spitting on us, so we had to leave."

"Spitting! Why?"

"I'm not sure. Some grudge about an old boyfriend. I don't think it helped that she was with me." He snapped the hair out of his eyes. "I guess they thought I was too much like a kid."

In fact, he *was* a kid, but he didn't really seem to me "like" a kid at all. Kids, for one thing, will never admit to being kids or even being like kids. He released Otis, and the dog leapt into the chair I was sitting on and curled up beside me, his head on my thigh.

I had a heavy, hardbound copy of *Great Expectations* open on my lap. We'd started to discuss it in class the week before, and there was a flurry of interest and excitement. At first I thought it was because students were actually reading the book, but it soon became apparent that because everyone had heard of Miss Havisham and knew about the dress and the cake and all the rest, they assumed they'd as good as read it. The discussion quickly melted into speculation about her character's emotional disintegration and slipping faculties, which had absolutely nothing to do with the facts presented in the novel and everything to do with current theories of agoraphobia, menopause, and even nutrition. Of course, one student suggested that Miss Havisham was suffering from allergies, a topic that fueled near-hysterical enthusiasm. I personally found Miss Havisham unsympathetic, possibly because I was jealous of her reclusive life.

When the phone rang, I asked Ben to answer it so I wouldn't disturb the dog. He picked up and said hello a few times. "There's no one there," he said, and passed me the receiver. "It must be your father."

"How did he know who it was?" my father asked.

"He's psychic." I was delighted Dad had called once again, especially since Ben was there to observe our chummy relationship. "How was your weekend on the Cape?" I asked with forced cheer, settling into a big chair.

"It was unbelievable. Great motel, beach over here, shopping mall over there, convenient to everything. Roger went swimming three times."

Roger again. So far, my father had managed to slip mention of him into nearly every conversation we'd had, and I was beginning to develop an intense aversion to the name. "Isn't it late in the season for swimming?"

"He's a rugged little guy."

"How little?"

"Don't be a wise guy," he said. "Roger's been through the mill, and he needed a break."

"I thought it was a romantic weekend for you and Diane."

"For Christ's sake," he whispered harshly. "Is that kid listening?"

Ben was at the stereo, leafing through a stack of records. "He's got his own problems," I said. "I wouldn't worry about him. How old is this Roger, anyway?"

"Early thirties, but he's in great shape."

I grunted. Younger than me and better-looking. It was impossible for me to mention anything about the appearance of anyone, male or female, in front of my father without inciting a hostile reaction. If I said a woman was attractive, he acted as if I was suddenly trying to claim heterosexuality to win his approval. And if I dared to mention that a man was fit, handsome, or even homely, he'd glare, shocked and furious, as if I'd just described a blow job in minute detail. "Anyway," I said, "I'm glad you had a good time. What's up?"

"I heard Agnes went down there last weekend. You didn't . . ."

"She doesn't know anything about it." I said it too loudly, for Otis jumped off my lap and ran over to Ben, the foolish tuft of fur bouncing on his head.

"Let's keep it that way. I don't like the idea of her running down there every five minutes. Who's this neighbor of yours?"

"Donald?"

"She's mentioned him three times in the last twenty-four hours. What's that all about?"

"He was nice to her, that's all."

"I don't like the idea of her hanging out with a gay crowd."

"I have to go," I said. My head was beginning to feel as if someone had slipped it into a vise.

"Listen," he said, "keep your ears open for a nice, cheap apartment in Cambridge. Roger can't afford much, but he's not going to move into some dump."

After I'd hung up, Ben continued to flip through the records, and neither one of us said anything. He had his back to me, a great relief, really, since it would have been too humiliating to face him right at that moment. I tried to reconstruct the portion of the conversation he'd heard, to see if he could possibly have made sense of it, but the whole thing was blurring in my mind, sloshing around with the dull throb of my headache. I dated my problem with headaches back to the disaster of coming out to my family, although the underlying neurotic response of developing a physical pain to mask something deeper probably went back to birth.

Coming out was, for me, the round of insults, anger, tears, recriminations, apologies, and regret that's pretty much standard fare for that particular rite of passage, assuming things don't go badly. Most of it doesn't bear repeating, which is a good thing, since I've buried most of it in an extraordinarily shallow grave. It might well be true that the unexamined life isn't worth living, but let's face it, cable TV makes it a lot easier to put up with.

What stands out most clearly in my mind is what happened a

month after I made my big announcement. I was living in Minneap-
olis at the time, having just dropped out of another graduate program in some subject I can't even remember. I'd found a job as a
desk clerk at a hotel, a semipathetic profession at which I'd become
an expert and which I later blamed, along with heredity, for the
premature failure of my eyesight. One day at work, I received a
package, a good-size carton with no return address. The box, which
I made the mistake of opening in front of my coworkers, contained
an assortment of shirts, underwear, ties, scarves, woolen hats, socks,
and gloves. Although a few of the items appeared to have been
worn, most looked new—the underwear was still in its cellophane
packaging, the shirts were still pinned and the socks still bound
together. It was a fairly dreary collection of goods, most obviously
sale items, seconds or factory rejects that looked faintly, disconcertingly familiar.

"Man! Look at this rag," a coworker said, and held up a check-
ered shirt.

It was at that moment that I recognized the contents of the
box. These were all the gifts I'd given to my father for birthdays,
Christmases, and anniversaries over the course of the preceding
eight or ten years. A look of shame must have crossed my face, for
even though I said nothing, everyone stopped laughing. I put the
stuff back in the carton and returned to work.

What continued to haunt me for years and what, I suppose, I
still hadn't gotten over was knowing that my father had been
keeping all of those ugly, bargain-basement gifts aside, in some
drawer or closet or in the back of some cabinet somewhere,
just waiting for the right opportunity to ship it all back to me.
As if he'd been planning for the day I'd do the truly unforgivable
and he'd be free to unload it with a clear conscience. I'd felt so
humiliated by what I came to think of as the Surprise Package, I
borrowed a friend's car, drove for miles one night, and stuffed it
into the Dumpster of a supermarket in a neighborhood I never
visited.

Ben turned on the stereo. Bordello piano, scratchy violins, and the throbbing vibrato of an overwrought soprano filled the silence. It was a recording of Libertad Lamarque, a tango singer who'd made her name in Buenos Aires in the thirties, a perfect choice for my overwrought mood.

"I think Otis is starting to respond to you more," Ben said without turning around.

Combined with the record, the comment was such an obvious attempt at consoling me, I cringed. "I think you're right," I told him.

"Louise says we're all strays—Otis, me, and her. Do you think that's true?"

"It depends how she meant it."

He turned around and looked out the window and away from me. "As a compliment, I think. I like Otis more because he was a stray. Barbara said the same thing. She loves dogs, but they can't get one because Agnes is allergic to all animals. Do you think that's possible?"

"No, no. Of course not. It's just . . ." I pointed to my head.

"That's what I figured. That's what Barbara figures, too. She said it all started when her father walked out on them."

"Oh, Agnes's troubles began before that."

Agnes had gone from worrying that she'd never find a husband to worrying that she'd lose the one she had, a worry she expressed by constant exaggerated concerns over Davis's health. Barbara had been the source of multiple miseries because she'd been a sickly infant and because Davis had always seemed uncomfortable with her and with the very idea of himself as a father. He'd once told me, when Barbara was still an infant, that he was afraid that being a father would make him less attractive to women, a comment that shocked me because it had never crossed my mind that women might find him attractive in the first place. Personally, I'd always thought that Davis's departure had been a slight relief to Agnes, at least in the sense that she no longer had to worry about him leaving her since he was already gone.

"Her allergies got worse when Barbara's father walked out," Ben said. "It happens a lot when men walk out on their families. That's a big advantage Louise and I have. Louise never gave my father the chance to leave us, because she left first."

I nodded in agreement. I was foolishly concerned with mentioning anything in front of him that might be taken as too loaded with intimacy. Even when I talked about Otis, I avoided words like bed, sleep, skin, and tongue. Father, I realized now, was another word I tried to steer clear of, unless I was talking about my own. But I decided to give it a try. "Do you think about your father much?"

"No," he said, too emphatically.

"Not even a little curious?"

"Not as much as everyone thinks. Besides, we probably wouldn't like each other anyway. That's the way it usually works out."

He was looking at the phone when he said this, a fact that made me think he must have heard more of my conversation with my father than I'd thought.

An hour later, when the sky had cleared some, I walked Ben halfway home. But when I got back to my house, it began to rain again, a heavy downpour that was like a faucet being turned on. I stood out on the front porch under the shelter of the roof and watched the water wash down the street, carrying leaves and trash to the clogged drains on the corner. One of the frantically thin mothers who lived next door ran along the sidewalk with a laundry bag slung over her shoulder, her long black hair streaming. I waved as she ran past, and she looked up at me and gave me the finger. A car sped by and sprayed the steps with water and rotting leaves. At the far end of the street, Donald rounded the corner. He was walking at a leisurely pace, carrying a monstrous black umbrella, practically the size of a small tent. He stopped a few houses down, picked a plastic milk bottle off the sidewalk, and tossed it into a trash barrel. At the porch, he made an elaborate production of ducking out from under the umbrella and closing it cautiously so that not one drop of rain touched the top of his head. The back of his coat was soaked, as if he'd been sprayed with a fire hose, but his Band-Aid—colored hair was dry, every strand in place.

I nodded to him and thanked him for inviting me to the cook-out. "Aw, what the hell," he said, shaking rain off the umbrella. "It turned out okay, didn't it? It's the first party I've had in a long time. I figured I had to break the ice sooner or later and face the world again."

He seemed to be referring to some personal crisis I thought it was probably best not to pursue. "How's your friend who had the accident?" I asked.

"Jerry? He's doing all right. They've got him in detox, lucky bastard, thirty days with nothing to do but watch TV and bullshit with a bunch of drunks. I'd like to know what happened to all those hamburgers, though."

"It's lucky Agnes brought the cookies," I said.

At the mention of my sister's name, his face grew serious, and he stared at me for a moment, perhaps to analyze the real meaning behind what I'd said. He drew his light eyebrows together but said nothing. We went into the dark front hallway of the house. It smelled faintly of cat piss, as it always did on rainy or humid days. When I first moved in, I'd spent an afternoon scrubbing at the floor with assorted cleaners designed to remove "pet odors," although the heavy chemical stench was remarkably similar to that of cat piss.

We stood silently fumbling with our keys, so close we were practically bumping into each other. When he had his door open, he turned toward me as if he was trying to prompt me to ask him something, but what, I couldn't guess. "Listen, Clyde," he finally said, "come in for a second, will you?"

I leaned my umbrella against my door and followed him into his apartment.

The living room was as unfurnished as I'd suspected. The speakers that had been in the backyard were disconnected and stacked up in one corner, and there was a lonely, spindly philodendron in a white plastic pot by the window. The brown sofa had a tangled, graying bedsheet and a pillow on it. Show me a man who sleeps on his sofa, and I'll show you a man willing to keep an open mind about the possibility of life on other planets. I followed Donald down a narrow, dark hallway that wound around under the staircase to our apartment. Instead of ducking forward or stooping to pass, he leaned back awkwardly, like a dancer going under a limbo stick. He lifted up one of the kitchen chairs and dumped a pile of clothes onto the floor. "Sit down," he said, gesturing with his hand. "Let me get you a beer or something."

"I'd better not," I said.

"Teaching tonight?"

"I have some reading I should catch up on."

He nodded and then shook his head in dismay. "Freaking work, man. It rots, doesn't it?"

"Well . . ."

"I know, don't tell me—I'm lucky to have a job. Hey, believe me, I know. The point is, I figured out a while ago that you have to specialize in something. I trained for this job for eight months. Eight months at minimum wage, but look how it's paying off. Even if the stress feels like it's going to kill me sometimes."

I nodded. Attempting to convince people you can grow their hair back when it's a medical impossibility must be trying.

The kitchen was a good deal smaller than ours, the walls covered with milk-chocolate–brown paneling. There were a couple of calendars thumbtacked to the walls, both of them with pictures of food that were so glossy and sensual, they looked vaguely pornographic. I felt certain they must have been put up by the former tenant. The stove was heaped with pots and cast-iron pans that looked too old and rusty to have been used in the recent past, and most of the cabinets were open and empty.

Donald took off his topcoat and his lab coat, stood in the doorway of a room off the kitchen, and tossed them in. He went to the refrigerator and pulled out a plastic jug of diet Dr Pepper.

As he twisted off the cap, the stuff sprayed all over him, but he seemed only remotely aware of it. He shoved the bottle into his mouth and drained off the foam.

"I meant to tell you, Clyde ..." He paused. He contorted his face as if he'd swallowed a fish bone. Then he burped. "I meant to tell you I'm sorry about my friend Mark Greeley. Don't pay any attention to him."

"I'm not even sure what happened. He seemed a little hostile."

"Forget about it." He swept the clothes off the other chair in the room and sat opposite me at the little Formica-topped table. "He's just one of those white guys angry at the world because he can't get laid. Now he's got some idea about Harvard Business School. A total fantasy. He got kicked out of an air-conditioning-repair training program last year for threatening one of the teachers. He'll probably end up opening fire in a McDonald's, something like that."

"How do you know him?"

He held up his hands. "Can't tell you, man. We've got a rule about confidentiality for patients at the clinic. Guys get into a very weird thing about losing their hair. I see guys walking down the street, and I can tell from the way they carry themselves which ones are going bald. You see guys cowering when they walk into a room with overhead lights? There's a lot of hair on their pillowcases, I'll tell you that. It's all about ..." He grabbed his crotch and shrugged.

His doughy face grew grim again, and he stared at me as if he was pleading with me to drag out of him whatever it was he wanted to say. His dark eyes darted from my eyes to my mouth to my eyes to my nose, as if trying to piece together a whole face. I looked around the room for something to comment on and settled on a blurry photograph of a yellow cat taped to the refrigerator door. "So ... is that your cat?" I asked.

"Damn right it is. I thought he was, anyway. Until my old girlfriend took him with her."

"I'm sorry to hear it. He looks ... cute."

The photo was a close-up of a cat with his mouth open wide

and his fangs bared. It was a fierce-looking animal, like a wild beast you'd see ripping apart a zebra in *National Geographic.*

"Best cat in the world." He lifted up the bottle and glugged down almost half the soda.

"You must miss him," I said.

"Yeah, well, what are you going to do?"

"Were you and your girlfriend together long?"

"Nah. Not long. About three, four years. Six, actually." He looked me in the eyes, his features drooping slightly. His own eyes turned sad and watery, and for a moment I feared he was about to burst into tears. "I'll tell you something, Clyde—I can be honest with you, right?"

"Of course," I said, hoping he wouldn't be.

"She left me for another woman. Can you believe it? I couldn't believe it. All those years, and it turns out she was gay, whatever, lesbian. No offense."

"No, of course not."

"I mean, if I wasn't secure, you know, the thing would have given me a complex. You know what I mean? Some guys would be like: 'Hey, if she's really into girls, what does it mean that she was with me for six, seven years?'"

"I guess it doesn't say anything about you at all. She was just confused about who she was. Or she changed."

He gave me another of his surveying looks. "That's what the shrink said. She had me go to a shrink. I went six times." He snapped his fingers. "Cleared the whole thing right up. Now listen, I haven't told anyone else about this lesbian business, so don't go spreading the word." He lifted up the bottle, poured the rest of the soda down his throat, and threw the empty container into the sink. "And I sure haven't told anyone about the shrink, either. Those losers at the party would drop dead, not that they don't all belong there themselves."

"How long ago did you break up?"

"Almost a year. I'm pretty much over it. Couldn't care less, as a matter of fact. The way I look at it, we had seven or eight good years, so it was time for a change anyway. Even most marriages don't last ten years. Not that I could ever get her to marry me. Things started getting better when I moved into this place."

I nodded, letting my eyes wander around the gloomy kitchen. He'd tacked a green plastic trash bag over the window above the sink and lined up a row of frozen orange juice containers he was obviously using as drinking glasses.

"Hey, believe me, I know. The place is a dump, total house of horrors. But what can you do? I work, I come home, stuff a couple of pizzas in my mouth, and go to bed. I don't have time to fix it up."

"I can understand that." For a fleeting moment, I considered confiding in him about Gordon, out of solidarity. But I'd picked up two chicken salad sandwiches on my way home, and they were weighing down the pocket of my jacket. I was eager to get upstairs and devour them and forget about my conversation with . . . Dad. "By the way," I said, "thanks for taking such good care of my sister the other day. She had a nice time. My father was telling me that just this afternoon."

He was contorting his face again, stretching his neck as if he was trying to elongate it. He covered his mouth, gasped out another burp, and smiled.

"That's what I wanted to talk with you about. I wanted to ask you about old Agnes. You know"—he rubbed his hand over his face—"you know, I guess there's no shame in saying I found her a pretty interesting gal."

"Agnes is very interesting."

"Hey, look, I'll come right to the point, okay? I want to ask her out to a movie, but . . . I can tell she's shy, insecure, whatever. I don't want to do the wrong thing, end up offending her or anything. Give her a complex or something."

A truck went by on the street, and one of the pans on the heap on the counter shifted position. We both turned to look at it. It crossed my mind that if I told him Agnes was dating someone, that would probably be the end of that.

"Well," I said, "as far as I know, Agnes isn't a big movie fan." Recently, Agnes had decided that it was unwise to sit in a darkened auditorium surrounded by a bunch of strangers, any of whom might be carrying a gun or an airborne viral infection.

"What you're trying to say is: Forget it. Right?"

That was what I was trying to say. But in the brief pause opened up by his question, I realized it wasn't any of my business and, if nothing else, Agnes needed a night out. She'd found him cheerful. "I just mean, dinner might be a better idea."

"Hey, I like that," he said. He smiled broadly, his tiny mouth pushing aside his fleshy cheeks. "Dinner. To tell you the truth, I don't much care about movies myself. Listen, you want to stay and order out a pizza?"

"I'd better not. I picked up something on the way home."

"Sure. Look, you don't think the age difference is a problem, do you? I'm probably younger than she is. Thirty-four."

"Agnes is only thirty-seven," I said, lopping two years off her age.

"No kidding? Man, she must be using some good emollients, I'll tell you that. I had her pegged for thirty-five, tops. Here ..." He jumped up from the table excitedly and began rummaging through the drawers under the counter. "I'm glad I got up the nerve to talk to you. You don't have a pen on you, do you? I'm mighty glad, Clyde, 'cause I'll tell you, I've been thinking a lot about that sister of yours for the past few days. I've been missing meals over old Agnes. Here you go." He handed me a scrap of paper and a red crayon. "Just write down the number. New Hampshire, right? Boy, I haven't been out in the country for ages."

"I'm not sure you'd call it the country...."

"I can get into that rural scene. Gift shops, motels, the whole thing. It'll be good, for a change."

He was looking over my shoulder as I scrawled Agnes's number.

"Long distance," he mumbled. "Well, what the hell, the worst she can do is tell me to drop dead."

"I don't think she'll do that."

"Nah. Too much class, right?"

ALTHOUGH I HADN'T BEEN ABLE TO discharge Gordon from my heart and mind as effectively as I knew I should, I wasn't so thoroughly deluded that I was keeping myself for him physically. I did have a sex life, even if it was sporadic and pretty strictly limited to satisfying the basic biological demands. Strangely, though, I was reasonably content with it, a lot more content than I had been dating, a charade that promised more than orgasm and invariably delivered less.

The first months after Gordon moved out, I spent the majority of my time wandering around the house with a hangover. It wasn't that I started drinking, or even, truthfully, that I missed Gordon all that much. It was just that the sense of having been rejected weighed on me so heavily that I sometimes had trouble getting out of bed in the morning and sometimes didn't bother trying.

His departure and the emotions around it were confused with and sharpened by my mother's death. In addition to missing her, I'd had some guilty hopes that perhaps her death would bring my father and me closer. My big move in that direction had been taking him out to dinner one night a month after the funeral. We sat through most of the meal in glum silence, which I managed to convince myself was related to our shared mourning. Toward the end of the meal, he looked across the table at me with genuine kindness in his eyes. "I know I don't say this often, but I want to thank you," he choked out.

"For what?" I made the mistake of asking. This was exactly the kind of sentimental, lower-your-guard moment I'd been hoping for all evening, and all the years preceding it. My only regret was that I'd been too intimidated to initiate the outpouring of feelings myself. I was already figuring out polite, insincere refusals of the gratitude I expected him to heap on me for helping with the funeral arrangements and finding a doctor to write a prescription for tranquilizers to hold Agnes together through the interminable, morbid ceremonies associated with a Catholic death and burial.

"Well," he said, fingering the empty glass in front of him thoughtfully, "for not showing up at the wake with that friend of yours in tow."

"Gordon?"

"Whatever his name is. You didn't get a haircut like I asked you to, but I'm willing to overlook that because the other was more important to me."

Two days before my mother died, Gordon had left with a couple of friends for a week-long vacation in Saint Croix, a trip that marked the beginning of the end of our relationship.

"He was out of the country," I said.

"Yeah, well, a couple weeks from now, when I drop dead, I hope to God he's still out of the country. And don't wear that ring to my funeral, either."

"I've never worn a ring in my life," I said, not strictly true, but true enough, since I was pretty certain I'd never worn one in front of him.

"Oh, well, I thought you had. My mistake. Don't get bent out of shape."

When the check came, he insisted on paying for his meal instead of letting me treat, as we'd agreed. "I'd just owe you one, and we'd be going back and forth forever. Now that your mother's dead, we'll have even fewer reasons to see each other, so let's each pay our own way."

In any case, about six months after Gordon had left and I managed to finally drag myself off the bed, I began a long stint of going out with the friends of friends. These evenings involved sitting around an overpriced restaurant trading censored and exaggerated life stories with someone in therapy and the computer field. The rambling monologues talked any mutual attraction out of existence and passed along so much detailed information, it was virtually impossible to project fantasies upon the other person. Because the whole chore of dating was tied up with safe sex and getting to know the other person and being responsible about AIDS in some broad, metaphoric sense that had little to do with the realities of viral transmission, the evening usually ended with a chaste kiss and plans to meet again for a movie or a second dinner, just to make doubly sure that all spontaneity and lust were pummeled into crumbs before we got naked. I found these dates so frustrating on every level that I frequently went straight from dinner to some venue where I could engage in responsible, anonymous sex without the clutter of college degrees, family trees, and amusing tales of coworkers. It took me months to realize that I'd be better off skipping the dates and cutting right to the sex. It was a more efficient use of time.

I also discovered that while ugly black glasses and a slightly bedraggled appearance were a drawback in overpriced restaurants, they were an asset in the bulrushes, where they added a note of glowering menace that was highly prized.

Out of these groping encounters, I'd managed to acquire a couple of casual friends with whom I didn't have sex and a few semiregular sex partners with whom I wasn't especially friendly.

The star of this latter group was an amusing, infuriating man named Bernie. We'd met a couple of years earlier under the usual furtive circumstances, and although we probably hadn't seen each other more than a dozen times since, he'd become an important minor character in my life. Bernie, like most of my semiregular sex partners, had a lover. Richie, the lover, was a scrawny, neurotic housepainter to whom, I'd been told, I bore a striking resemblance, although, for obvious reasons, I'd never met him. Bernie and Richie had been together for ten years, and while Bernie claimed they fought constantly, it was apparent they'd stay together for life. It didn't take much insight to recognize that Bernie had initially been attracted to me solely because I looked like Richie. And certainly the fact that Bernie bore an almost uncanny resemblance to Gordon —Gordon before he'd become a gym enthusiast and chiseled his body into a more sharply defined but less interesting shape—was one of the main things that made him attractive to me.

Because Bernie was living with a lover, I had to wait for his calls rather than call him, lest I compromise the sanctity of his relationship. I heard from him once every few months, depending on Richie's out-of-town work schedule and Bernie's moods. In between meetings, I thought of him infrequently and always with the same slightly annoyed fondness: "The little creep," and so on, accompanied by a jarring erotic memory.

I hadn't heard from him since before Louise's arrival, when, a week or more after my encounter with Donald, he called.

"Hi, Clyde," he said in the bored, vaguely mocking tone that was typical of his telephone personality.

"Bernie," I said. I was always happy to hear from him, although it didn't seem right to express too much enthusiasm. Receiving one of his calls was like finding a small, unexpected check in the mail.

"What are you doing?" he asked.

As always, I answered truthfully. "Nothing."

I felt at a slight disadvantage talking with Bernie on the phone, because he was so completely at ease with the medium, like one of those people who seem to be natural-born swimmers or beautiful untrained singers. Even the way he held the telephone, balanced gracefully between chin and shoulder, made it seem as if the receiver were part of him. The majority of Bernie's life revolved around long phone conversations that bled into one another; he was like a chain-smoker lighting a new cigarette off the last one.

"If you're in the neighborhood this afternoon," he said, "drop by and we can have coffee."

A more honest way of phrasing it would have been, "Can you come by at two-thirty and fuck me?" But I suppose to reduce the sting of possible rejection—sometimes I had other plans, and underneath it all, he was an appealingly insecure guy—he always put it in less explicit terms.

Actually, I did have plans for that afternoon. I'd agreed to drive Ben to a used-record warehouse in one of the suburbs and then take Otis for a hike. But since Ben had overheard my humiliating conversation with my father, I'd been less eager to spend time with him. I scrawled a note for Ben explaining an emergency meeting at The Learning Place and left it near Otis's food. The dog sat up on one of the kitchen chairs, watching me, with his tiny head held high. It was an imperious pose, made only slightly less condescending by the foolish tuft of fur on top of his head. "I don't know why you care," I told him. "You're still going to get your walk."

He gave a pathetic whimper, lay down, and hung his head over the seat of the chair. This look of abject misery and the please-don't-abandon-me cry that went along with it had started to get to me every time I left the house. I went to him and stroked his head, and he immediately rolled over onto his back, legs splayed, soft belly exposed: Do with me what you will, but don't leave me here alone.

"I liked it better when you ignored me," I told him, even though that wasn't true. "I'm just going to get you some food, all right?"

Against all odds, I found that this kind of lie usually made me feel better about walking out on him. As if he understood what I was saying or would have believed me if he could.

Bernie and Richie lived in the North End of Boston, an Italian neighborhood of cramped streets, antique cemeteries, and sweeping views of the innermost reaches of Boston Harbor. Their apartment was on the top floor of an unimaginably narrow building that always smelled so strongly of coffee and heavy, roasting meat, I grew dizzy just walking into the front hallway. The other floors of the building were inhabited by an assortment of old couples and ancient widows, who appeared to accept the boys above with startling tolerance and eyed me disapprovingly whenever I rang the bell. I climbed up the creaking four flights of stairs that afternoon, and as usual, Bernie met me at the door with his cordless phone cuddled against his neck. He was a waiter at one of the many restaurants in the neighborhood, and I'd never once dropped in on him when he wasn't arguing with some coworker about scheduling conflicts or a maître d' who'd favored someone else's station the night before. Bernie seemed to exist in a perpetual state of outrage over minor insults and slights.

He nodded at me and shooed me down the corridor to the living room.

Bernie was a collector of anything made before the Second World War, provided it was overdone and gaudy. Ten years' worth of kitsch was spilling from every shelf and tabletop and window ledge: ceramic figurines and squeeze toys, plates, cups, tourist ashtrays and old magazines, religious icons, grotesque lamps, hand-painted signs and children's toys. I loved the cozy clutter of the apartment, all the useless junk and heavy furniture, which seemed to guarantee that he and Richie would be buried there forever in their troubled domestic arrangement. If only, I sometimes thought, Gordon hadn't been such a minimalist. I sank into one of the overstuffed chairs and tried to arrange my legs and crotch as provocatively as possible.

Bernie finally came into the room and nervously dropped down onto the sofa, talking as if he were still in the middle of his phone conversation and trying to get the wrapper off a pack of chewing gum. He was short, like Gordon, and with the same solid, chunky build—the build of a scrappy boxer who's been out of training for half a dozen years.

"I've been there for seven years, seven years, and I'm the best waiter they've got and they know it, and there's no way I'm going to put up with that *shit*." He had a way of drawling swear words, sloshing them around in his mouth and spitting them out, that made them sound like whole three-page monologues. "I mean, I won't work under those conditions, and that's all there is to it. Well, do you blame me? I mean, really, do you blame me?"

I shrugged and held up my hands. I'd learned that if I expressed too much interest in Bernie or lent him too much sympathy, he'd turn cool, as if I wasn't playing my part properly or was staking a claim on him that I had no right to.

"No, you wouldn't understand. Not that I expect you to. You're as bad as Richie." He popped three sticks of gum into his mouth and started to chew. "What do you think of this lamp?" he muttered through the gum. "I bought it yesterday at an auction." He pointed to a Victorian parlor lamp dripping with broken crystal prisms. The glass shade was shattered, and the whole thing was tossed into a corner carelessly. "A hundred bucks. Too much, but who gives a *ffffuck*. I mean, you only go this way once, right? If Richie's going to leave town for five days, I might as well go out and spend some money. Serves him right."

He sighed and looked around the apartment, jiggling his crossed legs anxiously. Today he was poured into a pair of tight blue jeans so spotless and carefully faded, it was obvious they were part of yesterday's shopping spree, and a puce collarless shirt with a zipper instead of buttons. He wore his hair in a jaunty, military-academy crew cut that, since the last time I'd seen him, he'd bleached a highly unnatural and unflattering platinum blond. Like Gordon, Bernie considered Madonna "a genius," although the only thing either ever praised her for was her ability to lure anyone she chose into bed.

I listened to his chattering, nodding from time to time and throwing in the occasional noncommittal murmur. For all his self-centered banter, Bernie was, at heart, extremely generous, and every now and then he let slip into his rant a complaint about a sick friend he was caring for or some unappreciative elderly neighbor to whom he regularly brought whole meals from the restaurant. After what seemed a reasonable amount of time, I cut him off. "So, Bernie, Richie's out of town?"

He looked up at me and stopped chewing, suddenly timid. "Right," he said. He took the gum and dropped it into one of the many nearby ashtrays and cast a sidelong glance down my body.

"It's awfully bright in here," I said, even though the sky was a steely, late-October shade of gray.

"You think so?" he asked.

I nodded. "Maybe you should lower the shade."

He got up and strolled to the window slowly, showing off his firm little behind in those new blue jeans. There was something irresistibly fleshy and languid about Bernie. His telephone obsession, his constant complaining, his unconvincing tone of moral superiority, all added to his charm. He struck me as being more completely comfortable with himself than anyone I'd met, reveling in his flaws and indulging his appetites.

I hoped that he and Richie never parted company. Bernie wasn't the type who'd do well on his own. Probably half the reason he invited men over to the apartment when Richie left town was that he was lonely without his lover. I've always found something heroic in people who desperately need the company of others and aren't afraid to seek it out.

He leaned over a table by the window and reached up to pull down the shade, his movements deliberate.

"Come over here," I said, and sat upright in the chair.

As he was crossing the room, the phone rang. His eyes shifted to the receiver he'd placed on top of a stack of yellowed *Hollywood Confidentials*, and he stopped. "Oh, to hell with it," he said, and let it ring. Which, all things considered, was about the highest compliment he could pay.

Out on the street, I buttoned my sports jacket against the wind, wrapped a scarf around my neck, and dodged my way through the five-thirty crowds of shoppers and office workers. I loved being in that part of town at that hour, especially when I was feeling satiated and still pumped up after an hour or so with Bernie, when I hadn't yet let my self-image drag my ego back to reality.

The streetlights had all come on and the cafés and pastry shops were lit up and the doors of the churches were open; the whole bustling neighborhood seemed filled with romance and sex, incense and cannoli. I wandered into one of the cafés and ordered an espresso and a block of some dense nutty pastry and ate leaning against the counter. Within minutes, I was buzzing with a combination of dizziness and nausea that was easy to mistake for euphoria.

I stumbled out of the café and into the bustle of Hanover Street. A brisk wind was blowing, lifting whole sheets of newspaper up into the air and sending them soaring. There was a traffic jam on the corner, one of those festering brews of angry shouts and blaring horns and fists reaching out of windows. As soon as a chill pierced my overcoat, I felt a kind of unfocused loneliness begin to lap at me, a wave of nasty disappointment and longing that felt as if it was going to pull me under. The horns sounded especially loud and threatening on the corner. Although I'd made a point of telling Bernie, before I'd even pulled off the condom, that I had to leave, he certainly hadn't objected. In fact, I was barely dressed before he'd picked up the phone and started to dial a coworker. That was the usual routine, but it had never before struck me as quite so abrupt and, if I let myself think about it, insulting.

I trudged on, wallowing in dejection, for about half a block, when I spotted Vance near the traffic jam on the corner, round and oblivious, crossing the street. His big raincoat was catching the wind and billowing out around his legs like a hoop skirt. He was leaning forward into the wind, in an apparent attempt to keep his tweed cap firmly on his head. He had the distracted, vague look of a man who wanted, above all else in the world, to be left alone, but I was suddenly so anxious and eager to talk with someone, I called out his name.

He looked up with a hurt expression, as if he'd just been insulted. When he recognized me, his big, pink face lit up with relief. "Clyde!" he said. "What are you doing on this side of the river?"

"Visiting a friend," I said.

"Oh, yes, yes. The trick with the boyfriend who goes out of town?"

"I guess you could put it that way." The depressing truth was that there really wasn't any other accurate way you *could* put it. To Vance, I'd bragged about and defended the efficiency of my nonrelationship with Bernie, but at this moment, the whole arrangement seemed only dreary. The cold wind and all that miserable traffic weren't helping matters any.

Vance had his briefcase in one hand and, in the other, a white shopping bag with a name scrolled across the front in an elaborate and illegible script. I asked him what he had in the bag.

"Bag?" He looked down at his hand. "Oh, nothing," he said. "I'm just walking home."

"Let me take you out for a drink," I said. "I owe you hundreds."

"To tell you the truth, dear, I'm a little uncomfortable in these clothes." The wind opened up his raincoat, and he yanked at his tight belt. "Cutting off my circulation," he said, and smiled wanly. A skinny teenager in a tight denim jacket knocked into him as he walked past, and Vance stumbled backward a few steps before catching his balance.

The idea that Vance might walk off and leave me alone on the street filled me with dread. I couldn't face my shabby apartment and Otis's pleading little eyes and the telephone staring at me and Marcus padding around the kitchen with Sheila glued to his arm. I felt suddenly as if I were sliding—somewhere—and literally couldn't get a grip. "I'll come to your place while you change," I said. "Then we can go out. It'll be good for you, a little rest and relaxation."

"Well." Looking up the street and then down, he seemed to be searching for an excuse. "All right," he said, none too brightly. He swung around and dumped the bag into a nearby trash barrel. "Nippy afternoon, isn't it?"

"It is," I said, and we headed off.

I resisted the temptation to look back at the trash barrel. The bag must have been full of take-out food Vance was planning to gorge on, and I felt guilty for having come upon him and deprived him of whatever goodies he'd been carrying home. Still, it was better than getting on the subway to Cambridge or traipsing around Filene's Basement in a daze.

"I suppose you must be starving," Vance said.

"Not especially. I ate right before I bumped into you."

"Ah. I figured after an afternoon of mindless passion you'd be depleted. Of course, it's been so long for me, I can't remember how that sequence goes."

Vance often drew attention to what he claimed was his celibacy, perhaps to underline his devotion to Carl. More than one mutual friend had said that Vance regularly spent at least as much money on his sex life as he did on restaurants. It was pure rumor and speculation, but personally, I hoped it was true. It seemed a much better investment than all those trips out to the suburbs. But he was right, I did feel depleted, even if it wasn't for the reasons he thought.

We walked in silence for a while, assaulted by the sharp wind and the swirling papers and leaves, and crossed over Atlantic Avenue to the waterfront. All of the crumbling docks there had been converted into condos with guardhouses and gated parking lots. The few aged fishing boats that remained, tied up to the pilings and bobbing in the wind, looked more like window dressing than anything else. The clean lines and awful little balconies of the dockside condos seemed frighteningly similar to those of Agnes's town house development. In a few years, the entire country would be thoroughly homogenized, with only a few sad little signposts left standing to distinguish one place from another. Nautical motif for the seashore, a pine tree theme for New Hampshire. I mentioned this to Vance, but he shrugged it off. "I find it comforting, especially since I don't really like Boston. Makes it easier to pretend I'm elsewhere." He adjusted the brim of his cap and looked out at the ocean. "I'm in a bit of a funk, Clyde. Carl's wretched mother and I had a fight last week, and we haven't talked since. I'm not sure I'll be much use to you, if you're looking for cheering up."

"I'm sorry," I said. "What happened?"

"Oh, she listens to too much talk radio. Poor thing doesn't sleep. Anyway, she went into a vile right-wing rant. I'd mind it all less if I thought she really believed any of it, but she's just trying to be trendy. I figured I'd punish her by not talking for a few days. Of course, I have to call her tonight because we've got tickets for some revolting dinner theater event this weekend. You pretend you're at a wedding, as if being at a real wedding isn't awful enough."

By this time, we were nearly at the aquarium, and Vance insisted we stop by the sea lions so he could get his nightly look at them. "Big, blubbery things," he said. "I have total identification with them. Swimming, swimming, but never getting anywhere."

I watched the fat mammals corkscrewing through the water for a few minutes and then turned my back to the pool. Since Otis had moved in with me, I was incapable of looking at any animal without seeing his sad, confused eyes and wondering what he was up to at that moment, which led inevitably to wondering what Ben was up to at that moment, and so on, right down to wondering what the hell I was up to.

The aquarium was closing, and noisy groups of children in parkas were rushing out the doors, with their parents chasing after them. I'd once taken Barbara and Agnes to the aquarium, but the outing had been a disaster; Agnes had been overcome by fumes five minutes after entering. "It smells so fishy in there," she'd gasped, as if there were something surprising in that.

As I was about to drag Vance away from the tank, I spotted Eileen Ash emerging from the aquarium on the arm of a tall, handsome man. She had on a knee-length Navajo-blanket poncho, and her light, gray-streaked hair was pulled off her face in a tight bun. She and the man, obviously her husband, were surrounded by laughing children pushing at them as they raced by, but they appeared to be floating along the windy concrete walkway in their own enchanted world. Eileen looked more beautiful than I'd ever seen her, her enormous green eyes flashing, even at a distance.

Despite the relatively small size of Cambridge and Boston, I rarely ran into my students outside of class, and I was always mildly embarrassed when I did. Being seen anywhere but at the front of the classroom undercut my already minimal authority. Eileen's husband leaned over and kissed her behind her ear. I turned away quickly as they walked past, although, from the looks of things, they wouldn't have noticed me anyway.

Vance came up behind me and put his arm around my shoulder. "Let's go. I've had my daily dose."

Vance lived behind the aquarium in an enormous and fantastically ugly concrete tower right on the edge of the water. It had been built about twenty-five years earlier and had quickly become the primary residence in Boston for lawyers and business executives of both sexes who were in the middle of divorce proceedings and for people like Vance, who loved the ocean breezes and the dehumanizing anonymity of living in an ugly concrete tower. His apartment had a spectacular view of the boat traffic in the harbor and the tiny green islands out in the bay. The airport was right across the channel, and at times the monolithic 747s seemed to be lining up for a landing on his puny balcony.

He'd had the apartment expensively decorated with a brick-red leather sofa and antique Turkish carpets and all manner of new furniture weathered to look old and old furniture refinished to look new. Everything in the apartment had been carefully chosen by someone paid to choose carefully, but the whole place reminded me of a suite in a luxury hotel—elegant, but with the air of rooms that have never really been lived in.

"Make yourself comfortable," Vance said as we entered. I sat down on the leather sofa and he handed me three remote controls.

"I don't know which controls what, but if you hit an On button you're bound to end up with some kind of entertainment. I'll be right back."

I sat fumbling with the controls and finally threw them all aside. I don't own any appliances that come equipped with remotes, and I've always been chagrined by people who do. One more modern convenience to separate me from that portion of the world that's too busy with careers and lovers and happy families to waste time crossing a room to change a channel or shut off a stereo. The living room and kitchen were antiseptically clean and smelled faintly of ammonia and furniture polish. Twice a week, Sergio, a young Brazilian, came to clean. Vance had a deep sentimental attachment to Sergio, even though he'd never met him face-to-face; his name and his accent on the phone had won him over. For the most part, Vance lived in his bedroom—eating, reading, watching TV, working on his computer—but he kept the door to that room locked, so Sergio wouldn't have to deal with the mess. "It's not his fault I'm a slob," Vance had said when I suggested he let Sergio into the bedroom. "The poor kid works hard enough as it is."

I settled back against the cool, soft leather and watched the planes trembling past the window with their cabins dimly lit, one flying cocktail lounge after the next coming in for a landing. I could see it all: the landing gear coming down, the slow, smooth descent, the puff of smoke when the wheels hit the runway. There's nothing more melancholy than watching airplanes finally give in to the pull of gravity, and I felt certain that if I sat there watching too much longer, I'd burst into tears.

Vance's telephone was another high-tech piece of equipment and looked almost exactly like the remote controls. After two attempts, I finally figured out how to use it and called Bernie. Busy signal. Since Bernie had call waiting, he must have been on two lines at once, one of his specialties.

Vance came out to the living room and I tossed down the phone, as if I'd been caught going through his mail. He'd put on a pair of black jeans and an immense green shirt that came down to the middle of his thighs. It was one of those artful outfits that smoothed out his bulges but, in doing so, made him appear as big and square as a major appliance. He'd replaced his tweed cap with a baseball cap that looked uncomfortably tight with his thick, curly hair sticking out around the edges.

"So where shall we go for our drink?" he asked. He went into the kitchen, opened a cabinet, and pulled out a bag of pretzels, which he began to devour by the fistful. "I know, dear, I know, I shouldn't be shoving these in my fat face, but I can't help myself. Shall we go to some trendy gay place where I'll feel ostracized because I'm a fat queen, or to some trendy straight place where I'll feel ostracized because I'm a fat queen?"

"We don't have to go anywhere," I said. "I just thought . . ."

"Oh, no, I insist." He sat down on the opposite end of the sofa, right on top of the remote controls. "Just give me a few minutes to recover. It's been a terrible week. Hectic at work and then all this trauma with poor Carl's awful mother. And if you don't mind me saying so, you look a little shopworn yourself."

"Shopworn?"

"Pale. And black circles even those ugly glasses can't hide. Too much excitement this afternoon, I suppose."

It was tempting to go along with him and leave it at that. I'd settled comfortably into thinking of Vance as the more troubled of the two of us: he had a better education and nicer apartment than me, a serious career, a pension fund and health insurance, but he also had a minimum of two chins. I have no doubt he took considerable comfort in the fact that I was six years older than him. I was open with him about most of my feelings for Gordon, but I tried not to wear any of my other miseries on my sleeve for fear I'd lose my imagined advantage. Still, I couldn't resist at least hinting at some of the strange loneliness that had made me thrust myself on him tonight.

"To tell you the truth," I said, "I got a little down looking at the planes landing."

He finished off the pretzels, crumpled up the bag, and turned to the window. "I know what you mean." He sighed. "It's a lovely view. That's why I spend most of my time in the bedroom, where I can't see anything but an overpass on the Central Artery. But you were a little down to begin with tonight, weren't you, dear?"

"Maybe a little lonely."

"You're spending too much time with that child. Children are depressing by nature because they're still so close to the birth trauma and getting off the tit and all that." He removed his cap and plucked at his mop of curls. For a moment, I was distracted by his unsettling resemblance to my dentist's grandmotherly receptionist.

"There's nothing especially depressing about Benjamin," I said.

"Little Benjamin is another one of those sad boys waiting for his father to acknowledge him. Like you and like me. Boy on the burning deck, all that. Waiting, waiting. Miserable waste of time."

He got up and slumped off to the kitchen. What Vance had told me about his past was that he'd grown up in a wealthy suburb of Chicago and been spectacularly unhappy for all but a few days of his childhood. His mother, whom he'd adored, had died when he was seven, and his father had promptly married a pious, self-righteous woman who resented Vance because, even at age eight, he looked exactly like his mother. Vance's father was a dashing, sporty man who began to pursue an obsessive exercise regime as soon as he found out his son was gay. A civil rights lawyer, he'd sublimated his homophobia in revulsion of fat. He played football, coached rugby, ran marathons, and, the year before, at age sixty, started participating in triathlons. Vance had invited his father and stepmother to his law school graduation. He rented them a suite overlooking the Charles and made reservations at all the best restaurants in town. They'd left for Cape Cod after one night, complaining of the heat and indigestion and leaving Vance with a two-thousand-dollar bill for the unused rooms.

He came back into the living room with a plastic bowl filled with steaming macaroni and cheese that he'd just heated in the microwave. He fell to eating it like a driven man, with no discernible pleasure. "I should offer you some, but I'm starving. Completely famished. I'd love to meet the kid, but children don't like me. They treat me the condescending way they treat portly old-maid aunts. Speaking of which, I had a long conversation with Mary Laird the other day, and she told me they're hiring at the school for next fall. I told her to keep an eye out for your résumé."

Mary Laird was the headmistress Vance had been urging me to talk with for years. "I'm not sure I'm ready for that yet," I said.

"You'd better get ready, dear. The school is about to force her retirement, and there goes your best chance at an interview. If she believes half of what I told her, she's convinced The Learning Whatsis is giving Oxford a run for its money."

"I'll think about it," I told him. "I just feel I should wait a little."

He took out his wallet and handed me Mary Laird's business card. "Don't think too much, or you won't do it. And I can't imagine what it is you imagine you're waiting for."

"I have an awful lot of unfinished business at the moment, between my father and my relationship with Gordon."

He picked up the bowl again and looked across the room at me with a glance that was so uncharacteristically hard and unforgiving, I recoiled slightly. "Unfinished business? You're deluding yourself, Clyde," he said harshly. But then, perhaps taken aback by the tone in his own voice, he smiled and fell back into his more familiar, self-mocking mode. "I'm ready to go now," he said. "One drink, and then I can come home and pass out."

VANCE AND I NEVER DID GO FOR A DRINK
that night. As we were about to leave, he decided he
had to call Carl's mother first to have things out
with her, or at least to confirm plans for their date.
I sat through the first few minutes of the discussion
and then excused myself. Vance's end of the conversation was an embarrassing mix of apology and restaurant review, all in such intimate terms I had the
feeling I was listening at the wall of someone's bedroom.

It was probably just as well; he obviously wasn't
in the mood for spending time with me, and I was
considerably less keen on the idea since he'd broken
the sacred trust of our friendship by telling me what
he really thought of my attitude toward Gordon. If
he hadn't recovered from his bout of honesty so
quickly, I might have told him what I thought about
Carl, Carl's mother, and so on, and the whole house
of cards would have come tumbling down.

I walked out of Vance's building and into the
clear chill of the autumn night. Planes were stacked

up, waiting to land, a line of lights in the sky stretching far out into the harbor. I still couldn't face sitting around my attic rooms, sharing my solitude with an abandoned dog for the rest of the evening, so I decided to walk home. I followed a circuitous route through the concrete wasteland of Government Center and then up the steep, winding streets of Beacon Hill. I usually find the cold New England wealth perched up on the Hill soothing. But that night, it made me feel even more like a castaway. Looking down from the top of Pinckney Street past the town houses with their gaslights and wrought-iron gates and the rows of shedding trees lining the sidewalks, I could see the lights of Cambridge reflected in the river and the cars streaming along the roads surrounding the city.

What I hadn't told Vance was that a few days earlier, on my walk to The Learning Place, I'd gone into a real estate office to get information on available apartments for Roger. The agent, a garishly good-natured woman with extraordinarily tiny feet and blue eye shadow, dragged out a notebook of listings and went through it with me, page after page, until we finally got into a range that seemed affordable. As far as I could remember, I'd never dealt with a real estate agent before, but even so, I could tell she was tossing out every cliché in the profession concerning the location, charm, and amenities of the apartments. "Now, this would be *perfect* for you," she kept repeating, as if we were old friends.

Finally, I had to confess that the apartment wasn't for me.

"For a 'friend'?" she asked, putting the word in quotes to let me know she was onto me.

"Actually," I said, "it's for my brother."

"What a nice thing to do," she said, transfixed by my generosity in the same glazed, inattentive way she'd been transfixed by everything else I'd told her.

I settled on a couple of listings for studio apartments and took down the information. But when I called my father the next day to tell him, he interrupted me before I had a chance to get out more than a few words. "Studio means one room, doesn't it?"

"One big room. With an alcove."

"You expect Roger to live in an *alcove?* He's going to want to entertain, start a new life. You'd better try a different agency."

"Listen, Dad, maybe I should give you a few numbers and Roger can call himself."

"No way. Diane and I want to surprise him by having the whole thing lined up. Try a different agency."

I didn't do that, but I did call the agent and make an appointment to look at new listings. For some reason, I felt I owed it to my father.

By the time I'd walked along the Esplanade and crossed the long, flat bridge over the river and entered Cambridge, I'd worked myself into a state of confusion about my loyalties. It didn't help that I'd entered the city near MIT and found myself surrounded by the school's curious mix of computer whizzes and frat boys, most of whom looked to be high-IQ social outcasts driven to the brink of insanity by impossible parental expectations and a diet of tortilla chips and compulsive masturbation. I decided to stop at the Hyatt Regency and phone Bernie, just to say hello and make a few lewd remarks that might bring on a trace of the amnesia I'd felt in his presence earlier that afternoon.

Architecturally, the lobby of the Hyatt was an amalgam of the Hanging Gardens of Babylon and Las Vegas: a brick atrium lush with exotic plants and flowering trees and coruscating with fountains, glass elevators, lasers, and, for good measure, a rotating cocktail lounge pasted on the top floor. I loved stepping into the bustle of the place with its extravagantly costumed employees and grotesquely overdone floral arrangements and that peculiarly flattering lighting that made everyone from the chambermaids to the alcohol-flushed guests look like extras in a credit card commercial.

I went to a bank of pay phones discreetly tucked into one corner of the lobby and took my place in a row of business-suited men and women, the men all mumbling into the mouthpieces and the women talking loudly. In hotel lobbies, women are usually calling home to check on their kids and the husbands they're about to betray with their business partners, and men are phoning their mistresses to make tortured, whispered promises that it's only a matter of time before they leave their wives. If the religious fruit-cakes in this country are really as concerned with saving the American Family as they claim, they'd be well advised to get off their Kill Faggots platform and start lobbying against pay phones.

A call to Bernie would have been right in the spirit of things, but as soon as my quarter dropped, I found myself phoning Gordon.

It had been a couple of months since we'd spoken, so it was perfectly appropriate for me to call him—which was what I found so depressing about our current relationship. He'd even invited me to his and Michael's pad a couple of times for dinner. The whole easygoing tone seemed designed to remind me that there was nothing unresolved between us, nothing that needed to be avoided or allowed to cool off.

Gordon answered with a burst of the pep-rally enthusiasm that had recently infected his personality. "Clyde! Hi there." To Michael, he shouted out something about the volume on the stereo. "Oh, never mind, he can't hear me. You'll have to yell. We just got the CD of that incredible new singer. Have you heard her?"

I said I hadn't, even though he hadn't identified her. Gordon and Michael had the world's most extensive collection of newly issued CDs, all carefully stacked in specially designed shelves in their living room. Every time I called, they'd just purchased a recording by a chanteuse who, through packaging and a good press agent alone, had manufactured a reputation as "the new Piaf" or "the new Dinah Washington." All had similarly bland voices that gave way to an ear-shattering belt on the last bar, as if lung capacity were equivalent to talent. It always struck me as odd that Gordon and Michael would be so eager to hear "the new Dietrich," let's say, since, as far as I could tell, neither of them had ever had the least bit of interest in listening to the original.

"She's incredible," he said, "has a six-octave range. She's supposed to be the new Yma Sumac."

Someone was bound to be, sooner or later.

Gordon again shouted for Michael to turn down the volume, and this time he did. "So how are you, Clyde?"

This inquiry was made just loudly enough for Michael to hear. Gordon took pleasure in having Michael know that I was still pursuing him, in my own maudlin fashion. You're always more attractive to a lover if you have someone chasing after you, especially someone who'll likely never catch up.

"I'm doing fine," I said. "I was thinking about you because I was over at Vance's—"

"Oh, God. That must have been uplifting. How is he? Big as a house, I suppose."

"He's about to start a diet."

"I'm tired of hearing *that*. It's all about that boy in San Francisco he's so obsessed with. That's what Michael thinks. I heard some interesting gossip about that boy the other day. I'll have to tell you sometime."

I didn't say anything. Now that Gordon was convinced his life was on track, he'd lost all patience with Vance and anyone else who hadn't heaved his excess baggage into the nearest incinerator. He tended to explain away friends' problems with extreme explanations, which, however unlikely, at least relieved him of any obligation to lend a sympathetic hand. I was sure he talked about me in equally disparaging terms, but perhaps I was flattering myself.

I could hear him tapping a pen against a glass impatiently. "So what's up?" he asked.

A reasonable question. "Not much. Marcus says hello, by the way."

"Oh, yum."

Gordon, like everyone else who didn't really know Marcus, was fascinated by him and seemed to derive some mild sexual thrill from the mere mention of his name. I encouraged the infatuation because I knew I earned a few glamour points by association.

Figuring it best to strike with my own agenda while his mind was still on Marcus, I said, "I was wondering if you'd maybe like to have dinner sometime?"

"Not out of the question. Let me check with Michael and see what his schedule looks like."

"Actually," I said, "I was hoping you and I could have dinner alone."

"Why, is something up?"

"Not really," I said. "It's just been a while since we've had much of a chance to talk." In fact, he and I hadn't been alone together since he'd taken up with Michael. It was a risky suggestion. I knew from my own experience that such get-togethers often slide into uncomfortable silences in which the person with the new lover contemplates his good fortune at being free from the old. But I felt such a strong, sudden conviction about seeing him, I couldn't resist bringing it up.

"I suppose we could do it that way," he said laconically.

And then—something I'd completely forgotten about—the coin dropped, making its unmistakable series of clangs and clicks.

"Are you at a pay phone?" Gordon asked incredulously.

"My line's been on the blink lately. . . ."

"Why don't we make it drinks, Clyde, if it's going to be just the two of us? That would probably be easier to arrange."

I'd crossed into the realm of irritant, right up there with someone making calls from a telemarketing company. The pay phone had obviously given my call a note of desperation that reminded him of every reason he'd left. I could see the way his mind was working: If Michael wasn't going to be around to see how desirable even a loser like me found him, it was probably better to plan something less time-consuming than a meal. We set a date, and then a mechanized voice came on, threatening to cut off the call.

"Hold on," I said, "I think I have another quarter."

"Look, Clyde, I have to get going anyway. Dinner's almost ready."

"Dinner?" I checked my watch; it was nine forty-five. "But you always have dinner before six o'clock, sweetheart."

"That was *years* ago, Clyde. Call me and remind me about our drink closer to the day, will you?"

Then he hung up, a frequent ending to our phone conversations when I'd attempted to get too intimate with him.

I felt someone tap me on the shoulder. The man standing at the phone next to me had his hand over the mouthpiece and was looking at me, bug-eyed. "I hate to bother you," he said, "but my call's about to be disconnected. You wouldn't happen to have an extra quarter on you, would you?"

I looked at the coin in my hand and then back at the man's distressed face and decided to hand it over. He thanked me with such exaggerated gratitude, I almost demanded it back.

I went out into the lobby, where the guests were parading around in their uncomfortable clothes, water was shooting up from pools sunk into the floor, and glass elevators were descending from the rooftop lounge. It was such a dizzying display, I sank into a soft leather seat to get my bearings and ponder the whole numbing circus. The more I thought about it, the clearer Gordon's life with Michael became: late nights at the office, long workouts, ten-o'clock dinners. Someone on one of the upper floors let out a tremendous shout of laughter, and one of the glass elevators dropped into view and deposited a load of merrymakers in the lobby.

As I ogled this crowd, I felt someone tap me on the shoulder again, and I looked up to see the man who'd asked for the quarter standing above me, grinning.

"Hey, listen," he said, reaching out to shake my hand, "thanks. It really saved my life. I had this business deal going, and I think that call settled it. I just needed the final three minutes to really seal it. I should have phoned from the room, but they charge an extra seventy-five cents for local calls."

He was a tall man with an angular face that had the tragic pallor that comes from trying too hard for too long to accomplish an impossible task. His dark, deep-set eyes immediately made me think about poor abandoned Otis.

"I should offer to buy you a drink," he said.

"Don't bother," I said. "It was just twenty-five cents."

Later, though, when he invited me up to his room, I had the feeling that it had been a pretty good investment after all.

⌒

When Ben came to walk Otis the next day, I immediately launched into an elaborate description of the emergency meeting at school that had forced me to cancel my plans with him, a description so detailed it could only have been invented.

"It's fine, Clyde, it really is," he said several times. "It was too windy anyway."

"Too windy to go to a record warehouse?" I didn't want him to let me off the hook quite so easily; wallowing in guilt usually helps to assuage it.

He shrugged. "We were going for a hike after. I guess you forgot about that."

I guess I had, so I didn't say anything for a few minutes. He was crouching on the floor, crumbling a heartworm pill into Otis's dish of food while the dog looked on with intense curiosity, head cocked, ears at attention. "We can schedule the whole thing for tomorrow," I said. "I've been checking the weather reports, and it's going to be perfect for hiking around the suburbs. And buying records."

"I can't tomorrow."

"Oh?"

"I have plans."

So far as I knew, he'd never had plans before. Instantly, my desire to go out hiking and shopping with him became violent. "I know you're just trying to punish me, all right? So I'll admit I feel guilty about screwing up our excursion. I apologized, didn't I? If you really want to know, there was no meeting—"

"But I *am* doing something else," he said, cutting me off.

"Like what?"

"Marcus and his girlfriend are taking me to a museum at Harvard. To see meteorites." He looked up at me and snapped his lank red hair out of his eyes. "Sorry, Clyde. We can go next week."

"Does your mother know about this?"

"They just asked me yesterday. I can't remember if I told her or not."

"Well." Certainly it was a good thing that Marcus was coming around some. "You can't bring a dog to the museum, you know."

"I was kind of hoping you'd take him out tomorrow. Do you think you could?"

Otis swallowed the last of the pill and licked his nose lustfully.

ALTHOUGH SHE DIDN'T MOVE IN, SHEILA, like most of Marcus's girlfriends, started living at our apartment in the casual on-again, off-again style of a student. Shortly after Marcus showed up with her at the cookout, a tube of expensive French shampoo had appeared in the bathroom; a thick appointment book—a leather-bound item that looked alarmingly like a Bible—was usually somewhere near the kitchen phone; great pots of stew or pasta sat rotting on the stove for days, meals that had been abandoned mid-preparation in favor of passion. Sheila's official residence was one of those rambling Cambridge apartments with four bedrooms, three baths, two living rooms, and, at any given moment, an indeterminate number of graduate-student occupants. Her exact age, however, remained something of a mystery. I could tell she was so young she'd turn angry and defensive if I dared to ask her, so I didn't dare ask. In a few years she'd no doubt start to feel old and get defensive about that. Only twenty-seven-year-old women answer questions of age with a blunt, numerical response. (It's never a problem to ask a man his age, since most men have deluded themselves into believing they're at their peak from twenty to sixty.)

Most days, Sheila and Marcus showed up at the apartment late in the afternoon, long after Ben had dropped off Otis and headed for home. Despite her gooey, flirtatious interest in Ben at the party, Sheila seemed too wrapped up in his dashing daddy to spend a lot of time socializing with anyone else. So when I heard about the planned outing to the museum, I immediately became suspicious.

Like Marcus, Sheila seemed to exist primarily on coffee. She stumbled in from Marcus's bedroom each morning in the long thermal underwear she apparently wore to bed every night—the pants too small and clinging to her long, flawless legs and the shirt riding up over her belly button—and started the water boiling. Neither of us had much to say to the other, so we usually pretended to be even more sleepy than we were and spent a great deal of time yawning and rubbing our eyes and muttering complaints about the weather and insomnia. In less than a month, our relationship had begun to look like that of a long-married couple, from the lack of conversation right down to the lack of sex.

The morning after Ben told me about the upcoming field trip, I lay on the sofa in the kitchen and, over the top of the newspaper, watched Sheila sweep her hair off her face and commence coffee production. She had unpainted, almond-shaped nails, but the tips of her fingers were always stained with black ink, curious since, to my knowledge, she didn't do calligraphy or write with a fountain pen.

"Mmmmm, cold," she mumbled. "God, another cloudy. Unhh, can't open my."

"I know, I know," I said. "Last night. Wasn't it, though? Freezing."

We suffered through a few more minutes of this and then let ourselves retreat to the comfort of silence. Finally, I gathered the stamina to ask her if she was looking forward to spending an afternoon with Ben.

"I am," she said. "He's got such a sweet, sad expression." She yawned and lifted her hair up off her face. "And I think it's important Marcus and I spend some time with him. Don't you? I mean, he can't really get settled into his dissertation until he's resolved *this*."

"That's true," I said. At least he'd taken the step of telling Sheila about his son, even if he hadn't come around to telling Ben himself. Marcus's options for confidants were limited; like most unusually handsome straight men, he had a hard time finding male peers who were willing to be seen with him, let alone listen to his complaints. "But," I said, "I thought the problem was that he can't resolve *this* until he's settled into his dissertation."

"That, too." Sheila stretched and sighed as if someone were massaging her neck. She didn't appear to think the Ben problem was any of my business. "Your sister called last night." She flipped her mane off her shoulders and shut her eyes. "I told Marcus to write down a message, but he probably forgot."

"Did you talk to her?" Something about the idea of Agnes talking to this sensual woman struck me as tragic and unfair.

She nodded. "She's coming to Cambridge this weekend for a date and wants you to take her daughter to a movie."

That idea struck me as even more tragic and unfair. "What movies are fourteen-year-olds seeing these days?" I asked. Sheila was probably closer in age to Barbara than to me and, being a grad student, could afford to take pop culture seriously.

But she shrugged and yawned. "I'll ask Benjamin," she said.

Later in the afternoon, I walked to Louise's office with Otis in tow. Every few feet, he stopped dead, his paws planted on the pavement. Each time I looked back, he was standing in the middle of the sidewalk, staring at me with a forlorn, not-so-fast expression in his big black eyes. "You're pushing it," I told him, "but it isn't going to get you anywhere." If I could deal with the change in the afternoon program, he could, too.

As I was dragging Otis through the front door of the building, two women stopped me. "We don't allow dogs," one of them said. She was a wan woman with the anesthetized expression of a poet. Cambridge was crawling with brilliant, medicated poets collapsing under the weight of hypersensitivity and inherited wealth. "Several people here have environmental disease," she said. "I don't think you'd want to be responsible for sending someone into an allergic reaction or a coma."

At that moment, nothing would have pleased me more. "I'm visiting Louise Morris," I said.

The women looked at each other, frowned, and walked on.

Louise was stretched out on her daybed under the sloping walls, staring up at the ceiling and running her hand through her hair. She gestured toward the chair behind her desk, muttered Otis's name, and let her hand fall lazily to the floor. As I sat down at the desk, I saw in the open top drawer a sandwich bag with a few roaches and with crumbs of pot clinging to the plastic.

The radiator beside the desk was clanging and gasping out heat, and the window was open, letting in a chilly breeze.

"Should I close it?" I asked.

"It gets too hot," she said. "Then I open it and it gets too cold. I don't know what to do." She sat up on the bed and tried to lure Otis onto the mattress, but he held his ground. She put her elbows on her knees and rested her face in her hands.

"I've been reading your mother's cookbook," she said.

"No wonder you look so exhausted. I thought it was from the pot."

"Probably a little of both. Has Agnes ever made any of the recipes?"

"Doubtful. She doesn't like to cook, and she doesn't like to eat. Food makes her anxious."

"Some of them sound almost tasty, in a musty, church-basementy way. I'm not saying anyone would publish them—I don't think they'd risk the potential lawsuits, for one thing. But it's admirable, Agnes doing all this just to try and earn your mother some posthumous appreciation."

"I don't deny it. But she's getting her hopes up in a hopeless situation." Of course, half of life seemed to consist of getting your hopes up in a hopeless situation, and I hadn't yet discovered what the other half consisted of.

A gust of cold wind blew in and scattered the papers on Louise's desk. I reached out to stop them from blowing away.

"It doesn't matter," Louise said. "They're all disorganized anyway. Like everything else in my life. How does that girl next door expect me to get anything done if she's talking all the time and throwing parties?"

As every other time I'd been there, the office next door was silent. If the wan, comatose woman I'd seen leaving the building was the resident poet, it was hard to imagine her speaking above a calculated whisper.

"Do me a favor, will you, Clyde? Call the geological museum and find out what time they close this afternoon."

"I guess you know about the outing, then."

She nodded. "Ben told me about it this morning, all very casual and oh-by-the-way. I couldn't be happier about it," she said, and lay back down on the daybed.

～

My real estate agent's name was Taff. She had a desk in a bright, storefront office on Mass Ave, halfway between my apartment and The Learning Place. When I left Louise that afternoon, I stopped in for my appointment with her.

I'd fallen into a relationship with Taff in pretty much the same way I fell into all my relationships, from the most superficial to the most intimate. It had started out as a matter of convenience—she happened to be free when I'd initially walked in—and quickly escalated into some strange form of loyalty. I didn't especially like her, and I could tell she wasn't crazy about me. She realized immediately that I was conflicted and confused about the apartment search for my "brother" and would never bring in more than a few hundred bucks for her in any case. There were several other agents in the office with desks near Taff's with whom I probably would have had an easier and more productive rapport. But once Taff and I had made our initial, coincidental contact, I couldn't abandon her for one of the robust, sarcastic women nearby, whom I occasionally heard saying things like: "You're desperate, he's desperate, you might as well make an offer." Then, too, there was a strong component of hostility in my loyalty, possibly because Taff was so closely linked in my mind to Roger; a part of me loved watching her smile harden when she saw me walk into the office.

"By the way," I said that afternoon, "what's Taff short for?"

"That's it," she said proudly. "Taff, just Taff, doesn't stand for anything." Possibly to get back at me, she added, "What's your brother's name?"

"Roger," I said.

Otis was prostrate on the floor at my feet, and at the mention of the name, he sighed. Taff pulled back her head and eyed the dog suspiciously.

Her blatant disinterest, bordering on outright disapproval, made me feel momentarily nostalgic for the days before I'd met this particular mutt and fallen prey to unconditional, remorseless, sentimental devotion. For most of my adult life, I'd been bored senseless by the skull-numbing stories people tell about their pets, stories that frequently sound more like hallucination than reportage: "He lies in bed with us and reads the paper." "He turns on the TV at six-thirty on the dot every evening." "She uses the toilet!" Now, when I was out walking Otis, I frequently stopped to chat with other dog owners and thought nothing of spending fifteen or twenty minutes discussing the minutiae of eating habits, bowel movements, and adorable little gestures made with paw or hirsute, gargoyle ears. I understood exactly what Taff was feeling toward Otis, even as I gave him a protective stroke.

"Roger's the prodigal son," I said. "My father's favorite. To tell you the truth, we never really got along. I'm doing the whole thing as a favor to . . . Dad."

"I'm beginning to get the picture," Taff said. "I suppose he wouldn't settle for anything in your neighborhood."

"I doubt he would."

She closed up the book of listings and shut her blue-lidded eyes for a moment. Her lashes fluttered slightly as she spoke, as if she were trying to force her eyes open but couldn't quite manage it. "You're just going to have to tell him he can't have everything. He can have space or he can have location, but in that price range, he can't have both. You don't have both, do you?"

"Not really. But my father doesn't exactly understand the housing situation in Cambridge."

Her eyes popped open. "Well, then just sit down and have a man-to-man talk with Roger and this father of yours and set them straight! I understand these things, Clyde; I have a sister who's the prodigal son in my family."

"I'm not especially good at man-to-man talks," I confessed. "I'm better at trying to please and then resenting it for a few decades."

She sighed. "I'll try to come up with something. Okay?"

She uttered this last word with a tone of finality that was about as subtle as a shove out the door. It was obvious she was trying to get rid of me, silly dog and all, but for the first time, I felt some affection toward her and thanked her profusely for her help and her advice, even though I had no intention of taking the latter.

When I returned to the apartment that afternoon, Marcus was reheating a pot of stew left over from several days earlier, stirring round and round dreamily with a wooden spoon as he stared out the window. I took a seat at the kitchen table and started to leaf through Sheila's appointment book. It was stuffed with movie reviews, editorials, and news stories she'd ripped out of assorted magazines and papers. In the back, there was an ad for an upcoming sale of men's sportswear at I. Magnin.

"Where's Sheila?" I asked.

"She had to head over to the library, make up for the time she lost this afternoon. She's a diligent girl."

"How was the museum?"

"Oh . . . great stuff over there. Boulders, crystals, granite slabs. I guess everything in life is interesting if you look at it closely enough."

He had his back to me, so I couldn't read the expression on his face. But his voice was more rueful and sad than usual. As I watched him stirring the pot, I noticed that the gas had gone out under it. I was about to say something, but it probably didn't matter all that much; Marcus ate dutifully but without any particular interest. The surprise wasn't that the burner had gone out but that he'd attempted to heat his food in the first place. Sweets were the only food he had a real passion for—ice cream, chocolate-covered raisins, napoleons—but like all men with that passion, he satisfied his cravings furtively.

"Ben's a funny little kid, isn't he?" he asked.

"How do you mean?"

"Quiet, sad. Smart, though; knows more about rocks than I know. It was the kind of thing my father used to do with us, take us to museums, give Otto and me a big lecture on anthropology, celestial navigation, evolution. Then we'd go home and he'd quiz us. I wasn't big on that. Otto retained a lot more than I did. He always did have more staying power than me."

"He even got married," I reminded him.

"He even *stayed* married. His oldest kid starts college next year. He'll probably finish his Ph.D. before I do."

Whenever a person gets honest about his faults, no matter how serious the faults or how dire the consequences, I immediately forgive him. My attitude probably accounts for the fact that I've spent more time confessing my own faults than trying to correct them. In any case, I immediately pitied Marcus his whole overwhelming dilemma.

"You just need to . . ." But I didn't complete the sentence. It seemed cruel to remind him of how much he needed to do.

He turned around to face me, his head at an angle, his hand still clutching the spoon. "I have to tell you something, Clyde. I have to say I didn't really feel anything for Ben. I mean, he's a nice kid, he's bright and all, but I didn't really feel anything for him. I mean, I didn't feel anything *special* for him."

"You just need more time."

"Yeah, I need more time," he said. "I need more time for everything. We're taking him to a play next week." He turned back to the stove and turned off the unlit burner, hoisted the pot onto a trivet, and served himself a bowl of cold stew. "I didn't really like that museum all that much, to tell you the truth," he said. "All those rocks. I've been tripping over rocks for the past ten years. Can't get around the damned things, can't get under them, can't get over them."

He sat down at the table opposite me, lifted up a spoonful of stew, blew on it to cool it down, and ate it. "She's not a bad cook, that Sheila," he said.

CLYDE?"

"Agnes. I thought you were coming to Cambridge this afternoon."

"I'm *in* Cambridge, Clyde. I'm at a pay phone in the store around the corner from you. Unlock the front door for me so I can dash in."

"Why didn't you just ring the bell?"

"I didn't want to stand on the stoop and have Donald see me and think I showed up an hour and a half early because I'm anxious about our dinner. I'd be sending the wrong message."

"Is Barbara with you?"

"She went to buy a tape or a CD or whatever it is with Louise's son."

"With Ben?"

"Mmm. Cute, isn't it? The two of them?"

"I suppose so. Listen, dear, while you're there, pick me up some toothpicks, will you? They're near the paper goods at the front. And a box of saltines, if you would."

"I'm not going *shopping*, Clyde. Please. What if

Donald walked in and saw me standing in line at the cash register? He'd think I was out of my mind."

Agnes looked around the living room nervously. "You don't think he can hear our voices through the ceiling, do you?"

"Oh, Agnes," I said, "just try to relax."

"I'm tired of everyone constantly telling me to relax! I'd like to know what's so relaxing about relaxation. Dad is always telling me to relax, but as soon as I do, he complains that their dinner is late."

I leapt on this comment as if it were money. "'Their' dinner? Whose dinner? Who's *they?*" I kept waiting for Agnes to bring up the subject of Diane so I could talk with her about the situation without having to take responsibility for giving away our father's big secret. But as quickly as she'd let the words slip, she retracted them.

"*His* dinner. His. Don't hold me accountable for every word, Clyde."

I brought her to the study on the top floor and told her to take a seat in one of the big, drunken chairs. She made a move in that direction, but instead of sitting, she started to pace back and forth on the slim strip of floor directly under the peak of the roof. She had on a remarkably stylish navy-blue suit, wool from the looks of it, with a jacket that was pinched in at the waist and gave a flattering curve to her hips. Her hair was as close-cropped as it had been the previous month, but there was a slight auburn tint to it, as if she'd conditioned it with henna. I scanned her body to try and find the piece of jewelry or the overdone accessory that would derail the whole wardrobe effort, but there wasn't one. If I knew nothing about her and had seen her—on the subway, let's say—perhaps I would have seen a trim, manicured woman in an attractive outfit, anxious but coping. But much of what we see in people's faces and forms is what we know about them, and it was impossible for me to look at Agnes without seeing an abundance of context—her divorce, her cookbook, and those big, useless vitamin pills she was trying so unsuccessfully to sell.

"Your suit is beautiful," I said. "It looks wonderful on you."

She stopped in the middle of the floor and tugged at the bottom of the jacket. "What's that supposed to mean?"

"No hidden meaning. The suit is lovely."

"Barbara helped me dress. She was very sweet about it, actually. It's not every day I have a date, you know."

In fact, it wasn't any day. To my knowledge, Agnes had been out on only one other date since Davis had left her. That had been with a chef who worked at a chain seafood restaurant in a mall near her condo. Shortly after they left the house, he'd made the insane suggestion that she calm herself by snorting coke with him. The experience had traumatized her in some profound way, and despite her evident loneliness, she'd turned down all other offers that had come her way.

Initially, Donald had suggested he drive to New Hampshire and take her out to dinner. But Agnes didn't think it was a good idea to let a stranger into her house, especially since she'd heard unconfirmed rumors that a woman on the other side of West-Woods had been murdered two weeks earlier. Rumors of murderers entering the complex and slaughtering residents in their sleep abounded. Some of the condos had security systems so complicated the owners had to take courses to figure out how to use them. A neighbor of Agnes's had started a drive to have the entire appalling complex—parking lots, swimming pool, and all—enclosed behind a twelve-foot fence topped with barbed wire. While the community was working to keep the outside out, there had been several domestic disputes inside that had ended in violence, suicide, and, in one case, homicide.

But watching my sister pace, I realized that she'd probably been reluctant to let Donald come to New Hampshire out of fear that my father would sabotage her date, pounding on the ceiling with a stick or having a seizure on the staircase. It struck me as a well-founded and sensible fear, even if she was unconscious of it.

"You're sure you don't mind baby-sitting Barbara?" she asked.

"Not at all. Is she still up for a movie?"

"Oh, probably. She spends every weekend in that eighteen-screen place near the condo. She buys a ticket and wanders from one movie to the next all day long."

"Alone?"

"Usually. She spends too much time alone. It's hard when you live out in the country."

I hated the thought of my niece burying herself in a cineplex or upstairs in her room with her microwave and her spray paint. The alienated essence of the picture reminded me too much of my own adolescence. I'd been much happier assuming that she had a circle of malcontent friends than acknowledging that she was outside of even the outsiders.

In the next half hour, Agnes and I picked our way through a minefield of topics that produced only minor irritation when we veered too close to anything real or significant. Finally, she collapsed into a chair, possibly out of exhaustion from walking back and forth in the path between the eaves. It was probably ridiculous to think that Agnes and I might ever develop a truly open and intimate relationship; for as long as I could remember, she'd faced life with a subterfuge of coded language. She turned her anger and frustration into reckless anxiety and dolled it up with enough nervous energy to fuel a jet. When I wasn't outright lying to her, I was carefully dodging the truth and reshaping the facts, like the biographer of a heartless Hollywood idol, or attending to a debilitating headache. It was as if all the things we shared, all our common longings, formed a wedge between us instead of drawing us together. If she and I had been able to discuss Diane, Roger, and the whole matter of my father's malingering and manipulation, it probably would have made both of us feel better. But we were holding on to the tattered belief that if we played things Dad's way for long enough, we might finally be graced with his acceptance and love.

Around the time she was due at Donald's, she pulled a wide roll of masking tape out of her handbag, arranged it so the adhesive side was facing out, and asked me to run it over the shoulders and the back of her jacket. She went into the bathroom and emerged ten minutes later surrounded by a protective bubble of Summer Meadow.

We exchanged an awkward kiss, and I told her I hoped she had a nice time.

Then, as she was about to walk out the door, the phone rang.

Agnes put her hand to her chest, as if a ringing telephone, like one of those intrusive special news broadcasts, could only mean catastrophe on a global scale. When there was no immediate response to my hello, I quickly hung up. "How do you like that?" I said. "No one there." I ushered Agnes out the door and down the front stairs before our father had time to redial.

Each time I saw Barbara, her face seemed to have changed. It had to do with the way her skin was settling on the bones of her cheeks and jaw and the way her complexion was darkening, losing some of its peachy innocence. She went to extravagant lengths to alter her looks, piercing her nose and shaving the sides of her head and plucking her eyebrows and slathering on black lipstick, but the changes underneath all the makeup and hardware were the ones that were working subtle, significant magic in transforming her into a young, nearly pretty adult.

About an hour after Agnes left, my niece lumbered into the apartment carrying Otis under her arm, as if he were an especially heavy algebra book. He looked perfectly content, tongue out and ears up. She kissed me on the cheek with the detachment of a dutiful child. She had on her inevitable overalls and flannel shirt and, over those, a waist-length pea jacket covered in lint and animal hair. Her own inky-black hair was shooting out from the back of her head, looking like she hadn't combed it in weeks or, more likely, had just spent a couple of hours carefully disarranging it.

She set Otis down on the floor, and he did one of his best tricks, one I was always describing to my dog-walk pals, a sort of backward hully-gully on his hind legs. Barbara and I looked on with rapt appreciation. I kept a few miniature Milk-Bones in my pocket, treats with which I could bribe him into loving me, or at least get him to hang around me with a panting, pleading look that I could interpret as love when I needed to. I tossed him one of these, and he hurried off to a corner to devour it.

"Did you and Ben have a nice time?"

"It was all right." She took a CD out of the pocket of her jacket and flipped it through the fingers of one hand with great dexterity, as if it were as light and flexible as a playing card. "He told me I'd like this one, but I kind of doubt it. Earl Hines. I'm not big on jazz."

"Why did you get it?"

"I didn't want to disappoint him. It was his attempt to show me something new. He looks up to me."

"You can always return it."

She put the disc back in her pocket. "I don't think so, Clyde. It wasn't that kind of purchase." She stood next to the kitchen sofa and let her body fall onto it in a big heap. "My mother go off on her *date?*" she asked, uttering the word with so much sarcasm, Otis looked up from his treat.

"She did," I said. "She told me you helped her pick out her clothes. Good choices."

Barbara frowned at this and, as if to shed whatever embarrassment I'd caused her, said, "It'll be her luck to get raped or something."

She stretched out on the sofa and rested her head on the knotty-pine arm. From the pocket of her jacket she produced a straw, stuck it in her mouth, and started to twirl it between her teeth. She looked sturdy and resilient lying there and, at least compared with Agnes, remarkably self-possessed and calm. Perhaps it was the self-possession that made me feel I could confide in her in a way I hadn't been able to confide in Agnes.

"Your grandfather . . ." I said.

She stopped twirling the straw and looked over at me expectantly. "Did he call here?"

"How did you guess?"

"I know the routine, Clyde. He was all worked up because Mom was leaving him and his girlfriend for one night. So she made them both dinner before we left town."

"That's what he called about. He couldn't find the food."

"Mom was so nervous she put the plates in the freezer instead of the refrigerator. I saw her do it, but I didn't say anything. Serves him right."

"So you and Agnes have met . . ."

"Diane? The past couple weeks, she's been coming up looking for ice around four every afternoon. Cocktail hour. I think she's living down there, but Mom keeps pretending she's a nurse. She ought to kick them both out. Grandpa's healthy as a dog."

Barbara's attitude toward the whole situation was so pleasantly matter-of-fact, I felt especially foolish at being suddenly and fiercely jealous that she and Agnes had met Diane. I didn't dare mention Roger; since Barbara hadn't brought him up, I preferred to assume he hadn't entered the New Hampshire picture yet.

I pulled out a newspaper and we went through the listings of every movie in town; Barbara had seen them all, some, even the ones she insisted were trash, as many as four times. So far as I could tell, she viewed movies with the same pragmatic contempt she had for school and, for that matter, her mother. Movies were for her a necessary evil, an unavoidable part of life and the insipid cultural landscape.

As a last resort, I checked the listing for the Brattle Theater, the one remaining revival house in town. "I'll bet you haven't seen this," I told her. *"Carousel."*

"Never heard of it."

"It's a musical. Technicolor. 'If I Loved You,' 'When I Marry Mr. Snow.' Sound familiar?"

"I don't think so, Clyde. Maybe we could rent a video."

"The theater has a balcony," I told her.

She brightened at the mention of this architectural wonder she'd heard described but never seen.

The Brattle is a compact theater with a soaring ceiling, busted-up seats, and a screen set at the back of a stage designed for live shows. The place had been renovated recently, but the floor wasn't pitched, the sound system was extraordinarily bad, and the movies were projected from behind the screen. It wasn't easy to see or hear the films, which somehow didn't detract from the lunatic charm of the place. The theater drew big crowds who thought nothing of waiting for hours in long lines in snowstorms or in scorching August heat. The audience was usually made up of fanatical cinema buffs who sat through triple bills eating vast quantities of messy food—meatball subs and fried chicken and entire four-course Indian dinners —while they talked back to the characters on the screen and carried on running political commentaries and lectures on cinema history.

"Weird," Barbara said when we walked in, but she raced up to the balcony, took a seat in the front row, and leaned over the railing to survey the crowd as it filed in. The theater's ventilation system was second-rate, too, and it was always strangely humid, as if the air were saturated with the sweat of all those hungry, excited filmophiles and the steam rising off their odoriferous dinners.

"What do you think?" I asked.

"It's great. Too bad they have to show a movie."

Eventually, the lights went down. The ticket collector, in the middle of a coughing fit, clomped to the front of the auditorium and pulled a set of heavy velvet drapes across the exit door. The film began, ran for a few seconds, and then sputtered to a stop. The lights went back up, and the picnic below picked up exactly where it had left off, with no signs of disappointment or disapproval. Barbara and I leaned over the railing together. "I wish I had something to throw," Barbara said.

"You do not. You're too old for that."

"I know." She sighed and rested her chin on the railing. "It's sad, isn't it? Growing up?"

It was at that moment that we saw Marcus and Sheila stumble into the theater. They were windswept and flushed, perhaps because they'd just run through Harvard Square, and they had the look of people aware of the way they complemented each other's beauty. Marcus was neatly tucked into khaki pants and a denim shirt, an outfit that Sheila had bought for him and had shown to me with embarrassing pride one morning over coffee, before she'd presented it to Marcus. At least she'd broken with tradition by buying him something other than underwear. She had on one of her thermal undershirts and, over it, a tweed sports jacket of Marcus's that was jauntily falling off one shoulder. She scanned the audience, took Marcus's arm possessively, and led him to a pair of seats in the middle of the third row, apologizing insincerely as they stepped over people. When they'd settled into their seats, Sheila flung her curls and nestled against Marcus's shoulder.

"At least my mother got over her crush on him," Barbara said. "That was even more ridiculous than most of the things she does. And I hate that girlfriend of his. I hate her! 'What makes you think they'd let you in?' Can you believe she said that to me? As if it's any of her business. She doesn't even know how many courses I'm flunking."

"I thought you liked Marcus."

"He's irresponsible, Clyde. He's a big baby, just like my father. He wants attention."

"Well." The description struck me as uncannily apt, and I tried to defend my housemate, hoping the defense would prompt Barbara to reinforce her criticism. "Ben's been spending some time with him. What does he think of him?"

"We don't spend all of our time talking about you," she said, piling all adults into one loathsome lump. "Anyway, he knows the only reason they've been spending time together all of a sudden is because Sheila thinks it's cute Marcus is Ben's father."

The lights went down, and Barbara groaned and settled back into her seat. She had her arms crossed over her chest and was squinting at the screen, as if she was having trouble making out the faded images.

I leaned over her and whispered, "Who told you he's Ben's father?"

"Ben did."

"When?"

"How should I know? Today."

Someone in the row behind told us to shut up, and Barbara turned around and gave him the finger. Our muted conversation couldn't have mattered all that much, since the audience downstairs was already commenting loudly on Gordon MacRae's performance as an angel polishing stars on a ladder in heaven.

The portion of the movie I was able to concentrate on was a good deal more dated—glorious music notwithstanding—than I'd remembered. Much of the dialogue was drowned out by the audience, who hissed and booed at every line that defended the wife-beating hero. Not that Shirley Jones fared much better; a roar of laughter greeted every one of her wholesome Technicolor close-ups. Barbara paid attention for about fifteen minutes, then slumped in her seat and fell asleep. I was so distracted thinking about Ben and Marcus, I wasn't sure when she regained consciousness. But for the last twenty minutes of the film—the scenes in which Billy Bigelow returns from the grave to try and make things right for his daughter—Barbara watched attentively. At the end, when the sound track swells with a heavenly choir doing a reprise of "You'll Never Walk Alone," Barbara and I, along with the rest of the jaded audience, collapsed in tears.

We watched Marcus and Sheila file out of the theater and then made our own way out. "Cornball," Barbara said, once we'd reached the street. "That actress gave me the creeps."

"But a nice voice, don't you think?"

"The inside of my head started to itch every time she sang. She reminded me a little of my mother."

It was a clear night, mild for early November, and the streets were crowded with students and tourists walking slowly in loud little groups. There was an acrobat performing at the end of one block and a little man in a Pierrot costume reciting poetry in the doorway of a shop. "Fake Shakespeare," Barbara said, after listening for half a minute. I tried to talk her into going to a coffeehouse for dessert, but she insisted we go back to the house. "My mother's probably having a panic attack because we're not back."

It was almost ten o'clock when we got to the apartment, but Agnes still hadn't returned. Barbara looked around the living room and sank into the one chair that didn't have a light anywhere near it. She crossed her legs, ankle on her knee, dropped Otis onto her lap, and picked up a magazine from a stack beside the chair. It was one of Marcus's unreadable academic journals. Barbara appeared to be studying the table of contents in the dim light. She fingered the tiny stud in her nose, turned to one of the articles, and, to my utter amazement, started to read.

Fifteen minutes later, she slammed the thing shut and threw it to the floor. "It's supposed to be about sex, but it's all statistics. I couldn't tell if it was about people or plants. That Marcus is such a *loser*. I can't believe he reads these things. 'What makes you think anyone would ever let *you* into college, even if you did want to go?' Can you believe she said that? My mother let her get away with it, too, just because she was with *Marcus*."

"I'm not saying Marcus is Ben's father, but how did he find out about it?"

Barbara shrugged. "He figured it out. You act as if it's a big deal. Who cares about their stupid father? You don't think my mother's going to sleep with Donald, do you?"

"It's only their first date."

"That's why she dragged me along—so she'd have an excuse to leave at nine." Barbara picked up another of the dull journals from the floor and started to leaf through it. "I hope she does sleep with him, though. Anyway, it would serve my father right. I guess you know he's getting married."

"I didn't know."

"Everybody's getting married. I don't know why they bother, since they're all so miserable once they do. Do you have any ice cream or anything?"

Agnes returned after eleven, nervous and apologetic. I brought her into the kitchen, where Barbara had fallen asleep on the sofa with Otis on her chest and a bowl of melting ice cream on the floor beside her.

"You had a nice time?" I asked quietly.

"I did," Agnes whispered.

Barbara shot up, wide awake. "Where've you been, Ma?" she asked in the whine of a six-year-old.

"We went back to New Hampshire," she said. "We couldn't find parking around here, and there's that wonderful steakhouse near the condo."

"Sorry I asked," Barbara said, and dragged her mother out the door.

BEN AND LOUISE USUALLY SPENT THEIR Sundays driving through the New England countryside. Ben, with his love of maps and geological surveys and meteorology, planned the trips, figured out the routes, and navigated, while Louise drove. Louise had an indifferent appreciation of landscapes, like someone who chooses a seat near a window with a view, but then turns away from it. The one time I'd gone with them—an ill-advised five-hour marathon drive along the coast of Maine—Louise had contentedly kept her eyes forward, except when Ben reminded her to look right or left to catch some striking vista. Mainly, she seemed satisfied to be with her son in an enclosed little world where no one could get to them.

The Sunday after Agnes's date with Donald, they stopped by the house early to pick up Otis. I waited for them on the front porch, half hidden from the street by the sagging branches of the pine tree. "Remember," I told the dog, "you don't have to do anything you don't want to do. Just call home and I'll come pick you up."

Otis looked at me warily.

I could see Donald through the windows of his apartment. He had on a heavy royal-blue bathrobe that came down to the middle of his thighs, and he was moving around the few pieces of furniture in his living room, dragging the sofa and a busted-up end table into something resembling a sitting area. He caught me watching him, gave a brisk salute, and then quickly rearranged his hair.

When Louise pulled up to the curb, I led Otis down to the street and watched, with a slight flare of resentment, as he leapt onto Ben's lap and began to lick his face. To my surprise, the inside of the car—the arrangement of the incomplete little family, the maps at Benjamin's feet, and the pack of cigarettes on the dashboard in front of Louise—looked the same as always. Somehow, given what Ben knew, I expected a change.

"Newport," Louise said indifferently when I asked where they were headed. "Though really I'd rather be going back to bed for about a month."

"Make sure you're wide awake for your big debut in class this week," I said. "My students can hardly stand the excitement of not having to listen to me for once. Not that they ever do."

"I wouldn't think of missing it. I've got the whole thing planned. Sort of."

Ben unfolded one of the maps and showed me the route he'd charted for them. Traitor, I thought. The door to their private world had been slammed in my face. When they drove off, I waved to Otis, who was looking out the rear window and barking.

Donald had emerged from his apartment and was on the front porch in his bathrobe, cradling a steaming paper cup in his hands. He nodded toward the street and said, "Nice couple, those two," in a genial, lighthearted way that made the accuracy of the comment all the more unsettling. Leaning against the porch railing, he looked out at the street, and sipped. He was wearing a pair of green ankle-high sneakers that clashed so loudly with the bathrobe, and looked so foolishly clownlike, it seemed unfair to even notice them. "What's she doing with Agnes's cookbook?" he asked.

"Louise? I'm not sure she's doing anything."

He glanced up over the rim of his cup with a look of hurt surprise. "She hasn't shown it to her publisher yet?"

"Between you and me," I said, "I don't think she has a publisher right now."

He shook his head. "No kidding. I thought she was a big shot. In her own little way."

"I doubt she has connections in the cookbook world. Maybe," I said with an unattractive smirk I usually manage to keep in check, "we should try to interest Julia Child. I've heard rumors she shops around the corner."

Donald finished off whatever he was drinking, crumpled up the cup, and stuck it in the pocket of his bathrobe. "Now, why didn't I think of that? I guess that's why some people teach at Harvard and some don't. I'm going to ask her next time I see her."

"Next time you see her? You've seen her before?"

He shrugged. "Not for a few weeks, now that you mention it. I help her carry her bags home every once in a while. Not that she needs much help, big lady like that." He shivered and bundled the bathrobe around his chest. "Your sister's got a great sense of humor, Clyde. I guess she'd have to, to go out with a guy like me, right?"

I was still reeling over Julia Child.

He put his arm around my shoulder. "Don't worry—it was a rhetorical question. Agnes and I are going to one of those comedy clubs next weekend. I figure it should be good for a few laughs. I just have to get up the nerve to ask her."

I'd invited Louise to talk to my class because even though she hadn't written a nineteenth-century novel—the ostensible subject of the course, after all—I thought it might breathe some literary life into the room to have a working author say a few words about her craft. It could, for example, drive home the point that a human being had actually struggled to compose the assigned work, a fact that might induce a few guilt-prone students to read a page or two. I felt a special urgency about making sure the students finished the semester having learned something, since there didn't appear to be any intramural romances developing. Nothing helped my teacher evaluations more than an in-class romance. The flirtatious rapport of a couple-in-the-making lit up classroom discussions and added a note of sex and glamour to the atmosphere that the other students could enjoy vicariously. Of course, the lovebirds always stopped attending classes as soon as they began dating in earnest or sleeping together, but they invariably showed up for the last meeting, holding hands and making everyone present, me included, feel as if something worthwhile had been accomplished over the wearying course of the semester.

I'd been extraordinarily, boringly apologetic in inviting Louise, but she'd assured me it was all part of her job and might, in the long run, translate into the sale of a book or two.

"I wouldn't count on that," I told her. "My students don't read the assigned books. A few of them bring in crumbling copies they had in college decades earlier, but most don't even bother with that charade."

"I think you're too hard on them, Clyde. You never read the assigned books when you were in college, and neither did I."

"True, but that was college, a whole other kind of distraction." For the most part, colleges have become companion pieces to day care centers, places to store people for a few years when they're at an awkward, inconvenient age. Your average college student is too old to keep at home and too young to start a career. Most parents are willing to accept that their offspring are in college to learn about "life," a term that's usually understood—correctly or not— as having more to do with sexual experimentation, drinking binges, and shopping than with Euripides. But my students had other options they could have pursued for their Thursday evenings; the fact that they'd voluntarily signed up for a literature class made me feel they had a greater responsibility to do the assigned reading, even if I was secretly relieved when they didn't.

I met up with Louise at her house, and the two of us walked to The Learning Place. It had rained for two days that week, and the fallen leaves were matted into damp pads on the sidewalk. The air smelled strongly, sweetly of decomposing matter. Autumn and the scent of rot always make me feel a special kinship with New England, a sense of security in knowing that my life is rooted in a particular time and place, however shallowly or unhealthfully. Louise, on the other hand, appeared to derive comfort from knowing that she didn't belong in one place more than any other. She was free to float across the whole vast continent with her few pieces of luggage and her son and their portable alienation. How much that would change now that Marcus had entered the picture, I couldn't guess. For days, I'd been longing to talk with her about my discussion with Barbara, but it all seemed so confusing, I thought it best to stay on the periphery, where I belonged. Besides which, Louise's weariness seemed to be increasing, and I didn't want to add to her distress, at least not until after she'd put in her appearance in class.

"I hope you're hungry," I said.

"They bring food?"

"The class has become a banquet, with gossip thrown in between courses to cleanse the palate. Last week, someone had huge platters of sushi delivered during the break."

"Maybe they'll have Indian food tonight. I'm in the mood for a nice hot curry."

Although I was nervous about having her make an appearance (whether for her sake or mine, I hadn't decided), Louise was perfectly composed. She didn't have any notes for the talk she was going to give, but she had brought along a copy of her first novel, in case a reading was called for. And she'd obviously dressed with care. She had on a starched man's white dress shirt, a pair of tight black pants, and tall black boots that laced up the front. Over this, she was wearing a long herringbone tweed coat with the sleeves turned up several times so that the lining formed elegant cuffs.

She'd bought the coat at a thrift shop I'd taken her to; but it was Ben who'd managed to talk the cashier down on the price, from thirty dollars to five. Her hair was tied into a loose ponytail and held in place with a rawhide lace. I was flattered she took the occasion seriously enough to dress for it, and struck with remorse that I hadn't made enough of the class to deserve such a display of respect.

"Whatever you do," I said, "don't let them ask too many questions. I'll intervene if they start hounding you about your bank accounts and medical records, anything too morbidly personal."

"I can handle personal questions. I always answer truthfully but with a grin, as if I'm lying. Everyone ends up confused. Me especially."

"What I mean is, don't let them push you around."

"That isn't one of my weaknesses," she said.

"No," I said, "it isn't." Still, you wouldn't have guessed it from the way she looked walking along beside me, small and slightly hunched, overwhelmed by the heavy coat and the big, gorgeous boots. She seemed to be sinking into herself.

When we got to the school, the sky was dark, with only hints of a rosy glow at the edge of the treetops. All the lights in the mansion were on, and from the front walk, the pillared facade and the golden windows were undeniably impressive, like those of some great institute of learning.

"But you made it sound like a third-rate high school," Louise said, looking up and sighing.

"The education, I meant, not the facilities."

There was a group of seven students standing at the back of the classroom, clustered around the ornate commode, talking and laughing uproariously. As we walked in, they gave a little round of ambivalent applause and then, for the most part, went back to their private conversations.

"I love these low-maintenance groups," Louise said quietly.

Brian, the divorced lawyer, was the first to speak up from the back of the room. "Hey, guy," he said. "We thought you weren't coming." A couple of weeks earlier, in defending a scene in a television movie I had read about but hadn't watched, I'd made my sexual preference clear, and since then, Brian had been addressing me in absurdly jocular ways, just to show there were no hard feelings about my being queer. "We thought we were going to have to run the show on our own tonight, Clyde."

"What's new about that?" I asked, perhaps a little less jovially than I'd intended.

There was more laughter, loud and curiously effusive. I thought I could detect a whiff of something tart and alcoholic—in the laughter if not the air itself. I showed Louise the layout of the classroom, introduced her to Edwina on the wall, and told her I'd make a few introductory comments before I turned the class over to her. She sat down, shyly, it seemed to me, in one of the bow-back armchairs at the side of the room, while I tried to establish my academic credentials by needlessly shuffling around some papers on the table at the front. The crowd at the nightclub in back cracked up at someone's hilarious comment and dispersed just enough to reveal that Tim, the aspiring actor, had converted the top of the commode into a full-service bar, complete with sweating ice buckets, glasses, cocktail shakers, and an assortment of pretty booze bottles. I had a dim memory that in the first weeks of class he'd somehow managed to bring his weekend bartending job into a discussion of Emily Brontë's prose style.

"What can I fix you, Clyde?" he asked, catching my gaze.

"Oh, fix him one of these," Eileen Ash said. "He makes a perfect martini. Then again, who doesn't?"

"I should hold off," I said. "Designated driver, all that."

"Oh, don't be silly. You're off the hot seat tonight. We're going to grill Louise." Eileen advanced toward the front of the room with the delicate caution of someone with only one sip left in the bottom of her martini glass. She had on a pair of slim beige pants that moved in silky ripples when she walked. Since spotting her at the aquarium, cuddled up to her handsome, bearded husband, I'd become more forgiving of her pointless statements in class; if I were as in love as she, I wouldn't bother to read the books, either. She pulled a seat up next to Louise's and, after telling her how honored the entire class was that she'd agreed to come, gave a thumbnail biography of each of the students standing around the bar at the back. "Of course we adore Clyde," she said. "He has a real knack for the group dynamics aspect of it all."

Although I'd hoped that having a guest lecturer would boost attendance, twenty minutes after the official start of the class, only one other person had shown up. Because half the students were already on their second drink I thought it best to get things rolling before anyone passed out or launched into a rambling drunken confession about a love affair or a murder.

I began by making some broad justifications for inviting Louise, trying to tie her work into the tradition of the novels we were supposedly reading, and hauling out, for the grand finale, the tired Jane Austen comparison that's been used on virtually every contemporary writer who hasn't attempted a war novel. I listed Louise's three books, her various grants, awards, and teaching credentials, and I even made the mistake of mentioning that she'd managed to raise a twelve-year-old son on her own while racking up her other accomplishments. The tidbit of personal information was the only one that seemed to arouse any genuine interest.

Before I'd come to the end of the introduction, Dorothea, the retired schoolteacher, cut me off mid-sentence.

"I understand she has a grant of some kind from Radcliffe," she said, "but I was just wondering if she's ever taught there."

"I don't think so," I said, "but we can ask her. You haven't taught at Radcliffe, have you, Louise?"

"I'm afraid not," she said apologetically.

"I only ask," Dorothea said, "because she looks very familiar to me and I thought perhaps I'd met her at a faculty-alumni gathering. I attend them regularly to keep in touch with my old classmates."

Brian shifted in his chair until he was in position to announce his alma mater: "I don't suppose you've taught at Yale, have you, Lorraine?"

"Maybe Clyde should list all the schools poor Louise *hasn't* taught at," Eileen said cheerfully. "Well, I just want to tell you"—she laid a hand on Louise's arm—"that I took a copy of your story out of the library"—she held up a battered hardcover edition of Louise's second novel—"and I thought your photo on the back was absolutely charming. It made me long to dive right in."

The copy of the book was passed around as I finished my introduction, and then I turned the class over to Louise. She took a seat behind the library table, looked out at the students, and gave a nervous laugh. "I don't suppose you allow smoking in here?" she asked in her raspy voice. Most of the class chuckled appreciatively at what was assumed to be a joke. They wanted to like her, and why not? They'd paid their tuition, so they might as well enjoy the show.

Louise got up from her chair and moved to the front of the library table. She leaned against the edge of it, folded her arms, and started to talk, in an effortless but impassioned way, about her work and her career and her struggles at making writing a central part of her life—crying baby, kitchen tables in sublets, long nights of self-doubt. She'd never talked with me about her work in quite this way, so different from her customary self-deprecation. I'd assumed that motherhood had been the guiding force in her life and writing a sometimes profitable adjunct. But sitting there in front of her, another member of the audience, I realized that I'd been misjudging her for years. The books were what stood square in the middle of her life, and all the rest, even Benjamin, fed into them. And maybe not even the books themselves, but the frazzled passion that drove her toward their creation.

Where, I wondered, was my passion? What had I been striving for in all the years Louise and I had been friends? I knew what Marcus meant when he'd said he felt as if he'd been stumbling over the rocks in his path for years. But he had a path, even if he wasn't advancing along it. As I sat there listening to Louise, I began to wonder if I had.

When Louise came to the end of her talk, a hush settled over the room, a comfortable silence during which we could hear the naked branches of the beech trees scraping against the bay of curved windows. I took this admiring quiet as a tribute to Louise, and I felt tremendously proud of my diligent, insightful students.

Eileen Ash cleared her throat and said that she had a question. "And this brings us back to the topic of our course on the Victorian era. Do you think it was so very different then—for the writers, I mean?"

But before Louise had a chance to answer, Mallory White stuck her head into the room. "If you could just hold that thought," she said.

In the past month or so, Mallory's attendance had been sporadic, and I assumed that she'd either worked things out with her husband or found a reliable, energetic lover in his twenties. She'd attended class the week before, so I was especially surprised to see her now. She had on black tights and an alpaca sweater that came down to the middle of her thighs, and as she crossed in front of me, she left behind the fresh-air smell of the cool autumn night.

"For once," she announced, "I have a legitimate excuse for being late. I was reading Louise's first novel, and I was so completely engrossed, I lost track of time until I finished it."

There was a murmur of enthusiasm in the room, and I found myself getting caught up in the excitement.

"As you probably know," Mallory went on, "I've been quite distressed this semester about my husband, so as you can imagine, I was very interested in the part of the book in which you discuss your affair with the married doctor in France. What I'm wondering —and you don't really touch on this aspect—is whether or not you and the doctor spent much time talking about his wife when you were together. Intimate things, I mean."

I knew that much of Louise's first novel was indeed based on her own experience. She'd gone to Paris after graduation to be an au pair and had landed in the middle of a domestic cold war. The mother of the child she'd been hired to care for was having an affair with a family friend, and it quickly became apparent to her that an unspoken part of Louise's job involved covering for the wife. Gillian, the narrator of the novel, finds herself in an identical situation. She becomes involved with the husband, a sweet, portly doctor, partly to assuage her guilt over her complicity in his wife's affair. But in real life, it was more complicated than that. It was true that Louise felt sorry for the cuckolded physician, but her feelings didn't prevent her from taking advantage of him. She didn't start sleeping with him, she'd told me, until after she discovered she was carrying Marcus's baby and was trying to figure out what to do about it. This, Louise had explained to me, had been left out of the novel, not because she wanted to disguise Marcus's role, but because she wanted to make Gillian a sympathetic character.

Louise looked up at the ceiling and then glanced in my direction, a fairly blatant appeal for help. I suspected she looked as distressed as she did not because she couldn't answer but because she could.

"Let's not forget," I said, "that this is a novel. And because it's a novel, we should stick with what's given rather than speculate on Louise's life. The whole world of these characters exists between the covers of the book."

Mallory considered my comment for a moment. "I see what you mean," she said, "and I retract my questions. But my point is this, Louise: did Clyde tell you how I learned about my husband's affair?"

"Not that I remember," Louise said.

Mallory recounted the story that she'd told at least two other times since September, a story that had already been acted out in a role-play session involving the entire class. If this particular telling of the tale was about to evolve into a relevant question, I certainly saw no signs of it. It was with mild satisfaction that I noted the other students shifting in their seats and sighing as they were forced to listen to the recitation of events once more, this time with new details that bore the stamp of exaggeration.

I looked at my watch; over an hour had passed already, and if I took a little control now, it might be possible to get things back on track. I suggested we wait on questions and asked Louise if she'd give a short reading from one of her books.

She went to her overcoat and took out the dog-eared paperback of her first novel and a pair of round, rimless eyeglasses, which I'd never before seen her wear. She hooked them behind her ears, opened the book in what looked to be a random fashion, and started to read a chapter near the end.

In the last third of the book, Gillian's doctor lover sends her to Nice and sets her up in a yellow room with an obstructed view of the Baie des Anges. He's offered to help pay for everything up to the baby's birth, but their agreement is that Gillian will accept responsibility for everything thereafter. And never contact him.

After the emotional tumult of the first sections of the novel, the intentionally farcical comings and goings and the layers of irony, the last third is refreshingly uncomplicated. For all the panache of the beginning, I suspect it's the simple portrayal of contentment at the end that accounted for what success the book enjoyed.

But it was strange and unsettling to hear the words of this youthful, optimistic narrator read in Louise's cracked, hoarse voice. Her glasses pinched the sides of her face, making her look as old as she sounded. She read for close to half an hour, and the class listened in polite silence. Tim was sitting with his elbows resting on his knees, as if he were hanging on her words—or trying to stay awake. When she came to the end of the chapter, Louise took off her glasses and put them into the pocket of her shirt and closed the book. "And that's the end of that," she said quietly.

There was a round of applause, more muted and sincere than the applause that had greeted our arrival, and Eileen wiped at her eyes and indicated to Tim that she wanted a refill. Throughout the reading, Brian had been shifting in his seat, crossing and uncrossing his legs with what I assumed was boredom. But now he pulled himself up in his chair and announced that he'd been impressed with the reading. "Fascinating stuff," he said. "But I've got a question for you," he added, in a tone that sounded harsh and lawyerly. "And I hope you don't take this too personally."

"Go right ahead," Louise said. "I wrote the book so long ago, I'm not the least bit sensitive about it. My own son told me he didn't think much of it."

"I know this is a novel," Brian said, "and all made up and none of it ever happened, total fabrication, but will you please tell me why it is that no one ever thinks about the father? I mean, the father of this kid in the book is just a disposable wallet and not much more. At least, that's what I get from what you read—haven't quite finished the book myself. Forget for a minute about the kid and whether or not he deserves to have a father or even know who his father is. What about the man? It seems to me the whole attitude is that as long as the alimony checks don't bounce, who cares? Dad? To hell with the sperm donor, as long as the tuition gets paid. And just for the record, Princeton is not an inexpensive school. I tried to get him to consider one of the state schools, but that ex-wife of mine talked him out of it."

Louise was sitting on the edge of the table at the front of the room, looking at the floor and nodding as she listened to Brian. A few coppery strands of hair had come loose from her ponytail and swung down in front of her face. She tucked them into the rawhide lace and looked up. She smiled at Brian, rather feebly, but she didn't say a word.

It was then that I noticed there were tears rolling down her cheeks.

I stood up. "I think we should take a break."

"Absolutely," Mallory said. "I was about to suggest it myself."

"I suppose some people are brutes by nature," Eileen Ash said.

Tim quietly asked Louise if she'd like a drink, and she nodded. "Scotch on the rocks, if you've got it," she said.

Brian stayed seated, obviously confused as to why no one was answering his questions. Edwina had retreated to the turn of the century.

We walked most of the way back to Louise's house in silence, listening to the Mass Ave traffic in the distance and the braying of the electric trams circling the Cambridge Common.

"I don't want you to think I'm having a major slip," Louise finally said, "just because I had one drink."

"Two."

"I only had a few sips from the second one. Which just goes to prove my point, so let's not count it."

"Maybe the reading wasn't such a great idea."

Louise sighed and pulled her coat around her neck more tightly. "I hope the class wasn't too mortified."

"My God! The only thing you could have done to please them more would have been to lie on the floor and reenact your baby's birth. Three people told me they thought it was the best class we've had, and Eileen Ash is going to invite you to her end-of-semester party."

When we got to her house, Louise hesitated at the gate.

"Once more around the block?" I asked.

She took my arm as we walked. "It wasn't only that man's question that set me off," she said, "although that settled it, I suppose. It was the book. It was so light and optimistic. So calm. I can't write that way anymore, Clyde. I'd even forgotten I once felt that way. What a foolish girl! Stupid! I was selfish, not telling Marcus. It's true. I could have written him, called, sent a photo. I was wrong, what I did with the doctor. I admit it. I admit it, all right? But my intentions weren't *bad*."

"I know, I know," I said, and reached over to wipe her eyes.

"I thought my kid and I would be enough of a family. I could write my books and scrape by, and I'd have a real purpose. It seemed so wonderful, the idea of having a purpose and a real family for once in my life. The rest of the world could go on its own way and to hell with it. That's what I thought. I was on a bus coming back from the clinic with my test results, people around me talking

a language I barely understood. I couldn't have been more alone—
the pregnant American girl with the ugly feet. But I didn't care,
Clyde. It was the first time in my life I wasn't lonely. I felt protected
from all that. I was going to do everything on my own. . . . Do you
understand?"

"Yes. I think I do."

"And I did. I did it on my own for years."

"But you decided to come east."

"Don't you see?" She was sobbing now, angry at me but leaning
against my shoulder for support. "I had to. I wish Ben's father *were*
some Australian or some Austrian I couldn't find again if I wanted
to. Or some fat French doctor. But he isn't. Who was I to decide
Ben couldn't have a father? And I was a bigger idiot to think I
could just come and fix it all, make it all right."

"They've been going out, haven't they? Marcus is making some
moves."

"Marcus called yesterday to tell me he wants to wait until after
Thanksgiving to talk with Ben. He can't help himself, he's just too
dug in. I wish I could leave tomorrow." She pulled a paper napkin
out of the pocket of her coat and blew her nose into it. "Ben knows
about Marcus, doesn't he?"

"I haven't talked with him about it, but yes, I'm pretty sure he
does."

"You see, it's exactly what I didn't want to happen, to have Ben
waiting on some ambivalent man. It's what I worried about most. I
wish I had had that second drink. And a third, too."

We'd circled the block and were almost back at the gate in front
of the garden. With all of the trees and the vines stripped of their
leaves, the yellow carriage house was plainly visible from the street.
The lights were on in the loft, and as we walked down the path to
the house, I could once again hear the phone ringing in a house
beyond the fence. We entered, and Ben came bouncing down the
stairs. "How was it?" he asked.

"Another triumph," Louise said, and put her arms around him.

ONE OF THE DANGERS OF ENJOYING A THING too much is that you come to depend on it, almost as much as you depend on the things you loathe and dread. Much as I hated to admit it, I'd come to depend on Ben's companionship. In theory, I was happy that Marcus—Ben's . . . father, after all—was getting involved, but I was concerned that ultimately Marcus would let Ben down. Or, to put it another way, I was jealous of their relationship. I felt rejected by Ben, and hurt that he hadn't confided in me, so I spent more and more time rejecting him: making sure I was out of the house when he showed up in the afternoon or, if I was in, making such showy, furious lecture notes as I read *Daniel Deronda* that he didn't dare interrupt me. Pulling back from him had left me ample time to wander around my low-ceilinged rooms, wondering what I was going to say to Gordon when we finally had our drink, an activity that made reading a biography of Jayne Mansfield seem positively productive.

But one afternoon, as I was studiously avoiding Ben, I ran into him.

I'd made an appointment with Taff that afternoon so she could take me to look at an apartment which, she'd assured me, was a promising prospect for Roger, a special listing that she was hanging on to for me, as a favor. But because I didn't want to show undue respect for either my real estate agent or my "brother" by being prompt, I stopped into a store on Mass Ave to peruse a rack of tabloids. I figured it wouldn't hurt to chew on a few scandalous bits of celebrity gossip so I could regurgitate them when conversation ran dry with Gordon. "Did you see the picture of So-and-so?" was all I'd have to say to start him off on a ten-minute monologue on weight gain, plastic surgery, and rumors of homosexuality, drug abuse, and eating disorders among the famous and fabulous.

As I was studying a picture of Jamie Lee Curtis and her mother —an entire evening's worth of material—I looked up and saw Benjamin strolling down the sidewalk. It was a cold afternoon, and he was wrapped in a bulky woolen jacket and a green plaid hunting cap. Stopping at nearly every tree, parking meter, and hydrant along the street to let Otis sniff and leave his scent, he looked ahead with a vague, ponderous gaze as he waited. Traitor, I thought, and went back to the tabloid. But when I looked up again, I saw two boys on Rollerblades speed past and nearly knock into him. They stopped with remarkable speed and grace and, skating backward with the pretty athleticism of dancers, circled around him as they apologized and exchanged a few friendly words. They had on light sweaters and fingerless gloves, all very bright and synthetic, and propped up on their big skates, they towered over Ben. He looked small and weary, a dead-end kid by comparison. Classmates, no doubt, but they looked as if they'd dropped in from some happier, more carefree planet. After a moment, they waved and pushed off. Ben yanked at the leash and continued on to the next meter.

What Vance had said about the odd sadness of children, with their curious mixture of sophistication and innocence, was true, but in some, the sadness was more apparent than in others, closer to the surface. How foolish of me to buy used tango records and musette waltzes for a twelve-year-old when he didn't even own a pair of Rollerblades! I tossed down the magazine and hurried out to the street.

Ben smiled as I approached, a look I chose to interpret as forgiveness for my recent detachment, and Otis stood up on his hind legs and pawed at the air.

I knelt down and popped a biscuit into Otis's mouth. "Where are you headed?" I asked.

Ben shrugged and pointed. "This way," he said, indicating a chilly row of stores, as if that answered the question.

"Me, too. I'm going to talk with a real estate agent about an apartment. You should come along. The agent's fun to listen to, talks a lot, has a lot of opinions. Her name's Taff. Imagine that."

"Taff?" He pulled his mouth off to one side of his face. "Is that short for something?"

"No," I said proudly, "that's it, just Taff, isn't short for anything."

We walked down a long block of dress shops and toy stores and banks and stopped at the corner to wait for the light. Sometime in the past month or so, Ben had grown, and the top of his head was above my shoulder now. I could see his cap bobbing in my peripheral vision. "You're moving?" he asked.

A bus rumbled past, the side plastered with an enormous advertisement for an over-the-counter allergy medicine. "Moving?"

"The apartment you're going to look at. Is it for you?"

He was peering up at me from under the brim of his cap, waiting for me to explain, the tips of his big, inherited ears pushed out by the band of the cap. It was one thing for me to go through with the whole convoluted procedure of trying to get in my father's good graces by hunting down an apartment for his surrogate son, but quite another to discuss it openly with a twelve-year-old whose paternal relations were even more unresolved than my own. "Is it for *me?*" I asked, as if there had been something ambiguous in his question. "Yes," I said, "it is."

I explained to Ben that they didn't allow dogs in the office, and told him to wait outside. Taff was sitting at her desk, chatting on the phone with a customer in the tone of malicious good humor that seems to be required of real estate agents. But she had on a blue cashmere muffler, just to show me, I suppose, that my tardiness hadn't gone unnoticed, that she'd been sitting around waiting for me, dressed and ready to go. She indicated a seat by her desk and had me sit there for at least five minutes while she finished the call, rifled through the drawers of several filing cabinets, and then disappeared into a curiously empty-looking room at the back of the office. She had a dozen or so photos lined up on her desk, smiling, gap-toothed children floating in the azure ether of the professional photographer's studio, and friends or relatives unfairly preserved for eternity in a moment of bloated inebriation at some seaside picnic. The human spirit, in all its wonder, seems to insist upon personalizing a work space, which only makes it sadder that everyone's family photos are interchangeable with everyone else's.

On the far corner of the desk was a hardbound copy of the most recent translation of *Crime and Punishment*, with a bookmark stuck somewhere near the middle. I'd been meaning to read this new edition for some time but had been distracted by my craving for true-life stories, unburdened by what Louise called the obfuscations of art. I picked it up and started to scan the inside flap. "I'm reading it for my book group," Taff said, coming up behind me. "This translation's much more lucid than the old Constance Garnett. Well, I suppose no one reads that anymore."

"I guess not," I said feebly.

"Ready to go?"

I pointed to Ben through the window and explained that he was coming with us. "I hope you don't mind," I said.

"I don't see why I would." She had a coat folded over her arm, a fuzzy item the exact lapis lazuli shade of her muffler and her eye shadow.

"It's slightly complicated," I said. "The thing is, he doesn't really get along with Roger, either. In fact, I don't like to mention his name in front of him. He thinks the apartment is for me, if you see what I mean."

"Well, really, Clyde, I don't care who the apartment is for or who he is. I made an agreement to show it to you, and that's what I intend to do. I suppose he's your 'nephew'?"

"I suppose so," I said.

The apartment was in a brick building a short distance outside Harvard Square. I frequently walked past it when I was heading to The Learning Place and more than once had admired the shady courtyard that led down to the front entrance. We walked up five flights from the lobby, a climb that left Otis and me winded but seemed to revive my nephew and my real estate agent. "No elevator?" I puffed.

Taff looked over her shoulder at me as we ascended. "None of that, thank God. Noisy and always breaking down, people getting stuck in the hateful things for hours at a time. Anyway, if there were one, the rent would probably be double what it is."

The apartment was a one-bedroom, but considering the size of the bedroom, the definition was more technical than practical. Taff, Ben, Otis, and I peered into the tiny, dark room from the entry hall. High on one wall, there was a window the size of a place mat, and dishwater-colored light was leaking through. Taff shuddered. "Isn't it charming? You could do a lot with a room like this, Clyde."

She didn't need to convince me. Although it was smaller than my own bedroom, the high ceiling made it seem roomier and considerably less claustrophobic. And there didn't appear to be any water stains on the walls.

"But here's the main attraction," Taff said, leading us into the living room. She noisily hoisted up a set of venetian blinds, and the room was flooded with sunlight. "This view is priceless. The Cambridge Common down here, Harvard Square over there. There's even a smudge of the river from this angle. You might want to make this the bedroom, and use the other for your study."

"When is it available?" I asked.

"January. So you'll have to let me know soon."

When I went in to check on the kitchen, I heard Ben ask her if they allowed dogs in the building.

"I don't think so." The shade dropped loudly. "Now, are you going to be living here, too?"

I ambled around the rooms, trying to imagine what Roger—or my father, at least—would think of them, weighing the pros and cons from a variety of aesthetic and financial angles. But since I had no idea what kind of furniture, if any, Roger owned, or what kind of income, if any, he had, I found myself picturing my own ragtag collection of sofas and chairs and functional, ugly bureaus tucked into the corners and my own ragtag life lived in the solid rooms.

"You're an expert on apartments," I said to Ben as we walked back to the house. "What did you think of it?"

"It's okay."

"Just okay?"

"More crowded than what you have now."

"In some ways. But it would be just one person, don't forget."

He mulled this over in silence as we crossed Mass Ave and entered the grounds of the Harvard Law School. "She's not sure they allow dogs," he said.

"Well . . ."

"Are you mad at Marcus?"

"No, no. Nothing like that," I said. "The truth is, it's not definite I'm moving. I've been looking around, that's all." The truth was, acting the part of apartment hunter had made me think that it might be possible to take some action, if not right away, at least at some time before I entered a nursing home. For a few minutes there in the compact kitchen, it seemed not only possible but desirable.

"Are you mad at *me?*"

I turned to look at him, but he was staring off at a group of students gathered in a circle, smoking cigarettes outside one of the libraries. "No! Of course not, sweetheart." And then, immediately regretting the "sweetheart," I tried to chew it up and swallow it in a fit of coughing. I took a handkerchief out of my pocket and blew my nose needlessly. "Why would you think that?" I asked gruffly.

"I don't know. You're not around much anymore."

"You think I'm avoiding you, is that it?"

He shrugged.

"I'm just happy you're spending more time with Marcus, that's all."

"Because he's my father, you mean?"

He stopped at a spindly, trussed-up tree that had been planted the previous spring. Otis lifted his leg and gazed up at us, looking for approval. Ben had put the question so simply and honestly, I didn't see any alternative but to answer with equal simplicity and honesty.

"Yes," I said. "I suppose that is why."

"But what does that have to do with it?"

"I figured you had enough going on at the moment, enough things you have to sort out."

"It's not like he's even told me or anything."

"He will. He's waiting."

He nodded and looked down at his dog. "What's he waiting for?"

"Oh. He's tangled up in a lot of unfinished business at the moment." So far as I could tell, Marcus had been tangled up in uncompleted projects, unfinished business, and unsettled relationships since birth. But it wouldn't do to get too critical of him, especially with his offspring. "It's a big adjustment for him, the idea of having a son. He's only known for a couple of months."

"I guess it's a bigger adjustment than for me, since I've always known I had a father, even if I didn't know who he was."

A group of militant dog owners had congregated on the green in front of the law school library. Harvard kept putting up signs about leashing and curbing, complete with cartoon drawings of defecating canines with lines slashed across them, but the owners kept ripping them down or smearing them with feces. I was sympathetic to the cause, but the dogs were immense and as brutally aggressive as their owners. "We'd better walk around," I told Ben. "Bullies and rogues." We dodged a black Lab and a rottweiler doing battle over a Frisbee. "If you don't mind me asking," I said, "how did you figure out about Marcus?"

"I could sort of tell," he said, "from the way he was avoiding me."

"That's the giveaway, all right. I could talk with him, if you like. Tell him you know. It might make it easier for him."

"I don't think so, Clyde. I don't want him to feel cornered into anything. The day we went to the museum, he kept telling Sheila about some old girlfriend who trapped him into letting her move in. He mentioned her three times."

When we got back to the house, Ben walked around the oddly shaped rooms, checking out the paneling and the cut-off closets. "The other place is nicer," he said.

"Yes, but it's smaller."

"But it would be all yours. You wouldn't have to share it with anyone."

"They might not allow dogs."

"You can't decide for that reason. By January, Louise and I might be back in California."

HAVEN'T HEARD FROM YOU IN WEEKS," my father said. "What's happening with Roger's apartment?"

"It's very promising," I said. "The real estate agent promised me there isn't a better one in the city for that rent. She promised me she's going to keep it for me."

"Too many promises, Clyde. Roger can't live in a promise. I take it you haven't bothered to get hold of the lease and all the rest?"

"I haven't had a chance."

"Too busy with that fake school?"

"That must be it."

I'd told Taff that Roger would take the apartment and had even given her a deposit. I'd spent a fair amount of time fantasizing about the place, but in a guarded, furtive way, as if I were coveting my neighbor's wife—or husband. I had to keep reminding myself the apartment was rightfully Roger's and that I'd already told my father too much about it to claim it for myself. Besides, moving into it would mean a whole shift in identity, and I wasn't sure I was ready for that.

"Look, Clyde," he said, "if you can't get this thing moving, we're going to have to work on it ourselves. Just give me the agent's name, and I'll do all the rest on my own. Not that I have the time. Not that I wouldn't appreciate a little cooperation from you."

"I'll have the whole thing settled right after Thanksgiving. I'll send the papers up. You've got nothing to worry about."

"It better be *right* after Thanksgiving."

"It will. What are you doing for the holiday?"

"Thanksgiving? What have I got to be thankful for?"

"I don't know. Maybe Diane."

"Well, that must explain why we're having dinner together. Your sister wouldn't think of inviting me. Not this year. She's too caught up with that goon. He was here the other night. Big, sweaty guy. She didn't even bring him down and introduce him to me. What's she—ashamed of me?"

"I better get going," I said. "I have a headache that's about to crack my head open."

"I'm sick of hearing about those headaches," he said. "Every time I talk to you, you've got a headache. It isn't normal."

Normalcy was one point I wasn't about to open for debate, so I accidentally tripped over the phone cord and disconnected the line.

As instructed, I called Gordon a few days before our date to arrange a time and place. He suggested we meet at a restaurant near his gym called Yellow Fin.

"You've heard of it, haven't you?"

"Sure, sure," I said. "Great seafood."

"I'm afraid I can only stay for a drink," he reminded me, as if I were planning to kidnap him.

Since graduating from law school, Gordon had crossed the river into Cambridge half a dozen times at most. He used to claim he found it a pleasant, stimulating place to live, but now, even setting foot inside the city limits depressed him. Cambridge was too leafy, too genteel, too collegiate, too straight, too square. Whenever he mentioned any of this, I denied it adamantly, not because I disagreed with him, but because I knew he wasn't criticizing the city's character so much as my own. I'd never been to Yellow Fin, never even heard of it. It was a safe bet I'd feel totally out of place there, but I wasn't about to suggest we meet in a dingy Cambridge watering hole where I'd fit right in.

It is true that there's a drab, earnest appearance people get when they've lived too long in a university town, a look that comes from living too much in the mind, or at least from living around people who live in the mind. Rock musicians and movie stars touring Boston often stay in Cambridge because they can walk the streets without being bothered. It's not that Cantabrigians are cool and sophisticated; it's just that they're more likely to hound Edward Said or Doris Grumbach for an autograph than Sharon Stone.

The Monday before Thanksgiving, I showed up at Yellow Fin ten minutes early. It was a gleaming place, all glass and mirrors, and unlike the restaurants Vance and I frequented, it had been designed with immense windows that made you feel as if you were dining in the middle of traffic. You could sit and watch the world go by, and more important, the world could watch you. I took a seat at one of the dime-size tables near the windows and studied my reflection in the glass, trying to get a grip on myself. My shirt, a striped thing in assorted shades of light blue, was a closeout-sale mistake, but there was nothing I could do about it now. The crowd behind me was made up of fairly young people who, judging from appearances, were used to spending money they probably didn't have. There were several tables of gay men talking in loud groups, and five or six tables with well-heeled straight couples admiring each other through candlelight, in that brief moment of radiant beauty that heterosexuals enjoy for a few months right before they get married.

When the waiter came to take my order, I told him I was waiting for a friend.

"A what?" he asked.

"A friend. I'm waiting for a friend."

"I'm sorry, I can't hear you."

He was a squat, homely boy with an expensive, wedge-shaped haircut and one of those superior attitudes that come from having a lover other people desire. I often had trouble making myself heard by this kind of waiter, and worried that Gordon would arrive in the middle of a display of my social ineptitude, I practically shouted, "Martini, martini," to try and get rid of him.

A few minutes later, Gordon came around the street corner with his gym bag clutched in his hand and a worried, distracted expression. I'd had a couple sips of my drink, just enough to make me feel a warm flush of nostalgia creep over me at the sight of him. Although he'd transformed himself into a five-foot-six-inch Adonis in the past couple of years, he still had the flat-footed, lazy walk he'd had as a plump law student. Gordon thought nothing of working out vigorously for an afternoon, riding a stationary bicycle for half an hour and climbing a phony set of stairs for forty minutes, but he complained bitterly if he had to do any genuine exercise like walking.

He stood by the maître d's stand and loosened his tie, then scanned the room for a full minute, scratching his neck with upward strokes of his fingers. When he spotted me, he waved enthusiastically and sauntered across the room with his gym bag slung over his shoulder.

"Not late, am I, pal?" he said. "I expected to see you at a table in the back."

"I thought I'd shock you."

I stood up and hugged him. It was the first time I'd seen him alone since he and Michael had moved in together, and I suppose I held him a little too close and a little too long, for I could feel him pull away—subtly, as if he'd just realized I had a head cold.

He was wearing a charcoal-gray suit and a white shirt with thin red stripes, which, despite the fact that it was the end of the day, looked like it had just been taken out of the cleaner's box. As he took off his jacket and draped it across the back of his chair, I couldn't help but admire the perfect symmetry of his flaring shoulders and rounded chest, even though the whole package looked too flawless and prefab to be sexually attractive. His hair was damp and his face was rosy; either he'd just scrubbed his skin under a hot shower or had had a bracing sexual encounter—or perhaps both at once.

When the waiter came to the table, Gordon smiled broadly, revealing the most discreet set of braces I'd ever seen. They discussed the virtues of various bottled waters for what felt like a good five minutes, while I lapped at the martini.

"As usual," I said when we were alone, "you look terrific."

"Aw, Clyde, I can always count on you for a compliment," he said. "You're a loyal fan."

"But when did you have the braces put on?" I asked. "I thought your teeth were perfect."

Gordon's smile faded. "I don't have the date on hand," he said coldly, and glanced around the restaurant.

I instantly realized my mistake: if I was going to be rude enough to notice, I could at least have had the sense to keep my mouth shut about it.

"Well," I said, "I guess what matters is that they'll be off soon."

"Three years," he said.

"Ah. Well." I sucked on an olive. "Good workout, sweetheart?"

This loosened him up considerably. He launched into a long discussion of his trainer and a whole new set of exercises he was doing to balance out the development of his shoulders and his pecs, as well as a specially designed program to reduce stress on his rotator cuffs and hip joints. I sat listening, mesmerized not so much by what he was saying as by the detail with which he was describing it, and by his conviction that I would be interested. He reminded me of a friend I'd had who loved to describe his solitaire hands, card by card.

When he'd finished reliving his routine, he reached into the open neck of his shirt and flicked at his chest with his fingers, explaining as he did that he'd recently removed most of his body hair with a depilatory that had left his skin irritated and raw. "It's been hell wearing clothes for the past couple days," he said.

"No kidding. Exactly how much hair have you taken off?"

He shrugged. "Pretty much all of it. What's the point in working out if you can't see your progress through the fur?"

"I've often wondered that myself. But I mean, you're not trying to say you took off *all* your body hair, are you?"

He smirked at me, smug and flirtatious. It was one thing for Gordon to invite a question like this, but another for me to ask it. He sat back while the waiter delivered his water.

"When did you start drinking?" he asked.

"Oh, Gordie, come on. I'd hardly call one drink drinking."

He raised his eyebrows and sipped at his water. "Whatever you say."

Gordon's mother was an illustrator who'd made life miserable for everyone in his large family for decades, first by staying falling-down drunk for twenty years and then by turning self-righteously sober. Outside of the occasional weekend vodka-and-poppers binge, Gordon rarely drank or did drugs. I felt like a sloppy lush under his scrutiny. "It was a momentary lapse in judgment," I said. "Tell me all the news, sweetheart."

"There's not all that much to tell," he said, and looked at his watch. It was obvious he was beginning to regret having agreed to spend time with me and had started to count down the minutes until he could leave. I myself was beginning to wonder why I'd suggested the get-together. It wasn't as if I expected our dissolved relationship to spring back to life. It wasn't as if I even wanted that. "Michael and I are going to Brazil in January."

"So I heard."

He looked up at me with sudden interest and smiled without revealing his teeth. He loved hearing that people were talking about him. Unlike me, he usually assumed they were saying flattering things. "I didn't know Vance knew about that."

Gordon preferred to think that Vance was my only friend, the only person who ever invited me out anywhere, the only person with whom I ever went out. While this was nearer to the truth than I cared to admit, it wasn't the whole truth.

"I went to dinner at Drew and Sam's a while back," I said. "They mentioned it."

"Oh, that," he said, and poured more water from the tall, slim bottle. "Mikey and I almost went to that, but we had another invitation we couldn't get out of."

I took a sip from the wide martini glass and let the thick, icy drink burn along my throat and splash down in my empty stomach. "They showed a video," I said, "of their trip. Awfully informative."

Gordon slammed his water glass on the table and stared across the flickering little candle with a degree of fury that I wasn't prepared for.

"All right," he said, "so it wasn't a *National Geographic* special. It wasn't a three-hour documentary on saving the rain forest. Well, guess what, Clyde—it wasn't supposed to be."

"I didn't say a thing."

"You didn't have to. I saw the video, and I can imagine what your opinion was. It wasn't a UN peacekeeping mission; it was a vacation." He knocked back the rest of his water and glared at me.

"All I said, sweetheart—"

But he wasn't about to let me finish. "At least have the decency to accept responsibility for what you meant. You don't have to be so critical of them just because they know how to enjoy themselves. Just because they don't live in some hovel in Cambridge with a straight man who's a colossal bore, no matter how pretty he is. They work hard, and when they take a vacation, they like to relax. Not everyone considers sitting in an attic and rearranging your collection of antique fans a good time."

Gordon's face had grown red and puffy. He was leaning over the table, glaring at me challengingly, so full of emotion, he'd forgotten to wrap his lips over his braces. I looked down at the table contritely, thrilled that I was still able to provoke so passionate a reaction. It was only in these moments of unbridled anger that the real Gordon, the Gordon I'd lived with for two years, emerged from imprisonment inside the polite, sculpted lawyer with the scrubbed face. And it was only in these moments, when his guard was off duty, that he allowed himself to acknowledge that we'd ever been lovers and that there was still some kind of connection between us.

"And another thing," he said, a good deal more quietly. "I wish you wouldn't call me 'sweetheart.' It's embarrassing. You're not my sweetheart, and I'm not yours."

I'd had enough of my drink to let myself lean toward him and reach across the table for his hand. "There, Gordon, there is where you're wrong."

He'd slipped back into control and looked around the restaurant stiffly, trying to make out exactly who was watching us and how he could catch the eyes of those people who weren't. But if people were glancing in our direction, it was only to make sure we were looking at them. "Our relationship has been over for two years," he said calmly. "Three, if you count the last year we lived together."

"Now, just a minute . . ."

"You never made a real commitment to me then, I happen to know you weren't faithful, and I was under the distinct impression that if I hadn't ended the relationship when I did, you would have found some excuse to end it yourself. If you want to be honest, you'll admit that you only really fell in love with me after I walked out. It's ridiculous."

What had appealed to me as passionate honesty moments before had crossed into dangerous territory. I could feel Gordon clawing at the protective skin of my defenses, and I tried to change the subject, but combined with the martini, my anxiety made me slur: "Now, about your worgout . . ."

He waved off the topic and adjusted his suspenders. "You just can't deal with rejection, Clyde. I'll tell you what Michael thinks."

"Michael," I said. "Let's not drag him into it. This is between you and me."

"Nothing's between 'you and me' anymore, Clyde. You just have rejection and love confused in your mind. That's what Michael says. Michael says it has to do with being rejected by your father and seeking his approval by trying to work it out through me. I can't remember all the ins and outs, but it's some theory like that." He stretched his neck and looked around for the waiter. "Where did he go off to? I promised Michael I'd be back before nine."

As mortifying as it was to think that he and Michael had discussed my neurotic behavior, it was worse to think that Gordon cared about it so little he couldn't even remember the demeaning specifics of what had been said. "I thought Michael was an accountant," I told him. "What's he doing dirtying his hands with psychology?"

"He's done a lot of twelve-step work. And let's not get into a whole dismissal of twelve-step programs, all right?"

He motioned for the check and sat back, rearranging the casual drape of his loosened necktie. I finished off the rest of my drink and felt a warm rush of blood to my face. I began to long for a bottle of aspirin.

As soon as the check arrived, Gordon returned to affability. "How is your father, anyway? Still milking that sore throat?"

"He's doing pretty well. He's got a new girlfriend."

"Well, at least someone's getting on with his life."

Outside on Columbus Avenue, Gordon turned up the collar of his suit jacket. He wasn't dressed for the weather, probably because all that bulky winter paraphernalia hid too much of his new form. Everyone I know who gets seriously involved in his gym membership starts to contemplate a move to southern California, where the weather is more conducive to wearing tank tops.

"Oh, I knew there was something I wanted to tell you," he said cheerfully. He looked over at me and scanned my body from top to bottom, the first time he'd really looked at me all evening. "That coat is very flattering. Anyway, it's about Vance. Or about that imaginary boyfriend of his."

"Carl?"

"Right. Turns out—and this is from a very reliable source— Carl is married, two kids, been living in San Diego for years now. Isn't gay, never was, whole thing is Vance's delusion."

"That can't be," I said. It had become quite cold, and I pulled a scarf out of my pocket and wrapped it around my neck. I took off my glasses and wiped them against my coat. "Vance would know by now. He spends the majority of his time with Carl's mother."

"Maybe she doesn't want to give up her meal ticket. And what makes you so sure he doesn't know? You think a little thing like a wife and two kids would prevent him from mooning over the boy for the rest of his life? You and Vance, Clyde—no wonder you two get along so well."

He adjusted the scarf around my neck in a tender sort of way, a safe gesture now that we were going our separate ways. He stepped out into the street and raised his arm; a taxi made a dramatic U-turn and stopped in front of him. "Michael wants to have you over for dinner soon," he said. He opened the door of the cab. "I'll have him give you a call. What are you doing for Thanksgiving?"

"Dinner with Agnes and her boyfriend."

"Boyfriend! Everyone's in love." Then he got into the cab, waved, and sped off.

I'd wandered down Columbus Avenue for a few blocks before I realized that I had no idea where I was heading and had landed smack in the middle of a residential neighborhood. The martini, which had warmed me up in the restaurant, had started to make me feel chilled and hungry. I couldn't remember the last time I'd eaten. A kind of panic came over me, a conviction that if I didn't gobble down some food immediately, I'd pass out on the sidewalk. But there were no signs of any restaurants, just row after row of restored brick town houses, their lights spilling out of the windows and onto the sidewalk.

I headed toward Tremont Street, where I vaguely remembered there were rows of restaurants. I passed one after the other and peered into the windows, but I couldn't imagine walking in and sitting down, no matter how hungry I was. Inside, groups of friends were laughing, couples sighing. The mere thought of slipping into one of those places and trying to be inconspicuous made my eyes start to itch. Michael was probably right in his estimation of my psyche, but why did it have to be so obvious, even to an accountant? What's the point of having defenses if they're transparent?

I walked on and on, weaving in and out of the city streets, peering into one restaurant after the next. Finally, I ended up in Cambridge, where I slipped into a greasy sandwich shop. There was a line of bleary men waiting to order their sloppy solitary meals, and I took my place at the end of it.

OF THE HOLIDAYS DISCUSSED IN THE NOTES on my mother's recipes, Thanksgiving was the one that received the most attention. " 'Candied Potato Chips': A wonderful Thanksgiving treat to serve the gang when they first arrive and are too excited to sit down." "I love to give these unusual 'Raw Turkey Nugglettes' to the children, grandchildren, and 'cousins by the dozens,' right before I tuck them in at night." "It looks like squash, it tastes like squash, no one in the happy family will guess it's really leftover bread heels. A 'Soak 'n' Serve' surprise!"

The reality, of course, was never as bright as the fantasy depicted in those notes. There were no "cousins by the dozens," there was no gang and, certainly, no family that could reasonably be described as happy. For years, I'd been avoiding holiday dinners by claiming I was spending the day with "friends," a lie no one dared ask me to elaborate on. In fact, I spent most holidays alone, sitting through multiple showings of the longest movie I could find, usually a garish, unimaginably dull epic set in another century. I found it a comforting, surprisingly festive activity.

After my disastrous drink with Gordon, I stayed locked up in my attic rooms for several days. My reading had degenerated from movie star biographies to the lowest form of printed matter— memoirs by TV celebrities, only a small step above greeting cards. Half the celebrities I'd never heard of. Not that it much mattered: my impression was that, apart from a melancholic, desperate identification with the paper-thin characters they portrayed in front of the cameras on a weekly basis, most of the people in question had no idea who they were. But as Agnes might have said, the books helped pass the time—the time until I turned the apartment over to Roger and . . . Dad, and Marcus finally broke down and had his conversation with Ben.

I should have been reading for my class, but I wasn't even able to skim the first few pages of *Vanity Fair* without developing a migraine. My timing couldn't have been worse; after Louise's visit, three or four students were actually showing interest in the books listed on the syllabus. Somehow she'd broken through to them— or maybe they'd been motivated by dread of being dragged through yet another rendition of Mallory's tale of marital woe.

I love *Vanity Fair*, but considering its length, I'd stuck it onto the end of the syllabus almost as a joke. Among other factors, attendance usually dropped precipitously during the holiday season, and those students who did continue to come typically complained that they had too much shopping and cooking to do to bother with reading, as if they ever did bother with it. Fortunately, Dorothea had done her senior thesis on Thackeray forty years earlier, and the subject was fresh in her mind. She'd be more than happy to take over the class, exactly what she'd been bucking for the entire semester.

Rain was predicted for Thanksgiving Day, and when I woke that morning, the sky was slate gray, with low storm clouds gathering in the west. Louise and Ben had gone to Cape Cod for the weekend, leaving Otis in my care. He was under the blankets with me, tangled up in the sheets, a furry, breathing hot-water bottle. Most mornings since the weather had turned cold, I'd wake to find him under the covers, wrapped around my legs. "Move over," I'd say, and nudge him, hoping he'd stay put, almost exactly the routine I'd had with Gordon.

I had the house to myself for the rest of the weekend, not that I knew what to do with it. Despite Marcus's reluctance, Sheila had managed to drag him to New York to visit some friends of hers at Columbia. "She's rushing things," he'd said a few afternoons before leaving. "I don't like it."

"Rushing things?" I said. "I thought she was 'the one.' Besides, she practically lives here."

"True. But I don't like the idea she's so eager to have me meet her friends. Once you get hooked into that friend network, you're backed into a corner. The problem with a woman her age is that she's always got friends, friends everywhere. Why do they always have to have so many friends?"

In the end, though, he'd gone to New York, possibly because the alternative plan was staying in Cambridge, taking care of his son's dog, and having dinner with Donald, Agnes, and me.

It was disconcerting and strangely dislocating to stand in the gloomy entryway of the house, dog by my side, bottle of cheap champagne in hand, and knock on Donald's door. Only a few months earlier, nothing would have seemed less likely to me than spending a holiday in that grim apartment. It was even stranger to have my own frantic sister open the door, grinning, unusually composed, a pair of pot holders shaped like enormous fish stuck on her hands.

"I had a feeling you'd be late," she chided. "I told Donald to plan on it." She came into the hallway and planted a kiss on my cheek, knocking my glasses off my nose in the process. The entryway was flooded with the smell of roasting turkey and the toxic melon-and-lilies scent of Summer Meadow. Agnes knelt on the floor to pat Otis, but when the dog saw those big fish coming at him, he lay down and rolled onto his back.

"Does he think I'm trying to hurt him?" Agnes asked.

"No, no," I said. "That's a sign of love. Trust, love, devotion, all those dog things."

"You're just trying to reassure me, Clyde. I guess that's what family is for, isn't it?"

Since the last time I'd been in the apartment, the living room had been transformed. Or if not quite transformed, at least furnished. The brown log of a sofa had been replaced by a big puffy love seat with enormous cushions that looked as if they'd been inflated with helium and were about to float away. Opposite the love seat was a set of plump matching chairs and, in front of it, a glass-and-chrome coffee table. The lamp shades, the slipcovers, and the walls were all the same maddeningly vague, creamy beige.

Certainly it was an improvement. Still, the pieces of furniture were so uninvitingly far away from one another and placed so exactly at right angles, they appeared to have been set in place according to a master plan and then nailed down. There were two pictures on opposite walls, identical prints of an autumnal field with a flock of birds flying over it. Your basic Father's Day card, blown up, stuck in a plastic frame, and hung a few inches from the ceiling. There was a big fake Boston fern in a basket plunked on the top shelf of an empty, laminated-wood bookcase.

"It looks like a whole new apartment," I said.

"Well, Donald wanted to feel as if he was settling in," Agnes said, "so I got a few magazines and we worked on it together. I've done some interior decorating professionally, you know."

"I didn't know."

"E and A Resources has had a few calls for interior design." This comment was uttered with what struck me as astonishing self-confidence, the very same kind of self-confidence, in fact, with which Donald spoke about his own unlikely business. Even if it was misplaced confidence—it was a stretch to call cleaning someone's oven interior design—it was a pleasant switch from her usual self-flagellation. "Donald's been through a lot," she said. "He's just starting to come out the other side." She pulled off the big pot holders and sat down on the arm of the love seat. "It was a shock to him when that girlfriend left him. After almost twenty years."

"Twenty years!" I sank into one of the chairs, and the cushions rose up around me.

"They were sweethearts since junior high. I don't know if he told you," she said softly, "but he developed some health problems when he found out she'd turned into a lesbian." I assumed this meant he'd had a variety of nervous breakdown. She looked up at me apologetically. "Not that that has anything to do with you."

"I'm just happy you found each other," I said.

"I'll always be grateful to you for inviting me to that cookout, Clyde, even if nothing comes of this relationship."

I was pleased to see she'd already rewritten history and had me, instead of Marcus, inviting her. If I played it right, I could probably claim responsibility for arranging the whole relationship, assuming it didn't end tragically. "But something's come of it already, hasn't it, sweetheart?"

"Yes, yes, it has. I just wish I could have introduced him to Mom." At the mention of my mother, her eyes filled with tears and she leaned against the back of the love seat with a deep, exhausted sigh. "Do you think she would have approved? He's younger than me, and between you and me, I don't think his income is that high."

"I'm sure she would have approved, if she'd seen how happy he's made you."

She stood up and walked toward me, to embrace me, I suppose, but she tripped on a little throw rug and nearly kicked Otis. He whimpered and raced out of the room, and Agnes retreated to the arm of the love seat. "I wish you could find someone, Clyde. I really do. You couldn't convince Gordon to come to dinner?"

I felt my jaw clench. If I spent enough time with her, Agnes always hit my rawest nerve. But it was my own fault. I'd encouraged her to continue thinking of Gordon and me as a couple because it had served my own distorted perceptions so well. For the past few days, as I lay under my blankets devouring one insanely banal memoir after the next, I'd been trying to reorganize things in my own brain and kick the brawny little brat out of my thoughts once and for all.

"We haven't been together for years," I said.

"I know he moved out—"

"Agnes, Gordon has a new lover. Someone he lives with. In fact, the lover's not even all that new. They've been together for more than a year now."

"Lover," Agnes said vaguely. She twisted one of the pot holders as if she were trying to wring it dry. "It's like Davis getting remarried, isn't it?"

I resented the comparison. Even Gordon didn't deserve to be compared with Davis. "Well . . ."

"But if you look at it the right way, it's a relief. I'm relieved Davis is getting remarried. I really am."

She *looked* relieved, even uneasily happy. She had on a belted green dress that brought out the color of her eyes and showed off her legs. Although she frequently covered them up, Agnes's legs were her best feature, pretty and unexpectedly shapely. She looked around the room, from the windows to the doorway, to make sure we were completely alone. "I want to tell you something," she finally said, "about . . . Dad." She went to the bookcase and moved the fake fern a fraction of an inch to the right, stared at it from a different angle, and moved it back. "I'm glad he's not here, Clyde. I know he wouldn't have come even if I had invited him, but I'm glad I didn't invite him. I wouldn't have been able to enjoy myself for one minute."

I looked over at her, standing there beside the bookcase, nervously fidgeting with the phony plant. For years, I'd been waiting to hear her acknowledge some flicker of doubt about our father, encouraging her to utter some word of criticism that wasn't framed as a concern about his health, but now that she had done so, I felt oddly alone, as if she'd abandoned me in the middle of a crowded train station.

"About that nurse of his," I started.

"I know all about her," she said. "I've known all along."

"You figured it out?"

"He told me," she said. "He told me about her, but he made me promise I wouldn't tell you."

"But, Agnes, he told me himself, months ago. It doesn't make any sense."

"I don't care about that. It doesn't matter to me anymore. What matters is that I told you. Now he doesn't have it hanging over our heads."

There was a loud crash from the kitchen, a heavy pan hitting the floor, and Donald shouted one of his odd, invented curses. "I hope Barbara didn't do that," Agnes said, and hurried out.

I sank back into the chair and stared at the birds flying above the autumnal field, so absurdly close to the ceiling that they appeared about to fly right into my apartment upstairs.

"I'm sorry we don't have a dinner table," Donald said, "but I nearly went broke on the rest of the furniture. Or let's just say I would have gone broke if I hadn't maxed out my credit cards."

He'd lined up the platters and bowls of food on the coffee table, and we had served ourselves and were eating with the plates balanced on our laps. Donald and Agnes were sitting on the love seat, their shoulders pressed together. The only time I could remember seeing Agnes and Davis actually touch in public was when they'd been instructed to kiss by the priest who married them. And even that had been an awkward, embarrassing moment; Agnes had stepped on the hem of her dress and lurched toward Davis, and he'd ended up kissing her abruptly and grudgingly.

"I think this is much more comfortable," Agnes said. "It's like a big picnic."

"I hate picnics," Barbara said.

For once, Agnes had convinced Barbara not to wear her overalls. Instead, my niece was squeezed into a denim dirndl that came down to the middle of her thighs and, underneath, a pair of black tights with great jagged holes in the knees and the shins.

"Oh, honey, you're just saying that. You used to love them. When your father was away on business, I'd pack a basket, and you and I would go out to Salem Willows, right by the ocean. Don't you remember?"

"I remember we saw someone get shot there."

"Don't look at me," Donald said. "I've never been near the place."

Agnes jabbed a potato with her fork and dropped it onto Donald's plate, mumbling something about the weight she'd gained since they'd started going out. Donald cut the potato in half and stuffed it into his mouth.

"We never saw anyone get shot, honey. We heard the gun go off, and we didn't find out about the murder until later. But you used to beg me to take you there. You'd go picking wildflowers and bring me a little bouquet. My allergies must have been better in those days."

"That whole idea is so humiliating, Mom. What kind of freak would pick wildflowers for her mother?"

Otis was sitting in front of the coffee table with his eyes glued to the turkey, apparently waiting for the right moment to sink his teeth into it and carry it off, bones and all. I reached down to pat his head, and when he turned around and looked at me longingly, I slipped him a thread of meat from my plate.

"Hey, Clyde," Donald said, "what do you think of this: I've been trying to talk your sister into coming to work at the clinic."

"Ah," I said. "Well. Long commute, isn't it?"

"It's only half an hour," Agnes said. "Nearly everyone at West-Woods commutes to the city."

"You know," I said, "I've never been entirely clear what you do there. At the clinic."

Donald put his plate down on the coffee table, mopped at his mouth with a napkin, and commenced an impassioned tirade against minoxidil, hair transplants, and a variety of gruesome surgical procedures, all of which he described in minute detail. "That's what we *don't* do," he said, and for the next twenty minutes, he related the finer points of The Program, the foundation of treatment at the clinic. Each patient was first given an in-depth evaluation, in which strands of hair were plucked from the head and sent to a laboratory in Duluth for analysis. The Program itself consisted of a series of treatments that began with scalp massages, shampoos, heat caps, and ice-water rinses and progressed to ultraviolet lamps, injections of herbal extracts, and electric shocks from something Donald affectionately called the "stun gun." Most patients were expected to show up three times a week for half-hour sessions. "But only for the first year," he assured me.

"What kind of license do you need for this?" I asked. I was still trying to picture the "stun gun."

"Driver's," Barbara mumbled.

"Donald has degrees from the Trichological Association of America," Agnes said.

"It's a Swiss organization," he told me.

Each patient was given an individualized at-home hair-care regime for the few hours a week when they weren't at the clinic, a series of scalp tonics and shampoos, follicle stimulators and deep-breathing exercises. When I suggested that the home program sounded like a full-time job, Agnes dropped another potato onto Donald's plate and said, "Well, Clyde, it all depends on your priorities. If you cared more about your appearance, you wouldn't mind washing your hair every once in a while."

"I'm going to shave every hair off my head," Barbara said, "and have my scalp tattooed with a picture of a guy giving the finger to the world."

Donald burst out laughing. "Call me if you do, kid. We can use your photo for one of our ads: *Don't let this happen to you.*"

Later in the day, while we were lingering over cups of instant coffee Agnes described as "Vienna Mint Almond Mississippi Mud Mochaccino," Donald carried the dinner plates into the kitchen and returned wielding a platter with what looked like a chocolate-covered brick in the middle. He set it down on the coffee table and looked at it doubtfully. Agnes lit up. "Mom's Peanut Butter Holiday Roll!" she exclaimed.

"That's what it's supposed to be, but I gotta tell you, I couldn't get the damned thing to roll as much as your mother suggests."

I had a slim memory of this recipe—a jar of peanut butter, eight or nine different kinds of sweeteners, a pound of margarine, a few boxes of smashed-up cereal and assorted crackers, all rolled together and coated with a can of watered-down frosting.

Donald sawed off four thin slices and served them. My slice was surprisingly heavy, like some dense metal used by NASA. It lay on the plate, an unwholesome shade of brown, slick and damp, as if it were sweating or oozing oil.

Donald coughed over his first forkful and put down his plate. "Heavy on the sugar," he said. "I wonder what that Julia Child's going to make of this item. Maybe we should leave it out when I give her the book."

Agnes looked at her plate sadly, then put it down.

"I don't care," she said.

Donald put one of his big arms around her and pulled her close. "What is it, sis?" he asked.

"I don't care what it tastes like. Making that was one of the sweetest things anyone's ever done for me."

"It's the sweetest thing anyone's ever eaten," Barbara said. But she passed her plate and asked for a second helping.

Later in the afternoon, Barbara and I went upstairs to feed Otis. She carried him in her arms with his head on her shoulder, as if he were a baby, his hind legs tucked against the incipient roll of her stomach. "I'm turning into a blimp," she said as we climbed the stairs. "Have you noticed?"

"As a matter of fact," I said, "I haven't."

"Really? Then maybe I'm not. Not that I care one way or the other. Sometimes I'd like to turn into a huge, sloppy pig, so disgusting everyone would want to throw up just looking at me."

"Oh, come on," I said. I opened the door to the apartment, and Barbara set Otis on the floor. He embraced her leg, begging her to pick him up again. "Look at that. You're trying to be a menace, and even fifteen-pound dogs love you."

She stooped down on the floor, the holes in her leggings stretching open wider, the pale flesh of her legs bulging out more. She let Otis lap at her face. "If my mother and Donald get married, I hope they wait until I'm seventeen and have moved out. I don't think I could take twenty-four hours a day with him."

She picked Otis up again and carried him into the kitchen, sat down on one of the chairs by the phone, and put her galoshes up on the table. She started to leaf through Sheila's appointment book, with a look of disgust. "If I wanted to get into college, I could, you know. It's not like 'They'll never let me in' or anything. They'll let anyone in, as long as you meet the age requirement." The answering machine was blinking, and she hit the playback button. "As soon as I turn seventeen, I think I'm going to move into some kind of dyke commune—" But she was cut off by my father's recorded voice.

"Clyde. Where's your sister? It's two in the afternoon. Tell your sister to get the hell up here. I need her to take me to the hospital. I think I had a stroke."

His voice was calm, not that much different from the way it always sounded, although perhaps a little more shaky. I checked my watch. It was after three. Barbara and I looked at each other for a moment.

"Want me to play it again?" she asked.

I couldn't tell anything from his voice. Wary as I was, a knot

266

tightened in my stomach. I picked up the phone and dialed his number. It rang five times, and then his answering machine picked up. He didn't have a message, just a long silent pause and then the beep.

"What do you think?" I asked my niece.

"Hard to say. He could be faking or he could be dead."

"You shouldn't joke. Why do you suppose he didn't have Diane take him?"

"Maybe she dumped him. Should I go get Mom?"

I thought it over for a few minutes as I paced around the kitchen, with Otis's black eyes following my every step, and decided to go north on my own. If it was a crank call, there was no need to spoil Agnes's day with it. And if it wasn't, there was no reason I couldn't take care of things as efficiently as my sister. I told Barbara to tell Donald and Agnes I'd gone off to see a movie.

"Better tell them it's a long one," I said. "Very long."

AFTER BARBARA HAD GONE DOWNSTAIRS, I called my father again, and once again the only answer was the silent, portentous machine. The heat came on in the apartment—a deep whirring from somewhere in the basement and then a blast of warm stale air that blew up from the grate in the floor and sent the dust balls into a frenzy. It was drizzling now, and what little light there had been all day had thinned to lifeless gray. From the kitchen window, I could see the back porches of the triple-decker houses up and down the street and their muddy backyards, in one of which a muddy, miserable German shepherd, tied to a stake in the ground, barked at nothing in particular, his breath coming out in puffs. A dog in the rain in late November, not a cheering sight. I stood over the grate and let the heated air drive away a chill.

There was a chance that my father actually had been stricken. Ever since he'd reached his current inconclusive level of incapacitation, my chief fear had been that he might die before we had a chance to work things out, resolve our differences, and acknowledge the mutual love dormant under the crust of hostility. I hated to admit as much to myself, possibly because I didn't like the image of me it conjured up, dangling somewhere at the end of a thin thread of hope. But ultimately, who can resist hope, especially when it's hope for something as amorphous and meandering as love? Gordon had spelled it out for me all too clearly.

I'd heard plenty of stories of deathbed reunions and tearful final moments in which the family gathers around the gasping stern patriarch and all sins and slights are forgiven, anger is washed away, and blessings are handed out like chocolates. Even spiritual awakenings frequently occur in the final moments. There's a long list of famous hedonists who renounced their worldly ways with their last breath and were discovered with their cold, stiff fingers wrapped around a crucifix.

Otis was sitting on a chair with his head hung down, watching my every move, anticipating abandonment.

"Don't give me that look," I told him. "I'm not in the mood."

He sighed deeply, one of those mournful, longing sighs that seemed to fill his whole body with misery.

"You can come if you want," I told him. "You can go in my place, for that matter. But don't complain if you end up getting left in the car for hours."

I put on a raincoat and ran upstairs to my study. I'd left the envelope containing the lease Taff had given me on top of a book-case. I stuck it in my vest pocket and headed out.

As we pulled away from the curb, Otis stood up on the seat with his paws on the dashboard, panting and wagging his tail, checking out what had become familiar surroundings from a new perspective. It wasn't until we got onto the highway that he settled down on the seat and curled into a ball, his eyes trained on me. Then I realized that I had brought him not for his own sake—because I didn't want to leave him alone in the apartment—but because there was something in all that devotion and unconditional love drifting over from the other side of the front seat that I desperately wanted.

There was no traffic, and no cops were in sight. It was just the empty highway for miles, lined with slick, stripped trees and empty, ugly housing developments and shopping malls. My vision was blurred by the rain on the windshield and the fog on my eyeglasses. I took the glasses off and followed the loud lines along the pavement.

Surely if one of those deathbed conversions was good enough for God, it ought to be good enough for me.

Since this visit might technically count as an emergency, I felt justified in forgoing the visitors' lot routine and pulled into Agnes's driveway. I snapped Otis's leash in place and gave him a little tug to goad him out of the car. But as soon as we stepped onto the macadam, I heard the grinding rumble of the electric garage door. The garage door was one of the many supposedly modern conveniences that were part of the real estate package and general West-Woods "lifestyle," and like many of the conveniences, it had never really worked the way it was supposed to. I stood in the drizzle, coat clutched to my chest, and watched as the door made its agonizingly slow ascent. At the far end of the garage, my father came slowly into view: feet encased in polished black shoes from the fifties, legs in green work pants, broad chest, and, finally, grim, scowling face, bottom lip folded down in disappointment, disapproval, and disgust.

By the time the door had shuddered to a stop, I knew I'd made yet another error in judgment.

"What are you doing here?" he said.

"What am I doing here?" It was a good question, and for a moment I felt thoroughly confused. "Well, I don't know. I got a message on my machine saying you'd had a stroke."

"Don't stand out there shouting! You think I want the neighbors hearing all that?"

Overcoming the urge to turn and run, I stepped into the damp concrete bunker. When he moved out of his house after my mother's death, my father had sold the bulk of their furniture. What remained was stored in Agnes's garage, suspended on ropes from bolts he'd put into the ceiling. It was hanging above my head, all those chairs and bed frames, furnishings familiar from childhood. Otis had become adept at being led around on his leash, but he chose that moment to turn stubborn. I had to drag him behind me, and I could hear his nails scraping along the cement floor.

"And you didn't get a message saying I'd had a stroke," my father said. "You got a message saying I thought I *might* have had a stroke and to tell Agnes to get up here. I made a mistake. It was probably just indigestion. Where is she?"

"She's still in Cambridge."

"Well, that says it all, doesn't it? I have a stroke, and she's too busy with her boyfriend to come and take me to the hospital. Christ almighty. Some holiday. What the hell is that?" he asked, pointing to Otis.

"He's the dog I'm taking care of, for the kid who sometimes answers the phone."

"Not too obedient, is she?"

"He. Usually he is." Otis had planted himself in the middle of the garage floor. His head was slightly lowered, ears pulled back, and he was staring at me defiantly. "Come on," I told him, "don't make me look bad."

"Give her a kick."

My father opened the door to the basement and walked in. I realized as I watched him go inside that I hadn't seen him up and out of his chair in close to a year. He looked solid, almost robust, in his work clothes and his heavy shoes, as if he'd just completed a day of labor, though he was slightly hunched and walked with a barely perceptible limp. I gave Otis another tug, but he stayed put, staring at me with maddening willfulness. I scooped him up under my arm and carried him inside.

"Aren't you going to close the garage door?" I asked.

"Leave it open, in case I might possibly be expecting someone. Maybe." He turned around and looked at Otis draped over my

271

arm and shook his head. Never before had Otis seemed so much like an oversize lapdog, exactly the kind of insubstantial creature my father would expect me to be carrying around, like a surrogate infant.

"You're expecting Diane?" I asked.

"I didn't say that, did I? Who said anything about Diane?"

There was a big vinyl suitcase in one corner of the bedroom floor—Diane's, no doubt, although I wasn't about to ask at that moment. The basement was damper than the last time I'd been there, the air oddly hot and cold at the same time, as if there were a few weather systems battling one another in the small room. My father went to his chair by the window and lowered himself into it. "There's a bottle on the floor of that closet," he said. "Get it out and fill up the glass on the bureau."

I opened the closet and pushed aside an armload of suit coats and dresses. The floor was littered with my father's big, clunky shoes and slippers and an assortment of dainty pumps and sneakers, and there was a faint smell of stale, slightly rancid perfume. For as long as I could remember, my parents had maintained separate closets, bureaus, bathrooms, and bedrooms. There was something about the jumbled intimacy of the clothes on the rack and the shoes scattered around the floor that made me feel wretchedly sad for my mother and, at the same moment, happy for my infuriating father.

"And don't let that goddamned dog in there with you," my father called out.

"He's not in here."

"I'm not talking to you while you've got your head in the closet, Clyde. What kind of dog is she?"

I turned and stood up. "He. He's a mutt. Are you sure you didn't hide that booze somewhere else?"

"It's in there. Don't make me go look for it myself. I'm worn out."

I got back down on my knees and crawled deeper into the dark reaches of the closet.

"Who'd want a dog this size, anyway?" he called out.

"He isn't mine," I shouted. "I already told you that."

"I'm not talking to you while you're buried in there. Since when have you been a dog lover?"

Finally, I spotted the dark-brown bottle, hidden behind some dirty shirts. I stood up, and all the blood rushed out of my head. I grabbed onto the doorjamb. When I'd regained my balance, I filled his glass and set the bottle on the night table.

"Is she housebroken?" he asked.

"It's a he."

"A what?"

"A he; the dog's a male."

"What do I care about that? I just don't want her messing up the floor. You can't clean these carpets, goddamned AstroTurf, whatever it is."

I sat down on the edge of the bed, and Otis leapt to my lap. He stared up into my face with a pleading look that seemed to say, Let's go, let's go.

"Why do you do that, Dad? Why do you hide those bottles everywhere? What's the point of it?"

He looked at me, dog in my lap, and shook his head. He gulped down a healthy dose of his drink. "Just to keep things interesting," he said. "To keep people guessing. I don't like everyone knowing my business."

He switched on the television, and a picture flared to life, the gaudy halftime proceedings of a football game. He switched the channels until he landed on a home shopping network, shut off the sound, and glared at the screen with no interest whatsoever.

"I thought you were spending Thanksgiving with Diane."

"We spent some of it together. Then we had a fight. But she'll be back, you watch."

"So you came home and left that message about the stroke?"

"That's right. And Agnes wouldn't even come up here, wouldn't even leave her boyfriend to take me to the hospital. After all I've done for her, it's a pretty sad state of affairs."

I looked out the glass door to the little patio in back. It was raining now, big heavy drops pinging against the rusted grill. "I thought you might be happy for her," I said, "happy she met someone. He's not perfect, but . . ."

"That relationship isn't going to work out. Just like her marriage to that other loser didn't work out. I'm concerned about her, that's all. Going around with a big goon like that. And here's how she shows her appreciation. You have a stroke and you get left alone in a cold basement."

His bottom lip rolled down with a miserable life of its own. He flipped through more channels until he came to The Weather Channel, then turned up the sound and listened intently to a report of a storm somewhere on the other side of the planet. Otis looked over at the television, jumped off my lap, and lay down on the carpeting by the sliding glass door. As I watched those maps with puffy, computer-generated clouds swirling over them, I felt naked and alone without the dog protecting me. And then something occurred to me.

"You didn't get left alone," I said.

My father turned, gulped down a quarter of his drink. "What?"

"You didn't get left alone," I said. "I came, didn't I?"

"You what? I can't hear what you're saying, Clyde. You're going to have to speak up."

"Why don't you just turn down the volume?" But apparently he didn't hear that, either. I tried to make a case for myself in a louder voice, but I could feel something tightening up at the back of my throat and became panicked that I might start to cry. I couldn't remember the last time I'd shown any strong emotion around him. Even when my mother was being lowered into the ground I hadn't risked revealing the sorrow and regret I felt for all the things I hadn't had a chance to tell her before she died. A stony, distant demeanor was safest.

At least there was something I could offer. I reached into the pocket of my vest and took out the lease for Roger's apartment. But as I was about to turn it over to him, he pulled a pitcher out from under the bed and passed it to me. "Do me a favor, Clyde? Go upstairs and put some ice in this, will you? This booze is killing my throat. Not even a refrigerator down here. I've got to get the hell out of this dump."

I took the pitcher from him and put back the envelope. "Come on, Otis," I said. "We're going upstairs."

He'd fallen asleep on the carpet and was breathing deeply.

"Not too bright, is she?"

"He," I said. "Otis."

The dog looked up at me and then stretched his legs out in front of him and lay back down.

"Come on," I said. But once again, he ignored me.

"Look at that," my father said. "That's a useless dog. You haven't broken her spirit. She doesn't know who the boss is. You have to break their spirits or they never do a thing for you, and then they turn around and bite your hand when you're trying to toss them a bone. A dog like that, with a mind and will of her own, is useless."

But Otis looked so content lying there on the green carpeting, the rain streaking down the door behind him, I didn't have the heart to drag him upstairs with me. And if I called him again and he still didn't come, I'd look all the more ineffectual. So I told my father to watch him for a few minutes, and I climbed up the narrow spiral staircase.

That grim powder-blue condo with all the spindly white furniture had never looked more depressing. I stumbled into the kitchen and filled the pitcher with ice. The freezer was crammed with boxes of prepared dinners, frozen vegetables, cans of juice concentrate. I took out a package of frozen broccoli and lay down on the sofa in the living room with it pressed against my throbbing head.

I fell into some kind of stupor, and then I fell asleep. I don't know how long I lay there, but when I came to, half the ice in the pitcher had melted and the waxy cardboard of the broccoli box had turned soggy.

My father was seated in his chair by the window, and the television was still pumping out a loud, irrelevant weather forecast for some corner of the globe. He was snoring, his head thrown back.

I looked over by the door, but Otis had moved from his spot on the rug. I opened the closet, but he wasn't there, either. I shook my father's shoulder, and he opened his eyes wide, as if he'd been roused in the middle of a nightmare.

"Where's Otis?" I asked.

"Who?"

"The dog. Where's the dog?"

"I let her out."

"What do you mean, you let him out?"

"She wanted to go out, so I let her out. You didn't expect me to let her crap on the floor, did you?"

I looked out through the glass door to the cramped cement patio.

"He's not out there," I said.

"I let her out through the garage. The door back into the cellar's open. She'll wander in. What the hell time is it?"

I ran out to the garage. The door was still open, and rainwater was flowing down the badly designed driveway and into the garage, pooling in the center of the floor. There was no sign of Otis. I ran up to the winding roadway around the town house and called him.

My father shuffled out into the garage. "For Christ's sake, Clyde, stop that shouting. The neighbors will think you're calling for help."

OTIS SEEMED TO HAVE VANISHED INTO THE maze of houses and cars and parking lots. I searched for him for the rest of the evening and into the night, ringing bells and knocking on doors. The rain turned to slush and then wet snow. The later it got, the more desperate and bedraggled and deranged I knew I looked. Fewer and fewer people bothered to open their doors, fearing, I suppose, that I was one of the maniacal murderers rumored to be wandering the byways of WestWoods.

By the time my sister and niece returned to New Hampshire, it was late in the evening and I'd collapsed into one of the spindly wicker chairs, soaked and sneezing. Agnes rushed over to me. "Is it . . . Dad?" she cried. "Is he . . ."

"He's fine," I said. "Diane drove into the garage a while ago, and I think the two of them made up."

"No stroke?" Barbara asked.

"Stroke? What stroke?"

"No stroke," I told Barbara. "Indigestion."

Then, as if she already knew, Barbara came and sat next to me. "Where's Otis?" she asked quietly.

"He," I said, "is not fine."

I stayed the night in Agnes's living room, and in the morning, Barbara and I continued the search. But it was the day after Thanksgiving, and the shopping malls were teeming with frenzied buyers and the parking lots were spilling out onto the roadways and the roadways themselves were clogged with cars—traffic backed up for miles, exhaust fumes and blaring horns and the sizzle of tires on wet pavement. Late in the day, Barbara offered to come back to Cambridge with me, so she could be there when I told Ben.

For the next two weeks, I drove to New Hampshire with Louise and Ben every day after school. We canvassed a broader and broader area, put up signs, contacted the animal shelters, talked to suspicious residents. But there were no leads. Through it all, Ben maintained an eerily composed demeanor, as if he was convinced the dog would suddenly appear around the next corner—pretty much what I was expecting, too.

Then, as we were driving north one cold afternoon, Louise said, "One of these days, we're going to have to stop coming. One of these days, we're going to have to stay at home."

"I know *that*," Ben said.

"It could be any day." She pulled off the highway and onto the wet gravel of the shoulder and turned off the engine. The car shuddered as a truck roared past. "We'll just have to decide arbitrarily, pull the date out of a hat. But I'll leave it up to you to say when."

We sat there in silence by the side of the highway with the traffic speeding by us and Louise's cigarette filling the car with thin blue smoke. And then, as Louise was about to turn on the engine again, Ben began to cry. He curled up on the front seat, sobbing, his hands over his face as if something inside him had cracked open at last and all of his composure had fled. The front seat shook with his sobs. A police cruiser flew past with its siren on, and Louise reached out to put her hand on Ben's back. In one move, he flung open his door, jumped out to the shoulder, and began to pound on my window. He was shouting something, loudly but incomprehensibly, and when he stepped back, I went outside. He pushed me against the trunk of the car with sudden, angry strength and kicked and kicked at my legs. I put my arms around him and buried my nose in his hair while he beat his fists into my chest. When I lifted my face, he knocked off my glasses and kicked them out onto the highway. And then we both stood there and watched as a truck sped past and flattened them under its tires.

"I'm not sorry," he said, in a voice of dull amazement. "I'm not sorry. I'm not sorry."

We got back into the car and Louise turned on the engine and pulled out into traffic. "Should we go home now?" she asked.

"Wherever that is," Ben said.

When I walked into the apartment later in the day, Sheila was in the kitchen, stuffing her papers and books into a big string bag. She was moving with a kind of ferocity and purpose I wasn't used to seeing in her, and I had the distinct impression she was preparing to make an exit. I sat down at the table and watched her for a few minutes.

"Where's Marcus?" I asked.

"Don't know," she said. She turned quickly, flinging all her curls at once. "Don't know, don't care. Doesn't matter. He's stalled. And you know what happens to a helicopter when the engine stalls? Drops like a stone. Well, there you have it. Stalled. All this going on with Ben, just when he needs a father most, and he still can't bring himself to sit down and talk with him. So what chance has he got with anything else in his whole stalled life? What chance is there that he's ever likely to make a commitment to me? I'm not interested in losers, Clyde, and I never have been. Anyway," she said, "he's too old for me."

This was a complaint I'd never heard from one of Marcus's girlfriends before, and as I watched her dash around the house, putting her things in her bag, I realized it was true. He was too old for her, too old for his dissertation, too old to become a father. He'd waited too long for his life to begin, and he'd passed the point at which he could jump-start it. That he'd wasted his brains, all the promise of his supposed intelligence, wasn't news; the real shock was realizing he'd squandered his beauty as well.

Eileen Ash's party was held two weeks before Christmas, on a clear, icy Thursday night. I'd talked to Louise a couple of days before, and although she'd agreed to come, she told me not to bother picking her up. "I'll meet you there," she said, in a curiously unconvincing voice.

In fact, I was a little hesitant to go myself, since I'd barely been functional for weeks on end, but I tried to make the best of it by reminding myself I'd barely been functional for most of my teaching career. And so far, it had been a backhanded asset.

Eileen's house was an immense Italianate monstrosity, tucked in behind a tall cedar hedge on Brattle Street. There were candles in every window, flickering prettily and hinting at the tasteful splendor of the Christmas decorations inside.

"You're not getting enough sleep," Eileen said, as she showed me into the living room. "I think you should go on sabbatical."

"I'm afraid they don't offer sabbaticals at The Learning Place."

"Well, of course they don't offer them, dear. You have to demand."

The living room was vast. So vast, the small gathering of students might have looked lost if it weren't for the string quartet Eileen had hired and the uniformed army of caterers rushing around, passing out drinks and filling the room with activity and the impression of holiday cheer.

"I've been dying for you to meet my husband," Eileen said. "He feels as if he practically knows you."

She took me by the arm and led me to a high-backed chair at one side of a roaring fireplace. In it was an aged, hunched man who scowled up at me from behind a thick pair of lenses. Unless he'd been struck by a stray, out-of-season bolt of lightning in the past two months, there was no chance he was the same man I'd seen Eileen cozying up to outside the aquarium.

"I loved your class," he said, as I shook his hand.

"You did?" I said. Senile, to boot, probably a tremendous convenience.

"No, no." Eileen laughed. "Ei." She sat on the arm of her husband's chair and kissed his cheek. "That's what he calls me. Ei."

"She loved it," he said. "She's going to sign up for another class next fall."

"Unless he takes a sabbatical," Eileen said.

"Oh, well," her husband said. "They'll pull in somebody, won't they?"

Off the street, he clearly meant. "They usually do," I said.

"There are two people I want you to meet," Eileen told me, as she led me away. "They claim they're enrolled, but I've never met them before, and as far as I know, I've made nearly every class."

"That always happens," I told her. "A few people sign up and then don't show until the final party. I've never been able to understand it."

"I see what you mean. Probably using the class as a cover for some more nefarious activities. With each other, for all we know." This thought seemed to cheer her tremendously. "I'll say one thing for them, they're hungry."

I waited for Louise to arrive—through cocktails, through dinner, through an elaborate bûche de Noël that looked like an extraordinarily well-bred cousin of my mother's holiday roll. I wandered off into the library and called her, let the phone ring a good dozen times or more. Somewhere around the tenth ring, I realized, with uncharacteristic certainty, that the phone was ringing in an empty house. That sometime since I'd last spoken to her, she and Ben had packed up their belongings and driven away, as unceremoniously as they'd arrived.

When I got home that night, Marcus was sitting up at the

kitchen table, poring through one of his academic journals in the yellow light of a single, dim lamp. "How was the party?" he asked.

"Oh, pretty much what you'd expect: string quartet, lobster bisque, chorus girls jumping out of a cake." He nodded appreciatively, not hearing a word, eager to get on to the serious matter of updating me on his current state of mind. But I didn't much care if he was listening or not, and I went on anyway: "I think I've reached my limit with The Learning Place. Vance has a connection at a private school, and I've finally decided to follow up on it."

"Sure, sure," he said, as soon as I stopped talking. He put away the academic journal and folded his long, bony fingers on top of it. "I've made a decision, Clyde. I'm talking to Ben tomorrow. I'm walking over there first thing in the morning, bright and early, and I'm sitting down and talking to him. I was doing it all for Sheila before, but now that she's out of the picture, I see I have to do it for me. Him, too, of course."

He did look old in that dim light; handsome, of course—he still had a decade of good looks, providing he didn't lose much more weight or balloon up, grow a beard or start following fashion trends. But I pitied him for the first time ever as I heard his voice droning on somewhere on the other side of my thoughts. He'd misread his situation—in thinking he had forever to decide about his son, in thinking the rush of life would come to a standstill until he'd had time to catch up to it.

I'd misunderstood my situation, too. For years, I'd been assuming that my relationship with my father was unfinished and unresolved and had let myself drift into the becalmed waters of waiting. It wasn't until Otis vanished that I saw the cost of waiting and longing. Dad and I had finished all our business years earlier; we had nothing left to resolve. It was simply a matter of learning to live with the resolution.

I WAS A SNOWY WINTER, ALTHOUGH NOT an especially cold one. Beginning in January and continuing right into the middle of March, storms swept across the East, dropping wet snow that clung heavily to the trees and made walking and driving a misery. Sometime in the middle of February, I abandoned my car on a side street and didn't return to it until I felt certain I wouldn't have to worry about getting stuck in a bank of filthy slush. Anyway, I had nowhere to go.

In February, my father and Diane—who, as it turned out, was a retired nurse—were married. Agnes and I didn't find out about it until March, when they moved into an apartment in a planned and gated community about ten miles from Agnes. Birch Lane Brook was designed as a combination nursing home and cruise ship—twenty-four-hour health care available, along with nightly entertainment and two restaurants. Roger had arranged for the apartment. Whenever I felt aggrieved that Dad was a better father to Roger than he was to me, I only had to remind myself that Roger appeared to be a considerably better son than I'd ever been. Whether Roger moved to Cambridge or not, I never learned. My father and I didn't talk to each other for a long time after Otis disappeared, and when we started to talk again, it was mostly about the weather.

Agnes had wept profusely at the news of the secret marriage and declared that if *she* ever remarried, she wouldn't invite our father and his new wife to the ceremony—or at least she'd wait until the last minute to invite them. But secretly, I think she was relieved to have him out of her house. In addition to having her food bills cut in half, she could now entertain Donald without fear of intrusion and recrimination. Shortly after word came out about the marriage, Agnes quietly put away my mother's recipes, and she didn't mention them again for months.

I waited for news from Louise, a letter or a phone call or even a postcard, but none came. Eventually, I decided she'd slipped back into the anonymity of her drifting life. I assumed she'd gone back to California, someplace more familiar to Ben, warmer and more welcoming to her.

In the spring, I taught three courses at The Learning Place. I had a monthlong vacation in front of me before the start of the fall semester. Vance's connection with Mary Laird hadn't proved quite as useful as he'd promised or as I'd hoped. She kept referring to the adult ed center as The Learning Porch. She did assure me that they'd put my name on a list of people they could call in at the last moment, in case of sickness, death, or suicide. "Something often comes up," she said cheerfully.

Originally, I'd planned to spend my vacation languishing in the hot, tidy rooms of my new apartment, lying in bed and reading with a fan blowing over my body, but right before the end of classes, I'd felt a surge of determination to make a stab at being in the right place at the right time for once. I called Taff and had her find me an apartment in Provincetown.

Louise's letter arrived the day I was leaving, a dry, hot Friday in July. There was no return address, but it was postmarked Florida.

I dropped all my bags and started to open the envelope, but the lobby of the building was hot and still, and I longed to get on the road and out of town.

It was close to four by the time I got to the tip of Cape Cod, though the sun was still high. Driving through the miles of dunes with a hot wind blowing sand across the road and the ocean a trembling mirage at the edge of my line of vision, I felt over-whelmed by a calm optimism and a desire to stretch out in the sun. All that empty sand and water seemed to be spread in front of me as I approached, and then the crescent of the town, a lunatic hodgepodge of wooden houses and piers pasted onto the thin strip of land.

Provincetown was hot and teeming, the streets a gaudy carnival of tourists and bicyclists, six-foot drag queens sweating through their makeup, fishermen in heavy boots, men in string bikinis, and bewildered families trying to buy T-shirts, all baking together on that tiny spit of land thrust out into the ocean. The boat for Boston was boarding, and day-trippers, sun-scorched and drunk, were dash-ing down the sidewalks to make the pier before they were trapped for the night.

I rented a bicycle and pedaled through the crowds and out to the beach. It was after six o'clock, and the parking lot was nearly empty. The tide had started to come in, and a breeze was blowing across the water and up onto the sand. There were a few pockets of people, topless women and silent men in sunglasses, all too content and weary to leave. I found a place to spread my towel up on the beach, protected from the breeze. Finally, I took out Louise's letter and read.

Dear Clyde, Greetings from Florida. I know—Florida in July, but not nearly as bad as you might think. I found a town on the northwest coast Ben and I could agree upon. Not quite the surreal-ist landscape Ben had hoped for and I had feared. A quiet, bleached-out town that's been here for a surprisingly long time.

(20 years.) Not a bad place to have spent the winter and not an expensive place to spend the summer. Come fall, well, we haven't decided. San Francisco probably. But I haven't ruled out staying put.

In April, when the winter people moved on, we moved into a place right on the beach. Condo with a balcony, but not so terrible. We're house-sitting, a job I wasn't in a position to turn down. I lost a few precious grand on that flight from the vine-covered cottage in Cambridge. Worth it, I think. It wasn't the dog. Or, it wasn't only the dog. It wasn't *only* anything, just all of it together. It was Ben's idea to leave. All that time I spent waiting for Marcus to make up his mind, and it never occurred to me I might be better off letting Ben do the deciding himself.

We have another dog. Forty pounds, snatched from the jaws of death at the pound. We decided we'd never find out what really happened to Otis, so we could make up an end to his story. What we settled on was this: He wandered out of Agnes's condo and through the back of those malls and out onto the highway. He was headed back to Cambridge. When he got tired, he took shelter under a picnic table in a rest area, and a boy and his mother driving to their farm in Maine found him. His tags had fallen off by then, and they decided to take him home with them. There are five other dogs at the farm, and they watch over him, but he's the only one who gets to sleep inside.

Yr frnd, Louise

I folded the letter and put it back in its envelope. A town on the northwest coast of Florida, a dog, a balcony on a beach that perhaps looked something like this.

I was drugged from the heat, drowsy and melting into the blanket. Hot wind was blowing up over the sand and through my hair, and across the wide expanse of water stretched out in front of me, a smudge of smog on the horizon. There was a small group of men nearby, sitting on tiny, legless chairs, umbrellas over their heads fluttering in the wind. They had a cooler filled with ice and beer, and they were passing around a joint. One, a round, pink man in a straw hat, was singing a slow, maudlin version of "Ten Cents a Dance" in a raspy, ruined tenor, and from the opposite direction, a man was walking at the edge of the water, dragging his feet through the foam. There was a boy with him, eight or nine, thin and sunburned, in an enormous pair of swim trunks. The boy ran ahead of his father, up into the dunes, then reappeared farther ahead. "I'm right here, Dad," he called. "I'm over here." The father waved, and the boy disappeared again.

They passed by me, and I watched them wander down the beach like that until they were two dark shapes in the distance. Eventually, they disappeared, and all I could hear was the pink man singing the same slow verses over and over in his soothing, ruined voice.